#NO FILTER

MAXINE MORREY

Boldwood

First published in Great Britain in 2019 by Boldwood Books Ltd.

This paperback edition first published in 2020.

1

Copyright © Maxine Morrey, 2019

Cover Design by Charlotte Abrams-Simpson

Cover Photography: Shutterstock

The moral right of Maxine Morrey to be identified as the author of this work has been asserted in accordance with the Copyright, Designs and Patents Act 1988.

Every effort has been made to obtain the necessary permissions with reference to copyright material, both illustrative and quoted. We apologise for any omissions in this respect and will be pleased to make the appropriate acknowledgements in any future edition.

A CIP catalogue record for this book is available from the British Library.

Paperback ISBN: 978-1-83889-826-7

Ebook ISBN: 978-1-83889-030-8

Kindle ISBN: 978-1-83889-031-5

Audio CD ISBN: 978-1-83889-033-9

Digital audio download ISBN: 978-1-83889-029-2

Boldwood Books Ltd.

23 Bowerdean Street, London, SW6 3TN

www.boldwoodbooks.com

For James

'That's it! I am totally going to jail. I'm going to get it wrong, owe thousands, not be able to pay, and go to jail!' I flung myself backwards with an overly dramatic sigh and lay sprawled on the paperwork I had been looking at. 'And seriously? Me in an orange jumpsuit? I don't care how on trend they are; I could never pull that off! Orange is so not my colour.'

Amy topped up her wine glass before reaching a hand down to grab my arm, tugging me in the direction of the sofa. I slid along the floor for a few moments in my prone position, like some sort of beached, four-legged starfish, until I eventually bumped into the furniture.

'I think that's more America, hon,' she said, yanking me upwards. 'I'm not sure what ours are like. Something much more subtle, I expect. And don't worry. I'll hide a file inside the first cake I bring you. You'll be out in no time.'

I paused in my clambering from the floor onto the sofa, and gave her a look. She made a sawing motion with one hand, accompanied by an over-exaggerated wink as she held out my wine glass. Flopping onto the couch, I took the glass and swigged a large mouthful, before laying my head back onto the soft cushions.

'Seriously though. I really don't know what I'm doing with this. I thought I was handling all this business stuff OK until now.'

'And you are!' Amy interjected. 'Your blog is doing amazingly well! I can't believe the difference in a year – it's incredible! Seriously, Libs, you should really be proud of yourself.'

I sighed. 'Thanks, Ames. And I am, and of Tilly. I couldn't have done it without her. But I'm so frustrated! I've taken on this insane learning curve and, for the most part, got the hang of things. I think. But this?' I kicked a piece of paper with my bare toes. 'This, I just cannot get my head round! Why does tax have to be so bloody complicated? They send you this stuff so that you are supposedly able to do it yourself, but write it in the most confusing language possible! How is that even remotely helpful?'

Amy just shook her head and took another sip of wine.

'So, what are you going to do?'

'I don't know. I guess I need to start looking for an accountant.' I twiddled the wine glass stem in my hand.

Amy leant over and bumped her head gently on my shoulder. 'You know; it is OK to ask people for help sometimes. We can't all be amazing at everything. Creating all this in such a short space of time is brilliant, Libby. Finding that you need some extra expertise in one area is perfectly acceptable, and perfectly normal.'

'I guess.' I put the glass down. 'Before I forget, I have something for you.'

Immediately, Amy sat up straighter in anticipation and her eyes watched me as I crossed to the other side of the room and picked up a small, but fancy, cardboard bag with intricately twisted rope handles and a swirly script logo on the side. Walking back over to the sofa, I plopped the bag down on Amy's lap.

'Did I ever tell you that going for it with this lifestyle blog business is the best thing that you've ever done?'

I laughed. 'You just like the freebies.'

'True,' Amy agreed, before letting out an 'ooh' of pleasure at the eyeshadow palette and perfume she'd just pulled out of the bag.

'But thanks anyway.'

'Any time. Oh!' Amy's eyes shone like those of a child who'd just won pass the parcel. 'Really? I can have this?' Without waiting for confirmation, Amy began excitedly spritzing the exclusive new perfume copiously on pretty much every pulse point she could reach, including mine.

Laughing, I lifted my wrist up to take another waft of the

fragrance. It really was gorgeous. I smiled as my friend rummaged in the bag, unwrapping the various goodies from their pretty tissue-paper packaging. The cosmetic companies often sent more samples than I could possibly use so I always made sure my assistant got some to review and regularly ran giveaways on the blog, as a thank you to my readers. But occasionally I still had extra goodies left over. Amy always loved a good freebie so when I had something spare, it meant I got to make my best friend happy.

As the fumes of Amy's fragrance enthusiasm began getting a little pungent, I pushed myself up and padded over to the doors that led out onto the balcony. Grabbing the handle, I slid the door to the side. Immediately, a warm breeze rushed in from the sea, dissipating the perfume, and bringing with it the screech of seagulls intertwined with chatter and laughter from the nearby bars and restaurants in the marina. I stepped out, grabbing a wide-brimmed, slightly battered straw hat off the nearby console table, and took a seat on one of the two wooden steamer chairs that resided on my balcony. Amy followed me out, wine glass in hand, the gift bag now swinging off her wrist.

If I was honest, the furniture was a squeeze and a trendy little bistro set would have been a better, more sensible option. I'd made the classic mistake of 'guesstimating' that they would fit perfectly on the balcony. They didn't and I'd ended up building them in situ like some sort of furniture Jenga, which had proved to be the only way of getting them both to fit on there. But I loved them. I didn't want a trendy little bistro set. The loungers were super comfy with full-length padded cushions, and reclined just enough without touching the glass. I could sit out here and read in comfort, watching the boats sway and bob gently in the marina, listening as the sound of waves bumping against the harbour wall carried across the water. Even in winter, when the wind howled and the sea reared up before crashing down forcefully onto the nearby beach, I would happily sit out here, wrapped up against the cold, just absorbing it all.

There was definitely no need for coats and scarves this evening. It seemed that spring had decisively handed off the baton early to summer and the new season was away and running. The evening was warm and the breeze soft as Amy and I, now having inelegantly climbed onto our respective loungers, sat back and sighed happily.

'Thanks for all this, Libs.'

'You're very welcome,' I replied. Forgetting my worries for a while, and with a smile on my face, I closed my eyes, soaking up the atmosphere as the gentle warmth of the setting sun caressed our skin.

* * *

Closing the Twitter app, I leaned over, grabbed my handbag and proceeded to tip the contents out onto my desk. Tilly, my part-time assistant, looked up from where she'd been leafing through the latest issue of *Vogue* that had dropped through the door this morning. She raised an eyebrow in question.

'Apparently it's national "What's in your handbag?" day. I thought we could join in,' I replied, poking the pile of stuff now in front of me.

'We?'

'Yes.' I paused, looking over at her. 'Why not? You haven't got a loaded weapon in there, have you? Or half a kilo of cocaine?'

'No! Of course not!'

'I'm joking, Tils. You just looked decidedly shifty when I mentioned it. It's fine if you don't want to do it, anyway. It's not compulsory.' I grinned, before turning my attention back to the contents of my bag. A tampon sat proudly in the middle of the pile. I chewed my lip for a moment, and then snagged the item out and put it to the side.

I noticed Tilly watching me.

'So, we can edit what's in there?' she asked.

I raised a brow. 'I don't think the world needs to see my emergency sanitary items. There's sharing and there's over-sharing.'

Tilly waited a beat before grabbing her own bag and turning it upside down on her own desk.

'Holy crap, Tils!' I laughed. 'How do you even carry all that without tipping over?'

'I keep meaning to clear it out and never seem to get around to it.'

'Apparently. Well, why don't you take this as an opportunity? Sort out what you want in there and then we can just post the "after" rather than the "before".'

Tilly pulled a face. 'I'm not sure you should be paying me for sorting out my handbag.'

I waved her protest away.

A grin slipped onto Tilly's face. 'OK.'

For the next twenty minutes, there were several exclamations of the 'Bloody hell, I've been looking for that forever' and 'Oh, I wondered where that had gone!' variety. By the time she had finished, Tilly's bag was about half a tonne lighter and the nearby waste-paper basket was overflowing. Artfully arranging each pile to look specifically unartfully arranged, but in a pleasing manner, we moved the lights over to the desk and photographed each one – the contents in sharp focus with the handbags themselves slightly out of focus in the background. Tilly emailed me her copy for the post, listing the items her bag now contained and their significance, if any, which I then added to my own piece, before quickly typing an introduction about the hashtag. Finally, I copied and pasted a bunch of hashtags we commonly used for blog posts, and added the #whatsinmyhandbag tag to the bottom. With the photos loaded, I ran the spellchecker then gave the text a final scan as a triple check. Satisfied that there were no errors, I pressed submit and the post went live on my Brighton Belle lifestyle blog.

* * *

'Do you still want to try that photo shoot on the beach tomorrow morning? I've just checked the weather, and it's looking good.'

Tilly and I were scanning the list of planned blog posts we'd compiled for the next few weeks. These were flexible to a degree, which allowed us to comment on any hot, relevant topic that came up, but planning was an essential part of running the blog. It didn't tally too well with the glamorous ideas that some people had of what I did for a living, but it was most definitely a necessary part. Like a lot of jobs that people only saw a small part of, there was a much bigger, far more mundane part to it.

'Ideally.' I nodded as I scanned my calendar. 'So long as you don't mind coming over early? I can get everything ready and packed in the car so that we can just go straight there and hopefully catch some good light, as well as beating the crowds.'

'Fine with me. I think it'll be fun! We've always stayed around the marina for pictures before, so I think it's good to try and incorporate some more of Brighton into the shoots. And who doesn't like the beach?'

'Great. Thanks, Tilly. Hopefully it'll all go well. With a bit of luck, we might even find we're naturals at this whole "on location photo shoot" thing.'

* * *

We most definitely weren't naturals. I heard the wave first. And then I saw it. Briefly. Very briefly. It was, in fact, just long enough for me to open my mouth, ostensibly to make some sort of noise signifying surprise, but in actuality it just ensured that I swallowed what felt like a third of the English Channel before the force of the water overtook me and unceremoniously washed me up onto the beach like some bit of old shipwreck detritus. Opening my mouth had definitely been a bad move.

'Libby!' Tilly's panicked voice came to me through the gurgly water sounds now filling my ears.

Spitting out seawater and goodness knew what else, I quickly stood, the shock of the cold water propelling me to move. Pushing my hair back from my face, I made to step forward, inelegantly wobbling on the uneven pebbles. The next wave crashed into the back of my legs and, unbalanced, I took another tumble. Thinking that a gradual ascent to standing might be more successful, I pushed myself up onto my hands and knees. From the corner of my eye I saw a nearby windsurfer, out for an early morning sail, fall head first off his board. At least I wasn't the only one taking an unexpected dip. Although admittedly, he was more suitably dressed for the water than I was. The pebbles of Brighton beach dug into my knees and I made ouchy noises as I got myself fully upright once more.

'Are you all right?' My assistant had now made her way to me and was staring. I could only imagine what I looked like but I did know it certainly wasn't the look we'd had in mind for this photo shoot. 'You have... umm...' Tilly hesitantly pointed at my head.

I looked back, blankly. 'What?'

'In your hair.'

'What? What's in my hair?' My voice kicked up an octave. I didn't especially want to know what was in my hair. But neither did I want what was in my hair to remain there. I put my hand up warily and felt around. Nothing.

'Can you get it?'

Tilly shook her head. 'I can't. I can't touch it!'

'What? You can't touch what? Where is it?' Visions of hideous things crawling about on my head now filled my mind. I bent over and shook my head but nothing obvious plopped out on the beach. I looked back at Tilly, hopeful.

She shook her head. Then took a picture.

'What are you doing?' I squeaked in horror.

Tilly turned the camera and showed me the screen.

Nope. Definitely not the look we'd been aiming for to showcase these pieces on my blog. Moments ago I'd been dressed in a full-length, organic cotton sundress, its laced bodice giving way to a floaty, bias skirt, all in the softest shade of lemon. My shiny, deep auburn hair had been swept artfully to the side, softly teased curls contrasting with the colour of the fabric. The image on the screen now showed that there was absolutely nothing artful about my current look. The dress was plastered to my body, its pale colour and fine fabric meaning that it had helpfully gone completely see-through the moment it got wet. My hair had returned to its natural poker-straight state and clung in strands to the front of the dress and my upper arms. I peered at the screen again for direction, then reached up. A piece of seaweed had wound itself around my hair and was now clinging to the side of my head, just above my ear. Tentatively exploring my hair with my fingers, I brushed against something slimy. Biting back a squeal, I tried again. Forcing my hand to close on the slippery tail, I yanked and felt it give. Flinging the offending piece of seaweed back towards the waves, I turned back to Tilly.

'Has it all gone?'

She peered around my head, moving me by the shoulder to check the back, 'Yes. All gone.'

'Thanks for your help.' I raised an eyebrow and grinned at her.

She looked at me, a sheepish look on her face. 'Sorry. Seaweed gives me the willies. It's all slimy and yucky.'

I shook my head at her, still smiling.

'What are we going to do about the dress?' Tilly asked.

I glanced down. She was right. There was no way I could walk about like this. Brighton might be known for its laissez-faire attitude but I personally drew the line at swanning about in an outfit that now left very little to the imagination. I leant across and took the bags and equipment off her.

'New plan. I'll go and find us a more inconspicuous spot and you nip across the road and grab us some coffees and something to eat. We can go over some stuff here until I dry out enough to not get arrested.

'Sounds good.' She turned to go. 'And I'm sorry about the seaweed thing.'

'Don't worry about it,' I said, handing her two reusable takeaway cups. 'Now, off you go. I'll be over here.' I waved the bags in the general direction of where I was headed.

'OK. Back in a bit.'

I sat down and pulled a pair of flip-flops from one of the bags. Slipping them on, I made my way across the pebbles to a spot that looked good and sat myself down. From one of the bags, I pulled an Oriental-style parasol and opened it, shading my pale skin from the strengthening sun. Whilst my brother had inherited my dad's 'one glance at the sun and I'm handsomely golden' genes, I'd inherited my mother's pale Irish colouring wholesale from the red hair to skin the colour of fresh cream. 'Golden' wasn't a word I associated with my skin when it came to the sun. 'Red and blotchy' would be nearer the truth if I ever bothered trying to acquire anything resembling a suntan. Which I didn't.

If I was honest, it didn't really bother me. Despite all the usual carrot top, ginger nob and other wholly inaccurate connotations my redhead status had inspired at school, Mum had always kept me positive about it all. Of course, when all my friends had been wearing tiny shorts and crop tops, their golden tans making their hair look blonder, legs longer and teeth whiter, there had been moments I'd ached to be the same. But, as I got older, I realised that I couldn't change what I'd been given so it would be better to embrace it rather than fight it. And in recent years, celebrity had been on our side. With Prince Harry and Ed Sheeran flying the flag for the men, plus the advent of the *Mad Men* phenomenon and actresses like Emma Stone and Julianne Moore, redheads were cool! I mean, we'd always known we were cool, but finally – *finally* – the world at large was also now getting the message.

I'd played on this aspect for my blog, Brighton Belle – I saw it as part of my USP. A lot of the blogs were run by gorgeous brunettes and beautiful blondes and, whilst a lot of beauty advice can be applied to everyone, I'd had quite a few emails from young redheads who were getting teased at school or just didn't know how to make the best of their fabulous colouring. Tilly and I shared the task of replying to emails and comments, but I always replied personally to these ones because I knew exactly what these girls were going through, and I'd ask them to let me know how they got on, if they chose to take my advice. When replies did come back, with the sender clearly in a happier place, it always made me a little bit teary and I'd send Mum a quick email, telling her about it.

People sometimes accuse bloggers of being vain, and that it is all 'me, me, me'. Some comments were downright nasty. The Internet could be a wonderful thing, but it certainly had its dark side too, allowing people the opportunity to be incredibly unpleasant whilst hiding behind a shield of anonymity. The days when I got a response from a reader who had been made to feel better about herself by trying something I'd suggested helped wipe all the mean stuff away. It reiterated to me that my blog, which was now my full-time job, had a purpose, and a good one at that.

Tilly returned with the drinks.

'Sorry it took a while. There's some sort of conference on at the

Brighton Centre and everyone's stocking up on drinks before they go in.'

'Not to worry. Have a pew,' I said, indicating the other side of the blanket I'd folded over several times to sit on.

We sat back and watched the surf splash to shore. The beach was getting busier now as tourists and locals on a day off came down to take advantage of the sun. The windsurfers from earlier were now further down the beach, pulling their boards on shore. At the end of the Palace Pier, the rides were beginning to move and Tilly and I watched as the Booster started to spin, the wire-enclosed pods on the end of its arms reaching out over the sea on every turn.

'Have you ever been on that?' Tilly asked me, pointing at the ride with her takeaway cup.

'No. You couldn't pay me enough.' I turned and looked at her from under the shade of my umbrella. 'Have you?'

She nodded. 'Sam made a big deal about wanting to go on it a couple of years ago. Then promptly threw up all over the place. Including me.'

'Oh, no!' I screwed my face up at the thought. 'And this is the same Sam you're about to marry? I hope he realises just exactly how much of a gem he's getting with you.'

'I remind him frequently. And he's banned from all rides now. At least if I'm in the vicinity.'

'That sounds like a very good strategy.'

'How's the dress?'

I looked down at the fabric of the skirt I'd spread out in the sun, my legs folded up and crossed out of the way underneath it.

'Definitely drying. My bum still feels pretty soggy though, which could be tricky. I'd rather not walk to the car with my knickers on display.' I glanced at the bodice. Its double-layer construction had at least helped make this part a little less embarrassing now it was drying in the warm air. 'The top will be OK. And I've got a scarf in here I can just sling round my hips to cover my unmentionables.'

Tilly laughed. 'I don't think there'd be too many people complaining.'

'I'd be complaining! Come on, help me make sure I get everything under wraps.'

We got to our feet, and I rummaged in my bag for a scarf.

Pulling it out, I tied it so that it sat low on my waist and covered my bum and the front of my dress, preventing anyone from seeing that today was, of course, the day I'd chosen to wear my tiniest pair of knickers. We gathered up our stuff and headed back up to the car. After loading the gear and ourselves in, I pointed the little Fiat back in the direction of the marina, and my flat.

Leaving Tilly to upload the photos and do any editing required, I grabbed my dressing gown and headed into the bathroom. Stripping off the dress and my underwear, I stepped into the shower.

With body and hair now free from sand and salt, I stepped out and began drying off. My eyes took in the small beach of sand in the bottom of the bath. Flicking the water back on, I rinsed it away. Not exactly the best start to the day.

'How did they come out?' I said, returning to the living room after blasting my hair with the hairdryer. I'd got the worst off but it was still damp, so I twisted it up and stuck a butterfly clip on the back to hold it out of the way.

'Good!' Tilly said, her eyes still locked on the screen. 'It looks like we got some good shots before you took a dip, so we can just go ahead as planned. I think this is really going to be a great aspect to the blog – you know, incorporating more of the city into the shots.'

'I hope so. I'm thinking we might need a bit more practice with location photography though.'

'Yeah, I think you're right. Sorry I didn't get to warn you about that wave. I didn't really notice it coming until it was too late.'

'Don't worry, no harm... What the hell is that?' My eyes fixed on the image now displaying on Tilly's laptop.

'Oh! The camera was set on burst mode. It was still taking pictures when the whole wave thing happened. I guess it caught you as you stood up.' Tilly giggled. 'I'm pretty sure the hits on the blog would go sky high if I put this one up!'

On the screen was a picture of me standing at the edge of the beach, soaking wet, eyes closed, just as I'd pushed my hair back. The yellow dress was plastered against my body, leaving little to the imagination. My mind whizzed back to the windsurfer. Oh God, please don't let him have seen anything!

'The only thing you're going to do with that is to delete it. Now!'

'Oh, Libby. I never thought I'd say this but you're no fun.'

I pulled a face at her.

'Delete. Now.'

The post dropped through the door and we turned at the sound. I heard Tilly pressing keys as I went to fetch it, my mind working as I did so.

'Although, we could do a sort of mini feature about the mishap – not with that picture though!' I flicked through the mail. Nothing interesting. 'Have you still got the one you took with the seaweed in my hair?'

'Yes... here.' Tilly brought it up on screen.

'Certainly not the most flattering shot but, if I crop the X-rated bit off, it might make a funny little story as an extra post. I'll set about writing that up, if you can finish off the main one?'

'No problem.'

* * *

As we'd started early in order to catch the light and the relative peace of the beach, I'd offered to let Tilly have the afternoon off. Once she'd gone, I was going to settle in and try to get my head around the tax paperwork. Again. A couple of days ago, I'd rung an accountant but within minutes he was talking in what seemed like an entirely foreign language, asking me things I didn't understand. Eventually I'd feigned someone at the door and hung up before proceeding to work myself up into even more of a state about the whole thing.

But today was a new day. If I could make even a little progress, it would go some way to making up for being washed up on shore this morning.

* * *

'You're going to love me!' Amy announced as I answered my phone.

'I already love you.' I laughed.

'Well. Obviously. I am fabulous. Totally understandable. But what I mean is you're going to love me even more!'

'Not possible, but tell me anyway.'

'I am going to help prevent you going to prison.' She paused for a moment. 'Really! Some people are so judgemental. You should have seen some of the looks I just got!' Her voice faded a little as she turned away from the handset. 'It's all right. It's only the one body,' she called to her colleagues.

I grinned, imagining Amy now doing the same. Most definitely not the shy type; if she could get a reaction out of someone with a bit of harmless fun, she was having a good day. Her corporate career was going well, but her latest position had also landed her in an office with some people best described as 'a little stuffy'.

'So? Why the love fest?'

'Because, dear heart, I was chatting to Marcus in the staff kitchen today—'

'Is this Marcus-that-has-been-asking-you-out-forever-Marcus?' I interrupted.

'The very same.'

I made a 'hmm, interesting' noise. Amy ignored me and continued.

'He was asking what I'd been up to lately, and I mentioned that, among other things, I had been drinking wine as a sign of comradery with my best friend, who was stressing over having to do her first-year business accounts.'

'Comradery? I believe the wine was your suggestion.'

'Semantics. Anyway, the upshot is that Marcus' brother, Charlie, is some sort of Risk Manager in London, but lives down here.'

'Right,' I said, not entirely following.

'But, he started off as an accountant before moving into Risk Management,' Amy clarified.

'Oh.'

'Marcus already had a chat with him and Charlie's agreed to pop round next weekend and take a look at your books.'

'What? Here? Aren't I supposed to make an appointment or something?'

'Yes, there. It's a favour to his brother. He was hoping to be able to do it this weekend but he's about to jet off to New York or somewhere equally glitzy for work.'

'Nice.'

'Quite.'

We both reflected for a moment on the glamour of jetting

around the world on business before I pulled myself back to the subject at hand.

'Oh, Amy. I'm not sure.'

'Too late. It's arranged. And poor Marcus would be crushed if it fell apart now.'

I paused.

'Amy?'

'Yes.'

'Why is Marcus pulling in favours for you?'

'Umm...'

'Seriously? You're finally going on a date with him?'

She lowered her voice. 'It wasn't that I was averse to him before. I just had to make sure I was over the whole John thing. Marcus is too nice to be used as rebound fodder.'

'But are you sure?' I suddenly realised that, despite being alone in my flat, I had also lowered my voice. I shook my head and returned to normal volume. 'I mean, please don't feel you have to do this to help me out. I'm sure there are plenty of other accountants I can try. Don't get into something you don't want—'

'Libs. It's fine. I do want. And he's taking me up to Nobu in London. So I definitely want! Also, this way, I know that you'll be getting good advice. You've worked too hard not to have the best people helping you when you need them.'

'You know, you are right. I do love you more.'

'See? I told you. It's just inevitable.'

'When are you going out with Marcus?'

'Tomorrow night. We're catching the train up to Town after work. Know something?'

'What's that?'

'I can't wait. After months of putting him off, I'm actually really excited to see how this goes.'

'I hope it goes brilliantly, Ames. Text me after, won't you?'

'Will do. And Charlie said he'll be round about half ten next Saturday morning. Is that OK?'

'Of course. Thanks for setting this up, Amy. And thank Marcus too. I really appreciate it.'

'Least I could do. OK, got to go. Talk to you later!' And she was gone.

I put my phone to the side of my workstation and allowed a small wave of relief to wash over me. Although I'd earlier decided on having another attempt at looking into the accountants, I'd procrastinated about it for most of the day. Now, thanks to Amy, there was something actually happening – at last. I smiled and let the worries of finance get pushed to the back of my mind for the first time in ages.

Opening a new email, I entered a familiar address and quickly typed an update of the situation.

Hi Mum
Looks like I might be able to finally stop worrying about all this tax stuff.
Got a chap coming round next weekend to take a look. Very relieved!
Love you xxx

Picking up a pile of notes from the side of my computer, I spread them out on the glass top of my desk and grabbed a pencil from the outsized 'Visit Chicago' mug my brother had brought me back from a medical conference.

'Is it for holding a beverage or for swimming in?' I'd asked.

'I believe they're marketed as multi-purpose.'

So, it now sat as a handy holder for all my pens, pencils, and other implements I might need close to hand whilst working, which was preferable to spraining a wrist whilst trying to use it for its primary purpose.

Pushing my chair away from the desk, I went over to where I'd set up my camera and the ring light I used for my YouTube channel videos. I checked the battery level on the camera. Fully charged. During my early days of doing them, I'd once forgotten to charge it and discovered that it had switched off halfway through a make-up tutorial, resulting in me having to redo the entire thing from scratch.

Sitting in front of a camera, recording videos that would then be sent out into the great unknown, hadn't come especially easy to me. Although I loved what I did, and loved sharing it with people, I had initially been entirely satisfied doing all of that via the blog. Taking photos of myself with certain make-up looks or wearing an outfit I'd put together had just grown organically. I'd always been looking to improve the blog, even when it had been just a hobby, so I'd worked on relaxing in front of a camera. After reading somewhere that the key was just getting comfortable with it all, and the secret to it was just practice, that was what I'd done. I'd practised, just snapping and deleting for ages until it had finally stopped feeling quite so awkward.

The video side of the blog was something I'd really had to consider. I hadn't been worried about the haters or the oddballs, or anything like that. It just hadn't seemed to me at the time that it was a direction I'd needed to go in. It had been clear that it was a popular avenue for many, with some blogs getting an incredible number of hits and their owners becoming recognised as 'celebrities'. I was happy for those bloggers. This was their main thing, and what they wanted to do with their life, so publicising it as much as possible and building a brand made sense. But when I'd first started the blog, it hadn't been my main thing. I'd been a PA, and I'd liked my job. The blog had just been something I'd enjoyed doing in my spare time, my hobby. I loved it when I got comments – and always made a point of replying to them. I knew that for however many views a blog got, hardly any of those translated into a comment. It was hard when there were so many things vying for attention – I was guilty of it myself in many cases – so I really appreciated that those people had taken time to leave a comment on the blog.

Gradually, I'd started getting more and more requests to do videos to show in real time how I'd created certain looks, to help readers recreate them at home. I'd talked it over with Amy, who had been all for it. Amy loved clothes and make-up as much as I did. We had pretty different looks – I tended to fall more into the Boho camp whilst she was definitely more Classic – but our differences in taste only strengthened our friendship and she'd been behind me from the start when I'd done my first video. I'd recorded it and then spent hours editing, learning the software, mostly through trial and error – a lot of error – as I'd gone along. Once finished, I'd shown it to Amy for her feedback. I knew she loved me enough not to tell me it was great if it wasn't, and risk me looking an idiot online. The next day, Amy had called round to my flat wearing the same make-up look as I'd done in my video. Exactly the same.

'I followed it, step by step,' she'd said. 'I love it! You were brilliant! You absolutely have to post this, and do more.'

Her positivity and support had been the boost I'd needed. I'd pressed the button to upload my first ever video, all the while feeling just a teensy bit sick. The response was amazing! My blog hits went up, the link had been shared and I'd started getting a bunch of 'thumbs up' on the YouTube channel.

By the time I'd done my second one, I'd relaxed a bit more in front of the camera and the views had gone up again. I couldn't help but get excited by the enthusiasm filtering through to me via the blog. I'd had an email from one of my viewers, saying that she had used my tutorial for her prom and it had sent her confidence soaring – in her own words, she had felt like the 'belle of the ball'. I'd actually cried when I'd read that.

Perhaps to some it was a frivolous pastime – a grown woman playing with clothes and make-up and sharing lifestyle tips. Who was I that people should listen to me? And I got that. I really did. I could understand how all of this might come across as a vanity project to those who didn't understand what it meant to me to share these things. Or what it meant to those women out there to gain that extra bit of confidence by discovering something new. Whenever I got a negative comment, or a dismissive sound was made in my hearing by someone who found out what I now did for a living, I searched in my mind for that happy email, and others like it, mentally reading it over. If I helped just one person feel better about themselves, then that was all I needed.

Flipping on the studio ring light and checking the camera's settings, I took a seat opposite them. I pressed a button on the remote control and saw a red light on the camera begin to blink.

'Hi, everyone! Libby here, and welcome to another video. Today I've got some fabulous products to show you and how they can be used to create a great summery look. Even better, these are all from a new range called "You Can Bee Natural" which is a small start-up company committed to using Fairtrade, fully natural, non-GM ingredients. You know I'm all about the natural and ethical when possible so I'm pretty excited to try these out. But, don't worry, you don't have to have these particular items to get this look, and I'll be chatting about plenty of other ways to adapt it to suit whatever you have in your own make-up bag. So, first off...'

3

The following day I was just in the middle of editing the completed video when my doorbell rang. Glancing down at the clock in the corner of my computer's screen, I guessed my assistant, Tilly, was finally done with tasting wedding cake. I got up and went over to answer the door.

'Hi! I'm so sorry I'm later than...'

She stopped half in and half out of the doorway and stared at me.

I shifted my eyes. I'd opted for a slice of chocolate cake for elevenses (it needed eating) and was just beginning to wonder if I should have checked my chocolate-to-face ratio before opening the door.

'What?' I asked, when Tilly still said nothing.

'That's it,' she replied.

'What's it?'

'That look. The one you're wearing. Is that for a video?'

'Yes, I shot one for it yesterday. Are you actually coming in?'

'Oh, right. Yes!' Tilly stepped inside and pushed the door closed as she slipped off her heels and the lightweight jacket she'd had on over her sundress. It was warming up out there now that the clouds were clearing but there was a definite breeze whipping in off the sea.

'Tea?' I called, heading off to the kitchen.

'Please!' she replied before following me through. 'So, did you just come up with this look yesterday?' Tilly had come closer and was now peering at me.

'Could you look at it on the video? I've captured a couple of stills for the blog too. It's just – and don't take this the wrong way – you're freaking me out.'

'Oh! Sorry! Of course!' Tilly stepped back.

'It's only that I've been through so many magazines, videos, and goodness knows what else trying to find the right look for the wedding, I was beginning to think I'd never find the right one. And then there it is!' She started smiling. 'Although, I might leave off the chocolate-cake crumbs...'

'It needed eating.'

'Of course.'

'Talking of which, how did your own cake-tasting go?'

'Good. Apart from the fact I might not want to eat another piece of cake again for several months. I think we finally settled on one. It was actually the first one we'd thought we'd go for, but Sam wanted to make sure. You know how it is?'

'You mean he was hungry?'

'Exactly.' Tilly rolled her eyes. Tilly's fiancé, Sam, was always hungry. It led us to wonder where he put it all as he was skinny as a beanpole but the amount of food he could consume was staggering.

'Come on. I'll print off those stills for your wedding file, and then we can get on with some tasks. The most amazing box of goodies arrived this morning. I haven't had a chance to look through them properly so thought we could go through together and plan out some posts around them. If you choose which things you'd prefer to try, then I'll take what's left. Although, from what I've seen, they all look delicious!'

'Ooh, show me! Show me!'

We took our tea and headed back into the living room to get to work.

* * *

At precisely half past ten the following Saturday morning, the door-bell rang and I opened my front door to find the light almost entirely blocked out by a very tall, slightly serious-looking but entirely gorgeous man. He wore smart dark-wash jeans, a slim-fit short-sleeve shirt, that only half hid some serious guns, and a messenger hybrid laptop bag hung from a strap slung across his broad chest. His dark blond hair was short and neat and a cleanly shaven, lightly tanned face highlighted the most strikingly blue eyes I had ever seen.

'Hi.' I smiled. It was kind of hard not to.

'Hello.' He half smiled and shifted his weight. 'I'm looking for Libby Cartright.'

'That's me.' I paused momentarily. 'Are you Charlie?'

He nodded, as though relieved to have me confirm his identity. 'I am.'

'Nice to meet you.' I held out my hand and he shook it firmly. 'Please, come in.' I stood back to let his sizeable bulk through the doorway, the top of his head missing the frame by barely an inch, then closed the door behind him. 'Thanks so much for doing this,' I said, turning to him.

He gave a little shake of his head. 'Not much choice in the matter. My brother's got the real hots for some girl in his office. I was roped in to do this so that he could get her to go out with him.'

'Yeah,' I said slowly. 'That girl is my best friend.'

A brief flash of awkward horror showed in Charlie's eyes. 'Oh.'

'Look,' I said gently, 'I realise that you've been forced into doing this. I'm absolutely sure that you have much better ways to spend your Saturday morning than doing boring paperwork for someone you don't even know. So, why don't we sort something out that suits everyone better? Or perhaps there's someone you could recommend to me, whom you trust?'

Charlie was looking at me now but hadn't replied.

I tilted my head to prompt him.

He took a deep breath and gave me a tight smile. 'I didn't mean for that to sound bad, about your friend, I mean. I'm... I... Look. Would you mind if I went out and came in again and we started from scratch?'

I wasn't entirely sure he was joking.

'It's fine.' I smiled at him and he seemed to relax a little. 'Are you really sure you're happy to do this? I mean, it's obviously out of hours so perhaps you could give me a rough idea of what your hourly rate is? Just so that I don't pass out when you hand me your bill?' I gave a little laugh to show him that I wasn't serious. Although I sort of was.

Charlie looked at me, a slightly confused expression on his face. 'There is no charge. Like I said, it's a favour for my little brother.'

Now it was my turn to look horrified.

'Oh, no! I can't possibly let you do that. Giving up part of your weekend to go over a stranger's accounts for free? It's just... not right!'

'Really. I don't mind. I know it might seem boring to you, but it's sort of fun for me. It's different from what I do in my everyday job now, so it's quite nice to get back to basics.'

He caught my look and a shy smile spread over his face. The gorgeous-o-meter dinged up another few notches. I smiled back automatically.

'I guess that sounds pretty sad to you, right? That I find accounting fun?' He shrugged his broad shoulders.

'No!' I answered quickly. 'Really. It doesn't. And honestly, I'm so thankful for you and your love of figures right now because I have absolutely no idea where to start.'

As I steered the conversation into an area Charlie was more familiar with, he seemed to visibly relax.

'Would you like a tea or coffee before we get started?'

'Coffee would be great. Thank you.'

'Come on through,' I called as I headed off to the kitchen to get the drinks on the go.

I indicated for Charlie to take a seat as I gathered cups and supplies. He did so, but within a moment was back up again, wandering over to the window to look across the harbour. I came up behind him with the drinks.

'Do you want to sit outside for a few minutes whilst we have these? There's a better view there.'

'Sounds great. It'll give a few minutes to let the caffeine get to work.' He gave a little chuckle. Add cute to the list.

I led the way to the balcony door and opened it.

'It's a bit of a squeeze but quite manageable,' I said, before realising that Charlie was substantially bigger than most people who sat out here with me. I led the way and took a seat on the farthest chair, sitting in a cross-legged position. Charlie followed and folded his frame into the other one. I let out a giggle.

'Sorry. I know it's not the most practical. They really didn't look that big at the garden centre.'

'It's fine. Cosy.'

'How long have you lived here?' Charlie asked, after a few minutes, as he rearranged his legs.

'Oh, quite a few years now,' I replied. 'I managed to get in before the prices tipped into insane territory, luckily.' I watched him subtly trying to get comfortable for a couple more moments as he nodded in response.

'Here,' I said, 'put your feet on the end of my chair.'

'Oh, no. Thanks, anyway, I'm OK.'

I let out a laugh. 'You are so not OK. Just put your feet on the end. I'm not using that bit anyway.'

He straightened his long legs out until his feet rested on the end of the other lounger.

'Better?'

'Better,' he agreed. 'Do you like it here?'

'I do. It's far enough away from the centre but also easy to get there when I want to. And I love watching the boats and the water. I think I must have been a sailor in a previous life. Or a fish.'

I saw an amused look cross Charlie's face.

'And do you live here on your own?'

I slid a glance to him and did my best to hide the smile that was itching to escape, but I needn't have bothered because Charlie got there before me.

'Oh, I didn't mean... that sounded like I was trying to... I was just...'

'It's fine, Charlie. Don't worry.' I waved my hand. 'I know you were just making conversation.'

He did a tiny head-shake to himself and took a sip of the coffee before giving me a smile that did a good job of mixing embarrassment and shyness.

'I'm sorry. I'm not very good at small talk. Luckily, Marcus and my best mate, Alex, are connoisseurs at it. They usually help cover any failings on my part when we go out.'

'You shouldn't think of them as failings. It's just that everyone has different skills. And that's good. It makes the world a more interesting place.'

'You don't think being unable to talk to a potential client without it sounding like I'm trying to chat her up is a failing?'

'No, I don't. I think you were just making conversation, which you've admitted isn't your speciality. And the fact that you still made the effort does you a vast credit.'

Charlie tilted his head at me, the vague shadow of a smile in those incredible eyes. 'Are you always like this?'

'Like what?'

'Finding a positive spin for things?'

'I do like to try. But between you and me, even I'm finding it hard to find something – anything – positive with this tax stuff. I can't tell you how relieved I was when Amy told me you were coming to save the day! Why does the tax office make it so difficult?'

He shrugged.

I pulled a face and laughed. 'That's a polite way of saying that it doesn't seem all that difficult to you.'

'No! Not at all. It's just – well, like you said – people have different skill sets. Mine happens to be numbers.'

'Lucky for me! Do you want to go in and start taking a look?'

'Sounds good.'

I let Charlie manoeuvre himself out of the chair and step back through the door. I unfolded my legs and followed him. Maybe two large loungers really were too much out there, I thought, glancing at them again as I reached for the door handle to balance myself. What I found instead was a very muscular arm. I looked up as Charlie took my hand with his and steadied me in through the door.

'You know, whilst it is cosy, I'm a little worried it's also an accident waiting to happen,' he said, glancing back at the balcony.

'Is that your official risk management opinion?' I grinned up at him, tilting my head back to meet his gaze, which was serious.

'It is. People pay a lot of money for that normally.' Humour suddenly sparkled in the spectacularly blue eyes.

'Do you take cheques or would you prefer cash? You know, avoid the taxman and all that?'

The humour spread from his eyes and enveloped his whole face. It had quite the effect and I was suddenly glad of the cooling breeze drifting through the flat from the open window.

'Come on. Let's go and see how we can get you paying as little as possible to him, legally.'

'Legally sounds good. I've been lying on this very floor, surrounded by paperwork, convinced I was going to end up going to prison for messing everything up and accidentally committing fraud.'

He laughed. It was a nice sound and I was relieved that he seemed to have relaxed a little. 'You really have got yourself in a state over this, haven't you?'

I pulled a face.

'Don't worry. I'm rubbish at small talk but I'm good at this. I promise. It's all going to be fine.'

Nearly three hours later and I was beginning to understand a lot more about tax than I'd ever thought I would, or could. Charlie was patient and kind and didn't treat me like an idiot if I needed something explaining more than once. He was also funny. Now that he was in his comfort zone, it seemed as if his natural personality had stepped to the fore. It made me a little sad that he didn't feel as though he could harness that in everyday social situations because, seriously, women would be falling over themselves for him. Not that they wouldn't be already but add this side of his personality and... hello! Charlie Richmond was, in fact, incredibly sexy. And he seemed to have absolutely no idea of the fact. A thought suddenly skittered through my brain – should I be worried that I had six feet five inches' worth of gorgeousness sitting next to me and all I could think about was getting my tax stuff in order?

'Did I say something funny?' he asked, the faint ghost of a smile playing on his mouth.

'No,' I returned, quickly deciding that telling Charlie what I was really thinking was probably a little too much sharing, even for me, on a first encounter. I had a feeling I wouldn't see him for dust if he knew my current thoughts. And I really needed my taxes done. 'I'm just happy that you were able to do this today for me.'

'Like I said, it's a pleasure. There's a few more things to go through but I can always come back another day or meet up some-where another time if you've had enough.'

'How about we take a break for a bit of lunch and then see how we feel after that? Unless you have other plans, of course?' I added, hastily.

'No, not at all. Lunch sounds great.'

'Do you have any preferences? Favourite places, or foods?'

'No. I pretty much eat anything.'

'OK. Let me grab my stuff and we can go. Here, put some of that on whilst you're waiting. It's scorching out there.' I tossed him a tube of sunscreen I'd been sent for reviewing earlier in the week. He turned it over in his hands, read the blurb and began unscrewing the top.

I slung my bag over my shoulder and grabbed my wide-brimmed hat. There was only a light breeze out there today so I was fairly confident that I wasn't going to end up chasing it halfway down the beach. Again.

'Ready?' I asked.

'Yep,' Charlie said, replacing the sun cream tube on the console table and turning to me with one hand on the front door catch.

'Oh, wait. You have some...' Automatically I reached up and gently rubbed in the blob of sun cream he'd missed on the top of his cheekbone with my thumb. 'There.'

'Thanks.' He nodded, not quite looking at me.

I blinked once, slowly. 'Sorry. I probably should have just pointed you to a mirror then, shouldn't I? Habit. I have two nephews so I'm always tidying them up. Obviously they're, umm, a bit smaller than you. That should have given me a clue, I guess.'

'It's all right. Thanks for tidying me up too.' Charlie gave a little smile and I returned it, all the while thinking that I most definitely needed to work on my boundary issues. I'd always been super tactile, and was, as I'd said, used to fussing after my nephews. It was only when I'd looked up and seen Charlie's diverted eyes that I'd suddenly remembered not everyone was as touchy feely as me.

4

We left the flat and headed down to the pathway that separated the residential buildings from the marina walls. On our left, the sun was glinting off the calm water that today had taken on a vibrant aquamarine hue.

'Look at that colour!' I enthused.

'Beautiful, isn't it?'

'So, you live in Brighton too, Amy was saying?'

'That's right. Just along the front, on the way back into town from here.'

We walked on another few steps before Charlie spoke again. 'Amy is the girl my brother has been nuts about for ages?'

I looked at him from under my hat. 'Nuts about?'

'Completely. I was so relieved that she finally said yes. For him, and me!' He chuckled. 'Can I ask something, though?' His voice was a little more serious now.

'Of course.'

'Why did she make him wait so long? I mean... Look, I know she's your friend, but he's my little brother. And yes, he's big enough and ugly enough to look after himself, but I just don't want someone playing games with him. Especially not someone whom he really seems to like. I know you're obviously going to side with your friend, which is totally understandable, but I get the impression you tend to say what you think, honestly.'

'I do, you're right. But I can put your mind at rest. The whole reason Amy's "made him wait so long", as you put it, is precisely because she didn't want to muck him around. Because she likes and respects Marcus too much to do that.'

Charlie seemed to consider that, then nodded as if in acceptance of my answer.

We were now walking along the raised wooden boardwalk that faced the marina. Restaurants lined the back edge and outdoor tables were nearly all full with locals and holidaymakers enjoying the weekend sunshine.

'Would you rather sit inside?' Charlie asked, having apparently already assessed that I wasn't the type for sitting in the sun.

'Do you mind?'

'Not at all. It's pretty busy out here anyway. It might be a bit less manic in there.'

We headed inside the restaurant and found that Charlie was right. Most of the clientele had chosen to sit outside in the heat rather than enjoy the cool of the air conditioning whilst they ate. The waiter showed us to a table and we gave ourselves a few moments to settle in before I took up the conversation again.

'Amy had a bit of a messy break-up some time ago. She was reluctant to see anybody for a long time because she was worried about rebounding. She had to say yes to Marcus when the time was right.'

'And what if he'd stopped asking by then? Given up?' Charlie asked, his eyes serious. From anyone else, I'd have taken this to be a bit of a smart-arse comment. But not here. My time spent with him this morning had quickly shown me that. This was just Charlie Richmond's logical mind wanting to see how things worked.

'Then I guess it would have shown that he wasn't as nuts about her as you thought, and that it wasn't meant to be.'

He fiddled with the menu, considering my words. 'You really believe in all that fate and "meant to be" stuff?'

'I'm guessing that you don't?'

Charlie let out a sigh. 'I'm not really sure that I can. I think that's the logical side of my brain kicking in – why I like numbers and why I'm good at my job. Fate doesn't play a part in it. It's all about probabilities. It can all be worked out in black and white.'

'But life isn't black and white. Even you must admit that?'

'I do. And maybe that's why I want as much as possible of it to be logical because sometimes there's something that comes out of nowhere, that throws you for a loop. For someone like me, who needs...' he paused and rephrased '... who likes to find reason behind things, something like that just completely fries my brain. It's almost impossible to process.'

I got the feeling that Charlie had a specific situation in mind. His eyes had taken on a sadness. I knew that it was too early to start questioning him as to what it was – that was to say, I knew it, I just couldn't help it.

'Something specifically threw you for a loop.' It was a statement rather than a question.

Charlie pulled his gaze from the menu.

'I'm sorry. I have no control sometimes. Feel free to tell me to shut up.'

His lips quirked.

'That's OK. I know exactly where I stand with you. I like that.'

I smiled, feeling the same way.

His eyes scanned the menu again. I guessed he wasn't actually going to answer me but was, not surprisingly, too polite to tell me to keep my beak out.

'In my second year of university, my best mate there collapsed and died on the running track. Fit as anything, he was. And then, out like a light.'

He hadn't looked up.

'Oh, Charlie, I'm so sorry.' My hand automatically moved to touch his. Again, with the touchy-feely boundary issues. Oh, well. But he didn't move it. He just looked up and let out a sigh.

'Something called HCM. Hypertrophic cardiomyopathy. Funny what you remember, isn't it? Apparently, it generally affects younger people and most of the time, unless it's something flagged in your family history, you don't know you have it until something happens.'

I didn't know what to say.

He reached for the glass of water the waiter had put down moments after we'd arrived and took a sip.

'Were you with him?'

He nodded. 'Right beside him. And I couldn't do anything. I've never felt so utterly useless in my entire life.'

'It sounds like there's nothing that anyone could have done.'

Charlie shook his head, then looked at me under his lashes. 'Do you always do this?'

My eyes widened. 'What?'

'Put people at their ease so they spill out their deepest, darkest secrets?'

I got the feeling Charlie Richmond wasn't used to opening up too often, and I didn't want to ruin the meal or, let's face it, lose my newly acquired accountant. Time to lighten the mood.

'The lifestyle blog thing is just a cover. Truth is, I'm actually a kick-ass secret agent. Being interested in people is my weapon of choice. Everything else makes far too much mess.'

The blue eyes sparkled with amusement.

'I'm sorry if I overstepped. I sort of have a habit of doing that.'

He waved away my apology before taking another sip of water. 'It just seemed such a waste. As I said, I like to try and reason things out. But this? There was no reason for it. It was just completely out of nowhere.' Sadness clouded the blue.

'It was an utter waste. I'm so sorry about your friend.'

He flicked his gaze to me and gave an almost imperceptible nod of acceptance.

I continued. 'It would be so nice if life worked like that. That there really was a reason for everything. Unfortunately, it doesn't, and there isn't. It's just bloody messy a lot of the time. I think all we can ever do is muddle through the best way we know how – whether that's by your way of finding as much black and white, linear movement as possible or my more... wishy-washy method.'

His face creased into a smile as he brought his gaze back from the middle distance it had been resting in. 'Wishy-washy?'

Looking back at him, I was relieved to see the sadness dissipated. 'It's as good a description as any,' I said, laughing, as the waiter approached the table.

'It is,' Charlie agreed.

We ordered our drinks and set about scanning the menu for lunch.

'What shall I have?' I pondered aloud, my gaze drifting from one yummy-sounding choice to another on the oversized menu I now held in front of me.

'Do you want bread and olives, or something else to get started on?'

'Hmm?' I said, peeking over the top of the card.

'I just wondered if you wanted some bread and olives to be getting on with? Whilst we wait for the rest?' He paused. 'Or do you not like them?'

'I love them! I just have a habit of filling up on them before my main course arrives.'

'I can ration you.'

Once again, I couldn't tell if he was joking or not. I decided to roll with it anyway.

'OK. Deal.'

I caught the tiniest of twinkles in his eyes at my response.

The waiter appeared at our table once again a short while later.

'Are you ready to order?' he asked. 'Or do you need a little more time?'

Unlike Charlie, I'd noticed that this particular waiter's gaze had rarely left us since we'd come in – or, more specifically, had barely left my lunch companion. I was pretty sure he'd be happy for this gorgeous man to sit there all day.

Charlie looked at me for an answer and I nodded. We gave our choices and the waiter scribbled them down before taking the menus with a flourish. He threw Charlie an extra-wide smile as he handed his over. Charlie smiled back at him in thanks, the further connotations of the waiter's attention apparently lost on him. A few minutes later the man was back with our drinks. He threw Charlie another couple of flirty looks, which again seemed to go unnoticed, then told us that our bread would be over in just a moment.

'I think you have an admirer,' I said, when the waiter was out of earshot.

'Hmm?' Charlie's brow creased in question as he lifted his beer.

It suddenly occurred to me that I had no idea as to whether Charlie was straight or gay. Either way, one gender was going to be sorely disappointed.

'The waiter. He's... extremely enamoured with you.'

Charlie raised one eyebrow at me as he took another sip.

'I just wanted to say, if you want to... you know... follow up on that, please don't stand on ceremony on my behalf. I mean, go for it.'

Charlie's eyes bulged as he began choking on his drink. Turning redder as he tried to stifle the coughing, he buried his face in a napkin and endeavoured to do it quietly.

'Are you all right?' I asked, even though he clearly wasn't.

He didn't answer.

'Shall I pat you on the back or something? Would that help?' I made to push my chair back and stand but Charlie's waved hand kept me where I was.

'I'm fine,' he croaked out, sounding anything but. 'Just went down the wrong way.'

He took another sip and it seemed to help. His face, thankfully, began returning to a more normal colour.

'Better?' I asked, concern in my voice.

He smiled at me. 'Much. Thanks.'

The waiter appeared and placed our starter nibbles down, along with a couple of fresh napkins. Apparently, he'd also witnessed Charlie's mishap.

'Thanks.' Charlie nodded at him.

'You're very welcome.'

I bent my head further as I took a breadstick and dunked it in the garlic dip we'd ordered. From my peripheral vision, I saw the waiter leave and head back to the bar. I risked a look up, my gaze quickly meeting Charlie's amused one.

'OK. I'll give you that one. But – and I don't know what you've heard – just so that you're clear – not that it matters on any level but purely because trying to be politely quiet whilst choking is a complete pain in the arse – I'm not gay. So, thanks for the offer of being a wingman – or woman – but it's not necessary in this case.'

'Oh. Right. Thought I'd ask. You know. Just in case,' I said, selecting another breadstick whilst deftly managing to avoid looking at my companion. Truth be told, I suddenly felt like a bit of an idiot.

'And please don't think I don't appreciate the thought.' I could hear the smile in his voice.

I risked a look. Yep. I knew it. There was a bloody great grin on his face.

I gave a small eye-roll. 'You see. This is why I work behind a screen. There's far less danger of me saying or doing something on the spur of the moment that, in that instant, seems helpful but soon after just makes me feel like a complete fool.'

'I can see how that might work better for you.'

I tilted my head a little and gave a resigned look.

Charlie laughed. 'Don't worry about it.'

'But I do!' I said. 'I always do this! I'm a nightmare!'

'Rubbish,' Charlie stated. 'You're natural. And – even when misguided – very thoughtful. It's refreshing.'

'It is?'

'It is,' he said, before taking a breadstick and chomping happily through it.

'So, is that true, then? What you said about why you started the blog? So you could hide behind a screen.'

'I wouldn't exactly call it hiding. Especially not with the videos I do.'

'No. Sorry. I didn't mean it like that.' He gave me one of those honest looks. 'You know what I mean.'

'I do. And to answer your question, no, not really. Although it's certainly a benefit. I'd had the blog for a few years but it was an intermittent thing. I was quite bad about posting regularly but it didn't bother me because it wasn't really something I was doing to get followers, especially. It was just something I was doing for me. Sort of a way of keeping a record of stuff that I'd read about, things I found interesting and products I'd discovered and really liked. I started getting a few comments and that was nice. They often asked if I could post more often and suggested some things that they'd like to see on the blog. I took notes, and said I'd see what I could do, but I had a full-time job, a boyfriend and a fairly busy social life connected to all that. I couldn't really see where I would find the time to fit in a more dedicated attitude to blogging.'

'Obviously something changed.'

'Yes. You could say that. I was Executive Assistant to a director of a tech company based here. It had done phenomenally well, and with the attention about the whole Silicon Beach thing, it just soared.'

Charlie nodded at the reference to the nickname Brighton had acquired in the last few years as more and more tech companies had begun basing themselves in the seaside town.

'Everything was going great. The company was doing well. I loved my job and I was good at it. And I know what you're thinking!' I said, holding my hand up. 'What with my faltering ability to engage my brain fully before my mouth goes into action, how could I possibly do a job like that?'

'Never crossed my mind.'

'You big fibber!'

He grinned and gave a little shrug.

'I knew it. Anyway,' I continued, 'again, most of it was online contact and, I don't know. It just seems to be more of a social affliction.'

'Affliction is a strong word.'

'You nearly choked to death earlier, thanks to me. I think it deserves a strong word.'

He gave a little head-shake and I continued.

'So, things were going well. Then an American company started showing some interest. My boss went over there a few times and had some discussions with them and it turned out they wanted to buy the whole thing. He wasn't prepared to give it all up so he got them to write in a proviso that he be part of the package, retaining an executive position in the new company.'

'That all sounds good. For him, at least.'

'It was great for him. Turns out, not so great for me.'

'If he was still an executive, surely he still needed an assistant?'

'And he got one. In America. Where the company was going to be based following the buy-out.'

'You couldn't go with it? Or you didn't want to?'

'Neither, really. I don't think I would have wanted to, if I'm totally honest. My friends are here. My brother and nephews are here. But when it came down to it, it wasn't exactly given as an option.'

'That's vague.'

'I'm trying to retain some degree of dignity.' I laughed.

Charlie frowned, that confused smile back on his face. I seemed to bring that out in him. A lot.

'My boss didn't want me to go with him.'

'But I thought you said you were good at your job?'

I opened my mouth to say something.

'And don't take that the wrong way – I meant that any boss of sense ordinarily does whatever they can to keep good staff. It's not like they're always that easy to find. Believe me, I know.'

'This was a little more complicated.'

'Oh.' Charlie sat back. 'I didn't mean to pry.'

'No. It's fine. And seriously?' I laughed. 'That'd be rich of me to object to you asking questions, wouldn't it? Anyway, as it's turned out, he did me a favour. Although I have to admit I didn't feel that generous towards him at the time.'

Charlie didn't say anything, clearly letting me decide as to whether I wanted to share any more.

'I was dating my boss. We'd been seeing each other for a couple of years and it seemed to be going well, like everything else. But when he went over to America for those trips, something changed. Long story short, he met someone over there. His new Executive Assistant.'

Charlie winced.

'Yes. It was a bit.' I finished the last of my drink. 'I'd love to say I had a dignified reaction to the whole situation.'

'I take it you didn't?'

'Not exactly. Let's just say I perpetuated the belief that redheads have a temper, culminating in a situation which may or may not have involved me stapling his tie to the desk.'

'Well, bearing in mind there are far worse things that you could have stapled to the desk, I'd say he got off pretty lightly.'

5

My eyebrows shot up and a bubble of laughter burst out of me. Accountants often had a reputation for being dry and boring but today was enlightening me to the fact that Charlie Richmond definitely wasn't boring, and the only thing dry about him was his wit.

'That's true. Although he was wearing the tie at the time of stapleage.'

He smiled. 'Stapleage? Is that a word?'

I shrugged.

'Still. It's been for the best and he was probably right in what he said – I wouldn't have been the right fit for the company there.'

'He said that?' Charlie's brow furrowed. 'Because of the relationship?'

I shook my head. 'No. Well, maybe a little but there was more to it.'

He said nothing, waiting for me to continue.

'Oh, Charlie! You've been in my company for a few hours now. I'm not exactly high-flying corporate material. I'm too... friendly!' I laughed. 'I think he was a bit worried that I might show him up with his new colleagues and friends.'

'Then it doesn't really sound like he deserved you in the first place. In any capacity.'

My smile broke through and I sat straighter. 'You know, I came to the same conclusion.'

'Good. It sounds like you had quite a last day at that particular office.'

I let out a sigh at the understatement. 'Still. It turned out for the best. I found some local bar work and decided to use the redundancy money to take a little break from working full time. With that, and my suddenly unexpectedly free social diary, I was able to concentrate on finishing the writing course I'd been doing and even started getting some magazine articles accepted, now that I had the time to devote to submissions. I thought doing a bit more on the blog would be good practice too, as well as it being a bit of a showcase for my writing. And the more I did it, the more I enjoyed it and the more hits I got. One post got picked up on a blog round-up and that really helped boost things. Advertisers started approaching me, which helped my income and as the blog continued to grow I started getting attention from brands, interested in possible sponsorship and collaborations.

'Getting a column in the local paper was pretty exciting, and I regularly write for a couple of other publications and their online sites too. I no longer do the bar work, by the way. Just so that you don't think I'm hiding any cash-in-hand stuff from my accountant.'

'I'm not sure you're actually capable of hiding much at all, from what I've seen.'

I frowned.

'It's a compliment.'

'Oh.'

'I take it everything was over with the boyfriend?'

'Definitely. I found out later they'd been dancing around each other for a while. She was some city girl high-flyer, same as him, so I'm sure they had much more in common than he and I ever did. I'm quite a people person generally—' at this I saw a glint of a smile in Charlie's eyes '—but, to be honest, I often felt a little out of place whenever I went to functions with him. They'd all be talking about stuff I have no understanding of, so I'd just sort of stand there most of the time, feeling a bit of an idiot.

'Did you ever tell him that?'

'What?'

'That you felt uncomfortable?'

'I tried.'

'And?'

'Nothing really. I mean, he couldn't make me understand the technicalities of the software business, or stocks and bonds, which is usually what the conversation swung around to. What was he supposed to do?'

'He was supposed to make sure you felt comfortable. To reassure you.'

'That's sweet, but it makes me sound a bit pathetic.'

'No, it doesn't.'

'I can look after myself, Charlie. I never failed to find the bar and a friendly barman or lady to chat to.' I gave him a cheeky wink.

'I have no doubt that you are entirely able to take care of yourself, or that you wouldn't have any difficulty in finding someone to talk to.'

'Just not in his social circle.'

'Then it was most definitely their loss. By not taking the time, they missed out on some very entertaining conversation.'

I tilted my head at him. 'I can't yet tell when you're being sincere and when you're taking the mickey.'

'In this case, I'm sincere.'

'Then, thank you.'

'You're welcome. And if you don't mind me saying so, I think the only idiot in that relationship was him.'

'Thank you. Again. I came to the same conclusion. Of course, it took me slightly longer and a lot more tears to get there.'

Charlie studied me for a moment, his expression unreadable, before taking the bill off the approaching waiter before he could put it down. Motioning for him to wait a moment, he then handed over a credit card.

'How much is my half?' I asked, rummaging in my bag.

'I'm getting this.'

I looked up, purse now in hand. 'Oh, no. You can't do that. We agreed I'd pay.'

Charlie frowned. 'We did no such thing,' he said calmly, taking the payment machine off the waiter, before putting in a pin code and handing it back.

'Didn't we?' I thought back. Actually, no, we hadn't. 'All right. Well, I meant to say that before we started. You're already doing the accounts as a favour. I'd feel better if you'd let me pay for lunch at least.'

'All done now.'

I pulled a face.

He chuckled. 'Fine. You can pay next time.'

'Next time! I'm not waiting another year to pay you back. Or... wait! Are my books in that much of a state?' A hint of panic crept into my voice.

'No, they're fine. And I'm sure we can sort something out if you're that bothered about waiting a year to recompense.'

'Good. And good. Because I am.'

He did the cute little chuckle again. 'OK, then.'

* * *

We did sort something out. After lunch, Charlie returned to the flat and spent another couple of hours going over everything with me, which led me to deciding that I would take him out to dinner, along with Amy and Marcus, as a thank you to all of them for their help. I rang Amy the following day to ask her.

'Hey, how'd it go?'

'Brilliant! My accounts are in tip-top shape.'

And that wasn't the only thing in tip-top shape.

'Great. Told you we'd get it sorted out. At least I don't have to worry about learning how to bake a cake for file smuggling now.'

'I still don't understand how you can be glued to every single series of *Bake Off* and still have no idea how to make a cake.'

'I don't need to know. That's what bakeries are for.'

'Fair enough. Anyway. The thing is, I want to take you all to dinner as a thank you for setting up this whole accountancy bail-out thing.'

'Aah, that's sweet, Libs. You don't have to do that. Charlie quite enjoyed himself, from what I heard. Marcus had it on speaker in the car when he rang to say he'd done your books.'

'Did he?'

'Apparently.'

'What makes you say that?'

'Oh, he was just going on about how nice it was to get back to basics and how...' Amy paused. 'Ohmigod! You like him!'

On the other end of the phone, alone in my flat, I flushed the colour of a beetroot.

'I did. He's very nice. Not like the other accountants I tried.'

'And just exactly how much of him did you try out?'

'Oh, ha ha! Look, do you want a free dinner or not?'

'Of course! When were you thinking?'

'I wondered about tonight?'

'Blimey. You are keen on him! Can't wait, eh?'

'Don't be daft. It's not that. I just thought it might be nice as it's a lovely day and I know Charlie can get home fairly late in the week. I mean, I haven't even asked him yet, so he might not be able to do it anyway but I just thought—'

'Libs!' Amy interrupted my jabbering. 'Just ask him and let me know.'

'Erm. Yes. Yes, good idea. I'll ring you back.'

'Talk to you soon.' There was a teasing note in Amy's voice that I tried to ignore as I brought Charlie's contact details up on my phone. Did I phone or text? Was phoning him a bit too much like asking him on a date? A little over-familiar? Or was texting more familiar than phoning? Oh, crap. For God's sake, it was just a thank you dinner with friends. I rolled my eyes at myself and began texting.

✉ Hi Charlie. Thanks again for the help yesterday. As you won't take payment, I'd like to invite you and Marcus and Amy out to dinner as a way of saying thanks to you all. I wondered about tonight as it's such a nice day, but obviously it's very short notice and completely understand if you have other plans. Thanks. Libby x

I took away the kiss. Then put it back. Then took it away before dropping a swear word in my head and putting it back in. I'd given Charlie a big hug in grateful thanks and relief when he was leaving and had a feeling he already had my character sussed to a pretty good degree anyway. I pressed send and put the phone down on the coffee table.

Picking up my tea, and a chocolate biscuit, I began reading an article on a new clothing company that had been set up along the lines of People Tree. I'd always been interested in this area of fashion and beauty. The concept and realities behind 'fast fashion' had been niggling away at the back of my mind for a while and then the Rana Plaza tragedy happened. Shocked, I'd sat and watched the rescue efforts on television, the friends and relatives holding photographs of their loved ones, waiting, hoping, sobbing. Their pain had been so tangible, so heart-rending that I hadn't been able to stop my own tears streaming. When the news broke that a woman had been pulled out alive seventeen days after the disaster, I'd felt more relief and joy than I'd ever thought possible for someone I didn't even know.

I'd read up some more on it all and discovered that the workers had already told the management about the huge cracks appearing in the building, but their concerns had been ignored and they'd been forced to go back in. I'd literally felt ill. All of that loss of life, that suffering, just so that richer countries could have access to cheap clothes and a tiny percentage of people could rake in obscene amounts of profit. And yet all of it could have been avoided.

I'd begun looking into things more, finding out who in the fashion industry was trying to help change things, and which companies were supportive of that change.

As my blog began to grow, I made this aspect part of my USP – the clothes I featured were pretty much all from companies who were completely transparent in their dealings, and could prove that their clothing wasn't made in sweatshops and that they had paid farmers a fair price for their materials. I was all for promoting the resurgence in home sewing too and was lucky enough to have a very talented friend, Tim, with a fledgling design and dressmaking business. Sitting chatting over coffee one day, we got to talking about how the designs from the catwalk filtered down through the industry until they hit the high street, and how well the character of Miranda had explained this in the film *The Devil Wears Prada*, completely burning the character of Andy in the process! Tim told me how once he'd been asked to make pretty much a direct copy of

Kate Middleton's wedding dress, with three weeks to the big day, when the bride had changed her mind about the dress she'd already bought after she'd watched the royal wedding on television.

'Of course, there are knock-offs being sewn up in factories all over the world within hours of anything like that being broadcast,' Tim mused. 'And I'm sure there were plenty of independent people like me being asked to do the same. Although I would hope most of them had longer than I was given.'

'You're amazing. I could never do that.'

'Yes, you could. You already have an eye for it. I told you I'd teach you.'

'Be careful, or I might take you up on that one day.'

'I live in hope!' Tim replied, a beating motion with his hand over his heart.

'Twit,' I said, laughing, knowing he was teasing. Mostly because Tim and I had the same taste in men.

'But you're on to something.'

'I am?' Tim asked, unsure.

'Yes! Look, there's all these gorgeous creations coming down the catwalk, but for most people they're completely off the scale, budget-wise. And eventually, versions will appear that are more budget friendly but at what cost elsewhere?'

'Where are you going with all this?'

'An idea for your blog!'

'My blog?' He frowned.

'Yes.'

'But that's just for fun, really,' Tim replied.

'It can still be for fun, but as a business you need a good website. Having a great blog will help draw readers and potential clients to it. It could showcase your talents even more and build your following, which in turn will help grow your business.'

'Spit it out, then!'

'What about doing a feature when the fashion weeks come around? You pick one item from a show that you love and then recreate it – obviously with your own twist. Using the original piece as "inspiration only".' I made air quotes with my fingers up by the side of my head, which gave the impression of doing bunny ears more than anything else, but Tim got the idea.'

'That's not bad. I like it!'

I beamed happily.

'On one condition.'

'What's that?'

'I make it for you, and you wear it.'

'No. You sell it once you've used it to showcase your talents.'

'I don't want to. It's a great idea, Libby. And it was your idea, so I want you to benefit from it too.'

'Tim—'

'Say you'll do it or I won't play.' Tim folded his arms across his bony frame and looked at me over the top of his trendy, thick-rimmed glasses.

I sighed. 'I'll do it,' I said, not quite able to stop the little smile that escaped. Tim really did make the most beautiful clothes.

'And you feature it on your blog.'

'That was always going to happen. I'll feature them all, and I'll keep the first piece, but the rest you sell. Deal?'

'No deal.'

'Why not?'

'It's only a few pieces a year, Libby, and the promotion I'll get from you looking fabulous in them is worth more than I could sell any of them for.'

'Flattery will get you everywhere.' I winked. 'You're sure?'

'I'm sure. And, bonus, I get to see you in your underwear when you come for fitting.'

'Oh, yes. Because that's a real draw for you.'

Tim winked back. 'Actually, I just live in hope that one day you might bring a gorgeous man with you and I can persuade him he needs something made to measure.'

'I'll bear that in mind, but don't get your hopes up.'

6

I took one look at Charlie walking through the door to the restaurant and decided that Tim would have an appropriately pink fit if I ever brought Charlie to a fitting with me. He wore smart khakis that made his bum look amazing, and a crisp white shirt, the sleeves rolled up to reveal gently tanned forearms with just the right amount of muscle to them. I hadn't looked at the menu yet but I was pretty sure several people in the room had already decided on the perfect dessert.

'Hi.' Charlie smiled as he took his seat opposite me, having said hello to his brother and Amy. They'd met properly earlier this afternoon when he'd dropped round to his brother's place, just after I'd spoken to Amy about the proposed dinner. Everything was arranged and Charlie had texted me back to say that they were all together and agreed it was a lovely idea. And now, here we were. And it was all very lovely indeed. For a while.

'So, you're not seeing anyone at the moment, then?' Amy asked Charlie, in an apparently casual way that I knew was anything but. 'I find that hard to believe. Couple of big, lovely blokes like you two and only one with a girlfriend. It seems a little unfair.'

'I don't mind.' Marcus grinned, his eyes giving Amy a teasing look.

I kept my face passive and gave Amy a kick under the table.

'Ow!' Marcus bent and rubbed his shin.

'Oh, no! I'm so sorry. I started getting cramp in my leg and...'

'No worries.' Marcus smiled and gave his leg a final rub.

Although I'd ended up making contact with the wrong person, I hoped the distraction was enough to give Amy the hint.

'So, was that a no?' Amy prompted Charlie.

Apparently not.

'Umm, no, not really. Work's kind of mad at the moment. Lots of travelling.'

'And he's picky as hell,' Marcus volunteered.

'Is he now?' Amy asked, intrigued.

'I'm not picky. I'm... discerning.'

'That's just a posh word for picky,' Marcus countered.

Charlie looked at me. 'Would you like a brother? I've got one going spare.'

I smiled. 'No, thanks. I already have one. He's more than enough.'

He returned the smile. Unfortunately, Amy took this as another cue.

'So, what do you look for, in your discerning manner?'

'Amy. Stop questioning the poor man!' I said, laughing but really hoping she'd get the message. 'I brought you all out to say thank you, not to start the Spanish Inquisition on Charlie.'

'Well, he definitely has a type.' Marcus clearly wasn't about to let it go now either.

'I don't have a type.'

'You totally have a type, mate.'

Charlie gave him the patient look that he'd given me a couple of times yesterday. I was sort of glad to see I wasn't the only one that brought it out in him.

'Do tell.'

'Every single girlfriend you've ever had have all been in the same line of work as you, give or take. And they've definitely all been high-flyers jetting off around the world, closing deals worth millions before breakfast.'

I felt my stomach twist. Amy caught my eye, her look now wary. I smiled, indicating that I was fine. She smiled back but it didn't reach her eyes and I knew that she knew I was completely faking it.

'Carly's an interior designer.' Charlie raised one eyebrow, indicating to his brother that he'd found a flaw in his theory.

'Yes, she is. She's an interior designer with a first in Economics from LSE who used to be in hedge funds but decided to change careers. She's still The Type.'

Charlie frowned briefly, and I wondered if he was only just beginning to see that he did indeed have a type. A type I most definitely didn't fall into.

'I think it's more coincidence than an actual choosing of a specific type, as you put it. They're generally just the sort of women that I meet. I spend a lot of time at work so naturally those are the types I spend the most time with and get to know. Besides, it's always good to have things in common like that, purely for conversational purposes, if nothing else.'

Amy nodded and smiled as the waiter came over to enquire as to whether we would be wanting dessert. I pretended to be studying the options but my mind was elsewhere. All I knew was that I suddenly had an uncomfortable, churning sense of City Boy déjà vu.

When the subject had come up yesterday, I'd told Charlie I didn't mind that I hadn't fitted in too well in Corporate Land. I'd brushed it off as if it didn't matter. And it didn't. Not really. What had mattered was that I'd been told by someone who was supposed to care about me that I didn't fit in. That I was too 'left field' for where the company was going. Whatever the hell that meant.

I hadn't shared any of it on my blog, instead putting on the sunny disposition that people had now come to expect of me, saying I was in an 'exciting place and ready for a new challenge'. Even Amy didn't know the whole truth. She'd been in her own difficult place and I wasn't about to ask her to deal with my upset too. To the outside world, I'd been fine about losing my job, my boyfriend and being told I wasn't good enough to ascend to the heights the company was now heading for – all on the same day. The only people that really knew how deeply it had hurt were my family. They were the only ones I felt safe enough to open up to, knowing I wouldn't be judged. I didn't have a perfect life, and my Instagram feed, for the most part, reflected that, unlike some. But even I knew that it was a curated version of my real life. Deep down I knew I was harbouring a fear that the real me might not be good enough for the world to see.

Glancing under my lashes at the man opposite me, I realised that even having a passing thought of dating Charlie Richmond was like a lactose intolerant wanting cheesecake. Sometimes things just weren't good together. At least not for very long. As delicious as it might initially be, I knew this particular dessert was off the menu.

* * *

I read the text from Amy one more time.

⊠ You're going to be great!

I hoped so. I knew this meeting could lead to great things for the blog, so I really wanted it to go well. Only, I wasn't used to meeting people on a more formal, businesslike basis and I was, quite frankly, terrified.

I'd caught an earlier train than I needed to. Much earlier, just in case. I sat in the carriage, staring out at the platform, not seeing anything of the Victorian architecture of the station. In my head, I was running over figures – subscriber numbers, amount of views, Facebook, Instagram and Twitter statistics, even though I already had them memorised. All of this was information that the cosmetics company would already have. If they hadn't been happy with those, I knew I wouldn't even be on this train worrying about it all, but I wanted to be prepared in case they asked me anything about them. I wanted to present myself as businesslike and competent, which I knew I was. But I was also wary of blowing it thanks to nerves. It almost didn't feel like me sitting there. I was wearing a suit, for a start. I'd never worn a suit in my life. The offices I'd worked in had all had smart dress codes but never formal to this extent. Obviously the company I was going to see – Gorgeous & Glam – already knew what my everyday aesthetic was and clearly felt that it was some-thing they could work with. But my day-to-day look of a Boho dress and loose-flowing hair didn't seem right. Not for this.

So, I had turned to Amy, who knew about these things, and we went shopping. I'd had doubts as to whether we'd ever find something that didn't feel as if I was entirely selling out but I should have trusted Amy – she had super styling skills when it came to the more formal side of things. I'd even jotted down some notes on doing a post about our trip because it had been far more fun than I'd thought. We'd found a gorgeous suit – all nipped-in waist and flippy skirt, my fears of boxy and rigid banished. My hair was tucked neatly into a chignon with some wispy bits at the front, for softness. All in all, I knew I looked the part and, although it was pretty different from my usual style, I might be able to get used to it for the odd occasion.

'Libby?' The deep voice broke into my thoughts, and I jumped.

Charlie's hand automatically reached out to my shoulder. 'Sorry, I didn't mean to startle you.'

'Hi! Oh, don't worry! I was miles away.' I smiled up at him.

'Is this seat taken?' he asked, pointing at the one next to me.

I shook my head. Charlie shoved his briefcase up onto the luggage rack and sat down next to me. He shifted position to get comfy and bumped shoulders with me.

'Sorry.'

He folded his legs in tightly against the seat, allowing room for the well-dressed woman now opposite him to sit comfortably. I was happy to notice that he wasn't one of those male leg-spreaders that took up every available bit of space, irrespective of whether someone else needed it or not. Although, to be fair, there was a seat opposite me that she could have shifted across to, which would have given her more room, what with my legs being somewhat shorter than Charlie's and my entire bulk being a lot less. She, however, seemed disinclined to move. I'd noticed her run her gaze over Charlie as he'd reached up to put his bag away earlier, so it wasn't a vast stretch to guess that she might have made strategic plans to sit opposite him rather than me. I could hardly blame her. He smiled at her briefly when they made eye contact as he settled in but, in general, seemed as oblivious to her attentions as he had done to the waiter's in the restaurant the first day we'd met.

'I—' He started to speak and was immediately interrupted by his phone beginning to ring. He rolled his eyes and pulled a face.

'Sorry,' he said again.

I took a sneaky peek as he pulled his phone out of his pocket and answered it, his voice low as he spoke. I smiled to myself. That made sense. Charlie was definitely not one of those types who would declare his business to everyone on the train, as so many others seemed happy to do. I turned my attention back to the platform and watched two seagulls fighting over a piece of dropped sandwich.

'So, where are you off to?' Charlie started again, returning his phone to his pocket as he did so.

I took a deep breath. 'London. I have a meeting with a cosmetics company today.'

Only my brother and Amy knew about the meeting. I'd been wary of telling too many people in case it all came to nothing, but it seemed right to tell Charlie now.

'Wow. That could be big, right?'

'Maybe. If it goes well, it could be great.'

Charlie tilted his head at me. 'Forgive me, but you don't seem as excited as I thought you would be for something like this. Which, bearing in mind your bouncy personality, is really saying something.'

'Oh, no, I am!' I said, turning in my seat to face him a bit more. 'I'm just really nervous. I'm worried I'm going to mess it up and, like you said, it could be great for the business. I don't want to let Tilly down.'

'Libby. You're not going to let anyone down. Just relax. Do what you do normally, and it'll be fine.'

'What I do normally is talk to a camera and when I muck up, I edit that bit out. That's the trouble with actually meeting people face to face – there's no chance to edit. If I trip over my words today, that's it!'

He smiled and I felt a warmth wash over me like a gentle sunbeam.

'What?' I said, unable to stop a smile forming on my face.

His hands reached out and covered the knot of mine as they gripped together in a tight little ball on my lap. His touch was cool, and the gesture calming. 'You're going to do great, Libby. If they didn't already know most of what they need to, you wouldn't even be going up there, so just relax and be yourself. That's what they want.'

'I suppose.'

'I know.'

I gave him a look under my lashes. 'All right, Mr Smarty Pants.'

He laughed and gave my hands a quick squeeze, just as his phone began to ring once more.

Rolling his eyes, he removed his hands from mine and reached for his phone. I smiled and glanced up, catching the visual daggers of the woman opposite him as I did so.

'What time is your meeting?' Charlie asked after he'd finished the call.

'Eleven thirty.'

'You know you're going to be up there way before then, don't you?' he said, glancing at the Patek Philippe watch on his wrist. I was hoping the woman opposite hadn't seen its brand. She was already burying me six feet under for just talking to Charlie. He was movie-star gorgeous, and built for strength. Add to that the Savile Row bespoke suit and a watch worth tens of thousands of pounds on his wrist, and I was seriously beginning to doubt my safe exit off this train.

'I know. I thought it better safe than sorry. Just in case they cancelled a train or something silly.'

'Good plan.'

'What about you? Don't you normally get a much earlier one than this?'

'Yeah. I'm heading off on a business trip first thing tomorrow so I wanted to get some packing done before I left this morning.'

'Oh,' I said, feeling an odd tingle of disappointment knowing that Charlie wouldn't be around at the weekend. 'Off anywhere exciting?'

'No, just back to New York again.'

I laughed. 'How tiresome for you.'

He chuckled back. 'That came out way more pompous than I was aiming for.'

'No, not at all.'

Charlie looked doubtful.

'OK, a little, but I know you didn't mean it like that.'

'Thanks.'

'Will you get to see any sights whilst you are there? Or have you seen everything already as you've been so many times?' I said, playing off his earlier comment.

He caught the meaning and gave me a little turn of his head. 'No, mostly it'll be work. I have a bit of shopping to do – Mum and Marcus give me lists each time! There seem to be a few more things on there this time so I'm thinking Amy might be getting in on the action now too.' He smiled.

'Do you mind?'

'No, of course not. Gives me something to do during any downtime.'

Under my lashes, I glanced at the woman opposite Charlie. She was looking at him in a way that told me she had plenty of ideas for ways to keep him occupied during his downtime.

'Is there anything I can get you?' Charlie asked.

'Huh?' My mind had drifted unbidden, and very unexpectedly, in the same direction as the woman's opposite.

'From New York? Can I get you anything?'

I fanned myself. 'It's quite warm in here, isn't it?'

Charlie looked at me. 'It's all right. It's probably just you being a bit nervous.' He waved his paper at me a couple of times. 'Better?'

Now I'd pulled my mind away from where it had been drifting, yes, it was definitely cooling down again. I nodded.

Charlie returned to our conversation. 'So, is there?'

I looked at him blankly.

'Anything I can get you?'

'Oh! No, I'm fine. I don't think there's anything I need, but thank you.'

'I don't think there's a single item on my list that anyone actually needs. Is there anything you want?'

I smiled. 'No, honestly. But thank you for asking. And if I think of anything, I'll let you know.'

'OK.'

'Unless of course Tiffany are having a 90-per-cent-off sale. In which case...' I laughed and he grinned.

'I'll be sure to keep an eye out for any sale banners and let you know.'

'That would be lovely. Thank you.'

We rode in silence for a little while, or at least as much silence as a train carriage allowed. Charlie's arm was against mine and I could feel hard muscle through the expensive cotton of his shirt. Subtle hints of his aftershave teased my senses. I looked across to see that his eyes had closed and his head was now tilted back on the seat. Returning my gaze to the passing landscape outside the slightly grubby window of the train, I focused on my meeting, feeling the nerves rush immediately back in.

7

The train shunted on one of the sharper bends and Charlie's bulk squished into mine. Asleep and relaxed, he didn't have a chance to brace himself.

I let out an 'oof' of surprise and he blinked a couple of times as he woke suddenly from the jolt and got his bearings.

'God, sorry, Libby! Are you all right?'

'I'm fine,' I said, waving off his concern.

'Nodded off.'

'That's all right. You obviously needed it.'

He pulled a face in return, before glancing out of the window. The sky-reaching towers of Canary Wharf were coming into view to the side as we got closer to the terminus.

'How are you feeling now?' Charlie asked.

'OK. I think.'

'You'll be great, don't worry.' His gaze flicked over me. 'I forgot to say, I like this look on you. I nearly didn't recognise you when I got on.'

'Thanks. It's a bit of a departure for me, but I thought I needed to try a bit more of a business look for this meeting.'

'Looks good.'

I returned his smile. From what his brother had said about Charlie's type, it was obvious that Charlie's tastes in women ran to the more polished end of the style range, rather than my more casual aesthetic.

As the train pulled in, eager passengers gathered their belongings and made their way to stand at the door, waiting for that magical moment when the beeping sound began and they could press the button and release the doors. Personally I always preferred to wait until the train had actually stopped, which reduced the opportunity for me to bump or fall, a situation always best avoided. I'd discovered this from past – and painful – experience. Charlie was clearly of the same mind as he had remained in his seat and was frowning at a message on his phone.

The woman opposite was now standing and making a point of smoothing her very gorgeous, clearly designer, dress, which clung to every perfect curve as if it had been moulded on her. She bent slightly, ostensibly checking the heel of her shoe, but in fact giving Charlie, and several other males who were by now paying full attention, a tantalising view of yet more perfection, this time in the form of curvaceous cleavage. Charlie glanced up from his phone just in time to get a full eyeful. I saw the blush hit his neck and travel full speed to his cheeks as he quickly pulled his gaze up, only for it to lock onto hers. An arc of a smile formed on her perfectly shaped, burgundy-red lips. Charlie responded with a brief, awkward smile of his own before the sound of the beeping doors seemed to release him and he shot up out of his seat and grabbed his briefcase, pulling it down from the rack.

Unfortunately, between his embarrassment and my nerves, neither of us judged the timing of this manoeuvre very well and as he yanked the case down, it swung and caught me on the temple. I staggered briefly and sat back down in my seat. From the corner of my eye, I saw the vixen opposite smile again, this time in amusement. Two teenagers passing behind Charlie giggled and moved towards the door. Charlie just stared. I stood up again, and it jolted him back into action.

'Libby, I'm so sorry. Are you all right? I wasn't looking what I was doing. I didn't...'

'It's all right, Charlie. It was just a tap. I was surprised more than hurt. Honestly,' I reassured him.

He shook his head. 'I can't believe I just did that.' He appeared to be speaking more to himself than to me. I thought I'd answer anyway.

'Really. I'm OK. Look.' I pointed to my head. 'No blood. No lump. Besides, I don't blame you.' I couldn't resist the tease, and lowered my voice. 'A flash of cleavage that impressive is bound to throw your attention a little.'

Charlie looked straight at me, those startling blue eyes wide, contrasting with the cute pink blush that now tinted his skin. He opened his mouth to say something but closed it again.

Laughing, I touched his arm briefly. 'I'm only pulling your leg. It was pretty hard not to see it to be honest, and, to be fair, she's been mentally undressing you for the whole journey so don't feel too bad.'

He frowned. 'I don't think—'

'Yep. She was. No question.' I gave him a wink and smiled at how even more adorable Charlie looked as he took in this information. 'You're definitely in there.'

'OK, you can stop now.' He pulled a face at me, laughter dancing in his eyes. 'You're enjoying watching me squirm far too much. I thought you were a nice person.'

'I am a nice person,' I said, accepting his unspoken indication to go before him off the train. 'I am so nice, in fact, that I point out potential dates for you!'

Charlie gave me a look. 'I don't think so. She'd eat me alive.'

Of that, I had no doubt.

We walked together along the platform, Charlie slowing his pace a little to allow me to keep up in the five-inch-heeled sandals I'd paired with my suit. As we headed into the main concourse, my gaze caught on the voluptuous goddess from the train. She was standing to the side, frantically wiping a magnificently aimed pigeon poop from her cleavage. I rolled my lips together and tipped my head down.

'Clearly one of those birds is the Lionel Messi of the avian world,' Charlie commented, his eyes facing forward.

I glanced across at him, trying to hide my smile.

'I feel bad laughing.'

'She felt no such compunction when I clonked you on the head, so I wouldn't let it bother your conscience.' He glanced over at me, a smile flickering at the corners of his mouth, making it look even more tempting than normal.

'I'm this way.' He stopped, nodding towards the Tooley Street exit. 'Which way are you going?'

'Hmm?' I yanked myself back to the moment, 'Oh. Underground.'

'OK. Well, I hope everything goes well. Not that I have any doubts about that, but, you know. Seemed the right thing to say.' He did his little chuckle thing.

'Thank you.'

'Honestly though. You're going to be great. I know you are.' He leant in and gave me a hug. He really was one of the best huggers I'd ever met. A part of me didn't want to let go as I breathed in his smell and felt the strength of his arms around me and his body close.

Bloody hell, Libby, get a grip!

Charlie pulled back and released me.

I nodded. I've no idea why. Nerves were getting the better of me, causing everything to go a little haywire, it would seem.

He looked at me for a moment, his brow creasing a little. 'Do you want me to come with you to the offices? I can wait for you.'

I smiled and touched his arm. 'No. I'm fine. Really. But thank you so much for the offer. It's really sweet of you.'

Charlie wrinkled his nose.

'What?'

'Sweet,' he repeated.

'What's wrong with sweet?' I asked.

'It's kind of on a par with being called nice.'

'Well, you are nice. And you are sweet.'

'Oh, God. Nice *and* sweet. I'm bloody doomed.' He placed his hands on my upper arms, turned me bodily in the direction of the escalators to the Underground and leant around, giving me a peck on the cheek. 'Good luck. Now, please go to your meeting, before you depress me any more.'

I started walking off, throwing Charlie a wave over my shoulder as I did so. Two seconds later, he was back by my side, snagging my elbow to stop me.

'What are you doing after your meeting? I just... I mean, seeing as you were up here, I thought we could maybe go for a drink or grab some food. You know, to celebrate your success.'

I couldn't help smiling at the confidence he was showing in me.

'That sounds great. But I'm actually meeting my dad a bit later. He's been promising to take me to Ocean for ever and finally arranged it for today, once he knew I'd be in town.'

Charlie pulled an appreciative face. 'Nice choice. Michelin starred.'

'I know! I can't wait!'

'OK. Another time.'

'Definitely.'

'Give me a buzz later and let me know how your meeting went.'

'I promise.'

'OK. Better go. Good luck, Libs.'

We parted ways, him heading out to the street and me down to the depths of the Tube.

* * *

'How'd your meeting go?' my brother asked.

'Really good, thanks,' I said, glancing around for somewhere to sit as, down the phone, I listened to him wrangle with one of the boys whilst talking to me.

'Great, you'll have to come round for dinner and tell us all about it. I'm just ringing to give you a heads up about tonight.'

I stopped walking.

'What do you mean?'

'You're meeting Dad tonight for dinner, right?'

'Yes,' I said, slowly.

'I've got a feeling he and Gina are bringing someone for you to meet.'

'What? No!'

'"Fraid so, sis. I did try to put him off but he's convinced you're going to "think he's marvellous". I believe those were his words.'

'Great.' All enthusiasm for the evening seeped out of me. 'Any chance you can ring him back and have another go at dissuading him? He listens to you.'

'I've got to leave for Theatre shortly but I can try if you want.'

Matt hesitated. 'You know it won't work though, don't you? Even from me.'

I let out a sigh. He was right and we both knew it. We'd tried, and failed, before with this tactic. Once he'd decided on something, it was hard for anyone to get my father to change his course. The only one who'd been able to do that was Mum.

'No. I know. It doesn't matter. I guess I'm just going to have to endure it, as usual.' I gave a little laugh, but, even to me, it sounded hollow.

'He means well.'

'I know. I just wish he'd stop.'

Matt made a sympathetic noise down the phone. 'So, the meeting?'

The smile bounced back onto my face. 'Really good, actually. Better than I could have hoped. They had some great ideas and I think it could be really exciting!'

'Sounds great. So, what happens now?'

'I'm going to think about it some more over the weekend. I have the legal papers to look at and sign if I'm happy. Which I am. Honestly, I don't think there's too much to think about. Affiliation with a brand like this is a fantastic opportunity.'

'Well done, Libs! I'm so pleased for you.' I could hear the enthusiasm in his voice and it made me smile.

'Thanks, Matt.'

'OK, I've got to get off to the hospital. We're both off duty this weekend. Fancy coming round for Sunday dinner?'

'That sounds lovely! I can relate the whole sorry tale of this evening for your amusement.'

He laughed. 'It might not be that bad. Who knows? Dad might actually have got it right and found you the perfect man.'

'We can always hope. Good luck this afternoon. Hope everything goes well.'

'Thanks, Libs. And well done today. I'll get some champagne in for Sunday so we can celebrate!'

'Oh, if you insist.'

We hung up and I wandered over to a nearby bench, shaded by a large plane tree. My enthusiasm and excitement at the successful meeting, and what that might mean for my business, had been

punctured. I tried to regain it, pushing my father's continual deter-
mination to marry me off and make me The Perfect Doctor's Wife to
the back of my mind, but it barrelled its way back to the fore again.
It didn't matter how many times I told him, the surprise dates still
kept showing up. Mum would have understood. I opened the email
on my phone and entered the familiar address into a new email.

Miss you.

I pressed send and returned the phone to my bag. Mum would
have been so excited about what I was doing now, with the blog,
with my life. She would have wanted to know all about it, how it
worked, what my plans were, and she would have adored all the
goodies I got to see and try.

She'd actually been the inspiration for my blog. It was from her
that I'd got my love of make-up and style. There was a picture of her
on my 'About' page, looking as glamorous as ever. With or without
make-up, she looked amazing, a beautiful smile on her face, always
ready to laugh. As a child I'd spent hours playing with her
cosmetics bag, taking the shiny, mother-of-pearl compact she kept
her pressed powder in, tipping it this way and that, fascinated by
the way the colours changed as it caught the light. I'd line up all the
items and she'd go through each one telling me what it was for.
Occasionally she'd pop the tiniest bit of lipstick on my lips from her
finger, barely a hint but it felt like the best thing in the world. I was
her little girl and, as much as she loved sharing these things, these
moments with me, she didn't want me growing up too fast.

When I was twelve, Mum started showing me a couple of tech-
niques, on the proviso that it was kept for special occasions only.
For my thirteenth birthday, she took me up to London shopping
and we spent hours at the make-up counters in Selfridges, eventually walking away with a Chanel lipstick and eyeshadow compact
wrapped carefully and handed to me in a swishy little bag. Mum
promised me that the following year, we would go again. It was the
first promise to me that she ever broke.

Two days after my birthday, a Saturday, we went to the beach for
the day, jumping waves, shivering in the sea whilst pretending that
it was all right once you were in. Having dried off, we met up with

Matt, who'd been elsewhere on the beach with his mates, for fish and chips in the restaurant on the pier. Once home, Mum mentioned that she had a bit of a headache from all the sun and excitement and was going to lie down for half an hour. Dad handed her a cup of tea. She smiled at him as she took it, resting her hand momentarily on his cheek. And then she closed her eyes.

Dad caught her before she hit the floor, the delicate china of the teacup smashing into a thousand pieces beside her as it hit the limestone tiles. Matt and I just watched, our bodies rigid, my hand gripping his until they were both a bloodless white. We didn't understand what was happening. We were sure of only one thing. Dad's distraught expression and desperate actions told us that something was very, very wrong.

Dad was a cardiac surgeon. There were bad days when he'd battled to save someone and lost the fight. On those days he looked tired and sad, almost defeated. He cared about every one of his patients. He never once forgot that they were individuals – brothers, sisters, wives, husbands, sons, daughters. That they were someone's world. But the look on his face that day was one neither of us had ever seen. He looked lost. Small. Shocked. Mum was his world and he couldn't save her.

The coroner concluded that Mum had suffered a brain aneurysm. There was no history of it in the family. It was just one of those horrible, unlucky, utterly devastating things. Dad hadn't married again. There could never be another woman for him like Mum. She'd captured his heart with her love and kindness, her beauty and laughter, and even in death it would still always be hers.

That wasn't to say he hadn't found company, although it had taken him many years. Initially he'd turned all of his focus on Matt and me. It had been easier with Matt, who'd already decided he wanted to go into medicine. Dad knew where he was with him. I was more of a challenge. He didn't really know what to do with a teenage girl who went decidedly woozy at the sight of blood and spent all her time reading about fashion and beauty. There hadn't been, and still wasn't, a day I didn't miss Mum horribly. God, what I wouldn't give to be able to talk to her right now. Even just for a minute.

My phone rang, jolting me back to the present. My eyes had

filled with tears as my mind had filled with memories. I rummaged about inside the bag for a tissue as I answered the call distractedly.

'Hello.'

'Libby?'

I hadn't checked the screen but I recognised the deep voice. 'Hi, Charlie.'

'Are you OK? You sound... different.'

'I'm fine.'

'Right.' His tone told me he was unconvinced.

'What can I do for you?'

'I was just calling to see how the meeting went.'

'Oh, right! Thanks, yes, it went really well, I think.'

'You think?' I could hear a smile in his voice.

'No, it did. I'm happy with what they want from me. They're happy with what I want from them. Everybody's happy.'

There was a pause on the line, and I pulled the phone back briefly to see if the call had dropped. Still connected.

'So why don't you sound happy?'

'No, I am. Honestly.'

'OK,' he said slowly, disbelief still clear in his voice.

'I was just thinking about something else.'

'But you have your dinner tonight to look forward to.'

Charlie was clearly doing his best not to pry by changing the subject, bless him. Unfortunately, with that particular topic, he was still onto a loser.

'Oh, yes. Dinner.' My attempt at enthusiasm morphed into sarcasm.

'Uh oh. Did the plans get cancelled?'

'I wish.'

'OK, I'm confused.' He let out a little laugh and the sound of it made me smile, knocking me from my wallowing.

'Long story,' I said, my voice sounding much more like my own again now.

'Good. I look forward to hearing it. Have you had lunch?'

'Well, no, but—'

'There's a great deli near here. If you can get back to London Bridge, I can meet you by the ship in Hay's Galleria – do you know it?'

I did know it.

'Unless you have some other plans, of course. I mean...'

'No. I really don't. Actually, that sounds lovely. If you have time?'

'As I'm going to be working all weekend, I think I'm entitled to a lunch break. So yes, I have time. Any preference on sandwiches?'

'I'll leave it up to you.'

'Uh oh. She's a risk-taker! I'll have to make a note of that.' He chuckled.

I smiled down the phone. 'Just choose me something nice. I'll pay you when I get there.'

'No, you won't. Lunch is on me. In celebration of your meeting going well.'

'Thank you.'

'OK. I'll get there as soon as possible.'

'Same here. See you in a bit.'

He disconnected and I returned my phone to my bag. Lunch with Charlie was an unexpected and very pleasant diversion before heading off to Dad's place, and the ensuing dinner for four.

8

Charlie had his back to me, gazing out past the whirring mechanicals of the nautical artwork, onto the Thames. I reached up and tapped him on the shoulder. He turned.

'Hi!'

'Hello!'

His intense gaze was fixed on me, and I could see he wanted to say something.

'What is it?'

'You... I... I don't know if I'm supposed to say this? But I think, knowing you, you'd want to know.'

'For goodness' sake, spit it out, Charlie!' I laughed.

'You have make-up... kind of here.' He pointed to a spot on his face, a little under his eye.

'I do? Oh, great. That's a brilliant advertisement for my blog, isn't it?' I wasn't annoyed in a vain way. Let's be honest, it wouldn't have been the first time I'd had smudged make-up. I was annoyed because I knew when it had happened, and I hadn't thought to check the state of my face following my emotional blip earlier. I balanced my handbag on the wall surrounding the sculpture, and pulled out my compact. Yep. Charlie was spot on. Repair work was definitely needed. I should have gone with waterproof mascara.

'Look, do you want to get some coffees whilst I sort this out? Here—' I reached for my purse, but Charlie put a hand on my arm.

'I told you, lunch is on me.'

I pointed to the deli bag he held in one hand. 'That's lunch. This is coffee.'

'Which is all part of the same meal. Now, come on, sit down here, do what you need to do, and I'll go and get the drinks.' He pulled out a chair from a nearby coffee shop's outdoor table selection and waited for me to take it.

'What would you like?'

'Tea would be perfect. Thanks.'

He nodded. 'Back in a sec.' He turned to go and hesitated. 'You know, I wasn't being... picky when I said about your make-up. I don't normally even notice stuff like that. It's just that I'd seen you this morning, so kind of knew how it was all supposed to look. And I just thought you'd probably want to know, as you were going on to dinner and stuff.'

'I know.' I caught his hand, and gave it a quick squeeze. 'If I'd seen later, knowing that I'd sat here and you hadn't said a word, I'd have killed you.' I smiled sweetly.

'Something to remember for the future.'

'Absolutely. Now shoo whilst I fix this mess.'

'Hardly a mess!' he said, squeezing my hand back briefly before letting it go. 'But I'm going, I'm going!' He grinned and I forgot all about my messy eye make-up for a moment. Charlie didn't do big grins a lot but when he did, it was kind of special. And yes, we were just mates. But heck, I wasn't dead! Purposefully I opened my compact and stuck it up in front of my face, blocking Charlie from view – sort of – and set about the repair work.

A few minutes later and he was back. Putting the takeaway cups down on the table, he unloaded napkins and stirrers, placing them alongside.

'I put some milk in already for you. Is that enough?' He opened the lid for me. It was the perfect colour. Of course it was.

He took a seat. 'So, did you sort out your—?' He stopped as he looked up at me.

I shifted my eyes. 'Please don't tell me I've smudged it again in the time it's taken for you to go and get these?' I began to reach down for my bag.

'No! No, you haven't. It's fine. I mean, it's perfect. It's like it was this morning. How did you do that?'

He paused, frowning.

'OK. I am perfectly aware that sounded like a weird question. I just didn't think you'd be able to make it look like nothing had happened so quickly. That's quite an art. You should do one of your videos on that. I know plenty of girls who'd love to know your tricks.'

I had no doubt that there were plenty of girls who'd love to know a few of Charlie's own tricks.

'Thanks. That's actually not a bad idea. I'll think about it.'

He nodded, taking a sip of his coffee, before quickly pulling the cup away. 'Christ, that's hot.' He took the lid off and sat them both on the table, allowing the drink to cool a little. 'So, tell me about this morning, and the meeting.'

I proceeded to do just that and felt the enthusiasm and excitement bubbling up inside me once again as I did. Charlie asked questions, checked things he didn't understand – his logical brain wanting to make sure it had all the facts, even if those facts were about cosmetics – and then congratulated me on the success of the meeting.

'So, what happens now?' he asked, echoing Matt's question from earlier. I gave him a similar reply.

'I'm going to think about it over the weekend, but I have the legal papers ready to sign here already.'

He nodded, a more serious expression coming onto his face.

'Have you read them all through?'

'No, not yet. They explained a lot of it in the meeting though. And if there's something I don't understand, I can just give them a call.'

'Do you have your own solicitor, you know, just someone who can run an eye over it? Make sure there's nothing been snuck in that you're unaware of.'

'No, I don't. This is kind of the biggest thing I've done so far.' I took a sip of my tea, pondering on what he'd just said. 'But I'm sure they wouldn't do anything like that.'

'Libby. They're Big Business. With capital "b" s. Never rule anything out. Not everyone is as nice as you are – in life or business.' He gave me a smile.

From some the comments could have been patronising. Charlie wasn't built like that, but he operated in this corporate world and knew what could happen. I didn't – yet. He knew I was excited about this deal, and just wanted to make sure there weren't any nasty surprises lurking.

'You think I should get someone to look over it?'

'It might not be a bad idea.'

'What sort of lawyer do I need for something like that?' I knew there were various specialities in law, but I didn't really have a clue as to where to start looking.

'Hang on. I have an idea.' Pulling out his phone from his pocket, he scrolled through his contacts and chose one. Pressing 'Call', then the speakerphone icon, he put the phone on the table. It rang twice before a man answered.

'Charlie! How are you?'

'Hi, Greg. I'm all right, thanks, mate. You?'

'Tired. As always. What can I do for you?'

'I need to pull in one of my favours.'

I glanced up and met Charlie's eyes, a warning expression in my own. He did a little head-shake thing and put his hand on my arm, reassuring. His warm touch, the gentle strength behind the gesture, soothed me. I knew there was something else too but I pushed that away, and concentrated on the conversation.

'I've got a friend who's about to sign a contract with a cosmetics company in conjunction with her blog. Would you have a minute to run your discerning eye over it and just check that everything's as it should be, before she does?'

'Hmm...' Greg pondered down the phone. 'This favour – is it a "whenever you've got time" kind of favour or the "I need it done like yesterday so that I can get her into bed tonight and she can show me exactly how grateful she is" kind?'

'Greg,' Charlie said, the warning clear in his voice.

'Oh, come on, mate. Give me a break. Mel and I have barely slept since the twins were born. If we ever get near a bed these days, it's certainly not to do anything that might involve creating another kid! You've got to let me live a little vicariously through my happily still-single friends. So, is she pretty? Of course, she is. Since when did you ever date anyone that wasn't?'

Charlie by this time had removed his hand from my arm and was now rubbing his right temple with two fingers, while studiously avoiding looking at me.

'Have you finished?'

'I suppose,' Greg replied.

'Good. So, can you do it?'

'Of course. When do you need it done by?'

'Have you got ten minutes now?'

'I knew it! It is the latter! You little—'

'Greg. Just so you know, the friend involved is right here and you've been on speakerphone the whole time.'

'Oh.'

'Yes. So, yes, we do need it done asap, but only so that she has all the facts before making a final decision. No other reason. And yes, she is pretty. But no, we're not seeing each other. Now, is that everything covered? Can we shoot round with the papers?'

'Of course. See you in a few.'

Charlie ended the conversation and risked a look at me.

'Sorry. I thought having him on speaker would be helpful in case he asked anything.' He pulled a face. 'Anything that might have been appropriate, at least.'

I laughed. 'Don't worry, Charlie. I know banter when I hear it. And besides, you said I was pretty, which I'm shallow enough to accept, be flattered by and make allowances for.'

He waited whilst I bent and retrieved my bag. 'You are pretty. And you're most certainly not shallow. Now come on, let's go and get Greg to look at this paperwork. Watching him squirm in embarrassment when he meets you will be amusing for a start.'

I stopped. 'Charlie Richmond. I wouldn't have believed it of you!'

He laughed and reached back, grabbing my hand to tug me along. 'Believe me, he's watched me squirm plenty of times and thoroughly enjoyed it!'

'Really. That sounds like an interesting conversation we need to have.'

Charlie smiled. 'Another time.'

'Spoilsport.'

'I didn't say never.'

'That's true.'

'So, what's with the change of heart about your dinner plans this evening?'

'Ugh.' I slumped my shoulders briefly as we walked. 'My dad has invited someone else along.'

'And that's a problem?' Charlie glanced at me, frowning briefly. 'You love people.'

'I do. But what I don't love is my dad trying to matchmake when all I want to do is have a nice meal together.'

'Matchmake?'

'Yeah,' I said. 'It's his thing. Well, it's his thing when it comes to me.'

'And you don't approve of his choices?'

'I don't approve of him doing it at all! Especially when it's launched on me as a surprise. I only found out there's someone else coming when my brother rang earlier to give me a heads up.'

'Look, maybe you're reading too much into it. Maybe it's just a friend of your dad's.'

'He told Matt that I'm going to think this guy is perfect. Or words to that effect.'

'Oh.'

'Yes. Oh.'

'Maybe he will be.'

I gave Charlie a look. He returned it.

'You never know,' he said, with a shrug.

I shook my head. 'That's not really the point.'

'No, I know. Just try and enjoy the food.' He made a gesture with his hand. 'This is it.'

The building housing the solicitors' offices was shiny and sleek with lots of glass, in line with much of the development of the area. Charlie held the door for me and we entered. He approached the building receptionist and announced who we were there to see, and that we were expected. Flashing him a dazzling smile, the receptionist asked him to wait a moment. She made a call on her desk phone and minutes later a man was exiting the lifts and striding towards us.

'Charlie.' He beamed and the two men shook hands. I was standing to the side, and half behind Charlie. I wasn't purposely hiding. It was just that with his sizeable bulk it was easily done.

'This is—'

'Libby!' Greg cut Charlie off and thrust out his hand as Charlie moved, realising he was blocking me.

I automatically took it, but my bemusement was about at the same level as Charlie's, judging by the look on his face.

'You know each other?' Charlie asked.

'No,' I said.

'Yes,' said Greg at the same time.

Charlie looked at me. I did a little shake of my head.

'Well, she doesn't know me, of course, but I definitely know you!' Greg enthused. He suddenly seemed to register our expressions.

'You have that lifestyle blog, don't you? Brighton Belle? Mel absolutely loves it! Always raving about it. You've seen her through some long nights with the babies!'

'Oh, I see! That's great! Thanks so much. I'm really glad she likes it.'

'She's not going to believe that I met you today! Come on, come up, come up, and we'll take a look at those contracts.'

'Are you sure you don't mind?' I asked.

'Of course not!'

We headed towards the bank of lifts and I stole a glance at Charlie as we did so. He caught me and gave me a smile.

'Are you OK for time? Do you need to get back?' I asked, quietly.

'Nope. No rush.'

I smiled, happy to have my friend beside me.

A short while later and Greg had gone over the contracts with us both, explaining anything that I wasn't entirely sure about. We'd agreed that it seemed a pretty fair deal for everyone concerned, and I now felt much better about signing it, knowing that I fully understood everything I was putting my name to.

'So, this could mean great things for the blog, then?' Greg asked.

'Absolutely!' I replied. 'But can I ask you to keep it under your hat until the announcement is officially made? Glam said something about wanting to do a bit of a splash reveal thing on all their social media so I'm sort of supposed to not tell anyone at the moment.' I pulled a face. I knew that this could put Greg in an awkward position if he was eager to tell his wife that he'd met a blogger she liked.

'Of course! I'll just tell Mel that Charlie dropped in to say hi and brought his friend with him.' A look crossed his face. 'Actually. I've just remembered. I owe you an apology, don't I? About what I said on the phone, I was just...'

I waved my hand in dismissal. 'Don't give it another moment's thought. Really.'

He smiled, a little bashful. 'Thanks. I'm definitely going to be asking whether I'm on speakerphone before I go off again, that's for sure!'

I tilted my head, smiling. 'Couldn't hurt to check.'

'Exactly.'

Charlie shook his head and then they did that thing that men do that wasn't quite a hug but sort of was, involving back slapping and handshaking all at the same time.

'Thanks again for doing this,' I said, shaking Greg's hand. My natural predilection to hug people was being sorely tested today but I'd done well this morning in the meeting and continued my effort now.

'Any time!' Greg said, covering my hand with his other one. 'Really. Any time. Anyone who can get Charlie out of the office to take a lunch break is OK in my book.' He gave the most unsubtle wink to Charlie I've ever seen. I couldn't help grinning. Charlie just rolled his eyes.

'I take lunch breaks all the time.'

'Sure you do.' Greg nodded, then swung his glance to me and immediately changed the action to a head-shake.

'Thanks, mate. I'll talk to you soon,' Charlie said as the lift pinged its arrival. The doors opened almost silently and he indicated for me to step ahead of him, following in behind. I pressed the button marked 'lobby' and the doors slid closed again and we descended smoothly back to ground level.

'I do take lunch breaks,' Charlie said after a moment's silence.

'I believe you.'

There was a pause.

'It killed you not to hug him, didn't it?'

I sighed. 'Totally. I told you I'm not made for the Corporate World.'

'You did well. But just for future reference, he wouldn't have minded in the slightest.'

'Thanks.'

I handed my visitor pass to Charlie and he dropped them off at the desk, thanking the receptionist as he did so. She treated him to another sunray smile and loaded a depth of meaning into her reply.

'Any time.'

Charlie nodded and quirked a smile. The hint of the blush on his face told me he hadn't missed the fact he'd just been hit on.

'Is there anywhere safe to stand next to you when I'm not going to feel like a third wheel?'

'Huh?'

'The train this morning, the receptionist just now...'

'Don't be daft,' he said before changing the subject. 'I have to get back to work. Do you feel better about the contract thing now?'

'Yes, I do. Though, to be fair, I only really started worrying about it when you said I should.'

'Oh, dear.'

'No, it's all right.' I laughed. 'I'm probably way too naive to be doing stuff like this anyway.'

'No. You're not.' Charlie's voice had a definite note to it that I hadn't heard before, a surety. 'You're more than capable. I never meant to make you feel that you weren't. I just don't want you taken advantage of. I've seen it happen and I don't want that for you.'

I nodded. 'No, I know, thank you. And I didn't mean that you made me feel that way. I know that I'm wading in here far deeper than I ever have before, so it's always going to be scary. I really appreciate your help, Charlie. I hope you know that.'

Impulsively I reached up and kissed his cheek. His freshly shaven skin was soft and smooth and that subtle hint of aftershave still lingered.

'Any time,' he said, repeating the phrase of the receptionist but with none of the meaning she had injected. His startling gaze flicked to meet mine for a moment before moving on to his watch. 'You all right from here?'

I rolled my eyes at him. 'Of course. Now stop skiving and get back to work.'

He laughed and turned to leave. Suddenly he turned back.

'Libs?'

'Yes?'

'Are you OK?'

I frowned and smiled at the same time. 'Of course. Why?'

'It's just that earlier... when I called... well, you just didn't sound like you. You sounded like you were upset. I thought the meeting had gone badly or something for a minute. But obviously it didn't. So, I'm assuming it was something else.' He shifted his weight and cast a glance around before focusing the hypnotic gaze back on me. 'I'm not meaning to pry. It's just that I hate to think of you upset. So, if there's anything I can do. Anything you need. Anything at all, let me know. OK?' He paused. 'Please.'

I nodded at him. My throat felt raw and tight, and I wasn't sure I'd be able to get any words out. I swallowed again and made an effort.

'It was just something silly, but I'm OK now, I promise. But thank you.'

Charlie nodded, his gaze resting on me for a moment before sliding to the ground between us.

'Now, get back to work before you get fired.'

He raised his head and gave his little half-smile. 'I'm a partner. It's not that easy to get rid of me.'

'But not impossible. And I'm not being held responsible.'

He shook his head at me, gave me a big hug and turned, setting off in the direction of his office.

'And have a good trip,' I called after him, suddenly remembering he was jetting off.

'Thanks.' He looked back. 'I'll be sure to let you know about Tiffany.'

'Perfect.'

He waved and continued on his way. I watched him for a moment, before turning and heading back towards the station and the Underground to begin the part of the day I was now dreading.

9

'Hello, darling! Come in.' Dad opened the heavy door of the Kensington town house dressed impeccably, as always, in his version of casual, which was a suit with his shirt open at the neck. Not wearing a tie pushed an outfit firmly into the realms of casual attire in Dad's eyes.

'Hi, Dad.' I kissed him on the cheek and stepped inside, my heels echoing on the pristine, white tiled floor.

'How was your morning? Did you say you were meeting a friend?' he asked, as we walked up to the next level and the sumptuous sitting room that overlooked one of the private parks.

'No. It was actually something for work.'

Dad didn't really understand the whole blog thing. I think as far as he was concerned, I was still the little girl playing with Mum's make-up. 'I was meeting with a cosmetics company. They want to work with me, and my blog.'

'Right! That's good, yes?'

'Yes, it's good.'

'Excellent. Now, what would you like to drink?'

And that was the end of the enquiry. Had it been Matt standing there, he'd have been questioned up, down and sideways about all of his latest operations and procedures. I got one question. I tried not to let it hurt and most of the time it washed over me. But just once, it would have been nice if he'd shown a bit of interest and pride in what I was trying to achieve. I'd built my own, now moderately successful business, from nothing. I'd just met with one of the hottest new eco-friendly names in the cosmetics industry who wanted to work with me, but it still didn't seem to be of interest to Dad. I thought again of how different things would have been if Mum had still been around. Then I concentrated on pushing those feelings back down again. They'd reared up unexpectedly once already today. That was enough.

'Libby?' Dad prompted as I gazed out onto the park and watched a nanny unlock the iron gate to the park and push a pram that probably cost more than my car through it.

'Sorry?'

'Drink?'

'Oh. I don't really...' I paused, considering the afternoon and the enforced blind date due later. 'Actually, got any champagne?'

'Of course.'

Two minutes later, I had a glass of fizz in my hand.

'So, Matt mentioned that we're now actually going to be four for dinner? Is that right?' Dad's expression barely flickered.

'Complete chance! Anthony's been working over in Switzerland for the last few years. We were just chatting and he mentioned that he hadn't been to Ocean, and was planning on going. Well, I thought it might be nice for him to have some company.'

I rolled my lips together to keep them from saying anything I couldn't take back and gave a short nod.

'I think you'll really like him. He's—' The sound of the doorbell interrupted his speech.

'Oh, that'll be Gina. She's probably loaded up with shopping and can't get to her key. Back in two shakes.'

I gave a little raise of my glass as acknowledgement and waited for him to leave the room before downing the entire thing. Moving to the drinks' cabinet, I took the bottle of Veuve from the ice bucket and topped up my glass. Somewhere inside I knew that this probably wasn't a great idea. I wasn't a robust drinker at the best of times, so heading straight in mid-afternoon having eaten nothing but the sandwich Charlie had bought me, I was pretty certain I was heading for Trashville.

The click-clack of Gina's heels alerted me to incoming and I turned back to the window, watching a designer-clad toddler wobble uncertainly around on the grass, his nanny inches behind, ready to catch any tumble.

'Libby, daaaaaarling!' Gina purred, her thick Italian accent infusing the words with a depth I could never hope to achieve. Gina could make ordering pizza sound erotic. She was very Sophia Loren – all curves and sex appeal. She had over twenty years on me, but still knocked me, and most other women, so far into the shade it was covered with permafrost.

'Hi, Gina. It's nice to see you.' And I meant it.

Dad hadn't seen anyone for a long time after Mum had passed away. She'd been his world, his rock, and, despite both having occupations in which they dealt with mortality on a regular basis, they'd never considered they didn't have many more years together. She was always so bright, so vital. To have that ripped away so suddenly – it wasn't something Dad could understand. He spent his life saving people, but he had to watch the one person he loved more than anything in the world die before his eyes, unable to do a single thing to prevent it.

Gradually, however, he did begin to see other women. They were always classy, bright, and reserved. Mum was both the former, but she'd never been reserved. She certainly hadn't been one for bottling things up. If something needed saying, it got said. She'd always said it was because she was Irish and that seemed as good a reason as any. Matt and I had inherited the same trait, and shamelessly used the same bloodline excuse.

So, it seemed strange to us that Dad had chosen to go for these demure types. We were never surprised when he didn't see them more than once or twice. And then Gina came into view like a thunderbolt, fizzing and popping. And Dad began to smile. He laughed, properly laughed, for the first time in what seemed like forever. I'd never be able to thank Gina enough for being responsible for that. For all Dad's chosen oblivion to what I was trying to do with my life, and his constant wish to set me up as Mrs Doctor Whoeveritmaybe – which I knew was only encouraged by Gina, one thing I didn't thank her for – I still wanted him to be happy. And she made him happy. He'd never marry again and had told her that and the arrangement suited her. But privately Matt and I were still of the 'never say never' camp when it came to that subject.

'So, has Joseph been telling you all about the gorgeous Dr Anthony DiMarco?'

'Nope! But I'm pretty sure he was about to,' I said, taking another drink.

'I told Libby that it wasn't planned or anything, we'd just got talking about the same restaurant.'

'Of course not!' Gina picked up, seamlessly. 'We just thought it would be nice for him to have some company.'

'If he's a gorgeous doctor I'm pretty sure that's one thing he won't be short of.'

'Well, you know how it is.' Gina waved a toned arm and the diamonds in her cuff bracelet caught the sunlight streaming in through the large Georgian windows. 'Everyone is so busy these days. Nobody has the time to meet anybody else! You are all so busy, busy, busy!'

So, definitely not by chance, then. Strategically planned. God knew what the poor man had been told. I imagined he'd felt that he had little choice, being asked to dinner by a senior, well-respected colleague. And, of course, he might not even be aware that he was being set up. After all, I'd only found out by accident. No, I was pretty sure this had been planned as an ambush on every front.

After another hour, I asked if it would be all right for me to go and have a lie-down, claiming that it had been a busy morning and that I wanted to be awake enough for dinner tonight. Nothing to do with the thumping headache I had and how the champagne now didn't seem such a great idea.

Closing the door, I pulled my phone from my bag and opened the email app:

Dad's done it again. I'd really been looking forward to this meal and spending some time with him and Gina but once again, they've added a fourth person to the party. Dr DiMarco this time, apparently. I know they mean well but I also know this wouldn't happen if you were still here. I just wish Dad understood me like you did.

Love you xxx

I undid the ankle straps of my shoes and slid them off, then slipped out of my suit and laid it carefully over the back of the over-stuffed armchair. The guest bedroom was decorated in a mix of soothing whites and soft greys and I could see over the rooftops as I lay in the luxuriously comfy bed. The sheeny thousand-thread-count sheets were soft on my skin and I closed my eyes.

* * *

A strange noise reached down into my dreams and I swam up to meet it. The noise came again. My mobile was ringing. Switched to vibrate, it was now dancing towards the edge of the bedside cabinet. I reached out and caught it, just as it dropped off the side. The screen was lit up with a picture of Amy pulling an ironic Kardashian pose, complete with duck-face pout and sticking-out bum.

'Hi.'

'Hiya! How'd it go? Are you OK? You sound weird.'

'I just woke up. I'm at my dad's.'

'Are you ill?'

'No.' I reconsidered the fact my head was still thumping a bit. 'Well, no, not really. I had champagne earlier, which was probably a mistake, but apart from that...'

'Libs, you know you're crap at alcohol! What made you think you could handle afternoon drinkies?'

'I know!' I sighed. 'But Dad's done his thing again and the "family dinner" has turned into yet another "let's try and find a husband for Libby" dinner.'

'Oh, no.'

'Oh, yes. Matt gave me a heads up earlier. If I wasn't so keen to go to this restaurant, I'd be on the first train home. The food better be bloody good after all of this.'

Amy made a sympathetic sound. 'But how was the meeting?'

'Really good!' I said, enthusiasm pouring back into me. I sat up and pushed a stray strand of hair out of my eyes. 'They're really keen, and it all sounds great. I have the contracts and Charlie took me to see—'

'Wait. You met Charlie?'

'Yes. Well, it wasn't planned. I bumped into him on the train this morning, so he knew about the meeting and called me afterwards to see how it had gone. He said he was just popping out for lunch so suggested a quick meet up. When I mentioned to him about the contracts, he came over all cynical businessman and insisted on getting them shown to a solicitor friend of his to check, and make sure they weren't trying to take advantage of me.'

'I see.'

'No. You don't see anything.' I knew from Amy's tone what she was hinting at. 'There's nothing between me and Charlie. I'm not his type and he's too reserved for me. But as a friend, he's lovely.'

'Um hmm.'

'Don't start, Ames, please. I've got enough to contend with, with Dad and Gina and their Doctors' Dating Service.'

'Sorry, Libs. You know I'm just teasing. You have to admit that Charlie is pretty hot.'

'Says the girl dating his brother. Classy.'

Amy laughed. 'Oh, stop. I think you're hot too, but I don't want to clamber into bed with you either!'

'I'm wounded. Anyway, we both know I don't remotely fit into his type box.

'You wore a suit today.'

'Somehow I don't think just changing my clothes is going to make that much of a difference. Besides, you know I've been there and done that when it comes to the whole Executive Type thing.'

'You have to admit Charlie is different from most though,' Amy prodded.

I paused. She was right. He was. 'True. But he was also pretty clear about what he looks for and he's never made the remotest move towards me so can we just put a lid on this forever, please?'

'Fine, fine. Tell me about this deal.'

I lay back on the down-filled pillow and told Amy all about the meeting, finding my own excitement building even more at her enthusiasm. By the time we'd hung up, the headache was almost gone and I was back to feeling more like my bubbly self. I pushed myself up out of bed and, ignoring the hotel-style slippers placed strategically by the bed each side, padded over to the dressing table and sat down on the stool. Hmm, not the best. My hair was a bit of scare-fest and my eye make-up was smudged yet again. Time for some major repairs. I pulled my bag over and set to work.

* * *

Dad paid the cabbie whilst Gina and I waited by the restaurant. Tucked discreetly in a corner of the West End, it didn't announce its presence, merely quietly resided. It had no need for flashiness. The owner was the youngest chef to ever have been awarded two Michelin stars – its quality spoke for itself. The door was opened for us, Dad stated his name, and we were immediately shown to our table. Having a father who had saved many a wealthy life in his time had its benefits. Dad mentioned that we were awaiting a fourth. The waiter nodded, and a few minutes later a man was shown over to our table.

'Anthony! So glad you could make it.'

'Joseph. Good to see you. Thanks for inviting me.'

Dad made the introductions. 'This is my partner, Gina.' Gina smiled warmly and took his offered hand. Her eyes didn't leave his face and it looked as if he were being sized up as an appetiser. I'd worried for Dad about this quirk initially until I came to realise that it was just her way. She was crazy about Dad, I knew. The whole vamp thing was just... well, just Gina.

'And my daughter, Libby.' The new arrival and I shook hands. A look passed between us that said, 'Well, this isn't awkward at all.'

The evening passed pleasantly enough, and Dr DiMarco seemed a nice enough chap, but it was clear that he had as little interest in being set up as I did. When Dad stepped out to take a call, and Gina conveniently excused herself at the same time, I turned to Anthony.

'I'm so sorry about all of this.'

'What's that?' he said, being terribly British and pretending that everything was just as it should be.

I gave him a look and a smile. He waited a beat and then returned it. 'It's all right. Don't worry about it. I'm sure your dad means well, for both of us.'

'Quite.'

'And the food's been delicious! I'm just not really looking...'

'No! No, it's fine! I'm not either! My father seems to think I should be, though.' I pulled a face.

He laughed. 'Like I said, I'm sure he means well.'

'Yes. I think he does.'

Anthony seemed to be considering whether to say something else.

'What is it?' I asked.

He glanced around. 'It's just that you seem a really nice person—'

'Uh oh!' I interrupted.

He laughed and seemed to relax a little. 'Well, it's just that I wouldn't want you to think it's any reflection on you.'

'Oh, don't worry about it!' I said, resting my hand briefly on his arm. 'Really, it's OK. I've been through enough of Dad's set-ups now to deal with it all. Please don't think I'm offended. I'm just sorry that you were put in an awkward position.'

'I'm gay.'

'Oh!' I looked at him, a smile beginning to tug at my lips. I could see my reaction reflected in my dinner companion's expression.

'I'm so sorry,' I said, and then my hand flew up to my face. 'I mean, about all this, not about you being gay.'

He laughed then, really laughed, and squeezed my hand. 'It's fine. I'm guessing your father didn't know.'

'No, he can't have. He's hopeless when it comes to this sort of thing with me, but he'd never have put you in an uncomfortable situation like this, knowingly. I mean, even more uncomfortable than it already was!'

'Like I said, I'm sure he means well. And I enjoyed the company anyway, as well as the food.'

Dad and Gina were heading back to the table and I could see them smiling to each other at the fact that we were chatting. Anthony was right. They did mean well. But I still really wished they wouldn't do it.

10

I rang the doorbell and waited. Behind me, cars and buses made their way along the busy seafront road. The honk of a car horn made me turn. A driver was waving his arms at a double-decker bus as it pulled out from a stop. The bus driver made no acknowledgement and continued manoeuvring the vehicle along the road. Heat and traffic were never a good mix. The door to the house opened just as I was turning back to face it.

'Hi.'

'Hi. Come in,' Charlie said, stepping back and allowing me entrance into the Georgian town house. For some reason, Charlie always seemed to end up at my flat, so this was the first time I'd seen the inside of his place.

'Wow! This is lovely,' I said, glancing around, my hand feeling the smooth, carved wood of the banister as I followed him down the stairs. 'I thought all of these had been converted into flats years ago.'

'They were,' Charlie said. 'This was originally flats when I bought it too.'

'You converted it back?'

'Yes. Well, not me personally.' He gave me that half-smile. 'I can do a bit of DIY but this was a little more than my talents lend themselves to, especially as it has listed status. There are all sorts of codes and things you have to abide by, correct materials to be sourced, etc.'

'Big job,' I said.

'Yes. Very. But I'm pleased with the outcome.'

We were now in the kitchen. It was very modern and sleek, all white and steel. Large windows flooded it with light and a set of beautiful period doors opened onto a gorgeous courtyard garden. One blank wall held three large photographic canvases of city-sponsored graffiti, their bright hue a vivid splash of colour in the minimalist room.

I ambled over to the prints on the wall for a closer look. I loved the angles the photographer had captured and the colours seemed to bounce right off the wall.

'These are amazing. Where did you find them?'

Charlie threw a look back over his shoulder. 'They're, um... they're mine.'

'Yours? You took them?'

'Um hmm.'

'Charlie, they're stunning!'

He came over to me and we both stood looking at his creations for a few moments.

'Do you have some more I can see?'

'I... I suppose. They're on my laptop. You can have a look through when we've finished your stuff, if you really want to.'

'I do really want to!' I enthused, grabbing his arm.

'OK.' He gave me a look of bemusement. Something I realised he did quite a lot.

I waved my arm around the room. 'This is gorgeous, Charlie. You've done an amazing job. It's hard to believe it was ever flats.'

'Thanks. I had a great project manager; I have to say. Really kept everything on track and all the workmen were brilliant. People always give builders a hard time, but I never had a problem.'

'Were you here much, when all the work was going on?'

'A certain amount. I like to keep an eye on things. Not that I didn't trust my project manager, but just because I get excited about projects.'

'You've done this sort of thing before, then?'

'Nothing quite on this scale. But I have done up a couple of smaller properties in the past. This was definitely an eye-opener though. I learned a lot.'

'So, would you do it again?'

He glanced around. 'I'm not sure. The grade listing of it was definitely a bit of a pain in the backside at times, trying to get just the right supplies, so I'm not sure I'd do something like this again.'

'I sense a "but".'

He glanced at me, smiling. 'I'm hoping to build my own house one day. I think it would be amazing to have things just as you like.'

'You sound like you have some ideas already.'

He wobbled his head. 'Maybe. A few. It'll be a while yet though anyway. Finding the land down here is a challenge for a start.'

'You'd stay around the area, then?'

'I'd like to.'

'That's good.'

He smiled at me.

'Well, it'd be a right pain for me to bring my accounts halfway across the country.'

Charlie let out a laugh. 'Cheers. Nice to know that's the only reason you'd want me local. Would you like a drink?'

'Please. It's roasting out there today.'

'It's definitely a warm one,' Charlie said, reaching into the fridge. 'There's some apple juice. Is that OK?'

'Sounds perfect.'

'It's organic.'

I nodded. 'Even better.'

'What?'

'Nothing,' I said innocently, shaking my head as I reached for the glass he offered. He held the drink up just out of my reach.

'Oi!'

'What was that look about?'

'What look?'

He fixed me with those eyes.

I let out a sigh and smiled. 'All right, I just didn't have you down as the organic type. Last time I saw you, you were inhaling a Big Mac, large fries, and a Happy Meal.'

'I'd been stuck on a delayed train for two and a half hours. I was hungry.'

'Fair enough.'

'I got the juice from the local farmers' market. The lady selling it was really chatty and sweet.'

'Oh, really?' I raised an eyebrow.

'Not like that,' he said, pushing the drink at me, with a smile. 'She was old enough to be my grandmother. But once she'd got me talking, I could hardly come away without buying anything, could I?'

'Charlie, how much did you buy?'

He hesitated. 'A crate.'

'You're such a softie.'

He looked at me.

'I'm not saying that's a bad thing. You can't help being a pushover.' I winked. We both knew that wasn't true. Not in all aspects anyway. There was no way Charlie Richmond would be in the position he was in if he were a pushover in the world of finance and risk management. But in other aspects he was soft as a brush.

'OK. Come on, we can go upstairs and look at this stuff.' Heading out of the kitchen, we started up the stairs. 'And just remember, if I wasn't such a pushover, as you put it, you wouldn't be getting your finances checked over for free.'

'Hey, I offered to pay,' I said, half turning round, the stair I was on meaning I was now more on eye level with Charlie.

'I'm teasing you. You know I enjoy doing it. Keeps me out of trouble. Come on, up you go.'

He tapped me on the behind with a file folder.

'Oi.'

'Get a move on, then.'

'I'm going, I'm going.'

The drawing room was just as beautiful as downstairs, but here the period features were more obvious with plaster roses around the chandelier, and a stunning fireplace that, for now, stood empty but that I could just imagine crackling with the warmth of a real log fire. The majority of the room was white with yellow accents resulting in a light, airy feel. The addition of some modern pieces of furniture made a pleasing mix of old and new, but also lent it an air of famil-iarity. It wasn't just a gorgeous room to admire. It was a home.

'Take a seat.' Charlie pointed at one of the overstuffed couches as he put the file and his drink down on the glass coffee table in front of it, before taking a seat next to me.

'This is a beautiful room,' I said, twisting round in the seat to view more.

'Thanks.'

'You have great taste.'

'As much as I would like to take the credit, it was mostly the work of an interior designer, not me.'

'Oh. But you must have had a say in the matter? I mean, if you're going to live here, you must have had some idea as to what they were going to do. Otherwise it could have been something you completely hated.'

'No, we discussed things. And... actually by the time the house was ready for any sort of decoration, Carly and I had been going out for a little while, so she'd got to know more of how I was – am – and what I like, and don't like.'

'Oh. That was handy.'

'It was,' he agreed, leaning forward to swipe the folder from the table. As he did so, his shirt rode up, exposing a glimpse of tanned lower back and the silvery traces of an old scar.

'So, what happened, then?' I said, distracting myself from the view.

'To what?'

'To you, and Carly, was it?'

He shook his head.

'What?'

'You just make me laugh. There's no preamble with you, is there?'

I pulled my mouth to the side. 'Would you prefer preamble?'

'No. Not really. And definitely not from you. It wouldn't suit. You are who you are.'

'Now you know why my ex didn't want me to go with him to his swanky new position in America.'

'No, I still think he missed a trick there. But his loss is our gain, so I can't be too hard on the bloke.'

I laid my head on his shoulder in an exaggerated gesture. 'You say the nicest things.'

'That's because I'm a pushover,' he said, without turning to look at me, but I knew he was smiling.

'But you're a lovely pushover.'

'And you're going to hurt your neck if you don't stop arsing about.'

I pulled my head upright and grinned.

'You didn't answer the question.'

'What question?'

'Stop stalling.'

He pulled my laptop off the coffee table where I'd laid it when I came in and rested the computer onto his knees.

'I'm not stalling. She got a job in London. Is this thing password protected?'

'No.'

'It should be.'

'Oh. Well, set one up for me if you like, but don't forget to tell me what it is.' I veered the conversation back to the original topic. 'London's not that far, and you work up there every day. There must have been something else.'

Charlie was tapping away at the keys. 'No, not really. It just wasn't working. It wasn't anything particular. There just weren't any... sparks, I guess. What's that look for?'

I hadn't realised that the surprise I'd felt inside at Charlie and his ex not having sparks had transferred onto my face.

'What look?'

'Stop stalling.' He threw my earlier accusation back at me, his eyes showing that he wasn't as serious as his tone made him sound.

'OK. It's just that I've been around you when women are sparking left, right and centre. I was at risk of flash burn that day in London what with Miss Cleavage on the train and the Any Time Receptionist.'

Charlie was shaking his head.

'I just find it a bit hard to believe, that's all.'

'Sometimes it's just not right, Libby. We're still friends. She actually rents an apartment I own in London.'

'Oh. Well, that's good. I mean, about you still being friends. Not about it being not right.'

He smiled. 'Yeah, I know. And yes, it is.'

'OK, password is set up. It's "champagne" at the moment but you can just change it to whatever you want.'

'Ooh no, that's good! I'm keeping that!'

'OK. Is the finances file on here?'

'Should be. Tilly said she'd labelled a folder "Charlie" within the main finances folder so it was easier for you to find. Although, bless her, with the wedding coming up, her mind has been a bit all over the place at the moment, so let me know if you can't find it.'

I got up and wandered over to the window, looking out onto the garden below.

'Can I ask something else?'

'I have a feeling you're going to anyway,' Charlie said, without looking up, his concentration on the screen as he tapped keys and drew his finger across the trackpad.

'Is it difficult being here? I mean, bearing in mind your ex had so much input into this place and now you're not... together any more.'

'Nope. It was always my house, Libby. Like you said, I had the final say on things. We weren't especially serious. It's not like we went and picked stuff out together. She didn't break my heart and I didn't break hers. It was fun while it lasted, but that's all.'

'OK.'

'She needed someone a bit more...'

'A bit more what?'

He lifted his head and looked at me. 'I remember a time when my Saturday afternoons were peaceful and not competing to be part of the Spanish Inquisition.'

'I'm just making conversation.'

'As is your wont.'

'Fine. We can sit here in silence, then, if you prefer.'

He laughed. 'Yes, right. Like that's going to happen.'

I narrowed my eyes at him. He smiled and looked back down at the laptop.

'She needed someone more like you.'

'Female?'

'No. Chatty. She's pretty quiet. I'm not exactly known for my extrovert personality. She needed someone to bring her out of herself more. Whom she's now found, I'm pleased to add.'

'You're not a total introvert. You just take a little longer to get to know people.'

'No, I know. But sometimes people need a bit of... va-va-voom to help them along, you know?'

'Va-va-voom?' I said, unable to stop the smile breaking on my face.

Charlie's fingers had stopped moving on the keyboard and his eyes were now focused intently on the screen.

'Va-va-voom!' he repeated, so quiet this time I could barely hear him.

'Charlie?'

'I... err... nothing. What?'

I frowned.

'Charlie?' I said again, moving towards him.

He snapped the lid of the laptop shut.

'Charlie?' I repeated, more serious now. 'What's the matter?'

'It was you.'

'What? What was me? What's going on?' I sat on the sofa and reached for the laptop. He moved it away momentarily before releasing it.

His gaze settled on me. 'It was you on the beach that day.'

I opened the laptop and frowned at him. 'Has that apple juice you bought been fermenting or something because you're making no sense whatso— Oh, my God!'

'It was in the folder with my name on it. I... I just opened the file.'

The computer was snapped shut for a second time.

'What the hell was she thinking? I'm so sorry, Charlie. I told her to delete that the moment I saw it!'

I dropped my head into my heads and felt my face burning.

'I can't believe this.'

'Really no need to apologise, Libs,' Charlie said, his hand gently rubbing my back. 'I'm sure it was just a mistake.'

'Of course it was a mistake!' I said, jumping up and pacing to the window. 'I'd hardly have let you at the computer knowing... that... was in there, would I?'

He didn't answer, so I turned. 'Wait, what did you mean when you said it was me on the beach that day?'

Charlie took a deep breath.

'Are you going to come and sit down?'

'No, I'm not done pacing yet.'

'OK. But that rug is silk and was shipped over from India. It cost me a bloody fortune so do try not to wear it out.'

I glared at him, but I couldn't make it stick. Those striking blue eyes were focused on me, and filled with amusement.

'Come and sit down.'

'Not until you tell me what you meant.'

He let out a sigh. 'Are you going to go all redhead and erupt again?'

'I don't know yet. It depends on what you're going to say.'

'OK. I saw you on the beach the day that this was taken. I was windsurfing with my mate, Alex, and the wind had taken me a bit closer to shore. I glanced over and saw this girl in a really pretty yellow dress...'

My hands went to my face again. 'Oh, God, you were the wind-surfer,' I mumbled through my hands.

'And then you were under the water. I never really saw your face. The brief glance I got, it was sort of covered with your hair. Hence, I've never put two and two together before. As I turned, you jumped up out of those waves like a shark was after you.'

'It was cold!'

'I could tell.' He chuckled.

I glared at him again, this time meaning it. 'So not helping.'

'I guess that's when Tilly took this shot.'

'Not intentionally. The camera was in burst mode.'

'And then you seemed to lose your balance and went down again.'

'Bloody pebbles. Besides, I wasn't the only one who lost my balance, I seem to recall.'

'No, you're absolutely right. I was just recovering when I looked over again and there you were... on your hands and knees, looking like that!' He pointed to the now-closed laptop. 'Jesus, woman, I nearly bloody drowned because of you!'

'I was trying to get up!' I said, my pitch rising as I flapped my hands and colour flushed my chest and face.

'I know you were.' He looked over at me. 'Come on, Libs. You have to laugh about it. It's only me that saw this. And you can delete it now, if you like.'

'I'll be having some serious words with Tilly.'

'I'm sure it was an accident. Normally she's great at what she does, isn't she?'

'Yes, she is. But this? This is mortifying! I can't even look at you.'

From behind me, I heard Charlie move. He came over to the window, and began bending further and further down until I was forced to meet his eyes.

'You're going to put your back out.'

'It's worth it if it means we get past this.'

I turned away from him. 'I'm all right. Just mortally embarrassed.'

'Don't be. It put a smile on my face for the whole day.'

'You're really not helping, you know. At all.'

'Come on. It's done. And like I said, it's only me. There are worse people to have seen it, let's be honest.'

'When you were windsurfing, you were with someone else.'

'Yes.' Charlie saw my eyes widen. 'But he didn't see anything,' he added quickly.

'How do you know?'

'Because when I came up coughing and spluttering, having swallowed half the English Channel, I blurted out, "Did you see that?"'

'Oh, thanks.'

'Sorry. It was just rather unexpected early on a Friday morning. I wasn't quite prepared.'

'But he didn't?'

'No. Not a thing. Much to his disgust, I might add.'

'And to my relief.'

'And I only saw you from the back really, anyway. Mostly.' Charlie bent and pulled me towards him in a hug. 'Are we good?'

'Yes. I suppose so.'

'Come on, then, sit down. I've got something a bit stronger than apple juice in the fridge. I think we could both do with a glass now. Phew!' He picked up a magazine and fanned himself with it.

I looked under my lashes at him, trying to glare but not pulling it off.

'I think that might be the beginnings of a smile...' He tilted his head, as if studying me.

'I hope you have some big glasses.'

'They're normal-sized champagne glasses but feel free to top up as often as you feel necessary.'

'I really wish I wasn't so bad at drinking.'

11

Charlie reappeared a few minutes later with a bottle of champagne in one hand, two glasses in the other and a couple of bags of nibbly things clutched between his teeth. I got up as he came in and relieved him of the snacks.

'Thanks.'

We sat back on the sofa and he twisted the bottle's cork until it made a satisfying pop.

'I should have known there'd be no flamboyant flying of corks with you.'

His mouth twitched. 'No. Flamboyant isn't really my style.'

'I didn't mean it like that. Besides, Dad always says you lose half the bottle doing that anyway.'

'He's right. You can.'

Charlie poured me a glass and handed it over. I watched the golden bubbles chase each other up the glass, escaping and exploding as they reached the surface.

'What shall we drink to?'

'I wouldn't mind going with "unexpected waves" but I'm sensing you'll probably veto that one.'

'I'm going to veto you in a minute. Behave.'

'OK, OK,' he said, chuckling.

'How about to friendship?'

He paused for a moment and then nodded. 'To friendship.'

We clinked glasses and drank, neither of us really savouring the taste, instead just enjoying the fortifying hit of alcohol.

Several hours later, Charlie had finished the accounting stuff I'd brought him to look at and together we'd finished off the first bottle of champagne and started on a second. He'd also rung for a take-away, which was now hopefully soaking up some of the champers. I was, however, in my world, rather hammered.

'You all right?' Charlie asked, as we sat out on the patio in his courtyard garden, the heat of earlier now reflected back at us as the paving and planters became outdoor storage heaters, surrounding us with warmth.

'Yep!'

'Can Matt come and pick you up?'

I shook my head vigorously. 'Working.'

'Amy?'

'Marcusss-ing.'

'You know that's not a word, don't you?'

'It is now. I'll get the bus.'

'You're not getting the bus. Not in that state.'

'Excuse me? I am not in a state.' I was totally in a state, but I wasn't in enough of a state to not at least attempt denial at said state.

'If you say so. But I'm still not letting you loose on the night bus on your own.'

I let out a dramatic sigh. 'Fine. I'll get a taxi, then. Happy?'

'No. Not really. You're pie-eyed and you expect a taxi driver to let you in smelling like a brewery, and besides, you're still on your own whilst not entirely in control of all your faculties.'

'My faculties are just dandy, thank you. And I do not smell like a brewery.' I bent my head and started trying surreptitiously to find a way to confirm this.

Charlie studied me for a moment then shook his head.

'You can stay here tonight. There's plenty of room.'

'I can't.'

'Why not?'

'I didn't bring anything else to wear. Or my toothbrush.'

'So, just put that dress back on tomorrow. It'll only be to go back home in. And I have spare supplies for guests in the bathroom.'

'I am not going to do a walk of shame from your house, Charlie Richmond.'

He raised an eyebrow. 'Walk of shame?'

'Yes. I mean, we'll know it's not but to everyone else, it'll look *exactly* like a walk of shame if I'm in the same clothes.'

'Everyone else who?'

'Everyone who sees me.'

'Who's going to see you? And even if they do, they won't care.'

'I'll care!'

'Libby, you won't have done anything!'

'I know! That's what makes it even more annoying! I'll know that. And you'll know that.' I was now pointing at each of us in turn for emphasis. Suddenly realising this, I stopped and sat on my hands instead. 'But to your neighbours... well!' I pulled a face that I imagined said it all. Charlie looked at me but said nothing so I continued. 'So, unless I'm going to wear a sign that says, "This is not a walk of shame. I did not sleep with Charlie Richmond", then it's a no go.'

'You'd need quite a big sign to fit all that on.'

I blinked at him.

'And it wouldn't really do my reputation much good.'

'You have a reputation?' I asked, my eyes wide.

'No. But thanks for looking quite so surprised at the possibility.'

'No offence.'

'Some taken.'

I bumped my head on his arm as we sat on the bench, absorbing the sultry atmosphere of the late evening. 'I didn't mean anything by it. You're too nice to have a reputation.'

'Thanks,' he said, flatly.

'You're welcome,' I replied, completely missing the inherent sarcasm. And then I fell asleep.

* * *

Sunbeams tickled my face and I opened my eyes. Too bright!

Quickly, I closed them again. Rolling over, I breathed in the smell of clean linen. Now facing away from the window, I tried again with the whole eye-opening procedure. This time it was a little easier, although my head still pounded whichever way I faced. I took a deep breath, pushed myself up a little and let out a groan. It might smell like clean linen but it certainly didn't look like it. Almost half of the pillowcase was smeared in what had once been my make-up. I hardly dared look at my face.

I pushed the duvet back and swung my legs off the bed, bending my body up to follow in such a manner that kept my head from moving until the very last moment. I looked down. The fabric of my dress was all crinkly anyway so at least it didn't look as if I'd slept in it, even though I clearly had. I had absolutely zero memory of going to bed and, as I was still fully dressed, could only assume Charlie had deposited me there. Peering sideways and hesitantly in to the mirror, I let out a squeak. The same could not be said of my hair and make-up. Both positively shouted 'slept in'. I flopped down on the dressing-table stool and glanced around. My bag was on the bedroom chair. Leaning over, I snagged the strap and pulled it towards me, plopping it on my lap. I rummaged inside and found a hairbrush. A few minutes later, having argued with some knots and tangles, my hair looked slightly more presentable. My face, however, was another matter. I looked around the room and noticed the door on the far side of it ajar. Getting up, I crossed the room and gingerly pushed the door open a little more. En suite. Charlie, you star.

* * *

'Good morning,' Charlie said, as I poked my head out of the kitchen doors.

'Well, one of those is right,' I replied, shading my eyes from the sun.

He was sitting on a Penguin Paperback deckchair, reading the business section of a newspaper. The rest of it was strewn in various directions around the bottom of the chair.

'Bad, is it?'

'It's not the chirpiest I've ever felt, I have to say.'

'I know how to fix that. Come on.' He got up and walked past me back into the kitchen. 'Here,' he said, pointing to a glass of orange juice on the counter. Next to it stood two small tablets. 'Take those and drink that for a start, then we can get some breakfast sorted.'

'I'm not sure I'm up for breakfast, Charlie, thanks all the same.'

'Yes, you are. It'll do you good. Soak up the alcohol. Believe me, I know from personal experience.'

'I've never seen you drunk. I can't even imagine it.'

'You've only known me a short while. Give it time. And why can't you imagine it?'

I finished the juice and walked to the sink to rinse the glass. 'I don't know. You just don't seem the type.'

'The type?'

I lurched for one of the bar stools that stood in a military line against the large central island. 'Oh, I don't know, Charlie. It just seems like you wouldn't like losing that studied control you have about you.'

He pulled a face. 'You think I'm a control freak?'

I shook my head. That was to say, I rolled it from side to side as I'd now laid it on my folded arms on the worktop. 'No,' I said, my voice muffled. 'You're just... Charlie.'

'I see. That, of course, makes it a lot clearer.'

I pulled my head up from the counter and squinted at him.

'It's a good thing, though.'

'Uh huh.' He gave a little head-shake. 'Come on. You need some food inside you.'

'I'll throw up.'

'No, you won't. You'll actually feel a lot better. It's been scientifi-cally proven.'

I tilted my head back and looked up at him. For some reason it seemed even further to meet his eyes today. 'Is that true?'

'Absolutely. You can look it up.'

'I will.' There was every chance that Charlie was right, but frankly, with his quiet, studied demeanour, even when he was being funny, he could have convinced me of pretty much anything.

'Good. And then you can ring me and tell me how right I was.'

'Unlikely.'

'You're clearly sobering up. Let's go.'

I slid off the stool. 'Oh, I think I owe you for some pillowcases. Half of my make-up is now splurged all over the cover of one. I put it in the laundry basket in the bathroom.'

'No worries. I'll mention it to the housekeeping lady when she comes.'

'You have a housekeeper?'

'Well, not a personal one, no. But a very nice lady comes in and takes care of all that stuff.'

I pulled a face.

'What?'

'Nothing. I was wondering how you kept this place so nice.'

'Hey, I have skills, you know. I just don't have the time.'

I burst out laughing as the image of a six-foot-five Charlie in a frilly apron and feather duster popped into my head.

'And why is that funny?'

'No, no, it's not. I just sort of got this image of you in my mind...'

Charlie looked at me. 'I don't really want to know what that image is, do I?'

I shook my head, then quickly stopped in order to halt the feeling that my brain was rolling around in my skull like a pinball. 'No. Probably not.'

Charlie rolled his eyes at me, but I could see laughter in them. 'Come on. Time for your walk of shame.'

I spun round. 'Charlie!'

He turned me bodily back around. 'It's OK. I made you that sign you wanted. We'll pick it up on the way through.'

'Oh, ha ha.'

He shuffled me to the door, slinging his camera bag over his shoulder on the way as we stepped out into warm sunshine. I rummaged about in my bag for some sunglasses whilst he locked up. Slipping them on, I breathed an audible sigh of relief.

'Morning, Charlie.' A sultry, breathy voice drifted across on the warm breeze. We both turned in the direction it had come from. Greeting us was a sight that could only be described as a 'bombshell'. She had curves I could only dream of, and the fifties-style

sundress clinging to them did a fabulous job of enhancing everything she had going on beneath it. In contrast to the shiny platinum
hair that stroked her bare shoulders, her lips were full and pillarbox
red. Keeping them half parted, she focused dark eyes on Charlie.
She was utterly entrancing.

'Morning, Elaine.' Charlie nodded. 'How are you?'

I risked a glance at him from behind my sunglasses. The vision
in front of us had brought out his cute little half-smile and that faint
blush he was sometimes prone to.

'Fine, thank you, Charlie.'

The way she said 'Charlie' was incredible. There was a whole
invitation wrapped up in just his name.

'It's getting warm already, isn't it?' She wafted the glossy magazine she held and ran her eyes over his face. The colour remained
there.

He smiled a little more. 'Yes, it is. Going to be another hot one.'

'Maybe we could get together for a trip to the beach later. Take a
dip in the sea and... cool off.' She smiled. Frankly, if Charlie didn't
burst into flames there and then I wouldn't have been at all
surprised if *I* did.

'Oh, that sounds lovely,' he said, 'but we're actually off out today,
along the coast.' He squeezed me against him, his arm around my
waist.

We are?

Charlie's neighbour gave a smile as she turned herself a little
more, bodily excluding me from the conversation. I was glad of the
sunglasses, as I was currently looking far less presentable than I
generally managed. Wasn't that always the way? On days you felt
good, you wouldn't see anyone. But get a day when you felt like
death on the back burner, you could almost guarantee you'd run
into someone you knew. And it was even more likely to be someone
you would much rather have run into when you were looking your
absolute best. Like an old boyfriend, an ex-schoolmate who was
always snotty to you, or a smoking-hot neighbour of your smoking-
hot male friend. I mean, it wasn't as if Charlie and I were dating, so
there wasn't that aspect, but still...

'I didn't know you were heading out last night. You should
have called on me. We could have had some fun. Although it

looks like you might have had some without me.' She leant in and whispered the last bit as though I weren't there. Her eyes half closing as she smiled and pouted at Charlie, all in the same movement. Quite the achievement. And then my brain caught up and my mouth dropped open as I realised she'd just referenced my walk of shame! I knew it! This was exactly what I meant! Well, not exactly. I hadn't expected to be confronted with it quite so directly.

'Last-minute thing. You know.'

Wait! What? Charlie, no!

As I made to move Charlie almost imperceptibly tightened his hand on my waist, keeping me pinned there. Fine. But he better have a hell of an explanation for making me out to be someone he just picked up by chance last night.

'Another time.'

Charlie nodded.

'Bye, Charlie.'

''Bye, Elaine. Have a good day.'

She turned back and let her gaze drape over him from head to toe. 'Thanks,' she breathed.

Charlie kept his hand at my waist and began moving us down the path towards the street, heading over to where his car was parked. A resident's parking tag showed in the windscreen.

'Wow.'

'Yes. She is a bit.'

'Even you must be able to see that this one wants to get you into bed.'

He gave me a look and opened the passenger door for me. 'Yes. Thank you for that.'

'So, I guess you don't feel the same way?' I asked, when he got in.

'No.'

'She's stunning.' I paused, thinking of how she'd signalled with that incredible body that I, most definitely, wasn't part of the conversation. 'If a little rude.'

'Part of my objection,' he said as the engine awoke with a burble and Charlie manoeuvred the sleek car out of the parking space and pulled up to the junction with the main road.

'I don't think hooking up with her would be anything to do with manners, Charlie.' I laughed.

He turned his head to the right, looking for a gap in the traffic that was now building as people trekked to the seaside to take advantage of a Sunday with great weather. After a couple of minutes he pulled out, the throaty engine sucking in the warm air of the morning and growling in pleasure.

'You know I'm not really the hook-up type, Libs.'

'Really?'

He glanced across at me. The clear gaze was hidden behind a pair of D&G sunglasses but I could still see his frown. 'You must have worked that out.'

'Well, you just made me do the walk of shame and rubbed it in her face. So apparently you do hook up sometimes.'

He gave that little chuckle and another glance, this time accompanied by a smile, 'Yeah, sorry about that. I panicked. And you were just... there.'

'Much to her displeasure.'

'She'll get over it.'

'Not until she gets over you. Or under you. Probably both.'

He gave a little head-shake.

I grinned. 'Bloody hell, Charlie. You saw her, right? Most blokes would be tripping over themselves to get that sort of attention.'

'She's not my type.'

'Does it matter? I don't think she's looking for a long-term thing here.'

'Of course it matters. And she might not be, but I am.'

'Oh.' I pondered on that for a bit. 'So, you wouldn't have a one-night stand?'

A small sigh escaped his lips. 'It's a good job I know you're just nosy. You ought to be careful though. Some people might think you're offering.' He slid a glance to me momentarily, before switching his eyes back to the road.

'Yes, but you know I'm not.'

Charlie gave a nod as we rolled to a stop at a red light. 'I take it you're feeling a little better.'

I held up my hand and made a side to side tilting motion, indicating that things could easily go either way.

'It's just that most people aren't all that talkative when they're hungover.' The light changed and he pulled away. He didn't rev or floor it, but the burbling engine and throaty exhaust still caused a few pedestrians to glance round and cast their eyes over the sleek machine. 'You appear to be the exception.'

'Are you thinking back to a time when your Sunday mornings were peaceful and easy?' I said, picking up on his comment yesterday about his Saturday afternoons.

He smiled, his eyes fixed on the road.

'Yes.'

I tilted my head at him. 'And?'

'And they were quieter,' he said.

I made a mock-offended huff noise and looked out of the window.

'Quieter. But much more dull.'

I didn't turn my head but my smile got wider.

'Where are we going?' I asked as Charlie took the turn for the marina. 'I thought we were going for this magical hangover breakfast cure. I sincerely hope you're not expecting me to cook it for you in this state.'

Charlie laughed. 'No. I most certainly wasn't. I just thought you might like to change clothes. Then we can go and find some food.'

'Ahh. You can be really sweet when you want to be, can't you?'

Charlie looked across at me as we waited at the next set of lights. Below us to the left, the marina stretched out, and beyond it the sea. Sharp darts of sunlight flashed on the masts and the sea beckoned, blue and inviting.

'When I want to be?'

'Figure of speech. You're actually always sweet.'

'Great. We're back to sweet again.'

'What?'

'Nothing.'

'It was a compliment.'

'OK. But don't say it too loud.'

'Why not? Women love that sort of thing.'

'It makes a bloke sound soppy.' He glanced up at the lights, waiting for them to change.

'No, it doesn't.'

'OK. Take two blokes, one's all muscled up and hard core, but a bit of an arse. The other one isn't so ripped but is, oh, so sweet. Which do you think the woman would go for?'

I took a deep breath. 'That completely depends on the woman. It's not a fair question.'

Charlie laughed, and the sound of it made me smile. 'That's a cop-out answer, Libs, and you know it. We both know that 99 per cent of the time they'll go for the bad boy. Sweet is not usually that big a draw.'

'All right. Yes, some women like a bad boy, but not forever. Not for the special stuff.'

'I see,' he said, the lights having finally gone green, 'so they have their fun with the bad boy, and then when they're done with that bit, and ready to settle down, they head for the sweet, but rather dull, guy.'

'You're not dull!'

'I was speaking hypothetically, but thanks for that.'

'Oh. Whoops. But you're not, just to clarify anyway. And besides, none of this applies to you anyway.'

'Here we go, it's time for Libby's Logic. I love this part of the day.'

I flicked him on the arm and his smile grew.

'It doesn't apply to you because you're the best of both worlds. You've got the looks of the first and the personality of the second.'

'Dull.'

'No, not dull! Sweet!' I said, flapping my arms around as if that would help get my point across. I turned in my seat as we pulled into the visitors' parking area for my block of apartments. Charlie's face looked serious. He lifted a hand to remove his sunglasses.

'Charlie, seriously, you mustn't think—' I looked up as I launched into a pep talk. His eyes showed all the laughter his serious mouth had hidden. 'Oh, you little...' I flung open the door and began to get out. Charlie was out and around the car in seconds, holding out a hand in assistance.

'Thank you,' I said, taking it. Dealing with direct sunshine and manoeuvring out of the low-slung car was taking more effort than expected. Safely extricated, we made our way up to my flat and I let us in.

'You don't need to stay if you have something to do,' I said.

'Thanks for the lift and for doing that stuff yesterday, and I really am sorry about the mix-up with the files.'

'Not a problem. You're welcome. As for the other thing, don't give it another thought.'

I gave him a look. 'I won't if you won't.'

He shrugged. 'I hate to make promises I can't be guaranteed to keep.'

'Perv,' I said, lobbing a cushion at him.

'Hey, I wasn't the one posing for *Sports Illustrated* on the beach.'

'It wasn't posing! It was falling! And I take what I said back – you're not sweet at all!'

'Glad to hear it. Now go and change or whatever you're going to do. I'm starving.'

'Well, go and get something to eat, then. I might just flop here.'

'Oh, no. I need to prove to you this magic cure. Plus, I can't go home now. I told Elaine that we were going out along the coast all day. If she sees me at home, she'll think we've broken up.'

I gave him an incredulous look. 'Broken up? We're not even going out!'

'She doesn't know that.'

'I don't think I'm that much of a deterrent to her, to be honest, Charlie.'

'Nonsense.'

'You have no idea.'

'I know more than you think. But I understand your point. It wouldn't matter to her if I was going out with the hottest model of the moment. However, she knows it would matter to me. Therefore, all the time she thinks I'm with someone, she's less likely to actually try and do something about it.'

'What was this morning, then? I was standing right there and it didn't seem to bother her.'

Charlie shook his head. 'This morning was tame.'

'Bloody hell, Charlie. Maybe you should just go for it and let her get you out of her system.'

'I'd rather not, if it's all the same to you.'

'Because you're looking for something more?'

'I suppose so.'

I raised an eyebrow.

He took a deep breath before letting it out on a sigh. 'Are you ever going to go and change?'

'Yes, yes, all right. But this conversation isn't over.'

'Of that, I have not the slightest doubt,' he mumbled before a cushion caught him square on the ear.

12

I'd showered at Charlie's so ten minutes later, I was ready to go. Having changed my clothes and redone my make-up properly, I still felt pretty rotten, but at least I felt a little bit more like me.

'Better?' Charlie asked, looking up from his phone as I came back into the living room.

'Much.'

'Good. Ready, then?'

'Yes. I'm actually starting to feel a little hungry now.'

'Then I know just the place. Don't forget your hat.' Charlie threw my big straw sunhat at me like a frisbee.

'Thanks.' I grabbed my bag, slung it over my shoulder and followed Charlie back to the car.

An hour later we were sitting at a cliff-top café, looking out over the Channel, both full to the brim with English breakfast and two large mugs of tea each. Annoyingly, Charlie had been right. I did feel better for eating. Although I was keeping that snippet of information to myself.

'Are you going to admit it?'

'What's that?' I said, turning from the view.

'You do feel better, don't you?'

Argh!

I shrugged, keeping my eyes on the view. 'No noticeable difference at the moment. But it was probably a good thing to get some food inside me.'

'Pretty sure that was a big fat porker.'

I pulled another face but couldn't help smiling.

'Yeah, that's what I thought.'

'All right. Don't let it go to your head.'

'I'll try not to.' He gave me a look. 'But I'm glad you're feeling better. What do you want to do now?'

'I don't mind. Any thoughts?'

'We could just go for a walk if you were up to it? And I know a little teashop down the back lanes that serves the best cake for later, you know, just to keep up your strength.'

'Oh, so the cake would purely be for my physical well-being.'

'Of course. I mean, I'll have some too, in the interests of politeness. You know, just to keep you company. Be rude to let you eat alone.'

'Ah, that's so *sweet* of you.' I put a big emphasis on the word and poked my tongue out as punctuation.

'I'm all heart.'

'OK, let's go and walk this off and make room for cake.'

The tide was out as we made our way along the coastline at the base of the cliffs. The summer sunshine bleached out the whiteness of the chalk, making them almost too bright to look at. At least too bright when you still had the remnants of a hangover. We walked further out and began climbing over the rock pools, peering in to see what creatures we could find in each one.

'There's nothing in here,' I said, squinting at where Charlie had pointed. I'd been peering into pools on my own for the past twenty minutes whilst Charlie had wandered around taking photos, crouching over pools and getting so close that I was worried he was going to tip in head first. I'd wandered off across rocks warmed by the sun, leaving him happy in his pursuits, but he had now caught up with me and, upon hearing how little luck I'd had in spotting any sea life, was trying to help.

'Yes, there is. He's just buried himself in the sand a little.' Charlie crouched next to the pool and pointed.

'Doesn't sound like a bad plan to me. Maybe he had too much champagne last night as well.'

Charlie straightened up. 'Are you all right? I can take you home if you'd prefer, and you can get some rest.'

I stood up and tilted my head back to look up at him, the brim of my hat shading me. 'No, this is good. Honestly. It's nice. I can't remember the last time I did this.'

Actually, I could. It was exactly two weeks before Mum died. I'd never been rock-pooling since. Not until today. Of course, Charlie had no idea about any of that. Despite my chattiness, I rarely opened up to anyone about what had happened with Mum. Even my ex only knew that she had died young, and unexpectedly. Despite nearly two years of dating, I had never felt that I wanted to open up about that. And he'd never asked.

Charlie took off his sunglasses, his beautiful eyes focused on me. 'I'm pretty sure that was another big fat porker, Libby.' His voice was soft. 'Is everything OK?'

I felt the tears prick my eyes, hidden still behind the oversized glasses I'd grabbed on the way out of the flat. Suddenly I wanted to tell Charlie everything, and I didn't know why. But I did know that it had nothing to do with last night's champagne and everything to do with knowing I could trust him completely and utterly. And with wanting him to know.

'I'm fine!' I said, bailing at the last minute, squishing the tears back down.

'You're really on a roll with those fibs today.'

He held out a hand and I took it, my sandals dangling from my other one. Stepping across the rock pools, with Charlie steadying my way on the slippery rocks, we headed out to where the sand had formed into little ripples from the outgoing tide. We walked along next to each other, content in silence, the wash of the tide drowning out the sounds of families having fun as we walked further from the main beach and moved along the coastline.

I bent and picked up a large shell, washed clean by the waves. Turning it over in my hands, I smiled at the perfection of its shape.

'Isn't nature amazing? I mean, look at this. It's just so—' I let out a squeal as a mollusc began poking its head out to see what was going on with its home. Quickly, I brought my arm back and lobbed the shell out to sea.

Charlie raised his eyebrows. 'Impressive throw.'

'Yes, my brother is the one that throws like a girl in our family. My nephews hate playing ball with him.'

Charlie laughed, and so did I. And then I burst into tears.

* * *

Charlie's arms were around me before I knew it. He didn't ask what was wrong or tell me everything was all right, or that I was fine. He just held me and let me cry until I was ready to stop. When I did, I searched in vain for a tissue in my dress pocket, having left my bag in the boot of the car.

'Here.' Charlie offered me a freshly pressed, soft linen handkerchief. I looked at it for a moment. 'It's clean,' he added.

A laugh bubbled up inside me at his obvious, yet earnest statement and I flung my arms around his neck. His arms wrapped automatically back around me and in that moment I felt so safe, so secure I didn't want to ever let go. But I knew I had to. My embrace loosened, and Charlie's followed suit. I took the handkerchief still in his hand and tried to delicately wipe my nose. Accepting that as a loss, I blew it instead.

'I'm sorry,' I said, stuffing the hanky in my own pocket.

Charlie gave a small shake of his head. 'You don't need to apologise. What can I do?'

I looked up at him. His expression held such concern that I felt the tears fill my eyes again.

'My mum would have loved you,' I said, my breath hitching a little as I spoke.

'I'm going to take that as a big compliment.'

I nodded in reply, smiling at him through tiny prisms of tears. 'Mum loved rock-pooling. She'd bring us down here on summer evenings, helping us poke about in the pools, but gently so as not to disturb anything living in there too much. She had a never-ending sense of wonder at the world, and her enthusiasm transferred to everyone she came into contact with. Just her smile could lift you out of a bad mood. She didn't even need to say anything half the time. Her being there was enough.'

Charlie listened patiently. Mum really would have loved him. And if I wasn't careful, I knew it would be very easy to fall *in* love with him, which I knew would be a Bad Thing. We were wonderful as friends but lovers were quite another matter; I knew I was the opposite of his 'type', and I didn't want to lose him as a friend by attempting something that I already knew wouldn't work. It was times like this I missed Mum the most.

'I was right when I said you did remember the last time you went rock-pooling, wasn't I?'

I nodded. 'Mum took us shortly before she died. It was one of those long summer evenings that seem to go on and on. She'd packed a picnic tea and as soon as Dad got home we all piled in the car and drove here. Dad got to work on the big umbrella and we sat eating this feast, Mum and I taking most of the shaded spot before setting off to clamber over the rocks and see what creatures had been left by the tide. That day we'd made it into a competition, Mum and I against Matt and Dad. We were all scrambling over the rocks, trying to be the first to find something, and then Dad started making up all these daft names of things they had supposedly found which, of course, had disappeared by the time we came over to look. We were all laughing and I remember looking up from the rock I was perched on and seeing Mum and Dad laughing together. I remember the look on each of their faces. I'll never forget it. It was like...' I swallowed, and flicked a brief glance at Charlie.

'Go on,' he said, his voice soft.

I dropped my glance to my feet. 'It's going to sound corny.'

Charlie gently took my fingers and gave them the softest of squeezes. 'No, it won't. And who cares if it does?'

I lifted my gaze to him again. There was no judgement in his eyes. No expectation. Just concern. My gaze shifted to the horizon, hazy and indistinct in the heat.

'The look on their faces... it was like there was so much love in it, it was almost tangible. It felt like you could reach out and touch it. It was so real.' I swiped at my cheek as a tear rolled down it. Charlie's thumb caught another before I could get to it. His touch was warm and gentle and part of me didn't want him to ever stop touching me. I took a deep breath, stepping back from him as I did so, letting his fingers fall away from mine. All the emotion that the memory had evoked, plus the remnants of a hangover and a late night, was muddling my senses. I pulled my hat straighter and shoved my sunglasses back on. Behind their screen, I risked another glance at Charlie. His brow furrowed slightly as he watched me.

'So, where's this amazing cake place, then?'

Charlie waited a couple of beats before he spoke. 'Follow me.'

* * *

Tilly had the Monday off so it was Tuesday before I was able to tackle speaking to her about the shock contents of the accounting file.

'Morning!'

'Morning,' I said, a little less enthusiastically, as I let Tilly in the door. From the corner of my eye, I saw her slide a glance to me.

'How was your weekend?'

'Fine, thanks. Yours?'

'OK. Bit crazy with organising things for the wedding, of course. But that just seems to be par for the course at the moment.'

I smiled and nodded and walked on to the kitchen, where I proceeded to pour two teas from the Art-Deco-style teapot I'd set brewing a few minutes earlier, ready for Tilly's arrival. She followed me in.

'Is everything all right, Libby? You seem... a little quieter than usual.'

I handed over the mug.

'Thanks.'

I took a sip from my own and then looked back at Tilly. She appeared to be waiting for me to say something.

'Have I done something wrong?' She had by now paled a little and an anxious expression creased her cute pixie-like features.

'I took the paperwork and laptop to Charlie on Saturday so that he could go over those queries we had.'

'And? Have I made a mistake on some accounts stuff?'

'No. Not at all. That was fine.'

'So why are you looking at me like that?'

'Like what?'

'Like you want to explode but you're too nice to do so.'

I laughed in spite of the tension filling the air. 'I don't want to explode, don't worry.'

'But there's something?'

'OK. Remember the photo the camera took when I fell in the sea?'

Tilly frowned. 'The one when you stood up and everything was a bit, umm, see-through?'

'That's the one,' I said, my voice a little tight.

'What about it?'

'I thought I asked you to delete it.'

Tilly dropped her gaze to the counter top. 'You did. I know. It's just...' She returned her gaze to meet mine. 'Libby, you look super hot in it! I thought that one day, when you meet a guy you really like, well, believe me, he'd like to see it! So, I tucked it away in a folder for as and when.'

'I see. Well, as and when became Saturday.'

'You met someone on Saturday?'

'No. But as you had put that photo in the accounts folder marked "Charlie", he got rather more than he bargained for!'

Tilly's hands flew to her face. 'No! No, I couldn't have! I...'

My suspicion that Tilly was, like Amy and Marcus, subtly – or not so subtly – trying to push Charlie and me together was immediately dispelled by the look of shock and horror on her face. Apparently, this really had been an accident.

'Oh, Libby! I'm so, so sorry! I never meant to put it in there. I don't know what I was thinking! I must have caught it and dragged it in there accidentally when I was preparing the file for Charlie. Did he see it... properly? I mean, were you there and able to close it quickly?' Her question had a tone of hope in it.

'Nope. I was the other side of the room. I only knew when he suddenly lost the ability to speak for a few moments, and I took a look at the screen.'

Tilly's hands went back to her face. 'I'm so sorry!' she said again, the words muffled by her hands. Tears began to prick at her eyes. 'Am I fired?'

I let out a big sigh. 'No, of course you're not fired.'

A couple of tears released and streaked down Tilly's face.

'Oh, come here,' I said, rushing round the kitchen table and wrapping my arms around her, as stray tears soaked into my new silk blouse. 'Don't be silly. It's fine. I'm just a little bit paranoid about people trying to set me up lately, what with my father's attempts. And ever since Charlie came on the scene, Amy and Marcus have been dying to try and get us together. I didn't know if you'd been roped in.'

'No, honestly,' Tilly mumbled miserably against my chest.

'All right. It's OK now,' I said, handing her a tissue to dry her eyes. 'Is there anything you need to tell me, though? It's not like you to make a mistake like that. That's why I was sceptical. Is everything OK, you know, between you and Sam and stuff?'

'Oh, yes, yes. That's all fine. We just had a bit of a panic on Friday. Our photographer suddenly said he didn't think he was going to be able to make it!'

'What do you mean?'

'Apparently he's double-booked himself and only just realised. He contacted Sam on Friday, so he was trying to deal with it because he knew I'd flip out, but in the end he had to tell me. I guess I was more distracted than I thought. I really am so, so sorry about the photo. I never meant for Charlie to see it like that.'

I slid my glance to her.

'I mean at all!' she clarified, pausing slightly before she spoke again. 'But I do think you should keep it. I mean, seriously, Libs, you look bloody amazing in it. I wish I had one like that.'

'Well, if you like, we can go down to the beach once we finish our tea. I'll throw you in the sea and we can get you one of your own.'

She smiled for the first time since we'd started talking.

'So, is everything sorted now, I mean, with the photographer?'

'Apparently. After I'd gone off on one about it, he seemed to reconsider. Honestly, I was a total Bridezilla. I didn't know I had it in me.'

I shrugged. 'Needs must. So long as he's got his act together now. And next time, just tell me what's going on, OK? Don't just sit and stress there on your own. I might not be able to help but I'd like to try.'

'OK, I promise. I'm sorry. I didn't want you to think I was being unprofessional, bringing all this wedding stuff to work.'

'Tilly, you're getting married and there's a lot to arrange. Of course there's going to be stuff you have to do in the day. It's fine. I know you well enough by now to know you won't take advantage. And I did hope you knew me well enough to know you could come to me – about anything. I must be a worse boss than I thought I was!'

'No!' Tilly cried. 'Not at all! I was just desperate to prove how efficient and professional I was. And ended up proving the opposite.'

'Rubbish. The only thing you proved is that you're human. And I already know you're efficient and professional. So just relax, OK? The blog wouldn't be where it is without you.'

She gave me a hug and we headed on into the living room and settled down at our desks ready to tackle our individual to-do lists for the day.

13

'So, what else did you do at the weekend?' Tilly asked when we broke for lunch. We were sitting out on my Charlie-declared-hazard of a balcony, under a parasol, eating a pasta salad I'd made first thing this morning.

'I drank too much champagne in response to Charlie seeing that photograph and passed out on his garden bench.'

'You did?' Tilly laughed.

'I did.'

'And then what?'

'Then I woke up.'

'Where?'

'Where what?'

'Where did you wake up?'

'In Charlie's *guest* bedroom,' I emphasised. Although I was now sure Tilly hadn't put the X-rated photograph in Charlie's folder on purpose, it was clear she wasn't entirely unconvinced by Amy's prompts about him and me either.

'Oh.'

I laughed. 'Sorry. No juicy gossip for you.'

'Oh, well.'

'Although, I did meet one of his neighbours, Elaine. Boy, she's something!'

'Is that good or bad?'

'I think that depends on who you are. She's quite the bombshell, a real siren!'

'Wow. I'm guessing Charlie was just standing there with his tongue out, drooling?'

'That's the funny thing. He wasn't. Not at all.'

'Huh.'

'She's definitely interested in him though. And that's putting it mildly!'

Silence settled between us. I could tell Tilly was building up to something, though, because she kept fidgeting.

'What is it?' I said, eventually.

She looked at me, as if to say, 'What?' but saw immediately that I wasn't fooled.

'I just wondered if Charlie was gay.'

'He's not.'

'How do you know?'

'Because he told me the first time I met him.'

'You really do have boundary issues, Libs.'

I laughed. 'No, it wasn't like that. The subject came up.'

'OK. And you think he was being honest?'

'Absolutely. I'm not sure that Charlie knows how to be anything much but honest.'

'I've not met him a lot but, from what I've seen, yes, I know what you mean. It's just a little surprising that he's not with anyone. I mean, he's gorgeous! And especially when he's getting offers like that.'

'He's looking for something a bit more serious than that, apparently.'

'A man who turns down no-strings sex? Blimey.'

'Yeah. I know.'

'And you're not... you know...'

I tilted my head a little. 'I'm not what?'

'You know, interested in him.'

'No. And he's not interested in me,' I continued. 'We're friends. Good friends. But we're not for each other in that way. I'm pretty sure I'd drive him insane within a week. He already thinks I talk too much.'

'I'm sure he doesn't.'

I wasn't so sure but, as we weren't dating, it didn't really matter. Without the pressure of a relationship, Charlie seemed happy for me to rattle on without it causing him too much of a headache, despite his teasing.

'So, what did you do on Sunday? Just recover from the night before?'

'Pretty much. Charlie insisted that a humongous fried breakfast was the quickest way to do that, so insisted on us going somewhere to get something.'

'Although it's often the last thing you feel like facing, it does seem to work.'

'I know. It's so annoying when he's right.'

'So where did you go?'

'Oh, to a little place up on the cliffs, further along the coast.'

Tilly nodded. 'Seems a long way to go just for breakfast.'

I caught the hint of suggestion in her voice.

'Don't start.' I laughed. 'I've already explained this once today to Amy. We bumped into The Siren when we came out of his house. He panicked and told her we were going out for the day. He said if she saw him come back earlier, she'd be round. I think he's a little scared of her, to be honest!'

'Bless him.'

'I know.'

'So, we popped back here so I could change, got breakfast and then went rock-pooling, of all things.'

'Blimey, I haven't done that for years.'

'No, neither had I. It was nice, actually. Charlie was off taking photos, and I was poking around in pools and just swishing my feet in the sand. It was really relaxing; I have to say.' I left out the bit where I'd burst into tears and ruined Charlie's pristinely pressed, expensive hanky.

'Sounds lovely.'

I smiled. 'Yeah, it was.'

Tilly was quiet for a moment, and I could see the cogs whirring.

'You know, we could do an "everyday" blog post on that.'

'What?'

'The rock-pooling and stuff.'

'Oh, I don't know. It was just a quiet day, Tilly. I'm not sure people would be too interested in me spending half an hour trying to see an invisible crab.'

'No, they would, really! I promise.'

'I didn't take any pictures.'

'But Charlie did. Can't you get some off him?'

'He's over in Asia on a business trip now.'

Tilly looked at me. 'Err, hello? Email? WhatsApp?'

'I don't even know if he's got the photos with him.'

'You can ask.'

'OK, fine. I'll ask.'

I picked up my phone, and started typing Charlie a message.

✉ Hiya, hope you had a good flight. Quick question. Told Tilly about beach trip — well, most of it… She thinks people will be interested in the fact I went rock-pooling (!!). I'm not convinced but there we go. Wondered if you might have a couple of photos you wouldn't mind me putting up on the blog of the beach and stuff? Obviously I'd credit you! Not to worry if not, really doesn't matter. Have a fab day and talk to you soon. Xxx

I put the phone down and pulled my to-do list back up on my screen. 'OK, I've asked him. But I'm not sure—'

My phone made a clown car noise that signified I had a WhatsApp message. I picked it back up and clicked on the icon.

✉ Hello you. Flight was good, thanks. One of the flight attendants was very chatty… reminded me of you.

He followed this with a winky face.

✉ You're welcome to use any of the shots I took. Not worried about credit, Libs. I'll just put everything in a zip file and send it over and you can see if there's anything you like. Hope you're having a good day. Bloody sweltering here!

I tapped out a reply.

✉ Thanks, Charlie. You're a star. Sorry to hear about the temp — people don't realise how tough having such a jet-setting lifestyle can be!

I returned the compliment of the winky face.
His reply came straight back.

✉ Ha ha! Mind you, I suppose having changed my screensaver to that photo of you on the beach might be helping push up temperatures…

Smart arse.

✉ Touché!

Tilly saw me smiling.

'Everything all right?'

'Yes. Charlie's just being a smart arse. It seems he hasn't quite forgotten about the surprise contents of that file from Saturday.'

'It's hardly the sort of thing a bloke would forget in a hurry!' Tilly laughed, and then remembered that she had been instrumental in Charlie seeing it in the first place. 'I mean…'

I shook my head. 'He's just saying it to wind me up.' I pulled a face.

Tilly smiled.

My email notification sounded and I glanced at it. 'It looks like Charlie's sent the file of photos. He said just choose whatever you like and not to worry about credit, but I definitely want to make sure he's credited properly, and all the copyright stuff is on there.'

'Absolutely.'

'I've got some stuff to look at this afternoon, so would you mind going through these? Just choose what you think and I'll have a quick look before it goes into the queue for upload. I don't think it really needs much wording, but you know what you're doing with these posts so I'll leave you to it. I'll forward you his email with the attachment now.'

We returned to the relative coolness of the living room and went back to work. With news of the Glam deal filtering through, my blog was getting more and more hits and I had now been approached by several more companies interested in working with us. I wanted to sit down this afternoon and start looking at some of their proposals. Searching online for some more information on one of the companies, I glanced up and caught sight of Tilly's face.

'What's wrong?'

She snapped her head up. 'Wrong? Nothing! Nothing at all. I was just looking at these photos of Charlie's. Libs, they're amazing! He's really, really talented!'

'I know. He takes some lovely landscapes. I'm thinking about asking him if I can get a couple of prints for in here actually.'

'You should. Totally. But you know he doesn't just do land-scapes, don't you? His portraits are pretty amazing too.'

I smiled. 'Well, he did seem to manage to coax a little crab out to have his photograph taken, so I guess it's kind of portraiture.'

Tilly twisted her screen around to show me the one currently displayed on it. It wasn't the crab. The image was a black and white shot of me standing on a rock, one hand reaching up to the crown of my hat as the breeze ruffled it. My other hand held a bunched-up handful of skirt fabric as I looked down, navigating my way to the next rock.

'Did you pose for this?'

I shook my head. 'No. I didn't even know he'd taken it.'

'I love it. Can we use it on the blog?'

'Umm, I don't know. I guess. He said use whatever.'

'There are a few of you. They're all fabulous! He's better than a lot of the wedding photographers we looked at! I think he's even better than the one we booked!'

I smiled. 'I'm sure yours will be perfect when it comes to it.'

'Yeah. I know. It's just, you know, it's that one day, isn't it?'

'And it's going to be amazing. Now come on, find the little crab picture he took. He showed me that on the camera and it was really cute.'

'OK. Will do.'

I picked up my phone. The thread I'd started with Charlie earlier on the chat app was still open.

✉ Tilly wants to book you as her wedding photographer...

A reply came back within moments.

✉ What?!!!

I smiled. Poor Charlie. I could just imagine panic coursing through him at the thought of dealing with all those people, not to mention the responsibility of getting the Perfect Picture for someone's Perfect Day. I thought I'd better reply and put him out of his misery.

✉ She's just seen the photos you took on Sunday. There are a couple of me and she loves the look of them.

✉ Oh! Yes, hope you didn't mind. I had planned on showing you — just had to shoot off on this trip before I got the chance. I've not really done people before, and you were just there. I really liked the look of them too. Came out better than I expected.

A happy but surprised smiley face followed this declaration.

✉ I'm not entirely sure how to take that but OK! Ha ha! And don't worry, she has a photographer booked. Lucky for you, otherwise I think you'd be first choice!

Winky face.

✉ I meant the photos being better than expected, not the subject, you daft woman. As I'm sure you know!

Pokey tongue face. And then another message.

✉ But I'm glad she has someone booked. Couldn't
deal with the stress of herding a wedding party
and photographing a bride — talk about pressure!
Give me a high-risk assessment involving
billions of dollars any day — that I can deal
with!

✉ I'll remember that. Note to self — do not ask
Charlie to photograph my wedding.

✉ Thanks. I'd appreciate that.

I sent him a smiley face as a reward.

✉ Right, breakfast meeting tomorrow so better get
some kip. Have a good rest of the day. Say hi to
the others for me.

✉ Night, Libs xx

✉ Night, Charlie. Sleep well xx

'OK, these are the ones I thought about using.' Tilly peeped over
her monitor at me. 'Do you want to come and have a quick look?'

* * *

Cleaning was most definitely not my favourite job. On the other
hand, I did like things to be clean and tidy and, as I didn't have a
magical housekeeper lady as Charlie did, the task unfortunately fell
to me. I'd been at it for the last three hours and I was just peeling off
the Marigolds when the doorbell rang.

'Hi!' I broke into a smile when I opened the door to see Charlie
standing there.

'Hi,' he replied. 'I'm not interrupting you, am I?' His gaze flicked
to the bright yellow rubber gloves dangling from one hand.

'Not at all. If you could make it a couple of hours earlier next
time, you'd definitely be interrupting me, which would be perfect.'

He nodded, that shadow of a smile back on his lips. 'Duly noted.'

'Do you want to come in?' I stepped aside.

'Only if you're not busy.'

'No, I've literally just finished this moment. I was going to make myself a cup of tea as a reward. Would you like one?'

'Sounds perfect. Thanks.' He came inside and laid down the gear he was carrying near the console table.

'Have you been out taking pictures?' I asked, as I bustled off into the kitchen to pop the kettle on.

'Yes. I drove up the coast and took some of the sunrise around Beachy Head and Birling Gap.' He followed me into the kitchen.

'You've been up since dawn?' I turned to him, teaspoon in hand.

'Well. Bit before. I wanted to get in place for the sun coming up.'

'Wow.'

'What?'

'You're all chirpy. And you look great. And you've been up since dawn. Before dawn. Put all those words together and add me in the mix and it would be a different matter entirely.'

'Rubbish. You're always chirpy.'

'You've never seen me pre-dawn.'

'That's true,' Charlie replied, smiling as he took the mug I offered him. 'Thanks.'

I noticed the hint of blush colouring his cheeks. I hadn't meant anything remotely in the realm of where his mind had apparently gone but – well, he was a bloke, so allowances had to be made. And he blushed. I mean, really? How could I be annoyed at that? It was kind of adorable. But that didn't mean I was letting it pass.

'And that's not what I meant.'

Charlie chuckled into his tea. 'Sorry.'

I rolled my eyes. 'No, you're not.' I shook my head. 'Men. So, can I see what you took?'

'Of course, if you want.'

'Of course I want!'

Charlie disappeared and came back a moment later with his camera and a laptop and twiddled about uploading the pictures from one to the other. A few minutes later, he replaced the card in the camera and pushed it aside. I took a seat next to him at the small table in my kitchen and looked at the screen. The most beautiful shot of blush-tinted chalk cliffs appeared on it, followed by more shots, each one as striking, if not more so, than the last.

'Charlie, these are amazing!' I said, when we'd cycled through his morning's work.

'They're not bad.'

'Not bad? They're fabulous!'

He smiled at me, his bright blue gaze twinkling like the sunlight on the water outside. 'Thanks, Libby. I'm glad you like them.'

'Do you sell them ever?'

'My pictures? No! They're not good enough for that.' He took the tech bits and headed back into the living room. I trailed after him.

'Charlie, they are. Seriously! You should look into doing that.'

'I don't think so. I've never really considered...'

I waited. He didn't finish, but I got the idea.

'Because you don't think they're good enough or because you want to keep it purely as a hobby. Untainted by commercialism.'

He looked back up at me from where he was crouched, replacing his camera in the bag. 'You're making fun.' He smiled.

I plopped down and sat cross-legged beside him. 'No. OK. Yes, a little. But only because I know you can take it.'

'Fair enough.'

'Are you going to answer the question?'

He sat back from the crouch onto his bum, facing me.

'I just never considered it. Well, I did. But not in a real way. Just in a "that might be nice" sort of way. Once or twice.'

'I think you're an amazing photographer, Charlie. I really do. And I told you what Tilly said when she saw your photos from our day out.'

'Libby—' he reached for my hand '—I really appreciate that. But it's a massively competitive market. I just don't think I have the time to dedicate to looking into something like that as well.'

An idea struck me. I jumped up. 'You should start a blog!'

'What?' he said, pushing himself off the floor and towering over me once more.

'A blog. For your photography! You should start one!' I was gripped by enthusiasm on his behalf – which apparently I needed to be because he wasn't showing a whole lot himself, but then that wasn't really his way. I was definitely the show-every-emotion one in this friendship.

Gripped by enthusiasm for the possibilities of this new project, I suddenly realised that that wasn't the only thing I was gripping and let go of Charlie's arm.

'Sorry.'

'It's all right.' He chuckled. He was looking at me with that half-amused, half-bemused expression I'd only ever seen him use on me.

I stepped away a bit, linking my hands behind me, just in case, as I felt the excitement bubbling away inside me.

'So, a blog?'

'Yes!' I squeaked!

Oops! Bit too much excitement. But I was excited! I had memories of how it had felt starting my own blog and the prospect of getting Charlie set up was giving me flashbacks of that and it felt good. His photography was amazing and I wanted other people to realise that. Which they would, once they saw it.

He shrugged and held his hands up, palms upward. 'OK.'

'OK?'

'OK. Let's do it. Although I need to warn you, I have absolutely no idea about blogging.'

'That's all right. I know someone who has a bit of a knack for this sort of stuff.' I winked at him and he laughed. I grinned, seeing my own enthusiasm now beginning to reflect in his eyes.

14

I grabbed my laptop, sat on the sofa and crossed my legs, making a table for the laptop on my knees. Pulling up the Internet, I typed in the web address for a well-known, easy-to-use blogging platform. Charlie took a seat next to me.

'So, have you thought what you might want to call it?'

'It?'

'The blog?'

'Bearing in mind it wasn't happening until about five seconds ago, err, no, I've not had too many ideas yet.'

'Not to worry. We can just call it Charlie Richmond Photography for now.'

He nodded and made a gesture with his hands, acquiescing. Despite our relatively short acquaintance, it hadn't taken Charlie long to get the idea that once I thought of something I was kind of off and running.

'OK.'

I started typing. As I finished the second word, my phone rang and a picture of my brother in 'mad surgeon mode' complete with mask, scrubs and scalpel appeared on my screen. We all thought this picture was hilariously funny but then I wasn't a patient of his, and I could see how 'deeply terrifying' could also be an accurate description, depending on your perspective.

'Hi, Matt.'

'Hi, Libs. Are you busy? I need a huge favour.'

'Err, sort of, but ask me anyway.'

'Is there any chance of you taking the boys for a few hours? Maria's at work and the hospital just called and asked if I could come in. Bit of a crisis.'

I didn't need time to think.

'Of course. I can come and get them to save you time dropping them off, if that helps.'

'You're a lifesaver, Libs. Quite possibly, literally.'

'Yeah, right. I think we both know who has the genius for that in this family. Now get off the phone and get them ready and I'll be there shortly.'

'You sure? You said you were busy.'

'It's fine. I can carry on with it when they're here.'

'Great. Thanks, sis. See you in a bit.'

I ended the call and turned to Charlie. 'My brother's been called in to the hospital. I need to go and pick up my nephews for a few hours. But I can work on this later and give you a call.'

Charlie nodded, and shrugged. 'Or I could come with you.'

'Oh! Of course! I didn't mean to exclude you; I just didn't think you'd want to get roped into babysitting.'

'It's fine. I don't really have anything much planned. Especially now the weather looks on the turn.'

We both glanced out of the balcony door to see storm clouds building on the horizon. To the east, swathes of dark, ominous streaks reached down from them, linking the sea to the sky.

I smiled.

'Great. We kind of need to go now, though.'

'Ready when you are.'

I grabbed my keys, and we hustled out of the door, down towards the car park.

'I'll drive,' Charlie said.

'Are you sure?'

'Absolutely.'

And then I remembered.

'No. No way. Absolutely not.'

He looked at me, confused. 'What's wrong?'

'That!' I said, pointing at his car. 'Maybe you didn't get the full message. We are collecting two small boys whom I cannot guarantee to stay clean for more than ten minutes at a time and that—' I bent and pointed at the pale leather inside the car '—is not going on my tab. So, thanks all the same but we'll take mine.'

'Come on. It'll be fine. I take full responsibility.'

'Charlie, I—'

'Libby! I believe we're in a rush. Just get in the car. Please.'

I gave him a look. 'Fine. But don't say I didn't warn you.'

'I wouldn't dream of it.'

* * *

'No way!' Liam, my eldest nephew, pushed past my brother's leg as Charlie pulled to a stop on the drive.

'Awesome!' added Niall, his eyes big in his face as he took in the swanky car, its engine ticking quietly in cooldown.

'You realise I am never going to be able to get them in my own car again now, don't you?' I said to Charlie as he walked round to me.

'Hi, Auntie Libby!' The boys rushed over and both gave me a hug at the same time. 'Did you get a new car?'

'No, this is my friend, Charlie. It's his car.'

'I love your car! It's awesome!' Niall repeated.

'Thanks.'

'It's like James Bond's car,' his brother added, still gawping.

'Less gadgets though, unfortunately,' Charlie replied.

I'd forgotten Liam's James Bond obsession. There was a possibility we'd have to physically remove him from the car later.

'DB11. Very nice,' my brother said as we approached the front door, the boys trailing behind, heads still turned towards the car.

'This is my friend, Charlie Richmond. Charlie, my brother, Matt.'

'Pleased to meet you,' Charlie said, as the two men exchanged a handshake.

'Thanks for doing this, Libs. I hope I didn't interrupt anything...' I saw his eyes flick to Charlie, and I was pretty sure Charlie did too, but we both pretended to ignore it.

'No, not at all. Charlie had just dropped in to say hi, and then offered to drive.'

Matt peered towards the car and blanched. 'Oh, God. Pale leather.'

'I warned him.'

Charlie laughed. 'Really, it's fine.'

Matt handed over a bag of stuff for the boys, plus their booster seats, and thanked me again for taking them.

'I'm not sure what time I'll be done. Can I call you?'

'Sure. No problem. Have they had lunch?'

'No, I was just about to start finding something when the hospital rang. God, I sound like the worst father, don't I?

'Don't be daft. I've got stuff for sandwiches at home. I'll feed them when we get back.'

In the distance, a low rumble of thunder sounded. Niall looked up and then at his dad. I took the cue for distraction tactics.

'Right. Everybody ready for a ride in the James Bond car?'

A little chorus of 'Yeah's went up as two small boys bounced up and down. I gave Matt a hug and a wave and wished him good luck with whatever it was he was heading into at the hospital. His job and abilities held me in awe and I was glad that I could do something to help, however small.

'Right. Feet on the floor and hands on laps, please,' I instructed the boys as they got into the small back seat of the Aston Martin. Liam worked his own seat belt and obeyed and I helped Niall with his as Charlie got back in the driver's seat, and closed his door. I clicked in the belt and made to move away. Niall grabbed my hand, his little face full of concern as he looked at me.

'But my feet don't touch the floor!' he whispered.

From the corner of my eye, I saw Charlie smile.

'That's OK, sweetie. I just meant keep your feet down. Don't put them on the back of the seat or anything.'

'OK.'

The truth was they were both good boys and Matt and Maria had instilled respect for people and property in them from an early age. But they were still children and it was still pale cream leather in an Aston Martin.

I tipped the seat back into position and got in, waving to my brother as I closed the passenger door. Charlie started the engine and blipped the throttle a couple of times, the car letting out a throaty roar each time. In the back the boys cheered loudly. I slanted my glance to him.

'You're as much of a kid about this car as they are, aren't you?'

He gave me an incredulous look. 'Of course!'

He gave one more blip and pulled out of the driveway onto the road and headed back towards the marina, taking a longer route, apparently for the benefit of the boys, although I think the enjoyment factor was about the same for all three males.

Having pulled into a parking space, we extricated the boys from the back seat and I surreptitiously checked the interior for marks and rips. Relief flooded through me. I stood up and shut the door. Charlie was watching. He gave me a little head-shake and smiled. I shrugged and smiled back. He made it hard not to. Traipsing up the stairs, I held Niall's hand as Liam and Charlie followed close behind, my nephew firing questions at Charlie about the car the whole time. We entered the flat, and I put the boys' stuff down on the floor, opening the balcony door for ventilation as I did so. The impending storm had made the air thick and humid, and the gentle breeze of earlier had been replaced with an almost eerie stillness.

'Do not go near the balcony,' I said. As I always said. And they never did. Not once. But it didn't make me any less paranoid. 'Boys!' I said. 'Are you listening?'

'Yes, Auntie Libby.'

'Yes, Auntie Libby.'

'Right. Thank you. Lunch will be ready in five minutes.'

I'd already lost their attention to the toys that were coming out of the bag my brother had given me. Not surprisingly, they were cars.

'Charlie! Charlie! Come and play!'

I raised my eyebrows at him and walked through to the kitchen. From my position I was able to peer out and could see all three now spread on my living-room floor driving little cars around imaginary roads with varying amount of noise and squealing tyre sounds.

'Boys! Lunch is ready. Come and wash your hands, please.'

Nothing.

'Boys! Now, please.'

The car noises stopped, replaced by giggling. Charlie appeared at the door with a small boy tucked under each arm, each one wriggling and giggling in joy. I laughed as Charlie put them down.

'I'm just going to pull the balcony door across,' he said. 'It's started raining quite heavily now.'

'Oh, thanks!'

'Come on, boys, wash your hands, please,' I said again, and they did. Niall dragging out his little hop-up so that he could reach the sink, then replacing it back in the corner once he was done. He was well trained – albeit traumatically.

I'd got him the little step so that he could wash his hands on his own – he liked to be able to do whatever his big brother did, which included washing his hands at the kitchen sink before lunch. The step was just big enough and the more he grew, the easier it got for him. But, of course, I wasn't used to having it there and one day, shortly after I'd bought it, I forgot about it. Right up until the moment I tripped over it, sending myself flying and catching my chin on the worktop as I went down. It really was quite surprising just how much blood could come out of your chin. Shocked, Niall had immediately gone into hysterics, which was kind of annoying because I'd planned on that very same course of action myself and now felt unable to do so.

Luckily, it had been a family lunch so Maria had bustled the kids out of the kitchen, enabling me to have my mini hysterics in peace, at the same time allowing Matt to patch me up. All that remained from that day was a tiny little scar at the base of my chin and an ingrained reminder in my youngest nephew never to leave his hop-up out of place.

We finished lunch and the thunder was now gaining in both volume and frequency. I'd planned to take the boys out for a walk after lunch but the weather had other ideas.

'Can we watch a film, please?'

'OK. And then if the weather clears up we'll go for a little walk, all right?'

'OK,' they said, already going to the cupboard where I kept a selection of their favourite DVDs.

'We can start having another look at the blog thing, if you like?' I said to Charlie. 'If you still want to stay.'

'Sounds good.'

As I spoke, I noticed something glinting on the floor of the balcony. So that was where it was! I'd thought I'd lost it – the beautiful Mont Blanc pen my brother had bought me for my birthday last year. I grabbed a pad for notes, and made to go and get my pen from under the lounger. I stopped as the boys' voices rose.

'I want to see *Despicable Me*.'

'I want to see *Minions*.'

'*Despicable Me* has Minions in it, st—'

'Liam!' I warned him sharply.

He stopped immediately. Calling anyone stupid was a definite no-no in their house and their parents' house rules automatically transferred to mine.

Liam looked a little sheepish and reached for the *Minions* DVD.

'It's all right,' Niall said, picking up his brother's choice instead.

'I like Gru. He's funny.' He handed his older brother the case, and Liam quickly set about loading it into the DVD player. I gave a glance to Charlie, rolled my eyes, then turned back to dash out and grab my expensive pen before it rolled off somewhere and I really did lose it.

Everything went quiet as I bounced backwards off the glass. However, the preceding loud bang and slight crunchy noise my face had made as it impacted with the door Charlie had kindly drawn closed earlier was still resonating within my own head. Distracted by the boys, my mind had momentarily forgotten that little nugget of information. I staggered backwards and felt for the couch. Missing it, I found the floor instead. I lay there for a moment hoping that the dampness on my face was just my eyes watering. Through slightly blurred vision I saw three faces looking down at me.

'Awesome,' Liam said softly, breaking the silence.

Knowing my nephew's penchant for goo and gore, I had a pretty good idea that it wasn't just tears running down my face. I had missed out on the gene that dealt with such things in a sensible, controlled manner and, at his exclamation, felt a wash of ickyness flood over me. I was immediately glad that I was already on the floor. It saved a step in the proceedings. Charlie crouched down next to me.

'Boys. Why don't you go and watch your film? I'll be there in a moment.' I squelched down panic at the fact my voice now sounded all weird and nasally.

They remained staring at me. I didn't have the willpower to say it again and I was beginning to feel sick from what I was now absolutely certain was blood leaking into places it wasn't supposed to be.

'Right. Let's sit you up,' Charlie said, and, without waiting for an answer, scooped me up and moved us to the smallest sofa. The boys followed.

'Liam, would you be able to get me a cold flannel from the bathroom, please?' Charlie asked.

'Um hmm,' Liam replied, still not taking his eyes off my face. 'Do you want Auntie Libby's first-aid kit too?'

My brother had equipped me with this some time ago. I wasn't entirely sure if it was for the boys' benefit or mine. Worryingly, but in a way somewhat comforting, I seemed to be the one who had got the most use out of it so far.

'Yes, please.'

'OK.' He finally tore his gaze away and hurried off through to the bathroom.

Through my own streaming eyes, I saw Niall's face crease.

'What's the matter, sweetheart?' I forced the words out.

'You're crying, and your nose is all leaky and bumpy.'

Ohgodohgodohgod.

'Niall.' Charlie smiled at him, reassuringly. 'Auntie Libby's absolutely fine. She bumped her nose and sometimes when you do that, it bleeds a little. It's swollen because of the bump – that's why it looks a bit funny at the moment.'

Funny?

Niall looked at Charlie and then at me, then back at Charlie.

'She's going to be OK?'

'Of course. I'll make sure of it. I promise.'

Niall thought for a moment. 'You promise?'

Charlie nodded. 'I do.'

'OK,' Niall said quietly before climbing up on the sofa next to me and snuggling in for a cuddle. I mouthed the word 'thank you' to Charlie and he gave a little smile.

Liam returned from the bathroom with a cold flannel and the

first-aid kit. Charlie thanked him and took it from him, before very gently wiping my face with the cloth.

'Do you want to take your brother and watch your film for a bit whilst I clean Libby up?'

'OK.' Liam nodded and held out his hand to Niall. 'Come on, Niall. Let's go and watch Gru.'

Niall wavered. He looked at Charlie, his big green eyes full of concern. 'You're going to look after Auntie Libby?'

'I am.'

'You'll make her all better?'

'Promise.'

Niall studied Charlie for a moment then took his brother's hand and they headed off to sit on the other sofa in front of the TV. A few seconds later, the sounds of the film starting filled the silence.

'I'm just going to rinse this. I'll be right back.'

I nodded once gently.

'How are you feeling?' Charlie asked when he returned, gently laying the clean, cold flannel on my face.

I squirmed a little at the painful touch.

'Sorry.'

I tried to shake my head but, thanks to the pounding headache I had also now acquired, I opted for a little hand-wave as a gesture instead.

'That was quite the impact.'

'Mmm hmm.' I paused. 'Is my nose broken?' I asked quietly, doing my best to keep calm.

Charlie's hands were cool as he gently felt around my increasingly sore face. 'No, I don't think so. I think you just gave it a good whack. You have quite the egg on your forehead too. You don't do much by halves, do you?'

'Not my style,' I said, my hand gingerly touching my nose.

'You're very lucky you didn't break it.'

I raised my eyebrows in agreement then decided not to do that particular action again for a bit until the pain subsided.

'I'm no doctor but I think I can patch you up for now and your brother can check you out properly later. You managed to break the skin on the bridge of your nose and it's still bleeding a little. I'm going to put some butterfly stitches on it.'

'I'm sure it'll be fine with just a plaster,' I said, leaning forward to find one in the first-aid box. Charlie put his hand across the top, blocking me.

'No. It won't. It will bleed straight through. Trust me. Now sit still.'

'Pardon?'

'Please.'

I looked at him.

'Come on,' he said quietly. 'I promised Niall that I'd look after you. You're not going to make me break my promise to a five-year-old, are you?'

'Oh, wow,' I snuffled out. 'That's low.'

'Desperate times call for desperate measures.'

I gave him a look and sat back against the sofa, as requested.

A few minutes later my nose cut was butterflied up and Charlie had put a little square of gauze on the top and secured it with paper surgical tape.

'Have you got an ice pack?'

'There's a gel one in the top bit of the freezer.'

He headed off to the kitchen and I pushed myself gingerly up off the sofa. The boys were happily laughing at the Minions doing something and I walked over to the mirror on the wall by the front door. Charlie had done a good job of tidying me up. A white strip of gauze ran across the bridge of my nose, covering the stitches, and he wasn't joking when he said about the egg on my forehead. It really was quite the bump! A very fetching look. Not one I would be highlighting on the beauty pages of my blog any time soon.

'Is this what you meant?' I turned to find Charlie grinning at me as he held up a gel ice pack in the shape of the Mr Men's Mr Happy.

'That's the one.'

'OK. Now come and sit down.'

I headed over to the couch where the boys were and they shuffled along without taking their eyes off the telly. I sat down next to them and Charlie sat down next to me and gently laid the gel pack on my bump.

'Hopefully this will take some of the swelling down,' he said, quietly, so as not to disturb the boys' enjoyment.

'Thank you, Charlie. I'm so sorry about all this. I don't think I'm up to looking at the blog thing any more today, so if you want to go home, it's fine.'

For a moment, I thought I saw a flicker of something cross Charlie's face. But then again I had a bump the size of Pluto on my forehead and had recently made disturbingly horrid crunchy noises with my nose, so my vision and perception were probably somewhat off right at the moment.

'I think I'll wait here a bit. Just make sure you're all right.'

'I'm fine. It was just a little bump.'

'Libby. You ricocheted backwards about three feet. I'm staying.'

'OK.' I was too tired to argue and actually it felt sort of nice to have him there.

I turned my head back towards the television. The colours pounded my eyes so I closed them, laid my head back and just listened to the sounds of the film and the boys, big and small, laughing along.

15

A couple of weeks later I answered the door to my friend. 'So, how's your day—?' Amy stopped as she entered my living-room area and saw the disaster zone it currently resembled.

'I know it looks bad, but it's not. Honestly.'

'OK,' Amy replied, wholly unconvinced. 'What are you doing?'

'Planning.'

'I'm guessing you don't believe in notepads.'

'I'm a visual person.'

'Apparently. I've not seen this bit of the process before. I had visions of you drawing beautiful pictures in elegant notepads.'

We both glanced down at the separate piles strewn around my living room.

'Yeah. I don't really work like that.'

'No. I can see that now.'

'Can we come in?' Marcus' voice drifted from the front door.

I glanced at Amy.

'I left it on the catch.'

'Thanks. I'll be coming to you when I get robbed.'

Amy pulled a face. 'It was only for a minute. I knew they were coming up.'

'Woah!' Marcus exclaimed, stopping abruptly. 'I mean... umm... what a lovely flat!'

'Thanks,' I said, straight-faced. 'I'm just so glad I tidied up before you arrived. You should have seen it earlier – it was a right mess.' I made a 'phew' face. 'Coffee? Tea?'

Marcus plastered a smile on and nodded. 'Whatever you're making. Thanks.' British politeness at its best.

Standing behind him, Charlie smiled at me and gave a shake of his head, before nudging his brother. 'She's winding you up.'

Marcus looked between me and Amy, clearly unsure which way to step so as not to risk offending me and my possible lack of house-keeping skills.

'I'm planning some posts for the blog. I find this the easiest way to do it. Honestly, it really is much tidier than this normally. Take a seat if you can find one. I'd pick it up but I'm not finished yet and I've just got it how I want,' I called through from the kitchen.

'It's fine. We only dropped in on the way home to say hi and ask what you were doing tomorrow,' Amy said as I reappeared with mugs on a tray. She and Marcus had squashed onto one of the sofas and Charlie had taken a spare seat on the other one. I put the tray down in the middle.

'It's early for you to be home, isn't it?' I said, glancing at Charlie as I handed the drinks to Amy and Marcus.

'Train strike. I worked from home today.'

'Oh, yes. I forgot. That's a pain for you.'

'It was OK. I probably got more stuff done at home than I would at the office anyway. I really feel sorry for the people who absolutely have to get places, though.'

'And it did mean that he could pick us up from work in the Aston.' Marcus grinned.

I shook my head. 'Boys and toys.'

I leant over and handed Charlie his mug.

'Could you take that for me too?' I asked, passing my own.

He took it and put it on the end table beside him, his eyes returning to me as I stepped around the piles of items as if I were taking part in some sort of fashion-based assault course.

'So, what's happening tomorrow?' I said, stretching over a pile that now seemed larger than I'd first estimated. I glanced back at Amy for an answer as I hoiked up the hem of my skirt and prepared to make a lunge for the sofa.

'It's nothing special,' she started, her eyes darting to the gap and the pile I was trying to manoeuvre around, calculating as to whether she thought I could make it.

I could totally make it, I told myself. Amy sent me a warning look, which I ignored and confidently launched myself.

Abort! Abort! My brain began yelling but far too late for the warning to be of any use. Instead of my aimed-for spot on the sofa, I was now half sprawled on Charlie's lap. I scrabbled about hurriedly, trying to rectify the situation. Despite the blood now pounding in my ears from mortifying embarrassment, I could still hear Amy and Marcus laughing. I made another attempt at extraction but my foot was now caught in the fabric of my skirt and severely limiting my movements. I heard Charlie let out an 'oof' as I hastily shuffled about.

'Jesus! Watch your knees, Libby!' Two large hands wrapped around my upper arms, tipping me upright. I was now pretty much square on Charlie's lap, and looking directly into his gorgeous blue eyes. Judging by the look on his face, that hadn't exactly been the plan. I guessed his manoeuvre had primarily been about damage control rather than specified outcome but, for once, I was the one blushing.

'Whoops!' I said, scrambling inelegantly off his lap. I made to push myself off and my hand slipped, sliding up his thigh. His eyebrows rose and I felt his shoulders move as he stifled a laugh.

'Don't!' I whispered, risking a look at him as I clambered backwards and sat as far away as possible in the small stretch of sofa not covered in stuff, or Charlie.

He looked at me, innocently. Ordinarily I would have believed it, but I'd already felt the laugh rumble in his chest as I'd braced my hand against it in my attempts to extricate myself.

'Everything all right over there?' Amy asked, as I settled back and took the cup of tea Charlie was now passing me.

'Yep, fine. Slight misjudgement.'

'Apparently.'

I flashed her a warning look which she ignored, wiggling her eyebrows and grinning.

I pretended not to notice and hoped that Charlie hadn't either.

'You were saying something about tomorrow?' I said, hoping to divert attention.

'Yes, Marcus and I are going out for a meal, and we thought it might be fun if you and Charlie came along.'

Oh, no. Amy was up to something again. And clearly Marcus was in on the plot. For God's sake, I'd just ended up unintentionally sat astride the man's lap and now she was suggesting we all go out for dinner. The word 'awkward' sprang to mind.

'Just as friends, of course,' Amy added, helpfully, which only served to make matters worse.

I risked a glance at Charlie, unaware as to whether he had known about the arrangement before he got here. By the look on his face, that would be a no.

'What do you think, Charlie?' Marcus asked his brother, saving me from answering straight away.

'Sounds good,' Charlie said, not missing a beat.

'Libby?' Amy asked.

'I... yes, of course. Sounds fun.'

'Great.' Marcus then steered the conversation back to something sports related and Amy and I soon lost interest. I leant down and shuffled some piles around in order to make my exit from the sofa a more dignified one than my entry had been. Gathering the used cups, I placed them back on the tray and headed into the kitchen with them. I heard soft footsteps behind me.

'God, you should have seen Charlie's face when you fell on him!' Amy laughed, her voice low.

'Ames. Don't. I'm mortified as it is! And if tomorrow is about trying to engineer something between me and Charlie, I'd rather you didn't. We're happy just being friends, and I get more than enough of that sort of thing from my dad, believe me.'

'Libs, I'm just teasing you! I know you're embarrassed but it was kind of funny. I think you made his day!'

'Ha ha!'

'And no, tomorrow's not about that. We just like spending time with you both. There's a new restaurant just opened up in Preston Street and we thought it would be fun to all go together.'

Amy was right. The evening was fun and she even restrained herself from making any further hints at a possible romantic connection between me and Charlie. Since Marcus had pointed out his brother's very specific choices when it came to women, Amy and

I had both accepted that friendship was the best option for me
when it came to Charlie. And, glancing across the table as the two
brothers shared a joke, I felt a sudden whoosh of gratitude at having
him in my life at all.

16

I pulled into the space that Marcus, from the back seat, was directing me into and tilted my kerbside mirror to make sure I didn't scrape my wheels, especially now that I could see Charlie wandering down the drive watching the manoeuvre. He raised his hand in a wave and then waited until I'd parked and switched off the engine. Walking to the car, he opened the passenger door and held out a hand to help Amy. She thanked him and gave him a quick hug before Marcus piled out of the back seat and told his brother not to start trying to muscle in on his date, grinning as he did so. Charlie did a knuckle rub on the back of his little brother's head and got a punch to the arm for his trouble before Marcus took Amy's hand and began heading inside.

'Oh. Gee. You're welcome for the lift. Thanks for waiting,' I said to their backs, before rolling my eyes at Charlie.

He knew I was only joking. Although, going in together might have been nice, bearing in mind I didn't know anyone. Amy had already been introduced to Marcus and Charlie's parents, but I was a complete newbie and although meeting people didn't really bother me, it also felt a bit weird to just stroll up alone on this occasion.

'Don't worry. I'll take you in,' Charlie said, as if reading my mind. He was dressed in a white, short-sleeve shirt and stone-coloured cargo shorts. His hands rested in his pockets and his feet were bare.

'Thanks.' I smiled, shutting the door.

'Wait!' Charlie called suddenly as I made to move away from the car.

'What?' I stopped, the look on Charlie's face freezing me in place.

He moved closer to me. 'Your dress...'

'What's wrong with it? Is it not the right sort of thing? I knew I should have checked. Is it more formal than—?'

'Libby—' He placed a large hand on my shoulder, interrupting my word flow '—what you're wearing is fine. But currently it's shut in the car door and you're about to leave half of it behind.'

I looked down. Charlie was right. Two more steps and there would have been a large ripping sound swiftly followed by either wailing or embarrassed silence on my part. Possibly a combination of both. Pressing the button on my key fob, I unlocked the door, pulled my dress from it and closed it again. I flipped the fabric back and forth to check for marks, but luckily it seemed fine.

'All right?' Charlie asked.

'Yes. Phew!' I laughed. 'Nice save.'

'No problem.'

'Maybe I should stop wearing dresses and skirts with quite so much fabric in them if I can't be trusted to keep them contained.'

'You wouldn't be you if you didn't wear the things you do.'

I tilted my head up at him, and squinted, the sun shining in my eyes. Charlie moved and blocked it. I unscrewed my face a bit.

'I'm not sure how to take that.'

'It was meant as a compliment.' He looked down at my dress, and then the pavement. Everywhere but at me.

'All right, then. I'll take it as one.'

'Good. Come on,' he said. 'Do you want me to take something?' He frowned a little at me, as I juggled my car keys, the wine I'd brought as a gift, and my wrap.

'No, it's OK. I think I've got it,' I said, just as the wine bottle slid out of my hand and headed for the pavement.

Charlie's hand shot out and caught it just before it hit.

'Yes. I can see you've got it all under control.'

I gave him a look that told him not to be a smart arse, and a flicker of a grin flashed across his face.

We headed inside.

It was a bigger gathering than I had expected, but Charlie's parents were friendly and welcoming, soon whizzing Amy and I around and introducing us to the various friends and relatives attending the party. It quickly became obvious that Marcus got his outgoing personality from his dad and Charlie got his striking eye colour from his mum. She was less exuberant than his dad but just as fun and witty. I glanced over to where Charlie was now standing, his head tilted down a little and forwards in concentration as he listened to the man opposite.

'Oh, golly. Poor Charlie. He'll be lucky to get away now,' his mum said, coming to stand beside me.

I smiled as she did so. 'Bit chatty, is he?'

She rolled her eyes. 'Loves a good conspiracy, does our Graham, and is convinced the banks are behind most of them. Charlie's financial background means he rather gets his ear bent every time Graham sees him.'

'Oh, dear.'

'He's been stuck there for over half an hour now,' his mum said. 'You wouldn't be a love and rescue him, would you? Goodness knows how long he'll be there otherwise.'

'Me?'

'Yes. Would you mind?'

'No, of course not! I can certainly try, at least.'

His mum laughed and patted my arm. 'Graham's a little eccentric but he's not daft. If a gorgeous girl walks up and tells Charlie she needs to borrow him for a minute, he'll know he's beaten.'

I smiled and glanced over at Charlie. He moved his head, as if he sensed me watching him, and his gaze locked onto mine. There was a silent plea in his eyes.

'Looks like you were right,' I said.

'I know my Charlie,' his mum replied. 'He doesn't always say a lot but it's all there.'

I glanced back at her, unsure as to whether she was referring to more than the current predicament Charlie found himself in.

'I'll see what I can do.'

'Thanks. Last time he got stuck with him, he ended up "accidentally" spilling red wine on himself just to get away. Ruined a perfectly good, rather expensive shirt.'

I wound my way between the groups of people congregating on the large back lawn and headed towards where Charlie and his cousin were still engaged in conversation, although, from what we had seen, that conversation appeared to be mostly one-sided. Charlie had now moved and was leaning against the trunk of an apple tree, his head resting back but the intense eyes still focused on his cousin. I approached from the side and touched his arm. He jumped a little and I guessed that he wasn't as intently focused on the conversation as his demeanour indicated.

'Hello.'

'Hi,' he said, straightening away from the tree. 'You OK?'

'Yes, thanks.'

Charlie introduced me to Graham.

'Libby, my cousin, Graham. Graham, this is my friend, Libby.'

'Nice to meet you,' I said, automatically.

'Likewise.'

I made a point of wrapping my arm around Charlie's and felt him turn a little towards me. 'I hate to be rude,' I said, looking at Graham, 'but would you mind if I stole Charlie away for a little bit?'

'No, not at all. I'm sure I've bored him enough by now anyway.'

'Oh, I don't believe that for a moment,' I said, a little laugh accompanying my declaration. Graham smiled and a little blush tinged his cheeks. Clearly this was a family thing.

'Catch up with you later, Graham,' Charlie said, before steering us away towards a spot shaded by a medium-sized oak tree.

The blue eyes fixed intently on me. 'Thank you.'

'You're welcome. Although you should probably thank your mum. She's the one who planned the extraction mission.'

'Then I'll do that, thanks. I see she sent her best operative. Obviously I'm more important than I thought I was.'

I watched the sun and shade dappling on his tanned skin. I realised I was still holding his arm and made to release it.

Charlie covered my hand with his own, keeping it where it was. 'It seems you made quite the impression on my cousin. He's still watching us. If you let go now, he's going to smell a rat.'

I tilted my head back and looked up at Charlie. His voice was serious but his eyes weren't. Surrounded by people he knew, and with a beer or two inside him, no doubt, he was completely relaxed. He looked down at me, his face full of mischief.

I shifted my weight, unsure as to what else was shifting right at that moment. 'And so what, exactly, am I supposed to do now then, instead?'

Charlie moved and gently pulled me down onto the bench that half surrounded the trunk of the tree. He was still looking at me as though he wanted to say something, but he didn't speak.

'Charlie?' I said, eventually. 'Is something wrong?'

He looked surprised and sat back a little. 'Wrong? No. Why?'

'It's just that you look a little... funny.'

'Thanks.'

'I mean...' To be honest, I didn't know what I meant.

'Are you having a nice time?' Charlie said, effectively changing the subject.

'I am. Thank you for inviting me.'

'You're welcome. Mum would have started to think you didn't exist if she didn't meet you soon.'

'Oh?' I said, prompting him for more.

'Well, she's obviously heard about you.'

'She has?' I said, sounding a little alarmed.

'In a good way,' Charlie confirmed.

'All right.'

'She's always enjoyed meeting our friends. That's all.'

I nodded, without looking at him.

Charlie dipped his head down, and caught my eye. 'That's all. Don't worry.'

I held his gaze a moment. 'OK,' I said, seeing that really was all it was.

Why I had even thought for a moment that there might be anything more was just ridiculous. A couple of glasses of wine and the summer heat and I was already losing it. It was just that, occasionally, Charlie's undeniable yumminess caught me by surprise.

I'd opened my door all those days ago to an accountant who could fill in for Adonis on his days off. Obviously, I wasn't blind. I'd seen immediately how gorgeous he was, but I'd been doing a good job of being distracted by the accounts. Stealing a glance at him now, I could see that I'd done an excellent job of being distracted. Had it been too good? All right, Charlie hadn't exactly made any moves, but I got the impression that sometimes he wasn't as sure of himself as his looks and – oh, my – that body should make him. A little encouragement might have resulted—

'You're quiet.' Charlie broke into my thoughts.

'Am I?'

'Yes. Unusually so. What's wrong?'

I ignored the second part and focused on the former. 'That makes it sound like I talk all the time!' I said, turning to look at him.

'Well, you are quite chatty.'

I carried on looking at him.

'I'm not saying that's a bad thing. Not with you. It's nice. It's good. It saves me from having to think of anything to say.'

My mouth dropped open. 'So, you're saying I talk so much that you don't even have the chance to speak?'

'No! Not at all.' He searched my face. And then he saw it. The twitch on my lip. 'You little rotter,' he said, wrapping an arm around my waist and squeezing me up against him. 'You had me really worried I'd actually upset you then. Don't do that to me.'

'Sorry. But you were making me out to be rather a chatterbox.'

'You are. But in a good way.'

'You and your "good way".' I eased out of the squeeze, feeling a little warmer than I probably ought to.

Charlie released me as I started to move. 'Libs, are you all right? Maybe we should get you into the house. You look a bit flushed.'

'Wow, what an attractive picture that paints,' I said, standing up, away from what was possibly the main cause of the flushing. 'I'm fine, Charlie. Really. But I am going to nip into the house and get another drink, if that's OK?'

'I can get that for you.'

'No, it's all right. Like you said, it'll give me a chance to cool a little. Maybe I did get a bit hot out here. I shall take your advice.'

'Want me to come with you?'

Maybe.

'No, I'm fine. Go on,' I said, flapping my hands. 'Do your thing. Schmooze. Mingle. Whatever.'

He shook his head at me and laughed. 'It's my parents' back garden barbecue, not a power networking session.'

'To-may-to, tomato,' I said. 'Now, go! But try and avoid getting caught up in any more conspiracy discussions. There's no guarantee that your mum will be able to spare her best operative for a second mission today.'

He grinned at me, then gave a little mock salute. 'Understood.'

'All righty, then,' I said. A phrase I had never once employed before. Clearly my chatterbox brain was having a moment. 'I'm off.'

'All righty, then,' Charlie echoed, laughter in his voice.

I began walking away, then turned and stuck my tongue out in a show of maturity. I heard his laughter as I turned back, my eyes focused on where I was going, my mind having trouble focusing at all. I stepped through the patio doors and made my way to the sink. Filling a glass with water, I guzzled it down, trying to cool my body and my thoughts. Away from the heat and the alcohol, my thoughts seemed to fall back into order. I wasn't entirely sure what had come over me – although two large glasses of wine were a fairly good bet – but, thankfully, the moment seemed to have passed. I was just washing up the glass when Amy peered in.

'There you are,' she said, coming up to me. She tilted her head. 'You all right? You look a bit funny.'

'There's a lot of that going around today,' I mumbled, thinking of how I'd said the same thing to Charlie a short time ago.

'Huh?'

'Nothing. I'm fine.' I beamed. 'I just got a bit hot and needed a glass of water. Did you come in to get a drink?'

'No, I came to find you.'

'You found me!' I said, smiling as I flung my arms wide. 'Come on, let's go back out.'

Amy linked her arm through mine, her deliberate movements confirming that she was several steps ahead of me on the Slowly Getting Mildly Plastered Path.

'Do you want a quick glass of water before we go back?' I said, pausing a moment.

'No, I'm all right,' Amy said.

'OK.'

'Promise. I'm not going to get totally smashed at Marcus'

parents'. That would be a little embarrassing.'

I smiled and squeezed her arm. 'You seem happy.'

She turned, a fleeting veil of total sobriety enveloping her. 'I am, Libs. I really am.'

I gave her a hug.

'Better get you back to Wonder Boy, then.'

She grinned and we stepped back out into the bright summer sunshine.

* * *

'Best behaviour everyone, the police are here!'

'Sergeant Ford. Nice to see you.' Marcus smiled as his dad reappeared from answering the door with a new guest. I made a point of trying to avoid using clichés on my blog, but one popped into my mind right now; Sergeant Ford definitely fell into the tall, dark and *hello* category.

'Marcus, you little squirt. How are you?' The new arrival threw a tanned, muscular arm around Marcus' shoulders and gave him a manly squeeze.

'All right, thanks, mate. How's you?'

'Good, thanks. How's the corporate world? Still setting it on fire?'

'Every day.'

The latecomer laughed, his face radiating joy as he did so. 'Glad to hear it.' His eyes shifted briefly to Amy and me before fixing back on Marcus. 'Are you going to do the honours or shall I do it myself?'

'Ladies, this is Alex, Charlie's oldest friend.' He put an extra emphasis on the word oldest and received a flick on the ear in return. Laughing, he continued. 'Alex, this is Amy, my girlfriend, and this is Libby.'

'Nice to meet you.' Alex shook our hands. For a moment it felt as if his hand rested in mine a little longer as he met my eyes, smiling. I quickly dismissed it until I caught a glance at Amy, who gave me a look that confirmed I hadn't been imagining anything.

'So, you work with Marcus?' Alex asked Amy.

'Yes, that's right. Well, we're in different departments so I don't actually see him all that much at work, to be honest.'

'Probably just as well. Don't want you to get sick of him too quickly.'

'Oh, ha ha.' Marcus pulled a face. 'Hilarious. You know, if policing doesn't work out for you, you should go into comedy.'

'I'll think about it, thanks.'

Marcus grabbed a sausage roll from a nearby tray. 'By the way, you should really try these, Alex. They're amazing.'

'OK, th—' Alex didn't get a chance to finish his sentence as Marcus rammed the entire thing into his friend's mouth.

Alex's surprised expression quickly turned to mirth, as he attempted to chew and swallow the pastry without choking.

'Touché,' he finally replied when he could speak again.

Marcus took a small bow. Amy rolled her eyes at him, laughing.

'So, do you work with them as well, Libby?'

'No, I have my own small business.'

I was still getting used to telling people that my blog was my business as often they didn't really get it. A vaguer explanation was easier and generally did the job. But not this time, apparently.

'And what is it that you do?'

I looked up to reply, finding Alex's clear hazel gaze fixed on me along with one of the best smiles I'd seen in a long time, besides Charlie's.

'I run a lifestyle blog,' I said, waiting for the glazing over to begin. But it didn't.

'Oh, wow! That's great! Some of those are really big business now, aren't they?'

OK. That was new.

'Yes, a few of them have really taken off.'

'And that's your full-time job?'

'Yep.'

'So that must mean it's doing pretty well itself – oh, wait! You're *that* girl.'

'Excuse me?' I said, feeling my cheeks begin to colour.

He caught sight of three pairs of eyes looking at him, each wondering what was coming next. 'Oh, no! I meant, you're the girl Charlie was helping with her taxes, is that right?'

'Yes. He's helped me with various finance-y bits.'

'Charlie and I were out biking one morning a while back, and when I suggested going to grab a late breakfast, he said he had to go and help a blogger with her taxes. And he's talked about a Libby. I just didn't put two and two together until just now.'

'Oh.'

'Probably would have helped if he hadn't left out the fact that you were gorgeous. Now I can definitely see why breakfast with me was far less appealing.'

I gave him a look but his smile remained firmly in place, and in fact only widened when I looked back at him. 'I can also see why he might have wanted to keep that extra bit of information to himself.' I shook my head, still smiling, and looked away.

'So where is that ugly brother of yours, anyway?' He turned to Marcus.

On cue, Charlie detached himself from a nearby group of people. 'Alex! Glad you could make it, mate.' They exchanged a quick, brotherly hug.

'Wouldn't miss it.'

'Mum would be devastated if you did. Have you seen her yet?'

'No, not yet. She looked engrossed, so I didn't like to interrupt. I've been meeting these two lovely ladies and being assaulted by your baby brother.' He turned to Marcus. 'You know that's actually an offence, assaulting a police officer? I could arrest you for that.'

'Like to see you try, mate.' Marcus offered up his bottle in a salute and laughed.

'Still a cheeky little git, isn't he?' Alex turned to Charlie.

'Afraid so.'

'Luckily the other company has made up for it.' He grinned at Amy and me, his gaze resting a little longer on me. This time I was sure. As was everyone else, by the looks of it.

'Right. That's good, then.' Charlie smiled, his gaze resting on me for far less time than Alex's had. 'How was your shift?'

'Fairly quiet, thank goodness.'

'Would you excuse us for a minute?' Amy interrupted. 'We're just going to sit down for a bit.'

We are?

''Course. You all right?' Marcus brushed his fingers across the small of Amy's back.

'Yes, just need a little sit-down. These shoes, you know.'

I had a funny feeling there was nothing wrong with Amy's feet.

'OK. See you in a minute.' Marcus dropped a kiss on the top of Amy's head and let her go.

Amy took my hand and led me over to a bench overlooking an ornamental pond, its waters half shaded by the swaying branches of a willow tree. Plants and flowers, none of which I knew the name of, spilled around its edges, making it look lush and beautiful, providing hiding places for the fish that flashed in the sunlight.

'Oh. My. God.'

'What?'

'Alex is hot! And he's totally into you! You can't tell me you haven't noticed!'

'No. I did. I mean, notice that he's hot. That's pretty hard to miss.'

'And the other?'

'I don't know. Are you sure he's not just being friendly?'

'Yes, I'm sure. And I think you're sure too. You're just afraid.'

'I am not afraid,' I replied almost automatically before following up. 'Afraid of what?'

'Seeing someone again.'

'Of course I'm not afraid of seeing someone. Why would I be?'

'Because you got hurt. And, I don't know, it hasn't seemed like you've wanted to put yourself out there all that much since.'

'Yes, I did get hurt. But it happens. I haven't been avoiding things. I've just been really busy with trying to build the blog and business up. Time's just sort of got away from me. And it's not like I've really met anyone that's caught my eye.'

'Right.'

I looked at Amy. 'Wow. That was loaded.'

Amy let out a sigh. Glancing around first, she leant closer to me, her voice low. 'It's just that Marcus and I really thought something might happen between you and Charlie.'

'Why? Did Charlie say something to him?'

'No. Not that I know of anyway.'

'Then what made you think that?'

'It's just the way you are together. You get on so well, and clearly enjoy each other's company. Charlie's much more chatty with you than he is with most women, apparently. Most people even.'

I nodded. 'I think that's because he's not interested in impressing me. I'm just another friend. He's relaxed enough with his mates.' I nodded to where Charlie, Alex and Marcus were now laughing uproariously at something. 'I guess I just fall into that category which means he doesn't get himself tongue-tied trying to say the right thing. Which I'm happy about,' I added quickly.

'Are you?' Amy questioned.

'Of course!'

'He's pretty gorgeous.'

'Amy. We're friends. That's all. And I'm really happy with that. If something had happened and then went wrong, it'd just make it really weird and awkward with you seeing Marcus, and those two being so close, so I'm glad that it's this way. Honestly.'

'OK. I just wanted to check because Alex has hardly been able to take his eyes off you the entire time we've been sitting here.'

'Oh, don't talk rubbish.' I laughed it off, bumping my arm against hers on the seat. But as I glanced up and back at the group of men, my gaze immediately met Alex's. He held it and smiled at me. I smiled back briefly, but flicked my own gaze away, unsure. Amy was right. And I was completely out of practice with all this.

'Told you,' whispered Amy.

'All right, Miss Smug Pants.'

Amy laughed. 'Come on, let's go and rejoin the boys.' She stood up and pulled me behind her.

'Feet better?' Marcus asked, his arm winding around Amy's waist as we returned.

'Yes, thanks. Just needed a little rest.'

'And a little gossip?' he teased.

'I don't know what you mean,' Amy replied.

'No. Of course you don't.'

'Would you excuse me a moment?' I said to no one in particular. 'I'm just going to get another drink.'

'I can get that for you,' Charlie said.

'Oh, no, it's fine.' I touched his arm. 'Thanks, though. You stay here and catch up. I'll be back in a minute. Does anyone else want anything?'

They all answered in the negative. Apart from Alex. 'Actually, I'm getting a bit low. I'll come with you.'

Before I had a chance to think up an excuse, Alex had moved and was waiting for me to step ahead of him.'

'Oh. Erm, right. Thank you.'

Amy caught my eye and raised her eyebrows, a wide smile on her face. I sent her a blank look, which made her grin even more. She knew it was killing me not to be able to respond.

I walked back up the garden, aware that Alex was right behind me and not entirely sure how I felt about that. I stepped through the patio doors and made my way to the table where drinks had been laid out in the Richmonds' kitchen diner.

'What are you having?' Alex asked me.

'Oh, probably just an orange juice this time.'

'You're driving?'

'No. Well, yes. I drove here, but I'm getting a taxi home later.'

'Marcus and Amy seem like they're getting on pretty well.'

I smiled, happy for my friend. 'Yes. They do.'

'You seem pleased about that. I take it you approve of him, then?'

I looked up at Alex. He was grinning down at me. 'Are you teasing me?'

'Just a little. I know how women are about approving their friends' choice of bloke.'

'That's because so many of you are a pain in the bum!'

He laughed and I smiled, before focusing my attention back to the drinks table.

'You should really try the punch,' Alex said, coming to stand beside me. 'It's legendary.'

I turned to him, laughing. 'Legendary? Oh, dear, I'm not quite sure if that is good or bad.'

'It's definitely good,' he replied, expertly serving me a cup. 'So long as you're not driving.'

'No, I'm not,' I said, taking it from him. Suddenly I remembered what he did for a living. 'I'm really, definitely not! I promise!'

I could hear the earnest tone in my voice and saw that Alex hadn't missed it either. His brows shot up.

'I believe you,' he replied, laughing, something I was beginning to see that he did easily, and comfortably.

I shook my head and rolled my eyes at him. 'Sorry. I always get nervous around police. I feel guilty even though I know I haven't done anything!'

He grinned. 'Well, how about if I make a promise not to arrest you all afternoon? Would that make you feel better?' He hadn't moved since handing me the drink, and I could smell the tang of shower gel and see the outline of hard muscles under his semi-fitted T-shirt.

'Umm, if you extend that promise to include the evening too, then we might have a deal.'

He shifted his weight, apparently considering the option, his eyes not leaving my face. 'I may be persuaded to include the evening as part of the deal.'

'Oh, yes?'

'Maybe. It's all on the condition of good behaviour, though.'

'Oh, crikey. Then I'm sunk.' I chinked my punch glass with his beer bottle and took a large gulp. Immediately my eyes bulged and I looked in panic at Alex, who was once again laughing.

'Steady on! That's potent stuff!'

I batted him on the arm. 'You could have told me that before!' I said, once my throat returned to normal.

'I thought I did. I said it was legendary.'

'That could mean anything!'

'Sorry.' He laughed. 'I'll remember that you need specifics next time.'

'Isn't that your job? Accurate descriptions?'

'Absolutely. My apologies, normally I'm very—'

I cut him off. 'If you're about to say you're very good at taking down particulars I'm going to make you drink that entire bowl of punch.'

'You realise that would probably kill me!' His smile was wide as his eyes danced with mirth.

I took another sip from my own glass. 'I think you're probably right.'

'Come on, let's get you something else that you prefer,' Alex said, reaching to take my glass.

I moved it away from him. 'I didn't say I didn't like it.'

Alex was close to me, having leant in for the glass, which I was now holding out behind me.

'Told you. Legendary,' he said, his voice softer, his gaze drifting over my face until his eyes locked back onto mine.

'You're flirting.'

'You're beautiful. It's hard not to.'

'Thought you two had got lost.' Charlie's voice came from close by.

Alex stepped back and I suddenly realised I'd been leaning backwards a tiny bit more than I thought. Oh, dear. This wasn't going to end well. I felt myself tipping. I closed my eyes and hoped for the best, making a point to resist grabbing at the tablecloth and pulling everything on top of me. And then I stopped falling. I opened one eye. Charlie was looking down at me, his arms wrapped tight around my body.

'How many of those did you have?'

I pushed myself up and away, a little indignant. 'I've only had a couple of sips. I just lost my balance. I'm not drunk, Charlie!'

'I didn't mean it like that. I just... I should have warned you. That's all I meant. I didn't think you were drunk. I just know you can be a bit clumsy,' he explained.

I raised my eyebrows at him. 'Thanks. I think.'

He gave me a look and I immediately felt bad.

'Thank you. For catching me.'

'No problem.'

'You can always chuck a bit of lemonade in the punch to water it down if you like.'

'That's probably a good idea.'

'Do you not drink?' Alex asked, concern in his voice. 'I'm sorry, Charlie. I didn't know she didn't do alcohol.'

'Hello! Still here!' I piped up. 'And yes, I do drink alcohol. I'm just a bit rubbish at it.'

'Why didn't you say?'

'Because I didn't realise the punch was 98 per cent proof before I tried it! Although now I'll know to avoid anything you tell me is legendary.'

'Well, I wouldn't go that far,' Alex said.

I looked up and his eyes were twinkling with mischief. I rolled my own at him, but I couldn't help a hint of a smile breaking through.

'Dad's starting to serve the food,' Charlie said, breaking the moment.

'Oh, great. Some food would be perfect,' I said, turning to him. I stopped as I caught sight of the expression on his face. He met my eyes, smiled and it had gone.

'Come on. Let's get some food inside you. And, as for you,' he said, turning to Alex, 'you're a bad influence. She was fine before you got here. Honestly, upstanding member of the community, my arse. Get out there, troublemaker,' he said, rolling his eyes at his mate. Alex laughed, and made to step past us.

'You all right?' he asked, stopping briefly and touching my arm.

'Oh, God, yes! I'm fine. Please stop making a fuss, both of you. I already feel enough of an idiot. Now go! Get food!'

'No need to ask me twice.' He gave a quick squeeze on my arm and stepped back out into the sun.

Charlie stood aside so that I could go next.

I made a move to do so, then stopped, that odd, fleeting expression I'd seen on his face replaying in my mind. 'Charlie, is everything OK?'

He frowned. 'What do you mean?'

'A few minutes ago, I just... you looked...' I wasn't quite sure how to explain it. Charlie tilted his head, waiting for me to go on. Seeing that I was faltering, he stepped in.

'Everything's fine, Libby. I was just concerned about you for a minute.'

'Because you thought Alex was trying to get me drunk?'

'No, of course not. He wouldn't do that. Despite what I said just now, he really is a good bloke. I'd trust him with my life.' He paused. 'With... most things, really.' His vivid blue eyes met mine, complete honesty laid before me.

'I was just worried that you were thinking... something.'

His lips quirked. 'Nope. Not a thing.'

'Right. That's OK, then,' I said, still feeling a little unconvinced, but of what, exactly, I couldn't put my finger on.

'Good.' He looked at me. 'Are you ready to get some food now?'

'Yes! Most definitely.' That was pretty much the only thing I was sure about right now.

17

I'd found a spot near the end of the garden and was peacefully watching the sun set over the Downs. Marcus and Amy had been getting cosy and I was beginning to feel more and more like a gooseberry, until I'd finally made an excuse and left them to it. I'm not entirely sure they'd noticed I was gone, which was fine with me. I was so pleased to see Amy this happy. Marcus was obviously smitten and clearly good for her.

'Hello again,' a deep voice said quietly.

I looked to my side to find Alex standing there, the setting sun casting a warm glow on his tanned skin.

'Hello.' I smiled, before turning back to the view. 'It's gorgeous, isn't it?'

'It certainly is.'

I glanced over to smile at his agreement only to find he was looking directly at me, and not the view.

'Oh, very smooth.'

He grinned. 'Actually, that came out way more cheesy than it was meant to.'

'At least it's reassuring to know that you didn't intend to be that cheesy. Although, frankly, it was still a total cheese fest.'

'I can't argue with that. As much as I'd really, really like to.' He leant on the fence. 'It is a great view, though.'

The sun was dipping below the horizon now and twinkling

white fairy lights were swathed around every available tree and surface in the garden, lending it a magical air. I turned back to admire it in the gathering twilight.

'So, the Richmonds do this every year?'

Alex turned too and leant against the three-bar fence that separated the end of the garden from the fields, and the view beyond. 'They do. For as long as I can remember, which, bearing in mind I've known Charlie since primary school, is a pretty long time. Luckily for his mum, we take less supervision now.'

'That's debatable.'

He laughed, before taking a sip from his beer bottle.

'It's lovely that you've stayed friends for so long. It's easy to lose touch with people, especially when you go in different directions.'

'You're referring to that fact I don't earn shedloads in the City.'

I turned quickly. 'No! Honestly, I just meant that life easily gets in the way. And with Charlie's travelling and you – I assume – doing shifts, it's just really nice that you've managed to stay such good friends.'

'I know you didn't mean it like that.' Alex touched my arm in reassurance. 'I'm just teasing you. And yeah, I'm really pleased we have too. Charlie's a great bloke. One of those people who you know would do anything for you.'

'The kind of friend who'd help you move a body!' I laughed, then stopped abruptly. 'Oh, God. That was just a figure of speech, you know that, right?' Alex took a swig from his bottle of beer and raised an eyebrow at me in a 'maybe yes maybe no' kind of way. 'Argh! Do you always have this effect on people?'

'No. Not generally.'

'Great, it's just me, then.' I'd had a couple more glasses of punch and was beginning to think I shouldn't have. Even watered down it was having an effect on me. 'Maybe I should just stop talking to you.'

'I'd rather you didn't,' he said.

I gave a hesitant look up through my lashes, pretty sure that he was teasing again. But his eyes this time were more serious. 'I'd actually really like to talk to you a lot more.'

'Oh!' I replied, eloquently and full of wit.

'Is that a good "oh" or a bad "oh"?' Alex asked, smiling. 'It's a little hard to tell.'

'I think it's more of a surprised "oh", to tell you the truth.'

'OK, then. Well, so long as it's not a bad "oh", we can work with it.'

I giggled. Too much punch. Definitely.

'Sorry. I'm rubbish at drinking.'

'It's fine. You're not drunk.' He bent and looked into my eyes. 'You're not drunk, are you?' His voice suddenly a little more serious.

'No, I'm not!' I said, and gave him a playful push in the chest. My hand hit solid muscle and tingled with the heat from his body. I shoved my hand behind my back. 'Bloomin' cheek.'

'I just wanted to check. I mean, you don't look drunk. Believe me. Some of the sights we see on patrol in the city, especially Friday and Saturday nights. Honestly, you look like a nun compared to them.'

'Wow. Comparisons to a nun. Just what every girl dreams of.'

Alex laughed and caught the hand I had now returned to resting on the top rail of the fence.

'I apologise. You are most certainly not like a nun. Not at all.'

'You know you're making it worse now, don't you?'

'I am actually beginning to realise that.'

'Should I be asking if you're drunk, Officer?'

He smiled at the tease. 'Want me to do a sobriety test?'

'It could be worth it for amusement purposes alone.'

'OK. Hold up some fingers.'

I held up three. 'How many fingers am I holding up?'

Alex took my hand and made a big show of counting out my raised fingers, one by one.

'I believe that's cheating.'

'I believe you're right.'

'You are drunk,' I said.

'Not at all,' Alex replied. 'I'm over the limit for driving, yes, but I'm still in full control of my faculties and know exactly what I'm doing.'

His gaze drifted over my face. His hand still held mine from his counting stunt and he took a step nearer. I could feel the heat from his body. I shivered as it collided with the cooling night air.

'Are you cold?' he asked, concern in his voice.

'No. I'm fine. Really.'

Although now he mentioned it...

He placed his hands on my upper arms and I could feel the contrast between the warmth of his skin and coolness of mine.

'You're not supposed to lie to the police, you know,' he said, his voice soft as he dipped down close to my ear. 'Come on, let's go and get you a blanket or something.'

'I have a wrap with me. It's up there.' I nodded further up the garden.

'Let's find it, then. In the meantime, try not to freeze on me.'

I laughed. 'I don't think I'm in too much danger of that.'

His eyes flashed at me. 'Well, that's good to know.'

I opened my mouth to explain that wasn't what I'd meant but closed it again. Who cared? And maybe that had been exactly what I'd meant. Only I hadn't realised it until now.

'Best to huddle up for a minute until we find your wrap. You know. Just in case.'

'To be on the safe side?' I smiled at him.

'Exactly.'

'Well, you're the one who's used to taking charge in crisis situations, so I'll bow to your expert knowledge in this case.'

'I think that's a wise decision,' Alex replied, his face serious but his eyes dancing with mischief. He put an arm around me and pulled me in close, the heat from his body transferring to mine in more ways than I'd expected. 'Better?'

'Um hmm,' I replied, unable to formulate anything more complex than that right now.

'Good. Let's go and find the others and get you warmed up.'

Warming up right now was definitely not an issue.

* * *

I could guess at the knowing smile on Amy's face even before we got close to them. We'd known each other long enough for me to know exactly what her response would be to seeing Alex's arm resting casually at my waist.

'What did we miss?' Alex asked.

Marcus raised an eyebrow. 'Not much.' I saw his gaze flick from Alex's face to Charlie – a brief, almost imperceptible look. But I caught it. Talking of missing things, had I missed something here? No, of course I hadn't... had I? Suddenly I felt hot and uncomfortable. I bent down and made a show of fiddling with the ankle strap on my sandal, an action that forced Alex's arm to fall away from me. Returning to an upright position, I made an apparently casual glance in Charlie's direction. He was listening to something Alex was saying but as I looked at him his glance drifted and caught mine. He smiled at me, a moment of hesitation in the action.

'Everything all right?' he asked, moving a step away from the others and glancing down at my shoe.

'Oh, yep. I think I just had it on the wrong hole. Felt a bit slippy. You know.' It hadn't at all and I had no idea why, after feeling completely relaxed with him for the last few months, I was now acting like an awkward teenager.

'It's a lovely party,' I offered, when Charlie didn't say anything else.

'Glad you're enjoying it.' He smiled again. His gaze stayed on me. There was no flick to Alex as there had been from Marcus, or secret smile like Amy. I didn't know what to make of that. Or whether I should even be making anything of it at all! I let out a sigh. This! This was exactly the reason I didn't drink much. My brain was far too easily addled by alcohol.

'Are you all right?' Charlie said, his smile replaced with concern. 'You've gone a little pale.'

I gave him a look.

'OK. Paler than usual.'

'I think I'm just a little tired.'

'Do you want me to call you a taxi?'

'No. It's all right. I'll wait until we all go. I don't want to be accused of being a party pooper.'

Charlie let out a laugh. From the corner of my eye, I saw the others glance round. 'I don't think anyone could ever accuse you of being that, Libs.'

'That's a nice thing to say. I think.'

'It was a compliment, don't worry. I just meant that you're always fun. Bubbly. Definitely not a party pooper.'

'What do you say, Charlie?' Alex's voice pulled us back into their conversation.

'Sorry?'

Alex proceeded to explain that an off-road biking session had been arranged for tomorrow morning and Charlie was now taking part.

'Oh. Yes. OK. Right. Sounds good.'

I kept my eyes down.

'Oh, wait! No, I can't. I'm sorry. I promised Libby I'd take some photos for her blog tomorrow.'

'OK. Never mind. Another time.' Alex smiled, his gaze taking both of us in. I didn't know him well enough to read anything into his expression. If there was even anything to read into it. Oh, God, I really was getting myself in a mess here.

'You should go, Charlie. It'll be fun. There's no hurry for the blog pictures. Go biking.'

'No, honestly. You and I arranged this ages ago. I can't guarantee when I'm going to be around to do it again, with the various business trips I've got coming up.'

'Even more reason why you should go biking, then. In fact, I insist. If you come to the flat tomorrow, I'm not going to let you in.' I tilted my chin up at him in defiance.

He shook his head at me, a mixture of amusement and something else I couldn't quite place on his face.

'OK. I will risk life and limb and go mountain biking with these two muppets instead, then. Happy now?'

'Yes.'

'I'll call you and we'll rearrange the photography thing.'

'Perfect.'

'So, you've been doing some more photography then, mate?' Alex asked, 'That's great!'

Charlie nodded. 'Yes. It's been for a peaceful life more than anything else, to be honest. Libby wouldn't let up about it. I even have a blog now.'

'You do? That's excellent!' Alex turned to me. 'I'm glad you've been on at him about it. I've been trying to get him to do more about it for years. He's too good for people not to see his stuff. Who knew all it would take is a pretty face?' Alex winked.

'That wasn't all it took,' Charlie stated.

Alex raised an eyebrow and grinned. 'Well, no wonder I never got anywhere with getting you off your arse about it. I love you, mate, but there are certain things that—'

'No! I didn't mean... that.' Even in the half-light, the flush around Charlie's neck was visible. 'I just meant that Libby can be quite determined when she wants to be.' He glanced over and caught sight of my raised eyebrow. 'In a good way. Obviously.'

'Obviously,' I repeated, one brow still raised.

'Definitely.'

I gave him a look under my lashes. 'Thanks. I'm glad that nagging you until you do something just for a peaceful life can be done "in a good way".'

I was pretending to be in a huff, but I wasn't at all. And he knew it. Charlie had been thrilled about his blog and he was starting to get some great comments on it. The fact that he'd texted me at half past five in the morning on the day he got his first comment on a post was testament to that. We both knew he was just teasing.

'Of course. If you hadn't, I wouldn't have got the commission that I got yesterday.'

'You... what?' I grabbed his arm.

'I got a commission. Someone contacted me in the week. We finalised details yesterday. They want some shots of the city for their new apartment in London; they both grew up here and miss it. They have some specific places they want images of but want something different from the normal things you tend to see for sale. They came across my blog and liked my stuff. So, I kind of said yes.'

'You kind of... Charlie! That's fantastic! I can't believe you didn't tell me – us – before now!'

'It's not a big deal.' But even with his reserved manner, I could tell that Charlie was excited about this. It showed in those incredible eyes – they shone as he looked at me.

'It's a huge deal! I'm so proud of you!' I threw my arms around his neck, stretching on tiptoes in my flat shoes, and felt his warm arms wrap around me.

'Thank you,' he whispered, his voice soft and low in my ear, before releasing me.

'Well done, mate!' Marcus and Alex chimed, slapping his back.

'Of course, what he hasn't told us is that the commission is for a series at the nudist beach,' Marcus teased.

'It is?' Amy entered the conversation, a little worse for wear. Her eyes were huge as she looked at Charlie. 'Oh, no! Charlie! You won't like that! I don't think that's really your thing at all! Perhaps Libby could help out? She's much more outgoing than you.'

'Err, excuse me?'

'I mean, you could go and take some photos down there for him.'

'Ames, they want Charlie's photos, not mine.'

'All right, then,' Amy continued, warming to her theme. 'Then perhaps you could go when it's really quiet and Charlie could take some photos there, and you could be the "random sunbather"!' Amy looked incredibly pleased with this suggestion. I looked mortified. All three men looked thoroughly entertained.

'I have never gone, and will never be going, to the nudist beach, and, as much as I support Charlie in this venture, I am not about to strip off for him!'

'Well, I guess that answers my next question,' Charlie said, calm and studied as always, as if he had just asked me the time.

My mouth dropped open.

'You should see your face,' he said, a smile tugging at the corner of his mouth. He shrugged. 'So, I'm guessing Amy's idea is a nonstarter?'

'How much have you had to drink?' I asked him.

He smiled. 'Not enough. I'm pretty sure I should have started much earlier.' A fleeting expression clouded his features.

18

'Are you sure you don't want us to stay and help clear up?' I asked Charlie's mum, for the second time.

'No, dear,' she replied, patting me on the arm. 'But thank you for the offer. Charlie and Alex have moved the tables back to the garage for me, and I'll be setting the dishwasher to do its thing in a bit. There's really not too much else to do.'

'Well, if you're sure. Thank you again for having me.'

She caught my hand. 'It was a pleasure! It's lovely to meet you after hearing so much about you from Charlie. I have to say,' her voice dropped a little quieter, 'I thought there might be something more to you and Charlie initially. I mean, he's not the chattiest of boys, we all know that. That's just our Charlie. But I know you two have spent quite a lot of time together since Marcus started seeing Amy. Lovely girl, by the way. I do like her.'

'Me too.' I smiled. 'But just so you know, there's nothing between Charlie and me. I mean, other than friendship.'

'Oh, no! I know. I asked him. I mean, I was sort of hoping he'd say yes because he's always so cheery when he's been around you. I can see why too now. You've a lovely, sunshiny personality. It brings out the best in him. His dad brought me out of my shell too when we first met. I suppose that's what good friends do – bring out the best in each other. But, you know, I just thought I'd ask Charlie.

Encourage him along. He's a wonderful boy, but he does occasionally need a kick up the backside when it comes to women.'

I laughed.

'But he told me that neither of you were that way inclined towards each other, and just enjoyed being friends.'

'That's true. I don't think I'm Charlie's type anyway. I've never been the most academic in my family. I'm not sure we really have a lot in common in that area.'

His mum stopped in her tidying and looked at me. 'Being academic isn't everything, Libby. And from what I've heard and seen of you, you're a bright, beautiful and creative young lady.' She rested her hand on my cheek momentarily. 'Don't let anyone, including yourself, tell you any different.'

I smiled and nodded against her hand and closed my eyes briefly, thinking how much *my* mum would have loved Charlie's.

'Thank you.'

'In the meantime, I'll continue to live in hope that he finds someone just as lovely as you. I have to say, it's a bit of a shame, as I think you'd be really good for him.' She gave me a wink and I felt a hint of colour warm my chest and face.

'If it makes you feel better, I don't think Charlie's ever short of offers.'

'I don't doubt it.' His mum glanced over to where Alex, Charlie and his dad were peering up at some tree lights. 'I know he's my son, so I'm probably a little biased, but he is a very handsome boy.'

'I think that bias is perfectly acceptable. And yes, he is. No doubt about it. I think we just became really good friends super quickly – you know how that happens sometimes? And then, well, you don't look at your mates as potential boyfriends or girlfriends any more. You sort of go past it. I don't know. Does that make sense?' I fiddled with my hair slide and tried to decide who exactly I was trying to convince.

'It does, dear. It does.'

'And Charlie will find someone lovely who deserves him when the time is right.'

'I'm sure he will. So long as it's not that temptress that lives in the flat next to him!'

'Aha, the delectable Elaine! She's quite something, isn't she?'

'She certainly is. And I'm far too polite to say what.'

My eyebrows shot up and I rolled my lips together to stop the laugh bursting out. 'I don't think Charlie is planning anything in that direction, so I shouldn't worry.' I thought of our unexpected, but very enjoyable, day out along the coast that we'd taken for the sole purpose of helping Charlie avoid Elaine's further advances that day.

'Talking of directions, our Alex has hardly been able to stop looking in this one the whole time he's been over there.'

I glanced over at the boys automatically. As Charlie's mum said, Alex was indeed looking this way. She pulled a move and fluffed her hair, pretending to soak up the attention. Alex grinned, and waggled his eyebrows. Charlie followed his eye line, then punched Alex on the arm.

'He's as good as one of my own, that boy. You're in safe hands there.'

'Oh! I'm not... we're not...'

She looked at me, a smile on her face, waiting for me to say what I was trying to say. I wasn't entirely sure what that was myself so there was a good chance she might be waiting a long time.

Charlie's mum smiled at me. 'I know you're not. Yet. Unlike Charlie, Alex is more obvious when he's got the hots for some girl. I should know, I've seen them all come and go, over the years.'

'There's been a lot, then?' I laughed.

'Oh, no, not like that. I just meant I've watched these boys grow up and seen the various girls that have come in and out of all of their lives. I sometimes wonder when they might get around to settling down. They're all such good lads. They deserve to find the right one.'

'Maybe they're still happy looking.'

She waggled her head in a 'perhaps' way.

'Although I think you might be right about that with Charlie. He said something to that effect when I asked him why he wasn't interested in Elaine.'

'I'd agree with you there. Charlie's never short of offers, like you say. But some of the girls he's been out with? Well, you can tell they're not interested in the real Charlie. Just what he looks like and what his money can buy them. He fell for it a few times, too. I think he's learned that lesson now. It's made him cautious.'

'Poor Charlie. I hate to think of someone taking advantage like that.'

'Yes. It wasn't easy to watch, but it's difficult to say anything, as his mother. It can backfire if they think you don't like their choice of partner.'

'I guess so.'

'Perhaps you can keep an eye on him?'

I tilted my head. 'I think he's got things pretty sussed, to be honest. And whilst he's reserved, I'm sure if he made his mind up to do something, or see someone, nothing I could say would have much effect.'

'He can be stubborn when he feels he needs to be. That's true.'

I rubbed her arm in a gesture of reassurance. 'He'll find the right person. I'm sure of it.'

'I hope you do too, Libby. You're a lovely girl.'

'Thank you,' I said, impulsively hugging her. She returned it, laughing.

'Libs, you ready to go? The taxi should be here any minute,' Charlie called over.

'Yep.' I nodded and we made our way over to the boys. Marcus and Amy had left a short time ago and Alex, Charlie and I were getting a second taxi back to our respective residences. We said goodbye and walked down the path, watching as car headlights came down the road. The cab driver saw us waiting and pulled into the kerb. From the corner of my eye, I saw Alex make a small head gesture at Charlie, and Charlie got in the front seat.

'Where to?' the driver said.

Charlie gave him all three addresses.

'Any particular order?'

'So long as the marina isn't last,' Alex put in.

I turned my head. 'I don't mind being last.'

He moved his hand across the seat and brushed my fingers. 'Humour me.' In the half-light I could see his eyes were serious.

'OK,' I said, my hand tingling from his touch. If I was honest, that wasn't the only thing tingling. 'As it's you.'

His eyes hadn't left me, and at my comment he flashed a smile.

Charlie was dropped off first. He leant back through the seats and slapped Alex on the leg.

'See you tomorrow, mate.' He twisted to me and patted my knee – it was kind of all he could do from that angle. 'See you soon, Libs.' And then he got out.

'Charlie!' I said, pushing open the door and climbing out of the car, and probably not at my most elegant. 'Aren't you jetting off tomorrow night?'

'Yep,' Charlie agreed, taking the hand I was flailing as I extricated myself from the taxi.

'And you think you're allowed to do that without giving me a hug? I'm not going to see you for ages!'

'It's only a few days.'

I huffed at him. 'Well, I always miss my friends, however long it is. Even if you don't.'

The next moment I was dangling a foot in the air and enveloped in the biggest hug I'd ever had. 'Bye, Libs,' he whispered.

'That's better,' I said, when he'd put me back down.

He chuckled. 'Take care, and I'll send you some pictures from Singapore.' I saw his glance flick to the waiting car and back to me. 'Have fun and look after yourself.' He waited whilst I got back in the car then closed the door. I waved out of the window and Charlie raised a hand in response.

Traffic was light and it wasn't long before we were pulling up outside my block.

'Thanks,' I said to the driver, before turning to Alex to say goodbye. He beat me to it.

'Can you just wait here a minute, mate? I'm going to walk her up.'

The driver shrugged. 'It's your meter running.'

Alex looked at me and we exchanged a grin before getting out and closing the doors.

'So nice to find someone who has such joy for his job,' Alex commented.

'Maybe he's had a long day.'

He pulled a face. 'I think he's probably just a grumpy git.'

'Has anyone ever told you you're too quick to judge?'

'Has anyone ever told you you're too nice?'

They had actually, but I wasn't about to give him the satisfaction of being right.

'Yeah, I thought so,' Alex smirked.

'What?'

'You're very easy to read, Libby.'

'I am not!' I knew I was ridiculously easy to read. But it was the principle of the matter.

'OK. Maybe not. Maybe it's the extra training I've had in studying people.' He made a point of running his eyes over me in a comical way.

I rolled my eyes at him. 'Yes. I'm sure that's what it must be.'

He smiled that gorgeous smile and I couldn't help but respond in kind. 'You really don't need to walk me up. It's only just here,' I said, pointing. 'Like he said, your meter is running.'

'I'd prefer to walk you up for safety reasons. And I'd like to walk you up for... other reasons.'

'Other reasons?'

'Lead the way,' he said, not expanding on his comment.

I did so.

'This is me,' I said, stopping at my front door. 'Thanks for the security detail.'

He grinned. 'I live to serve.' He bowed, making a rolling motion with his arm, like some medieval courtier.

I shook my head, laughing. 'You're bonkers. And drunk.'

'Not at all,' he said, returning upright and gaining the height advantage over me once more. 'OK, maybe a little. On both.'

'You should get back to that taxi. It's going to cost you a fortune!'

'Probably. I'd much rather stay here with you though.' He moved closer just as I stepped back, suddenly feeling awkward. Alex pulled a face. 'OK. That came out totally wrong! I meant staying here now, not in there—' he pointed at the door '—staying. I wasn't implying that...'

'Good. Because you'd be in for a disappointment.'

He put a hand up over his eyes for a moment, then ran it back over his hair. 'This went much more smoothly in my head.'

I tried not to smile. 'I see. So, you had it planned, then?'

'No! Well, yes... I mean. Do you always have this effect on men?'

'Excuse me?'

'I never fluff up like this!'

'First time for everything.'

'I'm blaming you. You've scrambled my senses.'

'But apparently your cheesy line delivery system is still in full working order.' I looked up through my lashes at him, now unable to keep the smile off my face.

'That's pretty indestructible, thank goodness.'

He looked down at me and took a step closer, taking one of my hands in his. 'I really enjoyed meeting you today, Libby.'

'I enjoyed meeting you too.'

'Do you think there's a chance you might enjoy meeting me again, maybe tomorrow night, for dinner?'

'I think there might be.'

'Shall I pick you up here, say seven o'clock?'

'OK.'

He stood looking down at me, the smile fading a little, my hand still in his. 'I really want to kiss you goodnight, but I'm going to be a gentleman.'

'OK,' I said again, mostly because my thoughts were heading along similar lines and it was suddenly all getting a bit warm.

He bent close, placing a kiss on my cheek, soft and chaste, but when he pulled away I saw the heat in his eyes that I knew was reflected in my own.

'You should go,' I forced out. 'The meter.'

'I'd be happy to walk home if it meant staying longer with you.'

Feeling the shy smile on my face, I dropped my gaze. 'I'll see you tomorrow.'

He took a deep breath, and his own smile returned. 'I'll see you tomorrow,' he repeated, then quickly stole another kiss and grinned before jogging back towards the waiting taxi. Sliding the key into my lock, I turned as Alex called out, 'Libby, wait! I don't have your number.'

I wasn't going to be responsible for more time wasted on the grumpy taxi driver's meter. 'Charlie has it. You can get it off him.'

Alex nodded, then waved again, a big grin in place.

I shut the door, twisted the lock and put my keys in the ceramic bowl on the nearby console table. Glancing up at the mirror above it, I realised he wasn't the only one wearing a big grin.

19

It was late afternoon before Amy responded to my text, and when she answered there was an emoticon with a sad green face and a single word. Ouch.

I picked up my phone and replied.

✉ Is it bad?

The app told me Amy was typing a reply

✉ It's getting better. It started off at a 9 this morning but is about a 4 now. Marcus has been amazing looking after me.

A heart symbol followed this declaration. I smiled. A man that uncomplainingly saw you through a hangover with care and attention was a rare find.

✉ Good to hear. I hope you feel better soon, honey xx

I followed this up with a 'hug' gif.

✉ Thanks. Did you get home OK?

✉ Yep. Taxi with Charlie and Alex

A shocked-face emoticon arrived. Followed by a devil one.

✉ Ha ha! Hardly. Although...

✉ Although what???????

✉ I'm going out with Alex tonight for dinner...

My phone rang.

'You are?' Amy's voice was raspy, hinting at her fragile state, but my news seemed to have trumped the hangover. 'Where are you going? How did he ask?'

I laughed. 'I've no idea where we're going, and he just sort of asked. He walked me up to the flat and kissed me goodnight.'

'You kissed?' she squeaked, her voice cracking.

'Calm down, not like that. Just on the cheek.'

'Which cheek?'

'Behave woman!' I giggled back.

A squeal came down the phone. 'I told you he liked you! Oh, I'm so excited for you! What are you going to wear?'

'Thanks, I'm actually really looking forward to it. And I don't know yet.'

'You sound surprised about looking forward to it.'

'No. Well, I guess. Oh, I don't know. With everything else going on at the moment, and then this deal with Glam, work is going nuts. I suppose I just haven't thought much about anything in that direction for a while.'

'All work and no play makes Libby a dull girl.'

'You're calling me dull? Thanks for that.'

Amy laughed. 'Of course not! Just, you know, it's been a while. I'm happy for you. And Alex seems nice. Marcus said he's a good bloke. I couldn't get much more out of him than that.'

'Thanks. I'm not raising my hopes, but it might be nice to go on a date. Like you say, it's been a while.'

'It has... so what *are* you going to wear?'

'I've really no idea! I don't know where we're going. I'm going to have to hedge my bets, I think.'

'Or just go all out and knock his socks off.'

'Oh. I don't know. I don't want to set standards I can't keep.' I laughed.

'Rubbish. He's seen the floaty, day version of you. Now show him the vampy night version!'

'I don't have a vampy night version!'

'Of course you do!'

'And what if we go to a diner? I'm going to look ridiculous.'

'I've a feeling that Alex isn't going to take you to a diner on a first date. He'll be wanting to impress you. Don't you want to impress him?'

Did I?

'I'm not looking for anything... serious. You know that. And I don't want to pretend to be someone I'm not.'

'You're not. It's just clothes and make-up, Libs. I can't believe I'm telling you, of all people, that!'

'Argh, I know, I know.' I flopped down on the sofa.

'Can I ask you something?'

'Of course!'

'What if something serious comes looking for you?'

'Alex isn't serious.'

'You don't know that. But hypothetically. Not necessarily Alex.'

I didn't answer.

'You don't think someone will ever be worth the risk?' Amy's voice was soft and concerned.

My mind tumbled back to the look on my dad's face as he caught Mum falling that day. The pleading in his voice as he performed CPR. The stunned, shattered expression he wore as he helped bear her coffin at the service.

'It's not that people aren't worth the risk. It's that I've seen what happens when luck turns its back on you. That's what I'm not prepared to risk.'

Amy didn't reply but I heard her sigh.

'You should get some more rest.'

'I'm OK. Do you want me to come round and help you get ready?'

I kind of did, but I thought of Amy, more than likely tucked up in a blanket with Marcus fussing around her as she recovered from her party head – and what might have been a long night, judging by the way she and Marcus were locked together when they left.

'No, it's fine. But thank you for the offer. You just concentrate on recovering.'

'OK, if you're sure. And thank you. It's a shame you don't know where you're going. Can't you ask him?'

'I sort of like that it's a surprise in a way. Besides, I don't have his number. He's going to get mine off Charlie today.'

'Charlie! Of course, Charlie would know where Alex always takes his first dates to.'

'Err, hello? I may not be looking for lifetime commitment but please try not to make me sound like I'm just one of a long line. Even if I am.' I thought back to what Alex had said about how his goodbyes to women usually went so smoothly. Yep, I was definitely one of a long line. But right now I was, at least, first in that line.

'I didn't mean it like that, sorry.'

I laughed. 'Don't worry about it. And Charlie will be leaving for the airport by now. He's flying out today on a business trip.'

'Does he know you're going out with Alex tonight?'

'I suppose he does now if Alex got my number off him this morning when they went biking.'

'Right.'

'What?'

'Nothing.'

'Hmm,' I replied, having a good idea of what she was thinking. I opted not to mention yesterday's moment of alcohol-induced befuddlement on this point. It had cleared as quickly as it had arrived and all was back to normal in the Libby/Charlie world now. Thank goodness.

'Charlie and I are really good friends and that's amazing. I don't know what I'd do without him these days. Not just because of the advice he gives me with the business stuff, but just his friendship. Charlie just being Charlie. You know?'

'I do. He's lovely. Whoever does end up with him will be one lucky girl, that's for sure.'

'They will. Absolutely.'

'OK. If you don't need me, I have a nap calling my name. Have an amazing time tonight! I want *all* the details.' She hung on the word 'all'.

'Of course.'

'Now go! Vamp up!'

'We'll see.'

'Don't make me come round there.'

'Go and lie down now. Too much excitement's not good for you.'

'Oh, so true. Today anyway. See you later, honey. Love you.'

'Love you too. Feel better soon. Hugs to Marcus.'

'OK, bye.'

* * *

'Wow!'

I'd taken Amy's suggestion and gone for it. Rather than my more normal relaxed look, I'd chosen a watercolour print silk shift dress. One side had a thin strap and the other had a long floaty sleeve. It was shorter than I generally wore – by about two feet – and I loved it. I'd only worn it once, for a post on the blog, because there just hadn't seemed the right opportunity since. After scanning my wardrobe for about the fifteenth time, I'd gone back to this one. My first date in a very long time seemed as good a time as any to give it an airing. Pairing it with some strappy, nude-coloured sandals and a small metallic clutch, I was ready.

Now that Alex was here in front of me, without the fortification of yesterday's alcohol, I suddenly felt a lot more nervous.

'I'm hoping this is OK,' I said, waving a hand to encompass my outfit. 'I wasn't sure where we were going. If I'm overdressed – or underdressed – I can change really quickly.'

'No! No, not at all,' Alex replied. 'It's perfect. You look perfect.'

I gave a laugh that came out a bit weird. Probably not the elegant, sophisticated response the compliment called for. And clearly not the one Alex was expecting, by the brief flash of surprise I saw flit across his features.

'I mean, thank you.'

'You're welcome. You ready to go?'

'Yes.'

I pulled the door shut behind me and turned back to my date. He was looking at me with an expression I couldn't quite make out.

'What is it?' I asked.

'You.'

'Oh.' I shifted my weight.

Alex sensed something and brushed his fingers against my hand. 'In a good way.'

I smiled, glancing down then back up, flattered by his compliment and the way he was looking at me. He held out his hand and I took it, partly because I wanted to and partly because the towering skinny heels on these shoes combined with the stairs to my flat ran the risk of being an accident waiting to happen.

'That's quite some grip you have there,' Alex said when we got to the bottom. I glanced down at our hands and noticed his fingers were almost entirely white from where I'd slowed the blood supply as I clutched his hand. So much for the romantic hand-holding gesture.

'Whoops. Sorry,' I said, releasing his hand. He opened and closed his fist a couple of times to encourage the colour back.

He flashed me one of those easy-going smiles. 'Not a problem. I like a woman who'd give me a decent run in an arm-wrestle.'

I raised one eyebrow. 'Give you a run? I believe the words you meant to use were "beat me".'

He laughed. 'Is that so?'

'I'm a woman of hidden talents.'

'Now that, I don't doubt for a minute.'

I smiled, the slight awkwardness of the first date pick up dissipating thanks to Alex's perfectly timed banter.

'I'm sorry. I'm just a little nervous. It's quite a while since I went on an actual date.'

He stepped closer, his hand on the car door handle next to me. 'I know. First dates can be like that. But we had fun at the barbecue. You already know me, sort of. And you look amazing. So just relax.' I could smell the aftershave he wore, just a hint, nothing overpowering. His shirt was open at the neck and a slightly deeper tan ran above his collar line, a sign of his outdoor lifestyle, combined with patrol duties. His eyes watched me, a soft openness in their expression.

I nodded. 'OK.'

He opened the door and a problem immediately became obvious. Alex's four-by-four featured a high step up – one which certainly hadn't been designed for anyone wearing a short silk dress. I half lifted one foot, then swapped and tried with the other. Each time I came horribly close to showing way more than I planned. I turned back to face him. For the first time, he looked slightly unsure. And then the confidence bounced back onto his face. He stepped in front of the open car door.

'OK. Face me.'

'Huh?'

'Face me.'

I did so.

'I know this isn't ideal. But do you mind?'

'Mind what?'

Placing his hands at my waist, he swiftly lifted me into the vehicle. I made a surprised squeak as he did so and clamped my knees together in an effort to preserve my modesty as I was now sitting sideways with my legs hanging over the edge of the seat, out of the door.

'Oh. Mind that. Right.'

'Sorry. Maybe I should have asked Charlie if I could borrow his car. It's a little more impressive than this old thing.'

'Don't be silly. It's just about finding a solution. Which we have.'

'I have to say it's not exactly how I had imagined this going. I was going to be all suave and help you in.'

'You did help me in.'

'Yeah, but not quite James Bond, was it?'

'I'm not interested in going out with James Bond. Too flashy. Now,' I said, my knees still firmly clamped together as I swung myself to face forwards, 'are we going to dinner, or what?'

'We are. We most definitely are.' He pushed the door shut, pulled it open again when it didn't quite catch and slammed it a bit harder. I pulled the seat belt out and plugged it in as Alex slid into the driver's seat. 'Sorry. I really need to get a new car. It's finding the time to look lately, what with work and studying for my transfer to plain clothes.'

'It's fine, Alex. Honestly.'

'No, I've been meaning to for ages. It's good for hauling about my mountain bike and windsurfing gear but it's kind of getting a bit tatty now. It'd be nice to get something a bit newer and smarter.'

'Well, it's doing the job perfectly right now, so could you take me to find food, please? I'm starving!'

'Your wish is my command. The restaurant's not far at all, don't worry.'

20

Five minutes later, Alex was reverse parking the Jeep into a space I'd never have a hope of getting into. I waited whilst he fed the meter and then waited again, as requested, until he came and opened the door for me. In a reverse of earlier he lifted me quickly out of the car and placed me down on the road. I stepped away from the car and he gave the door another heave before locking it.

'I hope you like French food?' he said, holding out his hand for me to take.

'I do. Very much so.'

His smile widened at this information as he squeezed my hand quickly and gently.

'Good.'

We were outside a Regency town house that had been converted to a hotel with a restaurant in what would have been one of the front rooms. It was quiet, intimate and beautifully decorated, paying homage to its heritage but infused with a Gallic flair that had been married perfectly. Alex kept hold of my hand as we mounted the stone steps outside the house and entered the building. An enthusiastic waiter greeted us and showed us to our table, pulling my chair out ready for me. Once I'd sat, the waiter advised that he would return momentarily with menus and a wine list. I glanced around as we waited.

'This is lovely!' I said, taking in all the period details and the paintings on the wall. I squinted at the plaque underneath one, seeing that it was by a local artist and for sale, as were all the other prints in the room.

'I'm glad you like it.'

'I love that painting,' I said, pointing at one that didn't appear to be of anything specifically but with colours that melted together like the most perfect sunset. It made me feel tranquil and happy.

'Really?' Alex frowned at it, apparently not quite so enamoured with the art.

'Yes. Don't you like it?'

'Not really. But I guess that's the thing with art, isn't it? It's very subjective.'

'It is. But you do like Charlie's photography, I'm guessing, from your enthusiasm at the barbecue?'

'I do. He's definitely got talent, and I'm happy you've made him realise that. He'd never say it but he's over the moon about this commission. He doesn't always show a lot, but I've known him far too long for him to be able to hide much from me.'

I smiled. 'I'm happy for him too.'

'When we were biking today, he mentioned that he's decided to take a few extra days at the end of this business trip to go off exploring and taking pictures. He's never really done that before.' Alex fixed me with a look. 'You're clearly very influential.'

'Oh, rubbish!' I said. 'I just wore him down. He likes a quiet life. The blog thing was just to shut me up, like he said.'

'He wouldn't have done it if he really was against it.'

'Really?'

'Really. You're right. He's all for a quiet life but you don't get where he is by letting people walk all over you. Charlie has limits, like most of us. I think he just needed a push in the right direction from the right person.'

There was something in his tone and eyes that held the suggestion of a question.

'Come on, out with it,' I prompted.

Alex opened his mouth to speak just as the waiter glided back to our table, producing our menus with a Gallic flourish before telling us about the specials, every one of which sounded delicious. I was suddenly glad I hadn't gone for something incredibly fitted when picking my outfit for the evening. He left us to make our choices.

'Out with what?'

'I might not have your training, Officer, but I can tell you're dying to ask something.'

Alex smiled and shook his head. 'Hard to get anything past you, eh?'

'Oh.' I waved my hand. 'You'd be surprised, but go on.'

'That sounds like a story.'

'It is. But not one I'm telling right now. Stop prevaricating.'

His smile turned into a laugh. 'OK, OK. I guess… I just…'

I waited, not prompting him. He'd get there eventually.

He started again. 'When Charlie started talking about you, I thought there might be more to it than just friendship, you know. He certainly seems to enjoy spending time with you, but, like I said on Saturday, he never mentioned that you were beautiful. I guess I sort of assumed…'

I shrugged. 'Beauty is in the eye of the beholder and all that.'

Alex pulled a face. 'That came out way more blunt than it was supposed to. Sorry.'

It was my turn to laugh. 'Don't worry about it. I'm just wondering where this is going.'

He took a breath. 'I knew I wanted to ask you out the moment Marcus introduced us, but… I guess, I suppose I just wanted to make sure that I wasn't setting myself up for failure here…'

I waited for more, but there wasn't any.

'Are you asking me if I have a crush on Charlie?'

He pulled a slightly awkward face.

'You certainly have an interesting style of dating, I have to say.'

'Believe me, this wasn't how I planned on opening. I don't know what happens to me around you. I lose all my charm and sophistication.' The easy smile returned.

'Oh, I think there's still a little charm left there.'

He laughed and tentatively moved his hand on the table so that his fingertips brushed mine. I dropped my eyes to them, and then moved my hand, placing it on top of Alex's.

'Charlie is lovely and I've been metaphorically buried six feet under several times by women in the vicinity when we've been out places, and I can totally understand why. But we're friends. That's all. So this—' I waved my hands around, encompassing the conversation '—is all irrelevant. And frankly, as much as I love Charlie – as a friend – I'd really rather hear about you right now.'

Alex turned his hand so that it caught mine; his smile was soft and the expression was reflected in his eyes. 'Glad we got that out of the way.'

'I didn't realise it was even in the way.'

'It isn't now.'

* * *

I was enjoying myself even more than I'd expected. Alex was funny, smiled readily and laughed often. But having also enjoyed three courses and two glasses of wine, I was pretty much ready to pop by the time the waiter brought the bill. I lifted my clutch bag from my lap.

'I'm paying,' Alex said, without looking at me, concentrating instead on wiggling a credit card out of his wallet. 'Why do they make these slots just the tiniest bit smaller than the actual cards?' He shook his head as it finally came out before placing it in the little holder on the menu and put the whole thing to the side.

'I'd like to pay my share.'

He gave a little smile and took a drink from the chilled water on the table.

'That bad, eh?'

'Pardon?'

He smiled, but it didn't have the twinkle I'd already become accustomed to. 'Usually when the lady wants to pay her half it's because the date hasn't gone all that well.'

'What? No, it's not!'

'Or you're standing up for feminism.'

'Or you're making fun.'

'Not at all. OK, a little. But either way, I'd still like to pay. Call me old-fashioned. I asked you to dinner, and I'd like to pay, whether you enjoyed it or not.'

'Alex.' I raised an eyebrow at him. 'I did enjoy it. I promise. I think I'm just... used to different things. My last boyfriend... well, if I wasn't paying outright, we just split the bill most of the time.'

'Seriously?'

'Yes.'

'Right.' He paused. 'Was he a feminist?'

I laughed and shook my head. 'No, he was just tight. I like to pay my share. It makes me feel comfortable. And I like treating people when I can, but he kind of took the pee a bit. I never really saw it at the time. You know, you sort of think something's normal after a while. But after it was all over, little things start prodding at your memory, don't they? You begin to realise that maybe, once in a while, it would have been nice to have not bought my own birthday present or meal. And yes, I do realise that a few feminist fairies just died when I made that declaration, for which I am truly sorry.'

Alex laughed. 'I'm sure there's something magical we can do to revive them.'

My eyebrows shot up and a moment later, so did his. 'I didn't mean... I meant... honest to God, Libby. You're seriously ruining my belief at having the ability to be cool and suáve on a date.'

'Cool and suave are overrated.'

'They are?'

'In my opinion.'

'Well, that's the only one that counts right now, so maybe I'm in luck.'

'Maybe you are.'

He smiled slowly at my reply and the look he gave me set off little flip-flops in my stomach and chest. Of course, it might have just been indigestion. But I was pretty sure it was mostly Alex.

We left the restaurant, Alex automatically holding my hand as we descended the steps, watching my feet as I did so.

'Amazes me how you women walk in those things.'

'Don't you like them?' I asked teasingly as I reached the bottom step, staying on it so that, with its help and the shoes, I was more on a level with him.

'Now, let's not jump to any hasty conclusions.'

'That's what I thought,' I said, half smiling and walking over towards the car. In two strides, Alex was back beside me.

'So, if the wanting to pay thing wasn't a signal that this date was going horribly, does that mean you're not quite ready for me to take you home yet?'

'What did you have in mind?'

'We could go for a drink, or maybe a walk on the pier?'

'Well, you're driving, and I've had enough wine, so I think a walk sounds lovely.'

'Great. The pier it is, then.' We were back at his car. He opened the door for me. 'May I?' He tilted his head a tiny bit.

I giggled and nodded as he put his hands on my waist, ready to lift me up into the seat again. 'I'm definitely wearing a longer dress next time.'

Alex stilled, his hands remaining on my waist. I met his eyes. 'So, there's going to be a next time?' he asked, softly.

I felt the warmth of his hands on my skin through the thin silk of my dress, and the hard muscle of his upper arms where I'd rested my hands preparing for the lift. He was looking at me as he'd done at the table, and I was almost definitely sure that this time it wasn't indigestion.

'Maybe,' I repeated my line from earlier. His grip tightened briefly on my waist and he popped me up into the seat, but this time his hands remained there for a fraction longer than they had previously.

Alex drove the short distance to Madeira Drive and parked the car, coming around and helping me out. He grinned as he did so. 'I really should have warned you about the car.'

'I told you, don't worry about it. It all adds to the fun.'

I waited for him to lock up, then began walking leisurely towards the Palace Pier. Above us, stars shyly began to show themselves in the clear sky of twilight. Alex brushed my hand with his fingers as we walked. I took the hint and let him take mine within his own. From the corner of my eye, I saw him smile and he gave the tiniest squeeze of my hand in acknowledgement. It was nice. I couldn't remember the last time someone had held my hand like this. Someone who wasn't generally covered, to some proportion, in either mud or foodstuff, that was. At seven, Liam was becoming less enthused at holding anyone's hand, but Niall still reached up for mine when we went out and I loved it. Even on the times that we shared that hand hold with something unexpected and gooey. But there wasn't anything gooey about Alex. Not in a bad way at least. Slanting my gaze to him surreptitiously, I took in his profile, felt the little flip again, and smiled.

The pier was busy with locals, tourists and the usual summer influx of language students. We walked across the widening pavement, heading for the point where the pier itself began. I aimed for the thin panel of slats that ran close together in a pathway, ensuring my heel wouldn't get stuck, and we walked along, enjoying the bustle of the season. As we got around halfway, I stopped suddenly, looking down.

'Oh, no.'

Alex pinged back a little, still attached to my hand. 'What's the matter?' he asked, concern in his voice.

'My wardrobe choice has struck again.' I kicked one foot up, pointing at the slim heel of my sandal, then at the slats of the pier's floor construction. The narrow pathway had stopped, and some of the were gaps were a definite hazard to thin heels.

He smirked. 'I can always carry you.'

I raised my head, laughing. 'You most certainly could not! There is no physical way of carrying me that would not be bad. Have you seen the length of this skirt?'

Alex flicked his gaze down, let it linger there momentarily before bringing it back. 'Oh, yes.'

I gave him a gentle whack on the arm with my bag and he laughed. 'Look, it's only this bit. There's a plastic runner further up.'

I smiled and nodded but inside I felt a bit of an idiot. Apparently, it showed.

'What's wrong?' Alex said, pulling me aside gently until we were no longer so close to a speaker blaring out the latest summer pop fare.

'Nothing. I just feel a bit of a fool. I mean, I love this dress, and I love these shoes, but frankly, between you having to carry me various places, it's not exactly the elegant and sophisticated demeanour I had planned to go with for this evening.'

A gentle breeze was blowing in from offshore and a recalcitrant lock of hair escaped from where I'd put it earlier and now dropped down in front of my face. Before I had a chance to move, Alex was there, gently pushing it back, the side of his hand ever so gently grazing my face as he did so. I couldn't help but watch those hazel eyes as he concentrated on the task. He slid his gaze to meet mine.

'Elegant and sophisticated can be overrated too, you know. And personally, I am beside myself that you wore that dress. And those shoes. You look amazing. So beautiful. I've already had to resist the urge to arrest at least three blokes for leering at you.'

'I doubt they were leering. And besides, I know I'm not a policeman – woman – person – but even I'm pretty sure that's not a chargeable offence.'

'You might be right.' He smiled. 'See? Smart as well.'

'Please don't tell me you're the jealous type?' I was teasing but, in all honesty, I wanted to check.

He shook his head. 'No. I'm not. I promise.'

'OK. Good.'

'That's not to say I'm thrilled when blokes are blatantly undressing you with their eyes. Call me old-fashioned.' He shrugged.

'It's OK. Jealous isn't good. Slightly protective is rather sweet.'

He nodded and grinned at me under his lashes.

'What is it with women and sweet?'

'What is with men reacting so badly to it? It's a compliment. Get over it. Now,' I said, pointing at the wooden slatted floor, 'how are we proceeding with this?'

Alex glanced over, then back at me. 'OK, hold on.' He wrapped his arms around me, just under my bum, lifted me quickly and began walking further up the pier. Automatically, I gripped his shoulders and began giggling. Wine really wasn't my best friend right now.

'I'm sorry. Wine makes me laugh.'

I could feel his chest rumbling and looked down to see him joining me in the gigglefest. He pulled a face. 'I'm not sure what my excuse is.'

I turned my head and leaned back a little. We were already at least ten feet past where the plastic runner started.

'You missed the thingy.' I waved one hand at the floor. 'I can do this bit now. You can put me down.'

I turned back to find Alex looking up at me. 'Oh, you're no fun.'

I raised an eyebrow. 'I am lots of fun, I'll have you know.'

He waggled his eyebrows. 'Well, that's good to know.'

I wriggled. 'If you don't put me down, I'm going to call the police.'

He started laughing again and gripped me a little tighter. 'And if you don't stop wriggling, you're going to end up showing more than you would have getting into the car by yourself.'

My eyes widened and I stopped wriggling, instead holding myself bolt upright and super still. Alex laughed even more. 'You don't have to stop breathing as well!' He lowered me to the ground gently.

'I am never wearing this dress again,' I said, and then suddenly realised that Alex hadn't let go.

'Now, that really would be a shame.'

He watched me, as if waiting for a sign. Then, he lowered his head, his eyes on me as he did so, his lips softly brushed mine, tentatively, and—

'Sorry, mate!' the man said, as we both stumbled heavily. One of Alex's arms tightened around me as the other reached out to a cast-iron support pillar, steadying us from the collision. The man did seem genuinely apologetic, if incredibly drunk. Alex put a hand on my arm as I smoothed my dress and straightened up.

'You all right?'

'Yep.' I didn't quite meet his eyes. The moment was gone, knocked out into the darkness of the inky black sea. 'Come on, let's see if I can win you a teddy bear.'

Alex frowned. 'It's going back to the old-fashioned thing, I know, but aren't I supposed to win you one?'

'Ha! You can try! I am, in the words of my nephews, awesome at this.'

21

An hour later I had eaten too much candyfloss, shared a churro I didn't need any of, been deafened by too many beeps, whizzers and other electronic noises, and won the biggest Minion toy on the stall. Alex's shirt pocket also held a small stuffed animal that neither of us could work out the exact provenance of.

'How are you so good at that?'

'Practise. And, of course, natural talent.' I thought about doing a bow, remembered the limitations of my dress, and did a little curtsey instead.

'Of course.'

'What are you going to do with this?'

'Me? You won it!' Alex looked bemused.

'Yes, but I said I'd win it for you.'

'Right. You did.'

'You don't want it, do you?' I looked at him, an expression of bravery masking my disappointment.

'No, of course I want it. It's...' He stopped when he saw me laughing.

'Oh, that's so sweet. You should have seen your face!'

'OK. That's mean!' he said, grinning and scooping me closer.

'I'm sorry. I couldn't resist.'

He gave me that look again. 'I know the feeling.'

I tilted my head and pulled the Minion up, forcing us apart, before poking my head around the side of it. 'Seriously? Can you make use of it?'

He burst out laughing. 'Make use of a giant Minion? You're nuts!'

'You know what I mean. Is there somewhere you know that could use it? I can get my brother to take it to the children's hospital but I've already sent several up there. So, if you knew of somewhere... I was thinking maybe a women's shelter? I actually have some things I've been given for the blog that I can't use so I'd really like to send those too. If it's possible. I don't know if it is, but you know...'

'That sounds like a great idea. I'm sure we can arrange something,' Alex said. 'Thank you.'

I shrugged. 'It's nothing. I mean, really! I hate to think of what they've been through. And the boys have so many toys. I watch them play and it's such pure and simple joy...' I looked up and saw him watching me. 'Sorry, I've gone off on one, haven't I?'

'It's all right,' he said softly. 'I think I quite like you going off on one. It's... sweet.' He grinned, throwing my compliment from earlier back at me.

We headed back towards the car. The breeze had kicked up now, blowing in off the sea as we walked. Alex took the huge toy off me and stuffed it under his arm. Wrapping his other arm around me, he pulled me closer, just as he had at the barbecue. Once again, I felt the warmth from his body infuse mine. But this time, the heat factor had ratcheted up a notch. We walked in the direction of the car, neither of us in a particular hurry to get there. I was aware of Alex glancing around occasionally.

'Everything all right?'

He looked down at me, that easy smile on his face. 'Absolutely.'

I gave a quick glance, trying to see what he was seeing. 'Sure?'

Alex led me to the side of the pavement and I leant against the cast-iron balustrades that separated the promenade from the beach below. 'Everything's fine. Sorry, just habit. Situational awareness and all that.'

'That's understandable,' I said, 'although you are forgetting one thing.'

'I am? What's that?'

I grabbed the toy from where it was stuffed under his arm and shoved it at him. 'We have the Minions on our side!'

Having regained his balance after the surprise attack by an oversized soft toy, Alex, still laughing, took it back off me and spent a minute juggling it.

'What are you doing?'

He shook his head. 'I don't want to put it down on a grubby pavement so I'm trying to find a position with this bloody thing that lets me do what I want to do right now.'

I frowned, watching him. 'Which is?'

He didn't answer immediately but instead leant past me and wedged the toy between two parts of the balustrade's intricate design. Stepping back, he slid his arms around me and pulled me close.

'This,' he said.

One hand rested low on the small of my back whilst the other was around my waist, tight enough to make me feel wanted and loose enough for me to pull away if I chose to. I lifted my face to his. It was shadowed a little by the angle of the streetlights but I could see enough. That smile was in place, but there was something behind it now. Something more raw and immediate.

'I'd really like to kiss you,' he whispered, as he dipped his head and brushed his lips against my hair. 'In fact, I've been wanting to kiss you since about ten minutes into meeting you at the barbecue. But I thought that might be a little forward.'

'Just a little.' I smiled, pulling back so that I could see his eyes focus on mine. His gaze dropped to my lips before coming back to meet my own. 'But I think now might be OK.' The smile spread as Alex moved and I reached up to meet him. His kiss was gentle and soft, as he pulled me closer. My arms had been resting on his biceps, but as we kissed I slid my hands up and let them meet behind his neck.

Slowly we pulled away. His gaze held mine before I dropped it and smiled, suddenly feeling a little awkward that I was standing in the middle of the street, kissing a man I'd not actually known for very long.

'What?' Alex smiled.

'Nothing.' I shook my head, flashing him a smile as I tried to yank the Minion from the railings. 'Bloody hell, did you glue this thing in here?'

'Here.' He gave it a twist and a pull and the toy came out. Tucking it back under one arm, he held out his other hand for me to take. 'Didn't have you down as the shy type.' He grinned.

'Pardon?'

'You got all shy back there. I didn't have you pegged as that. From what I've heard, you're pretty outgoing. So, I can only conclude I'm not as good at kissing as I thought I might be.'

I shook my head without looking at him. 'Stop fishing.' I laughed. 'I'm just... I haven't been out with anyone for a while. I guess I just felt a bit...'

'Out of practise?' Alex supplied.

'Yes! Oh, God, did it show? It did, didn't it?' I let go of his hand and put both of mine across my face. 'I'm so embarrassed,' I mumbled through my hands.

'Don't be.' Alex's voice was soft and husky in my ear as he pulled me to him with his free arm. 'There's nothing to be embarrassed about. I was just taking a guess from what you said earlier, and what Charlie said about you not having dated for a while.'

I dropped my hands. 'Charlie told you that?'

He nodded.

'Great,' I said, raising an eyebrow. 'Talk about sounding like a pity date! That's the last time I tell him anything.'

'He didn't mean it like that. It was more aimed at me.' He cocked an eyebrow. 'Charlie's way of telling me to behave myself.'

I considered him for a moment. 'Is that true?'

He pulled a face. 'He's kind of protective about you, it would seem.'

'Sweet. But unnecessary. I can look after myself.'

'Of that I've no doubt.'

'But I am interested in the fact that he felt you needed to be told to behave yourself. Quite the Lothario, are we?'

Alex laughed. 'Not at all. Well, not these days at least.'

'I see.'

'I'm reformed.'

'Really.'

'Really.'

'But Charlie still felt the need to tell you to behave.'

'Old habits die hard, I guess.'

'I guess they do.'

I smiled and carried on walking, trying to work out how I felt about Charlie feeling the need to give Alex instructions about how to behave with me. I knew he meant well but I didn't really appreciate being talked about as if I were his little sister. Even my own brother didn't get involved in my love life. Though I imagined the fact that he knew I had a better hook and jab than he did had something to do with that.

'Don't be mad at him.'

'Who?'

'You. At Charlie.'

'I'm not. And can we please stop talking about Charlie? It kind of feels like he's on this date with us.'

'Heaven forbid,' Alex said as I leant against his car whilst he wrestled the toy into the back seat. He closed the door and came to stand in front of me. 'That would never do,' he said, leaning down for another kiss.

Away from the nosy gaze of wandering tourists and drunken clubbers, I relaxed and smiled against the kiss as Alex's hand traced up the side of my bare arm. Little ripples of shivery pleasure coursed through me. I wasn't sure whether it was from the slight chill now coming in off the sea or from the heat of the intimate touch but could hazard a guess. I felt Alex smile in response and when he pulled back, there was merriment in his eyes.

'See? Most definitely just the two of us.'

'Well, that's good.'

'I don't want to take you home yet,' he said, his fingers sliding down my arm and entwining with my own.

'What time is your shift tomorrow?'

'I'm on lates tomorrow.'

'Sadly I'm not.'

'Shame,' he said, a teasing look flashing in his eyes.

I stood straighter and gave him a playful shove. 'Now I understand the warning. I hate to disappoint you, PC McSpeedy, but I'm not a first date kind of girl. No matter how gorgeous the man involved is.'

A deep laugh rumbled in his chest and burst out. 'I didn't think you were. But you can't blame a guy for trying.'

'Watch me,' I teased back.

'OK. I apologise.' He stroked my arm. 'Don't tell you-know-who, will you? I promised him I'd behave.'

'So definitely no reformation of the Lothario, then?'

'No. I mean yes. That is... Oh, come on, show me a man who would turn down a beautiful girl offering to take him to bed, whatever number date they're on.'

'I didn't offer!'

'I know you didn't. It doesn't mean I don't live in hope.'

'Besides, I think you're wrong there.'

'I am?'

'Yes. There was an article in the *Telegraph* about how three quarters of the men surveyed would turn down first-date sex.'

'Really? When was this study from – 1953?'

'Funny.' I pulled a face. 'Actually, it was 2015.'

'Interesting.'

'Clearly you weren't part of the survey panel.'

'Clearly not.'

I laughed and shook my head, keeping my face turned away for a moment until I could feel my heart slowing down a little. I had a bad feeling that, reformed or not, Alex Ford might well have the ability to charm a woman who had never once slept with a man on a first date into doing just that.

'Everything all right?' he whispered, close to my ear.

I nodded.

'I'm sorry, Libs.' His voice was soft but sincere, the teasing note gone. 'I shouldn't have said—'

'It's all right, Alex,' I said, looking up, meeting his eyes. 'Really. I know I might seem a bit old-fashioned with my no-first-date-sex thing, but... that's just me. In fact, I know there's no "might" about it, what with Tinder and everything else, but that's just not my thing.' I pulled at some stray hairs the breeze had blown across my face, struggling to catch them in my fingers. Alex stilled my hand with his, gently lifting the stray hairs away and smoothing them back.

'It's not mine either. I promise. It used to be. I will admit that, but not now.'

I smiled.

'Come on, let's get you home.'

He pulled open the door, lifted me gently into the seat and walked round to the other side. Settling in, and turning the key, he leant over. 'By the way, it's Sergeant McSpeedy, not PC. I worked hard for that promotion.'

I flicked him on the arm with my clutch. 'Just drive.'

He laughed and backed out of the space, watching for the odd inebriated, veering pedestrian, and headed off east towards the marina.

22

'So?' Amy said as I answered the phone.

'Good morning to you too.'

'Oh, yes, yes, all that stuff. Come on, I'm on my tea break. I need all the details double quick!'

'What details?'

'Libby!'

I laughed and took a tip from Amy, making my way to the kitchen, and pulled two mugs out of the cupboard before flicking the kettle on to boil for tea for Tilly and me.

'It was... nice.'

'Nice?'

'Yes. Nice. Fun. We had a good time.'

'Oh, dear.' Amy's tone had more than a hint of sympathy to it.

'No, really! It was good.'

'What did you do?'

I filled Amy in on where we'd gone and what we'd eaten, et cetera, whilst deftly making drinks with one hand. Mobiles, whilst useful, were way too thin to tuck under your chin as you could with regular old phones. Although Tilly and I were close, I wasn't quite ready to be sharing the ins and outs, so to speak, of my sporadic dating scene on speaker phone.

'So, did anything happen.'

'There were a couple of kisses.'

'And?'

'And what?'

'Were they good kisses?'

'Yes.' I laughed. 'They were good kisses.'

'But not goooooooooood kisses.' Amy drew the word out, and made it sound all breathy and hot.

'Ames, they were very nice.'

'Oh, dear.'

'Will you stop saying that?'

'Are you seeing him again?'

'He said he wanted to.'

'Do you want to?'

'Yes. Of course. I like him.'

'Do you like him enough?'

'Enough for what?'

'Oh, come on, Libs. You *like* nearly everyone. You're a nice person. But do you *like* Alex enough to make it something more than that?'

'Blimey, Amy! We've only met twice. Just because you and Marcus are already halfway up the aisle already...'

'We are not!'

'You know what I mean.'

'Yeah... I do.' Her voice went all soft for a moment.

'Look. I've got a million things going on at the moment. I had a really nice time with Alex last night. I hope he had a good time too. But we'll just have to see how it goes.'

'Libby?'

'Yes?'

'You don't exactly seem thrilled about it all.'

'Oh, Ames. Really. He's lovely. He makes me laugh, and he's fun to be around. I'm just... I don't know, maybe a little distracted right now.'

'By work or someone else?'

'Work, of course. What else would it be?'

'Nothing. I was just... uh oh. My boss is sending me daggers. Tea break must be over! I'll call you later!'

'OK. Have a good afternoon.'

I tucked the phone in my waistband and picked up the drinks

I'd now made and walked back into the living room, placing one of the mugs down on Tilly's desk.

'Oh, thanks! I was just going to do that when you went off.'

'No problem. How's the scheduling coming along?'

'Good. Do you want to take a look at it and see what you think? I'm not sure about whether to switch these two things around.' Tilly pointed at a couple of bullet points. I rolled my chair round to her side of the desk and began reading through the list she'd begun compiling. We were pretty good at organisation but with her wedding and then a three-week honeymoon coming up, prep work was definitely key right now.

* * *

The early evening rays of the sun caught the twisted metal of the old West Pier, highlighting its sad state and showing its beauty all in the same moment. The boys were busy colouring in their superhero books as the rest of us chatted over wine and breadsticks. Dad and Gina had driven down from London, booking a room at the Grand for the night, and Matt and Maria had ensured that they both had the evening off.

My birthday dinner was a tradition that seemed to be upheld more by my family than me, but it was a lovely opportunity to get everyone together. And also the one time I could be certain my dad wouldn't try and find me a date!

Mum's passing so close to my birthday had made it difficult for a long time and each of us knew that she should still be here with us, celebrating. My family's insistence on doing this every year, moving shifts, schedules and everything else to ensure that it happened, made me love them even more.

Amy and Marcus came in, having scooted home from work for her to change in record time – something that normally took my dear friend a heck of a lot longer. In order for my nephews to be here, a stipulation that was non-negotiable, the event was always a little earlier than I'd normally have arranged. There was no sign of Charlie yet, but he had promised to leave early and said he'd get here as soon as he could. The boys ran over to Amy and gave her a hug, considered Marcus and soon began giggling at something he said, before running back to the colouring as the new guests came over to me and we exchanged more hugs and Amy handed me a gorgeously wrapped gift.

'Oh, Ames, you shouldn't!'

'You don't know what it is yet!'

'I know. But it looks pretty.'

She shook her head. 'I love that you're my friend. You're so easy to please. I can just give you a pretty box and you're happy. It's great!'

I shrugged, smiled and opened the gift – a cashmere wrap that we'd oohed over online and that was just as beautiful as the wrapping that had enclosed it.

'No Alex or Charlie yet?' Amy asked as Matt poured them both a glass of champagne after I'd thanked them.

'No, not yet. Alex had some mountain bike thing on today after his rest, and Charlie said he'd be here as soon as he could.'

Amy raised her glass to me. 'Happy birthday, Libs.'

'Thanks.' We clinked glasses and sipped our bubbly.

'I thought Alex might have spent the day with you. You know, young love and all that.' She giggled.

I pulled a face. 'A few dates is not young love, thank you very much! And for your information, he did offer but I'm up to my ears in work at the moment so taking the day off wasn't really an option. Plus, he'd had this thing arranged before he knew it was my birthday. I'm hardly going to ask him to change it.'

This time it was Amy's turn to pull a face. 'I would have done,' she said, honestly.

I laughed and glanced at Marcus.

He shrugged. 'Guess I'm not going mountain biking on your birthday, then.'

'Not if you want to see your next one.'

'Fair enough.' He grinned and kissed her on the cheek.

I rolled my eyes, but my smile told them I actually loved it.

'Charlie!' Liam's voice rang out and he bounded off his chair and ran across the restaurant.

'Hello!' Charlie dropped to a squat and laughed as Niall caught up with his brother and they both careered full speed into him.

'Have you brought your car?'

'Not today, I'm afraid.'

'Ohhh!' they chorused, sadly.

'Sorry about that. Another time though?'

'Yeeaaahh!' They jumped up and down, still half hugging him.

He stood and each boy grabbed a hand, pulling him over to show him their artwork. As he passed he raised his eyebrows at me. 'Hello, birthday girl. Be right there.'

I grinned and made a 'no problem' gesture. Charlie paused briefly to place a small turquoise gift bag in front of me. Amy's eyes widened as she mouthed the word 'Tiffany's!' to me. Surprise showing on my own face, I looked back up to Charlie, but he was already being tugged away by the boys.

Movement at the door caught my eye. Alex stepped through and gave a quick recce glance before his eyes rested on me.

'Oop. Here comes lover boy,' Marcus whispered.

'Oh, shush up, you.' I laughed and rapped him on the knuckles with a breadstick before standing and going to meet Alex halfway.

'Hello.'

'Evening. How's the birthday girl?'

'Fine, thank you. How was your biking?'

'Great, thanks. Did I miss much?' He nodded at the scene behind me.

'No. We've been waiting for you to turn up. Charlie's only just got here too.'

'Oh, good.'

'Thank you so much for the flowers this morning. They're beautiful.'

'My pleasure. I didn't really know what to get you.'

'You didn't have to get me anything.' I kissed his cheek and took his hand in mine. 'Ready to come and meet everyone?'

'Let's do it.'

I smiled and began to turn. Alex tugged lightly on my hand. 'Hey.'

I turned back.

'Don't I get a birthday kiss?'

I tilted my head at him. 'But it's not your birthday.'

'That's just semantics,' he said softly, sliding his hand around my waist and pulling me to him. His lips were warm and soft as they touched mine and I felt myself move closer.

'Who are you?'

Startled, we pulled apart and looked down in the direction of where the bold question had come from. Niall and Liam stood there studying us.

Alex flicked his eyes to me then back at the boys. I opened my mouth to speak but Alex beat me to it.

'I'm Alex,' he said, holding his hand out to them for a handshake.

Liam looked at it for a moment, then took it and shook it. 'I'm Liam.'

'I'm Niall,' said Niall, who had chosen not to shake Alex's hand but was instead winding his own into mine.

'Nice to meet you, Niall, Liam.'

Liam considered him for a moment longer. 'Are you coming to Auntie Libby's party?'

'I am.'

Liam looked at me for a moment.

'OK,' he replied, before wandering back to the table and taking an empty chair next to Charlie. Niall remained where he was, his big green eyes watching Alex.

'Come on, Niall. Let's go and introduce Alex to everyone else, shall we?'

Niall nodded and headed off towards the table, pulling me with him. I stuck out my hand and grabbed Alex's before he got left behind, tossing a look over my shoulder as I did so. 'Welcome to my family.'

Alex grinned and squeezed my hand in reply.

I'd seen Gina's radar begin pinging the moment Charlie had walked in and now, with Alex attached to my hand, it was working overtime. I'd introduced Charlie to Dad, and Gina. Matt and Maria had already met him a couple of times now and had clearly got him relaxed and chatting by the time I got to the table, which I appreciated.

'Everyone, this is Alex. Alex, my dad, Gina. Matt, my brother, my sister-in-law, Maria, and you've already met their boys, Niall and Liam.'

Alex shook hands with everyone, making easy conversation. Gina was clearly already sold on him. Even my dad gave me a little look that seemed to intimate something. I wasn't sure what but he seemed pleased so I just took it at face value and carried on.

Once everyone had taken their seats and the boys had settled a little more, a toast went up and champagne levels went down. Our orders were taken and we all munched on olives, breadsticks and sun-dried tomatoes as we waited for the starters to arrive. I saw Alex's eyes take in the Tiffany bag at my place setting.

'Are you going to open it?' Amy asked, trying to peer into the bag.

'Later, if that's OK?' I flicked my glance to Charlie. He nodded. As I turned back, I caught a glimpse of something in Alex's expression. A tightening of his jaw. But the next moment it was gone and I wondered if I'd seen anything at all.

'Alex, do you have a James Bond car?' Liam asked during a momentary lull in the conversation.

I saw Alex's glance flick to Charlie and then to me.

'No.' He smiled. 'I don't. Wish I did, though. They're really cool, aren't they?'

Liam nodded quickly in agreement. 'Charlie has a James Bond car.'

'I know he does. Nice, isn't it?'

'Mmm hmm.' Liam returned his concentration to his drawing and it seemed that his questioning was done.

'So, where did—?'

'Auntie Libby?'

Or not.

'Yes, Liam?'

'Is Alex your boyfriend?'

I could see smirks all around the table, including one on Alex's face.

'Umm, well...'

'I am,' Alex filled in.

'Oh.'

I waited. Experience told me that my eldest nephew and his enquiring mind weren't done with me yet.

'But couldn't Charlie be your boyfriend instead of Alex, Auntie Libby? Then we get to go in his James Bond car.'

A second of silence descended on the table.

'Ouch,' Alex said.

'Alex drives a police car!' I blurted.

Like a lot of small boys, Liam and Niall had an affinity for anything that had sirens.

'Are you a policeman?' Niall asked.

'I am.'

'Is your police car here?' Liam asked, his interest in Alex now a little more piqued.

'No. We have to leave them at work but maybe Libby could bring you into the station one day and I can show you all round it, if you like?'

Two small boys whipped their heads to me. 'Can we, Auntie Libby? Please?'

'I expect so. We'll have to ask your mum and dad.'

They quickly turned to Matt and Maria. 'Please! Can we?'

'Let's see how you behave this evening and I'll think about it,' said Matt.

Immediately the two sat up straighter and I had to turn my face away so that they couldn't see me laughing. The conversation moved on and Alex gave Charlie a smile that had a hint of tightness to it.

'Thanks, mate. Aston Martins and presents from Tiffany. Don't set any high bars for me or anything, will you?'

23

Charlie didn't say anything. His gaze flicked to me. I gently shook my head and gave a smile that felt awkward on my face.

Alex turned his hand and took mine within it. 'Anyway, I might not have the flashy car, but I think I'm doing OK.' His gaze lingered on my lips for a moment before he looked back at Charlie.

Charlie smiled, gave a brief nod and turned back to my dad, who began asking him about his house conversion. I studied him for a moment, the awkward smile still on my face. I knew it had never quite reached my eyes and I couldn't say why. I shrugged the feeling off and listened as Amy told us about a spa weekend Marcus had just surprised her with.

Full of delicious food and even more delicious champagne, I leant my head on Alex's shoulder. He bent his own to mine a little and whispered, 'I love my job but I really, really wish I didn't have to go to it this evening.' Alex was on lates and, although I'd known he was going to have to leave early, I'd been doing my best to avoid thinking about it. And now, content with food and company, I wanted to avoid thinking about it even more.

'I suppose it's too late to get someone to cover for you?' I said, not moving my head.

'Afraid so. If I could, I would, believe me.' His voice held the hint of a promise that sent a warm rush through my body. I smiled against him and I knew he felt it because he laughed softly and drew his fingers slowly over my hand.

'Alex...' I said, raising my head, 'what if when you finish your shift—?'

'Auntie Libby! Can we go and see the waves? Please!'

I turned and saw Alex's face take on a blank expression. There went the moment. Again.

'You can see them from here, boys,' I said reasonably.

The entire front of the restaurant, perched high on the promenade, was plate-glass window.

'It's not the same!' they countered. 'And you always take us to see the waves on your birthday.'

I glanced over at Matt. He shrugged. 'What can I say? If you will be their favourite auntie...'

I narrowed my eyes at him. He knew that I loved it when they declared I was their favourite and was now using it as a defence. Typical brother. I made to push my chair out. Alex looked at me.

'It's a tradition thing. I won't be long.'

'OK.' He gave me a quick smile then glanced at his watch. I knew Alex hadn't missed the fact that the boys had been intermittently climbing all over Charlie ever since we'd finished eating. They had, however, asked Alex some questions about being a policeman, which I took to be a good sign. They weren't my children, but I spent a lot of time with them, so I was still aware of who I introduced into their lives. Charlie's introduction had been a bit of an accident, but a happy one, it would seem, judging by the grins that all three of them wore as he now tickled them and they did their best not to squeal with laughter in the restaurant. I could see my dad and Gina exchanging looks that included me. The concept of me and a gorgeous, straight man who also got on with my family, but whom I wasn't dating, was clearly doing their heads right in.

'Do you want me to come?' Alex asked.

In my peripheral vision, I saw two pairs of eyes fix on me.

'Umm, it's kind of a thing that the boys and I do alone. Like I say, tradition.' I leaned into him. 'Please don't be offended.'

He gave me a quick smile. 'I'm not. But I will have to go in a bit. Do you think you'll be back?'

'Of course.' Quickly, I gave him a kiss and pushed my chair out, kicking off my four-inch heels as I did so. From my bag, I pulled a pair of fold-up ballet flats and slipped them on.

'God, you are prepared, aren't you?' Alex raised an eyebrow.

'Oh, she always carries them in there,' Charlie piped up.

We both turned our heads to him, slightly astonished that he knew the regular contents of my handbag. The look on his face showed that he was just as surprised as we were to realise he had this knowledge.

'I've no idea how or why I know that,' he said, looking at his champagne glass as if that might give him the answer. 'I have to admit, it's slightly worrying that I do. I don't think it's very good for my image.'

Alex gave a laugh. 'I'm pretty sure your image is just fine, mate. As usual. And if you start showing your feminine, understanding side too, the rest of us may as well hang up our boots, so at least give us a fighting chance, eh?'

Charlie snorted. 'Oh, don't worry. I'm not about to claim absolutely any understanding of women. Totally beyond my capabilities.'

'Beyond any man's, I think!' Marcus chimed in.

Amy and I exchanged an eye-roll.

'Come on then, pests. Let's go and see these waves.'

Some quiet cheering was quickly followed by me finding a small boy attached to each hand. We walked down the stairs and across the beach. The soles of my shoes were thin so there followed some inelegant manoeuvring over the larger pebbles of the beach and I wished, not for the first time, that our local beach was covered in soft white sand instead. I shamelessly used the children as support devices until we got closer to shoreline, where the pebbles became smaller and merged into sand.

The tradition of going to see the waves had begun when Liam was a baby. I loved spending time with people, especially my closest friends and family, but I always needed a bit of time to myself on this day amongst the celebration and the laughter, just to have a chat to Mum. It wasn't always aloud but the words were there and I believed – I knew – she could hear them. But it was always by the shoreline. The first time I'd done it, I'd said that I was 'going to see the waves'. I wasn't sure why. It just came out and then it stuck. My family understood and left me to do what I needed to do.

When Liam had arrived, I'd borrowed him and cuddled his warm, chubby little body as I stood at the tide line, wishing that my mum could be there with me, be there to hold her first grandchild. The following year, he'd toddled over to me and I'd picked him up and taken him with me again and a tradition of the boys coming with me had been born. They didn't yet understand the deeper meaning of this ritual but it didn't matter. Part of the tradition now was that time alone I got with the boys. I still sent up my wishes and love to Mum, but my nephews' happy laughter and giggles as they taunted the shallow waves had made what had once been so difficult a little easier to bear and now a moment of joy that I looked forward to. I'd felt bad excluding Alex, but I'd seen the wariness in the boys' eyes. I didn't want to push anything on them yet because, if things did progress with me and him, I really wanted them to like him. I shoved all other thoughts out of my head as the boys gripped my hands and pulled me to the edge of the sea and began dancing with the shimmering water as it chased them back onto the land, their laughter echoing across the beach.

With slightly soggy feet from a misjudged moment, the boys and I headed back up to the restaurant and reclaimed our seats. Maria smiled at me as they ran back to her and Niall wrapped his arms around her neck as she pulled him onto her lap to remove his shoes and dry his slightly damp feet.

'How were the waves?' Alex asked.

'Pleased to see us.' I laughed.

He smiled. I wanted to pick back up on what I'd been planning to say earlier but now it didn't feel right.

'What time do you have to go?'

I saw his expression cloud a moment.

'Not that I want you to go!' I added quickly. 'I meant, how much longer do I get to keep you for?'

'Not long, I'm afraid. I'd better head off soon.'

I nodded.

'I'll call you tomorrow, when I wake up.'

'OK.'

'I'm really sorry I can't stay tonight.'

I shook my head. 'It's OK. I mean, it's not, in that I want you to stay, but it's OK in that I understand that you can't. Because you have to work. I'm not sure shift work is our best friend right now. Bit of a pain in the bum, if I'm honest.'

He laughed at my rambling. 'It certainly can be. But I'm sure we'll find a workaround.' That promise was back in his voice, as his gaze leisurely drifted over my face before he leant closer and kissed me.

'Ugh!' Liam's voice came across the table. My nephew still hadn't fully grasped the concept of whispering. He had the whispered tone right, but the volume was generally still set to normal. My smile broke against Alex's lips. He pulled away and shook his head, resignation on his face.

'Sorry.'

He shook his head, smiling. 'I have to go anyway.'

'But you'll miss the cake!' Gina waved her hands. 'Two minutes!' she said and rushed off to accost a waiter.

'Babe, I really do have to go.'

Across the table, I saw Amy's eyebrows rise. I chose to ignore them.

'Don't worry. I'll save you a piece. Don't make yourself late.'

'Happy birthday to you...' The tune rang out with a line of waiters following a large cake, complete with candles and indoor sparklers. The other diners began joining in and I could see Alex torn as to what he felt he should do.

'Go!' I said and kissed him quickly. 'It's just a cake.'

He nodded, made an apologetic goodbye gesture to the table and headed off to the exit. I watched him go for a moment before my attention was drawn back to the cake now being lowered onto the table. Alex was pretty gorgeous but, boy, this chocolate-sprinkled creation looked almost as delicious as he did.

Amy and I were now sitting next to one another as Marcus and Charlie chatted and demolished enormous slices of cake between them. Though, to be fair, our own slices were hardly what one could call petite either.

I looked up to find her studying me.

'What?' I said, around a mouthful of utter chocolate yumminess.

'Babe?'

I made a non-committal face. 'It's affectionate.'

'Libs, you hate being called babe!'

'I never said I hated it.'

'You did actually.'

She was right and I knew this. For a long time, I'd never given it a thought if someone ever called me 'babe'. And then, a couple of years ago, the boys went through a phase of watching the film *Babe*. And, as could often be the case with small people, they chose to watch it over and over again. To the point where I became conditioned that upon hearing that word all I could think of was a little piglet. Admittedly, a cute little piglet. But a pig all the same.

'Oh. Well, maybe it just depends on who's calling me it.'

'Really,' Amy said flatly.

'Maybe.'

'Why don't you just tell him you don't like it?'

'I can't! I kind of just let it go the first few times because we've hardly been able to get together much, what with his shifts and holiday cover, plus all his studying for the detective exam stuff. Not to mention the craziness that is my work right now. I didn't want it to come out wrong when it's all so new anyway. And then it sort of seemed like I'd missed the moment to say, "You know what? Can you not call me babe, because all I can think of when I hear that is a pig?" It's a ridiculous reason, Ames! I can see that, even if I can't help it.'

'So? It might be a bit ridiculous, but that's you!'

I looked at her. 'Did that come out exactly how it was supposed to?'

'No, not really. But you get the idea. You're entitled to have your own preferences and reasons, however ridiculous they may seem to anyone else. We can't all be as logical as... say, Charlie!'

Upon hearing his name, Charlie looked up and gave a sideways glance at his brother. 'Have you any idea what I've done this time?'

Marcus pulled a 'not a clue' face.

'You haven't done anything,' Amy said, leaning across the table and patting his hand. I was tactile all the time. Amy was alcohol-induced tactile. 'Libby was berating herself for not always being the most logical, but I said that it was all right and that not everyone is like you. Not that you being logical is a bad thing. It's just a... thing.'

'Libby's logical when she needs to be. In business, for example.'

'Exactly!' Amy said, enthusiastically.

'If you were as logical as me all the time, you wouldn't be you. And that wouldn't do at all. We need your...' I saw a glint in his eye and smile curve onto his lips '... your va-va-voom to keep us all amused and on our toes!'

My eyes widened as I immediately realised what he was referring to. The last time he'd used that exact phrase was when what he'd now christened the '*Sports Illustrated* picture' of me had popped up on the computer.

He met my look with an orchestrated innocent one of his own.

'See?' Amy said, completely unaware of the double meaning Charlie had infused his reply with.

'What's she got to be logical about, anyway? Marcus asked.

'Nothing really,' I said.

'Alex calling her babe,' Amy filled in.

'You hate people calling you babe,' Charlie said, and then frowned. 'Something about a... pig?'

I slapped my hand to my forehead and forked an extra-large piece of cake onto my plate.

24

I was working way past my bedtime when the sound of my mobile's video-call ringtone caused me to scoot back around the desk, propelling my chair along with my feet until I got to a point I could reach out and snag the phone. Charlie's picture was on the screen.

'Hi!'

'Hello. How are you?'

'I'm fine. How are you, Mr Jet-Set? What time is it there?'

'Early evening,' he replied, smiling at my description of him. 'I didn't know if you'd still be up.'

'Tonnes to do. Working late. Aren't you out hitting the town?'

'It's far too early for that. Those in the know are aware that no one hits the clubs before eleven.'

'Oh, of course. Silly me!'

'Actually, I'm sat watching a bad film on HBO.'

'That sounds more like it.'

'Thanks.'

'No! I didn't mean it like that.'

'Right. But apparently I can't fool you into thinking I'm doing something cool even when I'm thousands of miles away.'

'Don't be daft. I already know you're cool.'

'Of course. Well, I did actually go to a club last night. Which is why I'm knackered and in front of the telly tonight.'

'You did?'

'Um hmm,' he said. The ice cubes in the glass he held clinked as he swirled the drink.

'Fab! Was that with people you're working with?'

'Sort of.'

I waited for an explanation but nothing further came.

'Did you have a good time?'

'Yes, actually. I was dreading it. I couldn't really get out of it when they said they were going but I was amazed at how good a time I had. Paid for it a bit today though.' He gave his little chuckle.

'Gosh. Sounds like it suits you over there in the Big Apple.'

'Yeah, maybe it does.'

There was a beat or two of silence as we both digested that.

'So, did you ring for anything or just to say hello?'

'Both, really.'

'OK.'

'One of the companies I'm working with here is a cosmetics business, but all into saving the planet too. They're pretty big over here and are looking to expand into the UK and Europe. I got chatting with them yesterday and you came up, you know, the blog and stuff. They asked me if I thought you'd be open to doing some reviews of their stuff. I said I had no idea, but that I'd ask.'

'Oh! Well, yes, of course. I'd love to take a look at them. I'm not going to screw things up for you if we find it's not really our thing though, am I? I'm pretty honest with my reviews.'

'That's no problem. They went and looked you up and watched hours of your videos, apparently, so they know the score.'

'Right! Well, then, yes. Of course!'

'Great. They're pretty excited so this will really please them. Thanks, Libs.'

I laughed. 'I'm sure you don't need my help pleasing the ladies, Charlie.'

'Oh, ha ha. I'll bring the stuff back with me when I come.'

'When are you back?'

'Couple of days.'

'OK. It feels like you've been away forever.'

'Yes. It's been a bit of a longer than usual trip this time. Various things to fit in.'

'But it's gone well?'

'Yes. Pretty productive.'

'Great.'

There was a pause.

'Alex seemed to enjoy your last date.'

'You've spoken to him?'

'Messaged.'

'I see. And?'

'And what?'

'What did he say?'

'Oh, just bloke stuff, you know.'

'I don't know.' I paused. 'You're not going to tell me, are you?'

'Nope.'

'So why even say he'd mentioned it?'

'Because I knew it would drive you nuts.'

'You know, you have this adorable, sweet persona thing going on, but it's all a façade. You do know that, don't you?'

'I do. But don't tell too many people, will you?'

'How many drinks have you had?'

'This is my first. I'm perfectly sober and aware of what I'm saying.' His grin made me smile.

'Maybe it's last night's alcohol still swilling through your veins.'

'That's always a possibility. There were an awful lot of champagne corks popping.'

'Were you celebrating something?'

There was a pause before he answered. 'No. Not especially.'

'I see. Well, nice for some people. I, on the other hand, have a cup of hot chocolate going cold. Far less glamorous, I'm afraid.'

'Still busy, then?'

'Yeah. Ridiculously so. Just trying to get ahead as much as possible before the wedding.'

'Wedding?'

'Yes. Tilly's.'

'Oh. Right. Of course. Thought there was something you hadn't told me there for a minute.'

'Ha! Definitely not.'

'Never say never.'

'Too late.'

'Well, I guess that's another plus for Alex.'

'Huh?'

'Nothing. Never mind. I'd better let you get back to it. Although you should really get to bed. You'll exhaust yourself if you keep working into the early hours like this.'

'Yes, I will in a minute, I promise.' Charlie's comment about Alex lingered in my head but I was too tired to decipher what he meant. 'I'm actually having trouble keeping my eyes open now.'

'Get some rest, Libs. You'll make yourself ill.'

'This from the workaholic.'

'Not exactly, but I've been there. It's not fun.'

'Harder when it's your own business on the line, though.'

'That's true. But you'll be no good to yourself if you burn out.'

'No. I know. I'm shutting my laptop now. Happy?' I smiled at him.

'Immensely.'

'And thanks for the networking, you know, in advance. I'm glad it's going well. Oh! And thank you for the pictures you sent over. I love that one of Times Square. I really need to get to New York one day. It looks amazing.'

'You're welcome. Yes, it is pretty cool.' His voice drifted off a little.

'You look tired. Get some sleep.'

'Yep. Just need to see how this terrifically dreadful film ends, and then I will. Promise.'

'Thanks for ringing. It sort of feels weird when I don't talk to you via some method every single day now!' I laughed.

'I shall endeavour not to let that happen, then.'

'Good.'

'Night, Libs.'

'Night, Charlie.'

* * *

Tilly and I were knee deep in bridal-themed items when the door-bell rang. I pushed myself up, stepped over my assistant and a plethora of beauty detritus and opened the door. A very tired-looking Charlie filled the doorway.

'Am I disturbing you?'

'No! Of course not!' I threw my arms around his neck and he hugged me with his one free arm. 'How are you? You look shattered. Shouldn't you be home in bed?'

'I tried that,' he said, coming in and putting the large box he'd been carrying down on the floor next to the console table. 'Couldn't sleep. Bloody jet lag. Thought I may as well come and drop this off.' He pointed at the box.

'Oh, are those the goodies from the company you were talking about?'

'Yeah. They said these are just a few samples to start off with, but that if you like this lot then they'd like to send you the whole range.'

'Great. Sounds like a plan.'

Charlie quirked an eyebrow as he surveyed the disaster scene currently standing in for my living room.

'Hi, Tilly. I almost didn't see you there.'

Tilly stuck her head up from under the swathes of fine netting we'd been fiddling with for some of the bridal shoots.

'Hi, Charlie. Blimey, you look knackered!'

Charlie gave a nod, amusement making his eyes shine. 'Thanks.'

'Do you want a tea or coffee or something?'

He glanced around. 'No, it's fine, thanks anyway. You're clearly incredibly busy. I don't—'

'Charlie, please. It'll give me an excuse anyway. I've been at this since six this morning so I think I deserve a tea break.'

He held my gaze a moment. 'Tea would be great, thanks.'

'Not easy to get a decent cuppa out in the States, is it?' Tilly's voice drifted up from somewhere amongst the tulle.

'No. Not really.'

'I'd have to take a suitcase full of teabags out if I lived there, I think!'

'That sounds like a very good idea,' Charlie agreed.

'Take a seat, if you can find one. I'll be back in a minute.'

'Do you want some help?'

'No. Really. I'd feel better if you just sat and rested.'

If I was honest, Charlie looked so tired that it had me concerned. I realised I'd only known him a short time, but I'd never seen him look this exhausted or strained in that time.

He didn't protest and found a small clearing on the sofa that he could squish himself into. When I returned, I moved a few bits from around the floor near his feet so that he could stretch his long legs out. He took the hint and gave me a smile as I looked up from the floor.

'So, what's all this, then?' He pointed at the pile to his right, encompassing Tilly, as he took the tea and sipped. His eyes closed as he did so, a brief smile of satisfaction on his face that made me happy to see. It was funny how something as simple as a good cup of tea could make you feel as if you were home.

'We've got a bridal special running on the blog this month – as wedding season is upon us.' I gave a wink to Tilly and she grinned.

'Sam's banned from looking at the blog at the moment. I mean, not that he does much, but, you know, just in case.'

Charlie looked confused.

I pulled a face. 'One of the local boutiques saw us announce the feature and asked if we'd be able to include some of their dresses in the shoots. We talked it over and thought some reportage-style shots of the dresses would be best rather than just standard photos to make it feel less formal and a bit more fun.'

'Sounds good. How's that going to work? Are they going to send models?' He waggled his eyebrows in mock anticipation.

I rolled my eyes and tossed a packet of chocolate Hobnobs at him. He pulled out a biscuit, dunked it and ate it in two bites.

'So?'

'That's the catch. Neither I nor the shop have the money to cover professional models. If we want to do it, we sort of have to model the dresses ourselves.'

Tilly grinned at this. I didn't.

Charlie gave me a look before returning to his tea. 'You don't seem thrilled at that prospect.'

'I'm just not sure I can pull it off. This one has the glowing bride thing all set.' I thumbed at Tilly. 'Me, not so much.'

'What's so hard? You put on a dress. You look pretty. You take a photograph. It's what you do all the time.'

'Not in wedding dresses.'

Charlie looked at me. I looked away. The truth was, I wasn't sure I could ever really see myself getting married. On that awful day

Mum died, I'd seen the pain that enveloped my dad, the grief that had seeped from every fibre. Part of that still remained. I knew it would never entirely leave. I wasn't averse to relationships but marriage? It was something I took seriously and, in my heart, I didn't know if I would ever be able to take that final step.

Confusingly, I knew that my so-called reasoning was ridiculous. I mean, Matt and Marie had the most wonderful marriage. He'd lost his mum too, seen what I'd seen, but it hadn't deterred him from seeking out love. And it wasn't as if I didn't want love. Of course, I did. Didn't everyone? And the thought that I'd love someone less just because I hadn't signed a piece of paper and put a band of metal on my finger was daft. I knew that too. But there was still something about it. Something more definite in my mind. And it was that that made me hesitant. Dressing up as a bride just didn't seem right knowing that I might not ever do it for real. I felt, I suppose, a bit of a fraud.

'Models do it all the time, for brochures and magazines, and catwalk shows,' Charlie stated, sensibly. Of course, he did.

'I'm not a model. I feel daft.'

Tilly looked over at Charlie and rolled her eyes.

'I saw that.'

She and Charlie exchanged a smile and he said nothing more, returning to drinking his tea whilst we set up some more still shots of make-up, lotions and accessories.

'What if we put this here, and that there? Do you think that looks better?' I asked Tilly a short while later.

'Oh, yes, and this...' She leaned over and grabbed another product that made an ideal set-up. She really was good.

'Where's that rose we had earlier?' I said, moving some of the netting and finding the remarkably lifelike silk rose I had in mind buried underneath. My glance drifted to Charlie, who had been exceptionally quiet, even for him, for the last ten minutes. His eyes were closed and the empty mug rested on his chest, slowly moving rhythmically up and down as he slept. I threw a look to Tilly and put my fingers to my lips. She frowned and stepped over to peer.

'Aww,' she whispered.

I carefully lifted the mug, halting suddenly as his hand moved and caught mine within it for a moment before slipping away.

Putting the mug on the table, I cleared the rest of the sofa. He'd twisted his body in his sleep, sliding down the sofa so that his legs were now at an angle to the rest of him. Crouching down, I hooked my arms under his legs and heaved. My first attempt succeeded only in putting me on my bum with a bump. I altered my position and tried again, hefting Charlie's long legs onto the sofa. They didn't really fit and hung over the end, but at least they weren't now at ninety degrees to his torso. He barely stirred. I leant over and delved under yet more fabric and grabbed the summer quilt I normally kept over the back of the other sofa. Laying it gently over his sleeping form, I went back to work.

When Charlie woke it was after seven and a warm, soft breeze was swishing the voiles at my balcony back and forth. Tilly had left and the room now resembled a living space once again, rather than the aftermath of a Bridezilla rampage. I was curled up on the other sofa, reading, when movement caught my eye.

'You should have woken me,' he said, squinting at his watch. His voice was rough from sleep, and his normally impeccable appearance was ruffled. It was a good look on him.

'You needed the rest.'

He sat up properly and rubbed his face with his hands.

'Go and splash some water on your face, if you like. Dinner's in the oven. It'll be ready soon.'

Charlie looked at me. 'Dinner?'

'Yes. I was cooking anyway so I did a bit extra. Unless you have plans.'

He shook his head. 'No, no plans. Apart from more sleeping. Are you sure you have enough?'

'Yep,' I said, getting up. 'I'm just going to check on it. I'll be back in a minute.'

Dinner was looking great, maybe a couple more minutes. I grabbed some plates out of the cupboard, gathered cutlery and poured iced water into two glasses, returning to the living room to place them on the coffee table. Charlie was nowhere to be seen but I could hear the tap running in the bathroom and guessed he had taken my advice to go and wake himself up a bit with a splash around. I put the cutlery down and turned to find Charlie coming back in.

'Anything I can do?' he asked. He looked a little brighter than he had done earlier and had obviously run his wet fingers through his hair to tidy it up. It wasn't as perfectly done as it usually was, but I sort of liked it for that.

'Nope. All done. Just sit there.'

'I could get used to this.'

'Ha! Unless you're thinking of employing someone, I shouldn't.'

Charlie looked up from the sofa and smiled. 'Thanks, Libs. This is really nice.'

'You haven't tasted it yet. You might want to reserve praise until then.'

He gave a little shake of the head. 'You know what I mean.'

'Hmm, five-star hotels can be so tiresome.' I raised an eyebrow. 'I hate having all that cooking, cleaning, washing and ironing done for me.'

'Granted. That bit isn't too bad. But it's not the same as being with friends. Having someone to talk to.'

'You're hardly Chatty Cathy at the best of times. Besides, you said you went out partying so don't give me the hard-done-by act.'

'Once. I went out once.' He grinned. 'And I apologise for not being "Chatty Cathy". What would you like to talk about?'

I gave his shoulder a gentle shove. 'Don't apologise. It's how you are. You wouldn't be you if you were all chatty like Alex.'

'That's true.' Charlie moved his fork minutely to the left on the table. 'He always was far better than me with that sort of thing. I imagine there isn't a shortage of conversation on your dates.'

I gave him a look. 'Are you saying I talk too much?'

'No... I...' He cleared his throat and then looked back at me. 'I'm just saying you like to talk.'

I could see the mischief in his eyes and narrowed my own at him. He gave me a smile. I flicked him with the tea towel and headed back into the kitchen to get dinner out of the oven.

25

Two hours later, after we had eaten and watched a film on Netflix, I could see Charlie's eyes looking tired again.

'Come on, you.' I gave him a nudge with my shoulder. 'Go home and go to bed.'

Charlie gave a stretch and scratched his hair, yawning and nodding at the same time. He stood, and I followed as he made his way to the front door.

'Thanks for the goodies. We'll go through them tomorrow.'

'No problem. Thanks for the food. And the use of your couch.'

'Any time.'

He leant down and hugged me. I squeezed him back, realising just how much I'd missed him. Even though I'd been busy, even though we'd spoken on text and video calls, it wasn't the same as having him physically in my life. Charlie had fast become, alongside Amy, my closest friend.

As he opened the door, he turned back. 'What are you doing about your photoshoot for the wedding dresses?'

'What do you mean?'

'How are you doing it?'

I blew a wisp of hair off my face. 'I don't know. Probably just take it in turns, or something. I might try and set up some shots with both of us in them if I can, but it'll just depend on how it's going and time really.'

'Do you want a hand?'

'Are you offering?'

'Yes. I'm off tomorrow. I could come and help you shoot. It'll be easier that way and you'll get more of the reportage feeling you were after. I was thinking about it during dinner.'

'Were you, now?'

He held up his hands. 'Hey, you're the one who encouraged this photography thing.'

'Yes, but you don't usually like taking people pictures.'

'Only because I don't always feel comfortable talking to people I don't know, in that sort of circumstance. I do actually like taking their photos.'

'Well, it would make things a lot easier and get it done quicker. But shouldn't you be trying to get over your jet lag?'

'I'm going straight home to bed now. If we say after lunch tomorrow, I'll be up by then and functioning, for the most part. Come on, let me repay you for dinner and for falling asleep on your sofa.'

I rubbed his arm. 'You don't have to repay me, or apologise, for anything. But if you really don't mind, it would be a great help.'

'Great. OK. I'll see you about two, then?'

'Sounds good. Thanks, Charlie. And sleep well.'

'I'm pretty sure that's a given.' He raised his eyebrows over sleepy eyes.

'Just text me when you're in, will you?'

He gave his little head-shake. 'Libs. It's a few minutes' drive.'

'Please. You're tired. And lots of accidents happen very close to home. You love statistics so I know you know I'm right.' I tilted my chin up.

'Fine. I will text you.' He bent and kissed me on the cheek. 'You're worse than my mother.'

'Thanks.'

'See you tomorrow.'

Ten minutes later, my phone cheeped at me.

✉ Home. Thanks for dinner. Going to… zzzzzzzzzzz

I smiled at his message.

✉ Thank you xx

A smiley face, followed by a sleepy one, came back, along with a couple of kisses. I switched my own phone onto silent and headed off to bed myself.

* * *

'Seriously? Oh, that's so cool!' Tilly said, when I told her the plan Charlie and I had made about getting pictures of the wedding dresses. 'It'll be like having a trial run for my wedding photos!'

I smiled, unable to resist being warmed by her enthusiasm.

'Do you think we could try that make-up look we'd decided on before, and see how it looks? I mean, I know it's not the actual outfit I'll be wearing, but it's as close as I can get.'

'Of course. That's a great idea. We can link back to it in the post, and give it another boost. I have a few emails to answer. Would you mind choosing a look for me too? If I have a different one, then that's two posts we can boost.'

'Good plan.' Tilly looked at me for a moment, studying me.

'Sweetie.' I laughed. 'You know what I look like. You sit opposite me every day!'

She flapped her hands. 'Oh, I know, I know, but I've never really pictured you in a wedding dress for some reason.'

'Well, that makes two of us.'

That made her pause. 'Really?'

'Certainly not at the moment. Which reminds me, Alex is coming round later after his shift so I need to make sure all the wedding-y stuff is out of sight. I don't want him thinking I've got ideas.' Charlie's comment about Alex and weddings was still lodged at the back of my brain.

'He wouldn't think that. You've only been going out a little while.'

'No. Probably not. But still.'

She thought about it for a moment. 'I do have a friend who's kind of obsessed with weddings. She's loving these posts, by the way. We've tried telling her it might not be such a great idea letting blokes see a tonne of wedding magazines piled up, but she says she's not planning anything. She just loves looking at them.'

'Then she should enjoy them. It's harmless enough and they are lovely.'

'See, I know that. And you know that. But men? Well, like you just said about making sure all of this is gone before Alex sees it. Innocent things can incite panic.'

'True. Right. OK. I'm going to get back to these emails. If you can get all the stuff together for both looks, then we can make sure everything's in place for when Charlie gets here. I don't want to keep him too long. I'm sure he's got better things to be doing. He just felt guilty for nodding off on the sofa, daft thing.'

'I don't think he'd have volunteered to do it if he objected that much, Libs.'

I looked up from my screen. 'The only reason I'm even friends with Charlie is because he was forced into coming to look at my accounts! This wouldn't be the first time he'd done something he felt he ought to or got coerced into doing.'

'Libby. He's six foot five and weighs about the same as a small tank. He's hardly a pushover.'

I returned to my screen and opened the first email awaiting reply. 'Physically no, but he's a sweetheart. It doesn't matter what size you are when you're a softie.'

'Oh, he can look after himself if he needs to, I'm sure. Right, let's find you a kick-ass make-up look to go with your wedding dress.'

Tapping away at my keyboard, I laughed at Tilly's phrasing and left her to it.

* * *

'Perfect!' Tilly stepped back from fluffing the veil and turned me to the mirror.

I didn't say anything.

'You're supposed to be a bride. A happy bride. It's not an arranged marriage to some stuffy Victorian banker.'

'Sorry. Yes. It just feels a bit weird.'

Tilly began spinning around the room, reminding me of a Disney princess, and I was more than half expecting her to start singing and calling birds from the window. Eyeing the large seagull that had just landed on the rail of my balcony, I sincerely hoped not.

The doorbell chimed and I hiked up the dress, paranoid about damaging it as I made my way to answer it.

'Afternoon. There's a parcel—' The postman stopped as he looked up and saw my outfit. 'Oh! Umm, congratulations. I'd better not keep you. I just need a signature.' He held out the machine for me to sign.

'It's not real,' I said. 'It's for a blog thing.'

'Oh. OK. Right.' He gave me a smile that showed he didn't understand in the slightest and returned to his rounds. I closed the door.

'Is that Charlie?' Tilly came out from the bedroom where we'd prepared the 'set' for the shoot.

'No. Just the postman. Who now thinks I'm some weird and desperate woman who dresses up in weddings gowns on a summer afternoon for no reason.'

'I'm sure he doesn't.'

'You didn't see his face.'

'Ah, who cares?'

I stood for a moment. She had a point. 'That's true. I'm going to get some drinks. Back in a sec.'

The door chimed again and Tilly answered it as I disappeared into the kitchen. I heard Charlie's deep tones rumble through. Tilly said something and he laughed. I appreciated her helping to make this a less awkward experience for all of us. That said, it seemed I might be the only one who was feeling awkward as I heard Charlie and Tilly laugh again. Best to just get it over with and hope that it didn't show too much in the photos. I put the three glasses on a tray, and plopped a couple of eco-friendly straws in two of them to help keep our make-up intact, then picked it up and entered the living room.

'Hello, sleepyhead.'

'Hi, Libs,' Charlie replied. He was crouched on the ground, pulling his gear out of his camera bag. Standing, he turned and made a step towards me, before stopping abruptly.

'Bloody hell.'

I raised my eyebrows.

'Sorry.' He shook his head. 'I just... I didn't expect... umm.' A hint of colour was forming around the collar of his blue and white checked shirt, altogether making up quite a patriotic mix.

'OK. But was it a good bloody hell or an oh my God bloody hell? Because if it was the latter I'd rather know now before posting it online for a tonne of people to have the same reaction.'

'No, it was good. Honestly.' Charlie seemed to have composed himself and was back to fiddling with his camera lens. 'Just took me a bit by surprise.'

I flipped out a hand to Tilly. 'See what I mean? I'm not even going out with him and he's freaked. Now you know why I can't have Alex seeing any of this.'

'I'm not freaked. I've just never seen you in a wedding dress. Although I think you'd be better off with a bouquet than a bar tray.'

I put the drinks down. Tilly was standing near Charlie, swishing the dress she had on. I still wasn't convinced a song was entirely out of the question. Best to get this done as soon as possible.

'Let's put some music on,' I suggested.

'Great idea!' Tilly agreed, scooting past Charlie to her computer. A moment later, Little Mix began filling the room, and Tilly was off dancing around. Charlie turned his head to me, both amused and bemused. I shrugged, a wide smile breaking on my face as Tilly caught my hand, pulling me along as she danced past me.

A couple of hours later, we'd both had three changes of dress and make-up looks and were pretty much winding down. It had been a lot more fun than I'd anticipated. It was hard not to be infected with Tilly's excitement, not only for the shoot, but also for her impending real wedding. I'd temporarily forgotten my hang-ups and just relaxed, enjoying the music, the laughter, and the company. I'd even forgiven Charlie for sneaking a shot when Tilly had insisted on making me wear a garter and I'd bent to adjust it. My protestations were countered with his and Tilly's claims that he was supposed to be capturing the feel of getting ready for a wedding.

'It's not a real wedding.'

'And I'm not a real wedding photographer, so that's perfect.'

I stuck my tongue out at him. And he snapped a picture of that too.

'I'm beginning to think encouraging you in this hobby might not have been one of my better decisions.'

Charlie widened his eyes and did a maniacal laugh. 'You've created a monster!' he cried, scooping me up with his free hand, and swinging me round.

'I think I might have!' I laughed, happy to see Charlie so relaxed. 'Now put me down, you big lump!' Charlie's arm had wrapped itself under my bum and my feet were now dangling some way above the floor. I steadied myself with one hand on his shoulder as the other rested on his chest. As I brought my gaze up from studying how far down the floor was, it connected with Charlie's.

'You're looking at me funny.'

'I was just thinking that you're going to make someone a bloody gorgeous bride one day.'

I made a dismissive sound.

'What?'

'Could you put me down, please?' I bumped my hand on his chest, but he didn't move.

'You can't argue with me. I have the photographic evidence.' He wiggled the camera he still held in his other hand.

'I appreciate the flattery but I'm pretty sure this is the last time I'll be wearing a wedding dress.'

The smile faded as his gaze rested on me for a moment. Then, gently, he lowered me to the floor, ensuring I was steady before letting go entirely.

'What makes you say that?'

'Because I just don't really see myself getting married.'

'Why not?'

'I just don't.'

'I didn't know you were against marriage. Isn't this all a little bit hypocritical, then?'

'No! I'm not against marriage at all. I think it's wonderful. I just don't think it's for me.'

'Why not?' he asked again.

I shifted my weight. 'Would it be all right if we had this discussion when I'm not wearing a wedding dress? It seems a little incongruous.'

He nodded. 'I agree. Do you need a hand to get out of it?' He made a movement as if to turn me around to see the back of my dress.

'Oh, yeah. Because that's going to happen,' I said, taking a step further away.

'What? If I was Amy, you'd let me help.'

I fixed him with a look, trying to ignore how attractive he was when laughter filled those clear blue eyes. 'The fact is you are not Amy.'

'But we're friends. Good friends.'

'True.'

'So, what's the problem?'

'There is no problem. But the fact is that I'm not about to stand in front of any man right at this moment, good friend or not, in a basque and stockings!'

Charlie's face changed. 'Basque and...' His patriotic colourway returned, and he gave a quick little nod before mumbling something about needing a drink and heading off to the kitchen.

26

'God, he's adorable,' Tilly stated quietly once he'd left the room. 'I'm still amazed he's not seeing anyone.'

I threw a glance towards the kitchen and then looked back at her. 'I think he's looking for The One. He's done all the other stuff and is ready to settle down.'

'And he can't find someone wanting to be that? Bloody hell, I could get him a whole line up by this evening.'

'I guess it's not so easy when you're shy like him.'

'He must meet people all the time through work.'

'I guess. I don't know. He's never mentioned anyone.'

'Maybe he's just super fussy.'

'Maybe. His parents seem really lovely and happy. I think he's holding that up as a benchmark.'

'I can't see him staying single for all that long, though. Can you?'

From the corner of my eye, I saw Charlie returning to the living room, his colour back to a light golden tan.

'All right?'

'Absolutely. I thought you'd be out of that. Or have you got comfortable in it now?'

'I'm just about to go and change.'

'Shame. Suits you.'

'So, I do the bride bit, and you do the blushing?' I teased him with a smile, which he returned.

'Ah, that's not fair. You took me off guard. You can't just throw out words like basque and stockings without warning a man!'

'He does have a point, Libs. I mentioned it once casually over dinner ages ago, and Sam nearly choked.'

'Right. Noted. Though I must say I fail to see how it might possibly come up again in the future.'

Charlie shrugged. 'Never say never.'

I shook my head and made to turn back towards my bedroom.

'I'm assuming you don't want any shots of you in the—'

'No! Thank you. Blimey, you really are out of your shell today, aren't you?' I laughed.

'Must be the company.'

Tilly grinned and gave him a squeeze, which he returned. It was good to see him relaxing. He'd seemed not only tired yesterday but tense. Mucking about with us and doing something he clearly enjoyed seemed to have helped him shake off whatever it was, letting his personality shine through. As Tilly said, it was unlikely that Charlie Richmond was going to be single for long, especially once this side of his personality got to be generally known.

'Right, I'm going to change and—' The doorbell chimed, interrupting me. 'Flippin' heck, it's been like Piccadilly Circus here today,' I said, pulling open the door and coming face to face with Alex.

'Bloody hell.'

'I wish people would stop saying that to me,' I said quietly, taking in the look of shock and slight panic on Alex's face. 'Hi. I didn't think your shift finished until later.'

'I... err... I swapped with a mate as a favour.' He was still looking me up and down.

'Do you want to come in?'

Alex brought his gaze up to meet mine, and I could tell he wasn't entirely sure about the answer to that question.

'Hi, mate.' Charlie came to stand beside me and took in Alex's face, and mine. 'The girls had a shoot to do for the blog on bridal stuff. I was giving them a hand.'

'For the blog?' Alex repeated.

'Yep.'

I saw the relief flood in. I knew I wasn't the only one who had spotted it and for some reason I suddenly felt a little bit ridiculous.

'I need to change. Charlie, can you...?' I wasn't sure what I wanted Charlie to do to be honest but I did know I needed to get away from Alex for a moment and get out of this dress.

When I returned a short while later, having changed into a lace-edged vest top and a floaty cotton maxi skirt, Alex looked up and smiled. No one missed the relieved expression on his face.

'Better?' I asked.

'Much.'

He stood and came up to me, sliding his arms around my waist and planting a quick kiss on my lips. 'Sorry about earlier. Just caught me by surprise.'

I shrugged it off. 'Don't worry about it. Purely for PR.' I gave a quick smile that felt a little tighter than perhaps it should have done. And then, because I was completely incapable of not saying anything when a situation was bothering me, I turned my face up to his and raised an eyebrow. 'It might have been nice if you hadn't looked quite so appalled though. Not exactly a boost to a girl's ego, you know.'

'Sorry. Like I said, you just... surprised me.'

'Charlie wasn't exactly expecting it either but he didn't look like he wanted to run off screaming.'

Alex grinned and pulled me a little closer, apparently enjoying what he viewed as banter.

'You're not dating Charlie.'

I leant back in his arms a little so that he got the full benefit of the look I fixed him with. 'You're cute, but you're not that cute. I've no plans to run off with you just yet.'

'Now who's bruising egos?'

'Ah ah!' I waved my finger at him. 'You can't have it both ways.'

Alex released an arm from around my waist and caught my waggling finger with it. Gently, he lifted it to his lips and kissed it. His eyes were on mine, shining with mischief and the unmistake-able look of wanting, as he kept it there. I knew where this was going, and, judging by the way my pulse had kicked up, I was pretty sure that Alex knew that I knew what he had planned. He kissed my finger again. His lips lingered and began to move, gently. My eyes widened and Alex grinned. I wiggled and pushed off his chest, stepping back.

Across the room, I saw Tilly and Charlie peering in deep concentration at the screen of his laptop. Tilly was making 'oohing' noises, and genuinely seemed to be engrossed, but I wasn't so sure about Charlie. I saw him lift his hand to the back of his head and give two scratches. His nervous tic that something was off. I'd noticed from early on that he did this whenever he wasn't sure about something or felt uncomfortable.

'How did they come out?' I asked, moving away from Alex to cross the room and peer upside down over the top of the laptop screen.

Tilly looked up, a big smile on her face. 'They're amazing! Charlie's amazing!' She laughed, squeezing his bicep, which admittedly took both hands.

Charlie flicked a glance to her, and gave a little wiggle of his head, smiling.

I scooted round and squashed up next to her to take a look. Tilly was right. The photos were fabulous! He'd taken plenty when we hadn't been aware, which for someone of Charlie's size, making us forget that he was there taking pictures, was a pretty good testimonial to his skills in this particular area of photography. The posed ones were gorgeous, but it was the candids I absolutely loved. And, of course, the silly selfie of the three of us, with Tilly and I standing on the bed, just to get up to the same height as Charlie, one of us at each of his shoulders. That had to be my favourite.

'That one's definitely going on the blog!' I said, pointing to it.

Charlie looked mildly horrified. 'What?'

'That one. I love it!'

'Me too!' Tilly added. 'It's fabulous! People love "behind the scenes" stuff.'

Charlie remained unconvinced. I looked over to where Alex was reading on his tablet. Sports news, if I had to hazard a guess. Normally he was pretty interested in his friend's photography, but I don't think he'd quite yet recovered from having me open the door to him decked out in full wedding regalia. Pictures of me wearing a big white dress probably wasn't anything he was in a hurry to see just now. But I needed his back up on this.

'Alex, what do you think?'

'About what?' he said, his eyes still on the tablet.

'This photo of Charlie. Tilly and I think it should go on the blog. Charlie disagrees.'

'What's the photo?'

'If you come over here, you'll see,' I replied, with studied patience.

Alex raised his eyes to me and took in the innocent look on my face. A grin slid onto his own. He laid the tablet down on the table and crossed the room, walking behind the couch to look over our shoulders at the image under discussion. Much to his relief, I imagined, there wasn't a whole lot of wedding dress on display as it was mostly our head and shoulders in shot. He laid a hand on his friend's shoulder.

'Sorry, mate, I'm with the girls. That's a great shot. People will love it.'

Charlie watched as Alex made his way back to his seat, snagging his tablet on the way.

'Some help you are.'

'What?' Alex asked. 'What's the problem?'

'I'm just not comfortable with having my photo on the blog.'

'What's wrong with my blog?'

'What? Nothing! Nothing, at all. I just meant... well, I'm just not.'

'He doesn't like having his photo taken. So, the thought of having a picture of him somewhere that a tonne of people might see it is frightening the crap out of him. That about cover it?' Alex asked.

Charlie gave him a look. 'I'm not frightened. It's a question of comfort level.'

'Oh, Charlie, mate. You take a sickeningly good photo, and you're flanked by two hot women. What's there to be uncomfortable about?'

I saw Charlie waver.

'Look. I'll get the blog post ready and let you see it before it goes up. If you're still not happy with the photo being out in the big wide world, and women drooling over their screens at our new photographer, then you can veto it and I'll take it off.'

'What are you taking off?' Alex asked, suddenly drawn out of his sports magazine.

I rolled my eyes at him.

'Behave. Or I'll go and put one of those wedding dresses back on.'

He made a zipping motion with his mouth and settled back on the other sofa.

'I want to fiddle a bit with these anyway,' Charlie said, 'but I can get them back to you later tomorrow, if that works?'

'Yep. That's fine. Amy's got plans with Marcus and this one's working,' I said, pointing at Alex, 'so I'll probably be working anyway.'

'OK.'

'But don't feel you have to rush, or anything. And don't you dare delete that photo of the three of us!'

'I promise.' He held up his hands in resignation.

'We're going to get so many comments once they take a look at him, you know that, don't you?' Tilly said.

I grinned. Charlie's horrified look was back in place.

'Yep!'

'I... err...'

'Don't worry, Charlie. Who knows? Maybe this mock wedding shoot might end up finding you a real bride after all.' I did a Disney Princess hand clasp and rocked side to side, fluttering my fake eyelashes.

He gave me a tight smile, but I could see the humour in his eyes. 'Smart arse.'

I pointed to myself, and did a wide-eyed 'me?' action.

Charlie raised his eyebrows, did a quick nod and pointed at me. 'Did your previous photographer die of thirst, by the way?'

I took the hint, and headed out to the kitchen to boil the kettle. I'd just finished filling it when the doorbell rang.

'Can someone get that for me, please?' I called as I began pulling out mugs and spoons.

I heard the door open and close and a male voice, which was shortly followed by a high-pitched wail.

'What? He can't!'

27

I put the tin of teabags down on the worktop and rushed back into the living room. Sam, Tilly's fiancé, stood near the door and Tilly was pacing up and down. She was currently on a path heading away from me. Alex and Charlie hadn't moved. Alex still had his head buried in his tablet, whilst Charlie was doing something that made him look busy but I suspected otherwise. He'd already scratched the back of his neck twice now.

'Hi, Sam.' I walked over and gave him a hug. 'Everything all right?' His expression, and Tilly's frantic pacing suggested that things weren't exactly tickety boo but I wasn't sure what else to say.

'Things are most definitely not all right!' Tilly turned sharply and began to pace in the opposite direction. 'My wedding is going to be a disaster!'

'It's not going to be a disaster. We'll sort something out,' Sam soothed.

'No! We won't! Do you know why? Because we're supposed to be getting married in three weeks and now we don't have a photographer!'

'That hardly makes it a disaster,' Sam replied.

Eeek!

I made to step across but too late. Tilly was off!

'Not to you, maybe! But this is supposed to be my big day! It's supposed to be perfect! All of it! With a photographer there to record Every Single Perfect Moment!'

'I thought it was supposed to be our day.' Sam frowned.

Oh, Sam, please stop talking.

Tilly turned and opened her mouth but I got there first.

'Look!' I said, cutting her off. 'Do you have your wedding book here?'

Tilly had been hauling the enormous file around for months. It was filled with contacts, cuttings, pictures, notes, recipes, and pretty much anything else that she had ever seen, or any thought that she had ever had, in connection with this wedding.

My assistant, distracted by my intervention, closed her mouth and looked at me.

'Yes.'

'Good. Go and grab it, then.'

Tilly looked at me for a moment, then walked over to her bag, and hauled the file out. I motioned to her to bring it over to the sofa and pulled her down next to me. The beautiful make-up that we had so carefully applied for the photo shoot was now streaked with tears and her false eyelashes were looking as though, given the chance, they might well make a break for freedom.

'He said he'd sorted the double booking out,' she said, her voice cracking.

Seeing my bouncy, fabulous assistant so unhappy made me want to get hold of that photographer and crack something else.

'I know,' I said, reaching out and stroking her hair. 'I know. But, like Sam said, we'll get something sorted. There's five good brains here. I'm sure we can come up with a great plan between us.'

She nodded, not looking at me. A tear plopped from the end of her chin onto my lap, swiftly followed by another.

'Oh, now, come here. It's all going to be fine. Just perfect,' I said, wrapping her in my arms and rocking her as she cried. 'You'll see.'

My head was resting against Tilly's but I lifted my eyes to meet Charlie's gaze. He was still sitting at the other end of the sofa.

'Do you think you boys could make some tea, please?'

The English and Irish sides of my heritage often differed but in times of crisis, they converged perfectly. What was most definitely needed here was tea.

Charlie stood, seeming pleased at being given something to do, rounded up Sam and dragged Alex into the kitchen on his way. I heard movement and talking, and soon laughter coming from their direction, which I was glad of. Distracting Sam was a good start for the boys.

When they returned, clearly having also raided my cupboards, judging by the assortment of biscuits accompanying the mugs of tea, Tilly had calmed a little and we'd tidied up her face and hair. She gave a glance at Sam. I scooted up and touched his arm as I moved past, encouraging him to go and sit by his fiancée.

'Sorry about earlier,' she said.

'It's all right.' He dropped a kiss on the top of her head and wrapped an arm around her shoulders.

I took a sip of my tea and slid Tilly's book onto my knees. Flipping to the 'photography' section, I found several lists.

'What do all these mean?'

Tilly peered over to see what I was looking at. 'Oh. Those were categorised in to how badly I wanted them.'

'OK. So, this person was your second choice, and so on?' I said, pointing a French manicured nail at a name on one of the lists.

'Yep.'

'Right. So, what about ringing these, and seeing if any of them have that day free still?'

'I don't think they will, but we could try. If you don't mind? I mean...' she glanced at the clock on the wall '... I am supposed to still be working.'

I waved my hand. 'Priorities.'

To be honest, I didn't think they would have space either. We were hitting prime wedding season and anyone worth their SIM card would have been booked long ago. Finishing our tea, Tilly and I split her final choice list into two and started making phone calls. Half an hour later, we'd been through all of them. Every single one was booked. I'd had a couple promise to call me back if anything changed but I didn't hold out much hope. The tears now shining again in Tilly's eyes showed me that she didn't either.

'Are there any more that you liked?'

She swiped her hand under her nose, and I leant and grabbed the box of tissues from the side of the sofa and passed them over.

Taking one, she wiped her eyes and nose haphazardly, then shook her head.

'All the others we considered just didn't seem to have the sort of look we were going for. They were all really staged, and formal. We want a more relaxed kind of feel, as well as some traditional shots. Ones that really capture our personalities.' Tilly flicked through a few of the pages in her file. 'It seems a waste to spend so much money on a photographer that you don't share the same aesthetic with. I think I'd rather just put those funds towards the honeymoon.' She let out a sigh, before continuing. 'I think the best thing to do is to send an email to everyone who is coming, explaining the problem and asking if, after the wedding, they can send us any photos they think are good. I'll set up a special email address for it, and then we can choose ones from them. Some are bound to be great!' I could see that Tilly was doing her best to pep talk herself more than any of us.

'Sounds like a great idea!' Alex said.

'I think so too!' Tilly smiled at him. Alex returned it and then shot a covert look to me and Charlie. No, we weren't buying it either.

'Or... I could maybe take some for you?'

Everyone turned to Charlie. A hint of colour began to show around his neck. He stuck a finger in his collar and pulled at it a little. Bearing in mind it was an open-necked casual shirt, the quirk was kind of adorable. 'I mean, if you really can't find anyone else.'

'You'd do that?'

Charlie nodded. His glance flicked briefly to me and I read the panic in it. Somewhere deep inside me, I felt an inexplicable shift.

'I mean, I've never done anything like this before so I feel it's only fair to warn you that the shots might not be great. But if you show me the kind of thing you want, I'd be happy to do what I could.'

I watched Charlie for a moment and surmised that him being 'happy' about it was probably an enormous overstatement. Alex caught my eye and I could see the same thought reflected in his expression.

'Of course! We could do that, couldn't we, Sam? Of course!' Tilly gushed. She jumped up and rushed at Charlie, bumping into him with a huge hug. 'Thank you thank you thank you!' Charlie's eyebrows rose in surprise and the corners of his eyes crinkled in laughter as he returned the hug. I saw Tilly's shoulders start shaking as tears of relief overtook her.

Charlie tightened the hug. 'It'll be all right,' he said quietly. 'I promise.'

Tilly and Sam arranged to meet up with Charlie, and show him ideas for the sort of look they were going for, and then I sent her home. It had been a pretty emotional afternoon for them both and I could see Tilly's telltale tics of when she got tired beginning to show. It was funny what you picked up when you worked so closely with someone every day.

'I'd better be going too,' Alex said as the door closed behind them.

'You have to help me!' Charlie sidestepped, blocking Alex's exit. 'I can't corral a bunch of wedding guests! I'll never get the shots she wants!'

Alex pulled his head back and shook it, confusion showing on his face. 'Then why did you offer to do it?'

'Because the poor girl is about to get married and has no photographer. And she was so upset and crying! I couldn't bear it!'

I felt the shift again.

Alex laughed. 'Mate,' was all he said.

'You have to help me,' Charlie said again, his tone definite. 'You're the one with experience in crowd control.'

Alex smiled and slapped him on the back. 'Fine. I'll help you. But I'm just saying now, if one of the bridesmaids is hot...'

I cleared my throat.

Charlie and Alex both looked at me.

'Joking, I promise.' Alex wrapped an arm around me and squeezed. 'Just trying to wind up the knight in shining armour here. I promise,' he said again, whispering it this time, close to my ear, his breath warm on my skin. He let go and dug in his pocket for his phone, bringing up the calendar. 'What day is it again?'

I told Alex the date. He scrolled through and his face lost its smile.

'I'm on duty. Sorry, mate, I can't do it.'

I frowned. 'But I thought you'd booked it off when I told you about it a few weeks ago? When I asked if you wanted to come with me?'

He threw me a sheepish look. 'I kind of forgot.'

I nodded. 'Right.'

'Oh, God!' Charlie sat down heavily on the sofa and dropped his head into his hands. 'Why did I say I'd do it? What was I thinking?' He pulled his hands down over his face.

I sat next to him.

'You said you'd do it because you're a good person and because you can do it. And you're also much better than that loser she hired in the first place!'

'Libby.' He shook his head. 'You know hordes of people aren't really my thing.'

'I do know that. So, I can help, if you want.'

'Really?'

'Of course. Besides—' I threw a glance at Alex, eyebrow raised '—my date for it cancelled on me anyway.'

'There we are, then. Problem solved,' Alex said, holding up his hands. 'I'd really better be going if I'm going to get to work on time.'

'I'll see you out.'

'I'm really sorry about the wedding thing,' Alex said when we'd stepped outside my front door to say goodbye in private. 'I guess I just got distracted with everything going on at the moment.'

'It's all right.'

'Let me make it up to you.' Sliding his arms around my waist, he pulled me into his warm, hard body. 'Dinner. Friday night. And I have the whole weekend off. Whatever you want to do.' He gave me a look that told me exactly what he wanted to do.

'Sure you don't want to find a hot bridesmaid?'

He grinned. 'Sorry, that just slipped out.'

'Old habits die hard, eh?'

'Something like that,' he said softly, as he bent his head. His lips brushed my throat and both of us stopped thinking about bridesmaids.

* * *

I dropped my earring for the fourth time in a row, and realised just how nervous I was about this evening as I glanced over at my friend.

'So, tonight's the night?' Amy giggled, stopping in on her way home from work. She was sitting on my bed, watching me move hangers about as I tried to decide on what to wear.

I made a point of pretending not to know what she was talking about.

'What do you think of this?' I asked, pulling out a floaty summer dress that seemed to chime perfectly with the warmth of the evening.

Amy ran the delicate fabric through her fingers. 'Hmm, it is lovely. But it doesn't really say "rip me off and sweep me away into ecstasy".'

I fixed her with a look. 'Sweep me away into ecstasy?'

She shrugged. 'I've got a very dramatic book on the go at the moment. There's a lot of that going on in it.'

I raised an eyebrow. 'I see.' I hung the dress back up. 'Well, I'm kind of glad it doesn't say rip me off because it cost a flippin' fortune. Things could get expensive!'

Amy grinned. 'Ooh! Sounds like you have some definite plans for this weekend...'

I pulled out another choice and held it up in front of her face, ignoring the insinuations of lengthy romps currently catapulting about in her head.

'What about this one, then?'

'Now that,' she said, 'is perfect.'

28

'I'm going to be a bit late,' Alex said, almost before I'd finished saying hello. He sounded a little out of breath and distracted and I could hear noise in the background over the line. 'Sorry. I know it's bad timing but something's kicked off. Can I meet you at the restaurant instead?'

'Of course. I'll just get the bus in and meet you there.'

'Great. I'm really sorry. Hopefully I won't be too much later than we planned.' I heard more noises in the background before he came back to me. 'Got to go. I'll see you later, babe.'

I made to return the sentiment but he'd already hung up.

Alex's shifts often overran so I wasn't worried. Thanks to everything going on in both of our lives right now, we'd actually had far fewer dates than most people who'd been going out for over two months would normally have done. I'd soon learned that his time-keeping wasn't always the best, thanks to his job, and had adjusted around it. It wasn't his fault and so it didn't really become a problem. But tonight was supposed to be special. As Amy had hinted at, not so subtly, tonight might well be 'the night'. Alex was off for a couple of days and, knowing that, I'd arranged to not work this weekend either, even though there were still a billion things I could be doing. This weekend was going to be about relaxing, being together, about us. That was the plan anyway.

Two hours later I was still sitting at the restaurant. Alone. It was a small, intimate affair, which, when there with a romantic partner, made it perfect. However, sitting at a table laid for two, when there was clearly only one of you, merely gave all the other diners a perfect view of you being stood up. The owner had kindly replaced the breadsticks after I'd gone through the first lot, but I hesitated in eating too many more. I had a feeling that his sympathetic refills might end up with me eating something close to my own body-weight in bread if I wasn't careful.

I'd had one text from Alex. It told me that he was still planning to make it, so I'd carried on sitting there. But after another hour with nothing from him, I was thoroughly fed up and close to the edge of livid. Even though I knew it was likely something out of his control, I was still the one sitting there like an idiot. I motioned the waiter over and requested the bill for the two glasses of wine I'd had. Glancing briefly at the owner, I saw a look exchanged between him and the server.

'There is no charge, madame.'

'Oh, no, really. I must pay for those.'

'No charge,' he repeated, smiling.

Horrified, I suddenly felt tears spring to my eyes. Their well-intentioned kindness was making me feel so much worse.

'Thank you,' I said, just so that he would leave and give me a chance to regain my composure. I'd had a stinking headache for the last half hour and now I just wanted to get home. I left a ten-pound note tucked under my empty wine glass as a large tip in lieu of official payment and, aware of the surreptitious glances of other diners, made my way to the door. I kept my head up and made it outside. The sticky warmth of the evening air hit me after the controlled coolness of the little restaurant and I made my way down the street. A flash to my right caught my eye and I turned to face the sea. Out on the horizon another flash lit up the water, followed by a far-off rumble.

'Perfect.'

The darkening sky blotted out the stars and did a good job of reflecting my mood. Making a couple of turns, I headed towards the bus stop and checked the computerised arrivals board. There was one for the marina due in four minutes.

The rain now fell heavily from the sky as the wind whipped at it, the bus shelter's roof proving insufficient protection from the forty-five-degree-angle torrent. I pulled my trench coat tighter around me, having long since given up any hope of keeping my hair or legs dry. I squinted against the rain at the arrivals board. It still said four minutes until my bus, even though I had now been standing there for ten. I gritted my teeth and silently cursed, turning to look up the road for my errant bus. As I did so, a minibus drove past, sending a plume of muddy puddle into the air. I jumped back, managing to avoid the worst of it. The van did a double toot, and I returned a very unladylike, but thoroughly deserved, hand signal. When I then heard another beep, I spun round, prepared to give them the same treatment, dropping my hand as I recognised the sleek shape now pulling to a stop in front of me. The window slid down silently and Charlie's frowning face looked out at me.

'Libs? What are you doing here?'

'Waiting for a train. What do you think?'

Charlie said nothing. I ran my hand over my eyes, and back over my now soaked hair. My shoulders sagged a little. 'I'm sorry. I didn't mean to snap at you.'

'Are you heading home?' he asked.

'I'm trying to.'

'Come on, get in.'

I threw a quick glance up at the board again. Still four minutes.

'Are you sure?'

'Of course. Get in before you're entirely soaked.'

I quickly ran round to the passenger side that was now a little open, thanks to Charlie leaning across, and slid into the warm, comfortable, quiet interior of the luxury car.

'Thank you. My bus seems to be stuck in a time warp somewhere.' I tried to smile. By the look on Charlie's face, he wasn't buying it. His eyes lingered on me a few moments longer and then, checking his mirrors, he pulled back out into the traffic.

I kept my eyes forward, but in my peripheral vision I could see Charlie casting glances at me. 'I'm assuming you don't want to talk about it.'

'Not much to say. Besides, you're Alex's friend and I don't want to put you in the middle of anything.'

'I'm your friend too, Libby. Don't forget that.'

I swallowed and then gave a quick nod. 'I know. Thank you.'

We drove for a few more minutes. 'Did you have a row?'

'No. For us to have had a row, both of us would have needed to be there.'

Charlie pulled up at a red light and faced me. 'He stood you up?' In the dim light of the car's interior, I could see the tension in his jaw and heard the studied control in the question. It wasn't a side I'd seen before. From what I'd seen of Charlie in the months I'd known him, he always played his emotions close to his chest. Terribly British. But, for whatever reason, tonight that façade had slipped a little.

'Yes.' I saw his brow furrow more deeply. 'But so far as I can make out it was a work thing. I think.'

'I see.' Those two words were loaded as the light changed and we headed closer to my flat.

'Charlie. I'm fine. Really. Please don't say anything. I'll handle this myself.'

'I told him to look after you.'

'What?' I could hear the sharpness in my tone.

Charlie lifted one hand from the wheel, scratched his neck twice then let it rest back on the soft leather.

'Don't be like that.'

'I'll be exactly how I want to be! And I don't need you telling people how they should and shouldn't act with me!'

'Look, Libby. Alex is a player. Always has been. I didn't want you to just be another notch on his bedpost!'

'It's not about what you want, Charlie! It's what I want and I'm quite capable of looking after myself, thank you! I'm not looking for anything deep and meaningful like you are. I've seen what happens. Who's to say that Alex wasn't going to be another notch on *my* bedpost?'

He didn't reply but the tension had spread to his whole body now. His fingers gripped the wheel as a thick, uncomfortable atmosphere settled around us. Suddenly I felt worse than I had all night.

'Charlie...'

'No. It's fine. You're right. It's up to you. I shouldn't have said anything.'

'I know you meant well and—'

'Libby. As you said, this is between you and Alex.' He pulled into the apartment's parking area and put the car into neutral. 'I hope everything works out the way you want it to.'

I felt tears stinging my eyes and I knew they were more for the fight with Charlie than anything Alex had, or hadn't, done. 'I don't think there is really anything to work out now.' I shrugged, the movement jostling one of the tears free.

Charlie flexed his fingers on the wheel and then gripped it again. After a moment, he dropped one hand and switched off the engine.

'I'll walk you to your door.'

'No. It's all right. Really. I'm just…'

Charlie turned his face to mine. 'Oh, Libs. Please don't cry. Especially if you're not going to allow me to tear him off a strip.'

I shook my head. 'I'm not crying over him. I don't think.' My temples were throbbing and I pressed a hand to one side. 'It's just one of those days. I don't feel quite right and now I've fallen out with you, which makes me feel worse than any of it.'

Charlie's hand cupped the side of my face, his thumb gently brushing another loose tear away. 'You don't get rid of me that easily.' He leaned over and kissed the top of my head. 'Come on. You need to get inside. You really do look a bit peaky.'

'You don't need to get wet. I'll run.'

Charlie ignored me and got out of the car. A few quick strides and he was beside me, his hand out ready to assist my exit. We half ran to the main entrance of the flats, collars up, vainly trying to keep the driving rain out.

I plugged my key in the lock and stepped inside.

'Do you want to come in?'

Charlie shook his head. 'No. Thank you. You look done for.' He bent and hugged me. 'Get some rest.'

I nodded against his shoulder. Pulling back, he gave me a smile but I could still see the tension in his jaw.

'I'm OK, Charlie. Really.'

He nodded once, gave a tight smile and wave then turned and began walking away, his back straight, long strides taking him quickly out of sight. I pushed the door closed, threw the lock and engaged the safety chain. Pulling off my coat and kicking off my shoes, I headed to the bathroom to grab a towel for my hair. Drying it off, I padded slowly to my bedroom, dropped the towel and unhooked my dressing gown from the back of the door. Snuggling into its cosy warmth, I wrapped it tight around me over my clothes and headed back into the living room. Picking up the remote, I flicked the TV on and flopped down on the sofa.

It was another two hours before I heard from Alex.

✉ Are you at home?

I looked at my phone and rolled my eyes. Which did nothing for the headache that had only increased in intensity since I'd got back.

✉ Yes. The restaurant didn't allow overnight camping.

Sarcasm might be the lowest form of wit but, frankly, I was long past caring.

✉ I really am sorry.

I didn't reply. Partly because I felt like crap and also because looking at the phone's screen was making me feel worse. It beeped again.

✉ Can I come round?

Wow. Seriously? I didn't reply.

A minute later, the phone rang. Alex's smiling face showed on the screen. Ignoring it would make all this a much bigger deal than it was. And the truth was I had a feeling that something had changed. Maybe it was the fact that this was supposed to be a great weekend, a special weekend, and things were already conspiring to make it the opposite. The rumbling storm outside and the rain pelting against the balcony window all just added to my feeling of something being off. Dad and Matt had always scoffed at the gut feelings Mum and I had had. But they more often than not turned out to mean something. Except we'd called them 'heart' feelings because we thought the phrase follow your heart always sounded nicer than follow your gut. I had one of those tonight. And I knew it wasn't just a case of too many breadsticks. I answered the call.

'Hello.'

'I'm down in the car park. Let me come up, please.'

'My car park?'

'Yes.'

'What are you doing down there?'

'Right now, getting wet. I just... think we need to talk.'

'Alex...'

'Come on, please. I won't stay long, I promise.'

My heart instinct got stronger. I told him to come up. Flicking off the television, I went to the door, opened it and leant against the jamb, waiting for Alex to appear. A moment later he turned the corner at the end of the hall, dripping from the rain.

'Oh my God!' Paler than usual with shadows under his eyes, his handsome features looked drawn and tired. His right eye was swollen, the bruise surrounding it beginning to bloom outwards. I stood back to let him in.

'Please tell me Charlie didn't do that.'

Alex screwed his face up momentarily. 'Of course not. Why would he?'

'I... I just...'

'Oh. Right. Of course. I should have known he'd be the first one you'd call. I guess I'm in the doghouse with him then too.'

I glared at him, stung. 'Excuse me?'

'I came up to explain that I was late because—'

'Late? You were a bit more than late! You didn't even show up!'

'I'm here, aren't I?'

'We weren't having dinner here! And now is not five hours ago!'

'So, you rang your knight in shining armour instead?'

'No! I was waiting at the bus stop in the pouring rain and he drove past.'

'Whereupon you told him your tale of woe?'

'What the hell is wrong with you? You're the one that stood me up and yet it's me that seems to be in the wrong!'

Silence settled heavily between us. Alex turned, his hand on the front door catch.

'I'm sorry,' he said, his voice lower and softer. 'I didn't realise you were actually in bed.'

I looked down at the dressing gown I was wearing. 'I wasn't.'

He turned back and I gave a quick flash to show that I was still dressed underneath.

'Nice dress.'

'Thanks,' I replied.

We stood there.

'So, what happened to your eye?'

'A lucky swing from a bunch of troublemakers.'

'Do you need ice on it?'

'I will, when I get home.' He met my eyes and the meaning behind that sentence was understood, if unsaid. This weekend was supposed to have been a turning point. An opportunity to get to know each other better. It was still shaping up to be a turning point but not the one either of us had envisaged. A look passed between us. The possibility that we could right this thing hovered in the air. But we both knew the truth.

'Do you think you should get it looked at?'

'Deb already gave me a quick check-over?'

I did my best to keep my tone casual. 'Deb?'

He nodded. His eyes ever so slightly averted from mine. 'She's one of the other coppers. Done all the first-aid courses.'

'That's handy, then.'

'Yeah. I... I didn't want to tell you about the trouble earlier because I thought you might worry and I was still hoping to make it. But then this happened and I was a bit stunned. Deb didn't think I should drive until I was sure I was OK.'

'Did you drive here?' My brain was processing Alex's words and the awkwardness of his actions, trying to put everything together.

'No... I got a lift.'

'Do you need one back home?' I already knew the answer. For some masochistic reason I wanted to hear him say it.

'Umm... no. Thanks. I'm OK.'

I raised an eyebrow, attempting innocent enquiry. The fact that my fists were balled, nails digging into my palms, probably put a dent in the act.

Alex straightened. 'What do you want me to tell you, Libby?'

'I'm just asking how you're getting home.' I forced my hands to open and did a palms-up gesture.

'By the look on your face, I'm pretty sure you know the answer to that.'

'Sounds like Debs is a great friend. That's good.'

'You can hardly judge me,' he replied.

'I beg your pardon?'

'You just told me Charlie brought you home in his bloody Aston!'

'That's completely different!'

'Is it?'

'Of course it is!' I yelled back. 'You weren't left sitting in a romantic restaurant for two and a half hours, subjected to pitying looks and whispered comments! If you didn't want any of this to happen, if you wanted to see someone else instead, you should have just told me, Alex! Not left me to feel humiliated at a romantic table for two!'

Alex dropped his gaze. 'It's not that I prefer her to you...'

'Please don't.' I held up my hand. 'Let's just leave it alone. OK?' My hand pressed to my temple in an effort to quell the pounding.

'Are you OK?'

'I'm tired. That's all.'

'I should go.'

'Yes. You probably should. You've already kept one woman waiting tonight. I'd hate for you to do it to another.'

He met my eyes. 'I didn't exactly plan things to go this way.'

'And yet they did. Goodnight, Alex.'

He held my gaze for a couple of beats then turned back to the door. He pulled it closed behind him and I stood there in the silence. A distant roll of thunder signalled that the storm was beginning to move off. I pulled the voile back from the balcony door and watched as lightning danced on the horizon. Letting the fabric drop back into place, I switched off the light, padded into the bathroom and cleaned my teeth. Stripping off the clothes that I'd so carefully chosen with Amy earlier this evening, I uncharacteristically left them in a pile on the bedroom floor to deal with tomorrow and crawled into bed.

29

The sun was warming the room, sliding in through a gap in the curtains, when I woke the next morning. I groaned. My nose was streaming, my throat was sore and the headache from last night had only got worse. Perfect. It was forecast to be twenty-eight degrees today and I was shivering and full of cold.

I forced back the duvet and made my way to the bathroom. Ideally I should take a shower, wash my hair and try and feel a bit more human. I looked in the mirror, grabbed my toothbrush and accepted that absolutely none of that was going to happen.

Having found some cold medicine in the cabinet, I squinted at the instructions and took the required dose, tipping out the last drops of the bottle before heading back into the bedroom to grab my duvet and ensconce myself on the sofa. Tucked up, I glanced at my phone. I ought to let Amy know about everything. And also tell her not to come round. I couldn't risk passing this cold on to her.

Amy always made light of her asthma but the truth was that she had a severe case, which had to be monitored. There had been a couple of scares and, having been with her during the last bad attack, I was now on high alert about it. She always told me not to worry but I'd never been able to forget the memory of her struggling for breath and the relief I'd felt at the sound of the ambulance siren screaming up to her door three years ago.

I clicked on the text thread already going between us and began a new message.

✉ Hi. Just to let you know I have stinking cold so don't come anywhere near me until I give the all clear xx

A few minutes later, I got a reply.

✉ Oh no! Bad timing or what? What about your sexy weekend plans! Is Alex still there?

So much for putting off the inevitable for a while.

✉ Hmm, it didn't really happen. He got caught up at work, long story short, we broke up. But all amicable.

I wasn't sure about the last bit but I didn't have the energy to go into everything right now. My phone began to ring. So much for that idea.

'Hi.'

'You broke up?'

'Yeah.'

'Why? How?'

'It just wasn't working. I don't know. I think we both felt it. Last night was just the final nail in the coffin.'

'What happened?'

'He got caught up in something at work and ended up standing me up at the restaurant.' I omitted the fact that it seemed a female colleague had also had a starring role. Honestly, I just wanted to burrow under my duvet and forget the whole thing.

'Oh, Libs. I'm so sorry.'

'It's OK,' I croaked. 'Obviously just wasn't meant to be.' This seemed to be a regular reprise when it came to me and relationships.

'You sound awful,' Amy said, after a pause. 'Is there anything I can do?'

'No, just keep away from me for the moment. That's all I ask.'

'It makes me feel like a terrible friend. I should be bringing you soup, and magazines and Lucozade.'

'I'm OK. Just vegging in front of the telly with the duvet. I don't really feel like eating at the moment anyway, so the lack of soup isn't a great loss.' I tried to chuckle, which then turned into a coughing fit. I squeaked an apology and hung up. When I'd finished, I texted Amy, apologising for the abrupt ending and said I'd talk to her later. She replied quickly and told me to let me know if there was anything I needed. I promised that I would before switching the phone to flight mode and burying myself in the duvet. Blearily I watched *Saturday Kitchen* for a while, drowning out the commentary every few minutes when I blew my nose.

Within a couple of hours, the wastepaper basket was full of tissues. I wriggled and wrestled with the quilt for a few minutes, trying to escape, and then grabbed the basket and headed into the kitchen, where I decanted my cold detritus into the larger bin. Whilst I was there, I flicked the kettle on and plopped a ginger and lemon teabag into a mug. As I waited for the appliance to boil, I poked around in the cupboards to see if I had any more medicine lurking. Nothing. There was a supermarket in the marina complex, but the thought of having to get dressed and head outside didn't exactly fill me with joy right now. Just standing up to empty the bin and make a drink had me feeling as if I'd run the Brighton half marathon. Right now, attempting to go and get groceries on a busy Saturday would feel like doing a full one while dressed as a giant penguin. I decided I'd have this drink, try and get some sleep and then hopefully feel a bit better and not need any more medicine, or at least feel well enough to make the expedition for supplies. I grabbed the now empty bin and my drink and returned to the living room. Snuggling into the duvet, I peeked my already-sore-from-blowing nose over the top and half watched bland television for another hour before finally falling asleep.

The clock showed just gone five when I swam up from sleep to the sound of my doorbell chiming.

'I'm coming!' I yelled, as it rang again. I say yelled. All that came out was a squeaky little croak as if I'd just throttled an adolescent frog. I kicked at the duvet and broke free, then tripped on the corner of it as I made my escape. The thud I made hitting the floor clearly carried as the doorbell rang again, this time accompanied by a rapping on the door, and Charlie's voice calling out.

'Libby? Are you all right?'

Great. I really wasn't in the mood to see anyone. I freely admitted that my normal, fairly perky, social skills plummeted when I was tired or ill.

'I'm fine,' I called back. Although what Charlie might or might not have heard was just a strangulated noise. I let out a big sigh and realised I was going to have to open the door, just in order to do sign language.

I pulled it open on the chain enough to peer through, but without letting any passing neighbours see me in my spotty dog pyjamas, no make-up and sporting a Rudolph-competition-contender nose. Charlie's concerned face focused on mine through the small gap.

'I heard a thump. Are you all right?'

'Fine,' I squeaked out. 'Duvet. Tripped.'

We stood there for a moment, neither saying a word. Me because it was pretty impossible to get any to come out, and Charlie because, me having just broken up with his best friend, he probably wasn't quite sure what to say. Which begged the question, why was he here? I shifted my weight and tilted my head a little in order to ask the question without having to strain my throat. He got the hint.

'I wanted to see how you were. You didn't reply to any of my texts and I tried calling but it went to voicemail. I was worried. Even more so when I heard that thump.'

'Phone's on flight mode. Sorry.'

Charlie winced at the rawness of my voice.

'Can I come in?'

I shook my head.

'Don't want you catching anything. Not feeling sociable. But thank you.' I gave him a look that I hoped conveyed more than I was able to rasp out.

The soft smile he gave me in return told me he understood my intentions.

'I rarely feel sociable and you put up with me all the time. I probably owe you.'

I shook my head before resting it on the side of the door, partly just to keep myself upright.

'Come on. I promise not to catch the cold. Scout's honour!' He did a little salute thing, holding up three fingers.

Keeping my head in position, I raised my eyebrows in question.

'Yes, I was in the Scouts,' Charlie replied, understanding, 'Proud owner of the Queen's Scout Award too, I'll have you know.'

I pulled an 'ooh, impressive' face. I wasn't entirely sure what a Queen's Scout Award was but, as Charlie was the proud owner of one, it seemed right to be impressed.

'Come on, let me in. I'm worried about you. You look terrible.'

I lifted my head up. This time my expression did not say impressed.

'You know what I mean.'

'I look a state. I don't have any make-up on.'

Charlie did a little head-shake. 'So?'

'So,' I croaked, 'I just... don't want you... anyone to see me not...'

He let out a sigh that had more than a hint of exasperation to it. 'Libby. I don't care that you haven't got any make-up on—'

'I do!'

'Well, you shouldn't!'

'I don't go anywhere without my make-up. It's my...'

'It's your what?'

'Armour.'

Charlie tilted his head. 'Libs. It's me. You'll never need armour with me. Please, just let me in. From the little I can see, and what I can just about hear, you don't seem well at all. I want to help.'

As I was about to reply, a neighbour who lived further down the hall, recently divorced and, let's say, enjoying her new-found freedom, often quite loudly, sashayed past on five-inch platform-heeled sandals. She gave Charlie a slow look up and down as she passed. Her glance slid to me. One perfectly shaped and shaded eyebrow rose at the sight that greeted her – and, of course, that had greeted Charlie. I'd been in such a hurry to stop his banging on the door, it hadn't occurred to me to give a cursory check in the mirror before opening the door. By the look on her face, I guessed it was worse than I thought.

'I'm assuming this look isn't going on the blog?' She smiled and gave me a wink.

'Not sure anyone is quite ready for this look just yet,' I replied through an assortment of squeaks and croaks.

My neighbour winced at me. 'You sound awful. Do you need anything?'

I smiled and shook my head, and mouthed thank you.

'Let me know if you do.'

She turned her attention back to Charlie.

'And if she doesn't let you in, come two doors down. I'll definitely not keep you standing at the door. In fact...' she lowered a voice that was already a whole octave beneath mine '... standing at all might be off the agenda for the rest of the weekend.' She flashed her eyes at him, a wide smile breaking out as his blush began to show.

She turned to me. 'He blushes? How cute is that?'

I smiled and she began to move off, hips swaying, dress fabric clinging tight across her bum. As she walked, she tossed her hair back and called over her shoulder to Charlie, 'Don't forget, now. I'm just down the hallway.'

Charlie did a kind of nod, and half-smile. This seemed to amuse her even more and a throaty laugh travelled back towards us. Charlie looked back at me, some desperation now in his expression.

'Please, for the love of God, let me in,' he whispered.

I wasn't about to feed Charlie to the cougars so I heaved a sigh and stood back from the door, removing the chain and opening it wide enough for his bulk to pass through. Just as I began to close it, we heard a voice drift down the corridor.

'Shame. You don't know what you're missing.'

Charlie took the door from me and closed it quickly. He stood with his back against it for a moment.

'Thank you.' The desperate tone had now been replaced with one of gratitude.

'She's actually very nice,' I rasped out.

'I'm sure. I'm just not certain I have the stamina apparently required.'

'One way to find out.'

'I'm pretty sure curiosity would definitely kill the cat in the search to answer that particular question.'

'No adventure.'

'I have plenty of adventure in my life, thank you. And I'd like to live to see more of it. Which, if I go two doors down, I don't think will be the case.'

'At least you'd go out with a bang.'

Charlie looked down at me, quirked an eyebrow and shook his head. His gaze dropped to my outfit. 'Nice PJs.'

I saved my voice and went with the sophisticated reply of poking out my tongue.

He laughed and placed his hands on my shoulders. They didn't exactly fit and his little fingers sort of rested on the top of my arm each side.

'Get back in that duvet, you.' Charlie turned me around and steered me towards the sofa, leaning in front of me, and whipping up the rogue corner that had been my undoing earlier, ensuring I couldn't trip again. I flopped into the softness with little protest and he folded it back on top of me, then tucked it under so that I felt like the filling in a well-wrapped burrito. I wiggled and forced my arms to the gap at the top and popped them out.

'Put your arms back in and keep warm,' Charlie instructed the moment I'd done so.

I shook my head and then frowned. It felt as if my brain were loose in there.

'Too hot.'

He gave me a look and then stepped past the coffee table, taking a seat on the edge of the sofa, in line with my hips. He laid a hand on my forehead before quickly removing it.

'You're boiling.'

I nodded, gently this time, keeping my brain in position.

'Have you taken anything?'

'This morning. Ran out.'

Charlie gave a nod. 'Right, I'm going to nip across and get you some medicine. Is there anything else you need or want?'

I couldn't have told you what was in my fridge or cupboards right that minute, and I cared even less. I gave the signal for no and smiled. He hesitated a moment and then disappeared into the kitchen, returning a few minutes later.

'You're out of bread and nearly out of milk. I'll get you some. Have you eaten today?'

'Not hungry.'

'You have to eat. I'll get you some soup.'

I pulled a face and hoped that he understood. He did.

'You have to eat,' he repeated. 'Keep your strength up.'

I made a noise of disagreement and buried my face in the pillow, just as the landline began to ring. Groaning, I folded the pillow around my head. Charlie said something but I couldn't hear. He pulled the pillow back for a moment.

'I said, do you want me to get that?'

I made a noise, the interpretation of which could have been anything. Charlie took it as a yes.

'Hello?'

I shuffled around in my cocoon so that I was facing up again. Charlie listened for a moment, then said his name and explained why he was answering my phone. That was to say he told the caller that I'd lost my voice. Not the fact that I couldn't be arsed to answer it.

'It's your brother,' he said, moving the speaker away from his mouth, when he noticed me watching him.

I gave a feeble wave. He told Matt I'd done so. I wasn't sure what my brother's reply was but it made Charlie laugh, agree, and glance in my direction. I frowned. He shook his head in a 'don't worry' kind of way. I listened for a moment more but they'd started talking cars and I lost interest. A few minutes later, Charlie nudged me and made the motion of writing. I pointed towards the desk. He headed off and I heard him asking Matt to repeat something. A soft beep a few minutes later signalled that he'd hung up. He came back around to the sofa.

'Your brother says hi. He'd been trying your phone too.'

'They OK?'

'Yes. They were just worried when they couldn't get hold of you. He's given me some tips on what to get to help with your cold.'

'I'm fine,' I said, feeling not very fine at all.

'You're not really, though, are you?' Charlie stated. He fixed me with those eyes and I had the awful feeling that lying to him might genuinely cause my nose to grow.

I opted for a shrug instead.

Charlie crouched down next to the sofa.

'I'm sorry about you and Alex.'

I let my gaze rise to meet his, then gave a resigned smile and eyebrow lift, the international expression for 'what can you do?'.

'Have you seen him?' I croaked. Alex's reaction last night when he found out Charlie had brought me home had surprised and confused me and I still wasn't quite sure what to make of it.

'Briefly,' Charlie replied eventually as he fussed a little with the duvet, determinedly avoiding eye contact.

'I never meant to make things uncomfortable. You are his friend, first and foremost.'

'You need to stop talking and rest.'

I kept my eyes on him, waiting for him to meet them, knowing he would read the question there.

He did. 'I dropped round on my way to the gym earlier.'

I tilted my head in further question.

Charlie looked everywhere but at me. 'I'd better nip over and get this stuff for you,' he said, standing.

'She was there, wasn't she?'

He looked down at me, his face a mixture of emotions.

'Please don't fall out with your best friend over this. It would make me feel far worse.'

He sat back down. 'Alex and I have very different beliefs when it comes to relationships. It's one of the reasons I wasn't thrilled at him picking you up at Mum and Dad's barbecue.'

'Picking me up?' I made to sit up but a large hand quickly came to rest gently on my shoulder.

'Sorry, that came out wrong.'

My stomach twisted as I forced the second question out. 'What were the other reasons?'

'Huh?'

'You said it was one of the reasons. What were the others?'

'Oh!' Charlie shook his head. 'Nothing really. Just a turn of phrase. Now you really need to stop talking and get some more rest.'

I opened my mouth to argue.

'Please?' Charlie said quietly, meeting my eyes at last.

Taking a deep breath, I snuggled back down in the duvet, signalling my acquiescence and pulling my arms back in too. For all my protesting earlier, they now felt cold. In fact, all of me was feeling cold. I clenched my teeth together to stop the chattering becoming too obvious.

'You're shivering.'

I unclenched my jaw, letting my body do whatever it wanted.

Charlie stood, grabbing the quilt off the other sofa as he did so. He snuggled the duvet around me again and then laid the quilt on top.

'Are you all right if I go and get this stuff? I could ask your neighbour to come and sit with you, if you like.'

My horrified look gave him an answer.

'OK. Just stay there. I won't be long. Can I take the keys, so that you don't have to get up to answer the door?'

I nodded and met his eyes. He gave me one of those sympathetic looks and it was the worst thing he could have done. A sob broke through and I made a weird noise that ordinarily would have been crying but thanks to my cold sounded almost inhuman.

Had I not had the cold, I probably would have gone round to Amy's this morning, had a good old stomp about, bawled at breaking up with Alex and then stuffed unhealthy food all afternoon whilst we watched romantic movies and sobbed together some more. But feeling rotten had screwed up my normal procedure for dealing with such things. And now Charlie was on the receiving end, with an added side order of squeaky croaks and the ever-present danger of a loaded sneeze.

'I'm sorry. Just feel a bit...'

'Shh.' Charlie perched on the sofa, brushed some wisps of hair away from my mouth and shovelled his big hands underneath me, duvet and all, pulling me up towards him until I was wrapped in a big, comforting cuddle. We stayed there for a while, Charlie freeing one hand occasionally in order to pass more tissue supplies and hold up the bin for me to lob spent ones into. Eventually, the in and out procedure became less and Charlie must have sensed that the tissues weren't the only things spent.

I was exhausted. He gently laid my duvet sausage roll back down and I looked up at him.

'You all right if I shoot up the road and get supplies now?'

I nodded.

He stood, then bent and squidged the duvet back in place around me.

'Comfy?'

I nodded again. 'Thank you.'

'You're welcome.' He smiled down at me. 'Text me if you think of anything else you need.' Charlie moved my phone closer to the edge of the table so that I could reach it. 'I won't be long.'

I heard the door click behind him. After another humongous nose-blowing session, I snuggled down in the duvet and decided to close my eyes for a little while, just until Charlie got back.

30

When I woke up, the sky was streaked with red and gold, the TV was on low and Charlie was sitting at the end of the sofa, my feet – somewhere in the folds of the duvet – resting on his lap. He was chomping down cashew nuts and a glass of what looked to be beer rested on the coffee table in front of him. Sensing movement, he turned and noticed me awake.

'Evening.'

When all that came out was a croak, I waved instead.

'You were out cold when I got back. It's probably the best thing for you, so I let you sleep. I got some medicine. You should take some now you're awake. Do you want me to get it for you?'

I shook my head. My bladder had followed the rest of my body in waking and was now demanding attention. My feet wriggled and kicked at the duvet until I escaped, ostensibly by being deposited on the floor. I felt Charlie lean forward from the sofa, so I stuck a hand out behind me and waved him off, signalling that I was OK. Between the coffee table and the sofa, I managed to haul myself up into a mostly upright position and blew my fringe up with a quick puff of breath. Standing was apparently on the list of Exhausting Things To Do right now too. My glance slid to where Charlie was watching me.

'You all right? You're swaying like a tall building in a high wind.'

OK. I'd thought that feeling was in my head. Apparently not. I reached out for the end of the sofa. Carefully I made my way across the room and towards the bathroom, using various pieces of furniture as impromptu crutches. I grabbed at the door handle, pulled myself in and sat down heavily on the closed loo seat to catch my breath, sounding more like Darth Vader on forty a day than a thirty-something, mostly clean-living woman. A few minutes later and I scraped together enough energy to do the necessary ablutions and clean my teeth. It made me feel mildly more human but my jammies were still sticking to me and I was pretty sure I probably didn't smell all that great either. I risked a quick sniff. Oh, wow. I leaned over and started the water flowing to get it to the right temperature while I stripped off.

Charlie knocked on the door. 'Are you having a shower?'

I said yes, but not a lot came out volume wise.

'Knock once for yes, and twice for no.'

I knocked once.

'For goodness' sake, don't slip over. Leave the door unlocked.'

I rolled my eyes and stepped out of the shower, grabbing a bath towel and wrapping it around me before yanking open the door.

'I am capable of taking a shower, you know.' My voice was mostly a series of croaks intermingled with the odd squeak, but it got the message across for the most part.

Charlie turned from where he'd begun walking back to the living room.

'I realise that,' he said, his sensible, even tone neutralising my grumpy sarcasm, 'but you're unwell and couldn't stand up straight for ten minutes if I paid you, so just be careful.'

I let out a sigh and gave a palms-up gesture that said, 'Fine, whatever'. Unfortunately, I hadn't taken into account the fact that I'd not secured my towel for self-support and the whole thing began unwrapping itself. It wasn't an elegant save, but it was a save. Just about. I hardly dared look at Charlie, who hadn't moved from his position. When I eventually raised my eyes, he gave a little shrug.

'Can't be that ill,' he said. 'Your reflexes are still pretty sharp.' His mouth was non-committal, but his eyes were laughing.

'If you were a gentleman, you would have brushed past that moment without mentioning it,' I forced out.

'On the contrary. If I weren't a gentleman, I would have added the word "unfortunately" to the end of my sentence. Which I didn't. Ergo, I'm a gentleman. Now stop straining your voice arguing and go do whatever you're going to do. Carefully!'

I obeyed his instruction to rest my voice and replied instead by rolling my eyes.

'Very mature.'

I gave him another look that told him how much I cared about that opinion. He smirked, shook his head and closed the door.

Annoyingly, Charlie was right about the whole shower thing and I felt decidedly wobbly about a minute and a half in. I slid down into the bath and opted for a sit-down version. Hardly ideal but it did the job and even if I didn't feel relaxed and invigorated, I did at least feel clean, which was a start. Taking advantage of every surface I could, I managed to get myself out of the bath without falling over, and into clean pyjamas. I sat for a moment, recovering from the effort of it all. A drip escaped from the towel wrapped around my head, and I shivered as it chased its way down my spine. Five minutes later, I'd blasted my hair into a state of semi-dryness, without any consideration of styling, a fact soon confirmed by a quick glance in the mirror. Had I had more energy, and felt less rotten, I might have been bothered. But I didn't, and the only person witness to it all was Charlie so it didn't really matter. It seemed that, as far as Charlie was concerned, I could spend two hours or five minutes on my hair and, to him, the result would be much the same. Which was just as well. Especially today. I picked up my dressing gown and made my way back towards the living room, shoving my arms in the sleeves as I did so. I got one in, but the second was proving impossible to find. Charlie looked up as I entered, making annoyed squeaks and getting crosser by the minute. I decided that it was probably a good thing I'd lost my voice just at this moment, as I yanked off the dressing gown and glared at it.

'Wow. Little flash of redhead there.' Charlie laughed, getting up off the sofa and bending down to pick up the dressing gown.

I gave him a look but he missed it as he was studying the clothing. He fiddled for a second and then held it out to me, ready to put my arms into.

'You had one of the sleeves inside out.'

I hesitated for a moment, but, despite the heatwave-temperature weather outside, I was beginning to feel a chill.

'Come on. Stop being stroppy and put it on.'

I gave him another look, making sure he saw it this time. He just laughed it off and nodded his head at the dressing gown.

I slid my arms in and Charlie tucked it over my shoulders before turning me around and tying the belt for me.

'You really are feeling rotten, aren't you?'

I shrugged, and pulled a fed-up face, showing that my hissy moment was over.

He gave a smile and steered me towards the duvet, which he'd neatened up and now sat looking all snuggly and inviting on the sofa.

Two minutes later, I was tucked in, sitting up and awaiting the soup that Charlie informed me he had warming up on the hob. He ignored my protests of not being hungry and of being tired and said I'd feel better for having eaten something. Plus, he added, I was due medicine and it was best not to take it on an empty stomach. Sensible Charlie. I loved him, of course, and I was so grateful for him coming round today, especially after everything with Alex. But right now, I didn't want soup. I wanted painkillers, and I wanted sleep. Both of which he was denying me until I ate something.

Once again, Charlie's rational, steady plan was, of course, correct. I actually did feel a little better for eating, and the cold and flu liquid medicine he'd got from the shops was soon kicking in and reducing the thumping headache to something in the more bearable range.

'Why don't you try and get some rest now?' Charlie said, after he'd taken our bowls out to the kitchen and stacked them in the dishwasher.

I nodded, and then stopped as it made the headache flare. Instead I scooted down inside the duvet cocoon and pulled it around me. Charlie crouched down next to me. I moved a little so that I could see him properly.

'I'm going to head off now.'

I'd been reluctant to let him in, but now a part of me wished he wouldn't go.

'I'd already made arrangements for this evening. It's a work sort of thing and I can't really cancel.'

'I'm OK. Thank you for everything.'

Charlie nodded almost imperceptibly, and pushed a tendril of hair I'd been trying to blow away back from my face. He seemed to be considering something.

'But if I can catch them, I might be able to rearrange—'

I stopped him by putting a finger to his lips. Which suddenly felt way too intimate for what I was going for. I quickly moved my hand and instead squished his lips together with a finger top and bottom, holding them closed. There. Much better.

Charlie didn't move. Admittedly, my having hold of his lips made that difficult. His blue eyes were focused on mine.

'Just go,' I croaked, smiling.

He made a noise that sounded as if it might have been an 'OK' so I let go.

'I was just going to say—'

I grabbed again.

'Mmmmnnnnnnmnmn.' He held his hands up in surrender.

I let go.

He twitched his nose and rolled his lips in and out a couple of times.

'Thank you.'

I gave a little nod against the pillow in acceptance.

Charlie stood, tucked me in a little more and then crouched down again.

I frowned in question.

'I hate this. You're normally so bouncy and full of life. I really don't want to leave you feeling so rough.'

'Just a cold,' I forced out. 'Now, go away.'

He made to stand, and I snagged his arm. 'Thank you.'

He gave me a big hug and a half-hearted smile, then made his way to the door.

'Call me if you want anything. OK. Or text me. Probably best. Save your voice. And I'll see you when I get back from my trip, if not before.'

I nodded.

'OK?' he called again.

I realised he probably couldn't see me nodding in the huge cocoon so I wriggled an arm free and stuck it up in the air with my thumb up.

'Good. Get some rest.'

I wiggled the thumb as answer.

The door closed behind him and I quickly pulled my arm back in and snuggled down.

31

It was three days later when I finally spoke to Charlie on the phone shortly before heading off to bed.

'Hello, you.'

'Libby?'

'You sound surprised. Did you mean to call someone else?'

'No! No, not at all. It just doesn't sound like you.'

'I promise it is.' I laughed, before proceeding to launch into a massive coughing fit. I muted the phone whilst I pulled it together.

'Still there?' I asked when I'd recovered.

'Yes. You OK?'

'Yeah, just the cough gets set off whenever I laugh.'

'I'll try not to make you laugh, then.'

'Good plan.'

'You know, you could probably boost your income for a bit whilst you've got this cold.'

'What?'

'Premium lines.'

I laughed down the line, before quickly smothering the cough with a sloosh of water.

'Is that advice in your professional capacity as my accountant? Earn a bit of extra cash by answering sex-chat lines?'

'Obviously it's your decision. I'm just advising you of all the options. Laying things out there for you to decide.'

I did a laugh-cough thing and tried again. 'So, did you ring for something, other than to offer me dodgy career advice?'

'No, just saying hello. I've ordered dinner so thought I'd see how you were doing whilst I was waiting.'

'How's the weather over there?'

'Bloody scorching. I went out to the park earlier and there were people dancing in and out of the fountains, just trying to cool down.'

'There's a park near the hotel? That's nice. Not all just skyscrapers, then.'

'Umm, it's Central Park. The hotel is just off it.'

'Oh, wow, OK. Listen to you, all Mr Local, calling it "the park",' I teased.

Charlie didn't reply. After a short pause he instead asked how I was feeling.

'Much better, thanks. Really. The voice isn't as bad as it sounds. I think it's all heading off into the distance now, thank goodness. Just need plenty of concealer on my bright red nose at the moment from all the blowing, but, apart from that, I'm getting there. I think someone giving me a good start on Saturday helped enormously.'

'My pleasure.'

'What, seeing me suffering and looking like I'd just shipped in from Scary Town?'

He laughed. 'Of course not. I just meant that I was glad to be able to help. And there was nothing Scary Town about you.'

'Charlie, I have mirrors. I was not sporting a good look.'

'You were sick.'

'I know. Which can be the only explanation for the fact that I even opened the door to you in the first place.'

'What, because you didn't have your make-up and hair done for the first time since I met you?'

'Something like that.'

'So? You still looked fine to me. I mean, not fine, obviously. It was clear you weren't well, but you didn't look hideous or anything, just because you didn't have any make-up on.'

'Gosh. Not hideous. Thanks.'

'You know what I mean.'

'I do. And next time I'm just going to send you down the hall to Rula.'

'You wouldn't do that to me.'

'Wouldn't I?'

'No. You value my financial skills too much.'

'There is that. But luckily I think Rula's only after your body, and not your mind. I, on the other hand, need the latter. Perhaps she and I could work out some sort of deal.'

'You realise you're saying all this out loud, don't you?'

'Of course.'

'You're making me feel so cheap.' He put an inflection into his tone that made me giggle, and then laugh, and then cough.

'Are you deliberately trying to kill me?' I asked when I'd got my breath back. 'You promised you wouldn't make me laugh.'

'You started it.'

'Actually, I think we can trace it back to your original comments about my voice.'

'OK. Point taken. Apologies.'

'So, how's the trip anyway?'

'It's fine. Meetings, a bit of schmoozing, that sort of thing.'

'I can't imagine you schmoozing.'

'No, it's not really my thing, I have to admit. But Lenny's with me, and he's excellent at it. So, it's all working out.'

'Did you say you had ordered room service?'

'I did.'

'Not having dinner with Lenny?'

'No. He... he had other plans.'

'He hooked up, is that what you're saying?'

'Yes. One of the women from the mixer thing last night. They hit it off.'

'Didn't you hit it off with anyone?'

'You know me, Libs. I'm not great at stuff like that.'

'Charlie, you're beefy and gorgeous and intelligent. I don't think you actually have to be great at doing anything. Just stand there and wait for them to trample you.'

He laughed. 'Thanks for the pep talk, but, like I said, I'm good.'

'Maybe you should tell them that too.'

'Libby Cartright, did you just make an insinuation about my sex life?'

'No, I made an insinuation that maybe you should get one.'

'My sex life is just fine, thank you.'

'Is it?'

Was it?

'Yes. But thank you for the suggestion. Although I imagine saying one is good is probably seen as a bit pushy.'

I raised my eyebrows in thought, even though he couldn't see. 'I don't know. Depends how you say it. If you went, "Hey, I'm great in bed," then yeah, big turn-off and setting yourself up for failure anyway—'

'Gee, thanks for the vote of confidence.'

'I'm just saying. But a teasing "I'm good"? I think you could probably get away with that.'

'I'll bear it in mind, thank you.'

'You're welcome.'

'How on Earth did we get down this rabbit hole?'

'I'm not entirely sure. Want to climb out?'

'Most definitely.'

'OK. So, when are you back?'

'Few days. Tilly sent me a message to ask when it was good for them to come over and discuss their wedding pictures.'

'What did you say?'

'I suggested Sunday. Hopefully I'll be awake enough. Prod me if I look like I'm going to nod off during it.'

'Me?'

'Aren't you coming?'

'I hadn't planned to.'

'Oh. I thought you were. I mean, I...'

'You know Tilly and Sam. You don't need me there for that, do you?'

'No. It's not that. I guess, I thought because you offered to be my assistant for the day that you'd be there. But it's fine. I know things are nuts for you. I've got a few things on my mind at the moment and wasn't really thinking.'

'Would you prefer me to be there?'

'If I say yes will it make me look like a complete loser and wimp?'

'No. Of course not. Why would you think that?'

'Because I'm a grown man and handle information and deals worth mind-boggling amounts but the thought of dealing with this wedding is giving me the sweats.'

'Well, there are worse things it could be giving you, so, in view of that, it's fine. Of course I'll be there. I can always make some notes whilst you're all discussing things so that we don't forget anything.'

'You're great, you know that, don't you?'

'I don't mind hearing it again from time to time though.'

Charlie laughed. 'You're totally great! A superstar.'

'OK. Now you're just taking the mickey.'

'Never.'

'Yeah, right. Hurry up and come back to Blighty. I owe you dinner for looking after me last week.'

'You don't owe me anything.'

'All right then, truth is I have a business question and I'm not sure what to do.'

'That sounds more like it. What's the problem?'

'It's OK. No rush. I'll just ask you when I see you.'

Charlie paused. 'OK.'

'Charlie?'

'Yes?'

'You don't mind me asking you stuff, do you? I mean, using you as an information tap?'

'Of course not!'

'It's just that you're here – I mean, when you are here – and whenever I ask you something, you don't make me feel like an idiot.'

'That's because you're not an idiot.'

'I know... but some people aren't like that. They feel that they have this power over you because they have knowledge that you don't.'

'Then they're the idiots.'

'OK.'

'OK.

'What are you doing now?'

'I'm sprawled on the bed. There's a sci-fi film about to start so I'm going to watch that with my dinner.'

'You should be out partying in the Big Apple. Make the most of it.'

'There's a thing tomorrow evening.'

'A party?'

'Yeah. I'm not sure whose exactly. It gets complicated sometimes as to the connection but someone's throwing some party at a place on the Upper West Side.'

'Ooh, swanky.'

'Yeah.'

'You sound thrilled.'

'I'd rather be here watching HBO.'

'Oh, Charlie! Go and enjoy yourself.'

'I enjoy myself watching HBO and talking to you.'

I smiled. 'You're hopeless, you know that, don't you?'

'No. I refuse to accept that diagnosis. I just prefer a quieter life.'

'That's true. I take it back.'

'And because you're worried if you don't, you might not get help with your taxes.'

'There is that.'

'You're a hard-nosed businesswoman underneath that bubbly, kind exterior, aren't you? Cold, hard steel.'

'Uh oh. Busted.'

He laughed, a deep rumbling that tickled my ear.

'You are going to be OK to do Tilly's photos, aren't you? I mean, we all know you're doing it as a favour, and that you've been travelling a lot lately.'

'Yes. My assistant knows that weekend is a no-go for anything. I've taken the Friday off too so that I can go over some things.'

I smiled at the slight nerves in his voice.

'They're going to be fantastic pictures, Charlie. I know it.'

'I hope so. Obviously I will be blaming my studio assistant if anything does go horribly wrong. You do understand that.'

'I'd expect nothing less from an artistic master such as yourself.'

The laugh rumbled gently over the line again.

'Have you got any more trips coming up?'

There was a slight hesitation before he answered, and I assumed he was thinking ahead in his calendar. 'No, things should start settling soon.'

'That's good, then, isn't it? I mean, I know you like travelling sometimes but...'

'Yes. There's been more than I anticipated lately.'

Down the line, I heard the doorbell to his room sound.

'Room service is here. Better go.'

'OK, go and watch your film and enjoy your dinner. And have fun tomorrow! I absolutely insist.'

'All right. I'll try. Now go to bed, it's late.'

'Yep. Heading off now. Night, Charlie.'

'Night, Libs.'

32

I was waiting for Charlie in the car park and heard the throaty engine before I saw him turn in. He pulled up to me and I scooted around to the passenger side and hopped in.

'Morning.'

'Morning. Ready to do this?'

'I am. Are you?'

'I feel better now you're here but... yes, I am.'

I tilted my head at him. 'Charlie Richmond, I do believe you're actually excited about this.'

A grin slid onto his face. 'I am. I really am. But I'm also totally bloody terrified about messing it up. It's a very odd combination, I have to say.'

I grabbed his hand. 'You're not going to mess up. Just do what you did with us in the bedroom...' He raised his eyebrows and I silently ran through the sentence again. 'Yes, OK. That came out decidedly different from how it sounded in my head, but still you know what I mean. Do what you did then, and what you always do when you go out taking photos, and it'll be great. It'll be amazing. It'll be—'

He laughed, clapping his hand over my mouth. 'I get the idea.'

'Mmmff.'

He removed his hand.

'Just psyching you up. All part of my assistantly duties.'

'Assistantly?'

'Yep.'

'Nutcase.' He grinned, then grabbed me in for a quick hug and dropped a fleeting kiss on the top of my head. Letting go, he put the car into gear and pulled smoothly away, heading towards Tilly's parents' place to start with some early morning getting-ready shots.

We pulled up outside the address and Charlie was out and opening my door before I'd finished undoing my seat belt.

'That's all right. Just start getting your stuff out. I'll be there in a minute.'

He merely held out his hand in response. Which I took and thereby made a more elegant exit than I would have alone. Charlie didn't let go of my hand as I stood, closer to him now.

'Thanks for doing this, Libs. I really appreciate it.'

'It's my pleasure, really. I think you're wonderful for offering to do it for them anyway – you have no idea how much it meant to them. Tilly didn't stop talking about you for a week. Frankly, I was sick of hearing about you by the end. I was kind of glad you'd had to go back to New York again.'

I tilted my head back up to meet his eyes and winked.

Charlie gave me an even look, bent quickly and placed a kiss on my forehead before taking the straw hat I was holding and plonking it down on my head. I shoved my hand up and pushed the brim back in order to see him.

He was smiling now. 'Like I said, thanks. Now, are you ready to be a packhorse?' he asked, leading me to the boot, which was full of camera gear.

I made an ee-yore sound.

He looked round at me.

I shrugged. 'I don't really know what noise a pack horse makes. It was the best I could do.'

He looked at me like he didn't know what to say, but I saw a flash of something in his eyes. My smile faded a moment.

'Is everything all right?'

Charlie looked away, back at the range of the stuff in the boot. 'Absolutely. Come on, let's get going.'

* * *

It wasn't hard to get the bridesmaids to smile for Charlie as they attended to their preparations. It was, however, a little harder for him to get the candid shots that Tilly and Sam were so keen on, due to the fact the women kept throwing glances his way. One particularly enamoured cousin began talking about some photos she'd seen where the bridal party were in their underwear – beautiful, tasteful black and white shots, that she was sure Tilly would love. I had a feeling that the benefit would be more for the cousin than Tilly as they were all laced into corsets and this particular bridesmaid certainly looked amazing in it, from the flash I'd seen earlier as she swooshed past, her robe left open and her cover-girl figure perfectly suited to the style.

I sneaked a glance at Charlie, trying to think of something to say to diffuse any feeling of awkwardness, knowing he'd be going as red as a signal beacon right about now. But he wasn't red at all. He merely transitioned over the suggestion by making others, giving directions and laughing at little jokes the girls were making as they flirted outrageously with him. It was as if he'd become someone else for the day. My stomach flipped a little as I suddenly realised I was hoping this new aspect of Charlie was fleeting. The fact that he was a little shy was one of the many things I loved about Charlie. It made him... him. I never wanted him to be uncomfortable, of course I didn't. But it was endearing that he wasn't always all super smooth. It was... refreshing. But today he was taking it all in his stride. And, for some reason, I wasn't entirely sure how I felt about it.

My phone buzzed in the pocket of my dress and I pulled it out.

✉ I know you probably don't want to hear from me, but I just wanted to say again I'm sorry how things went. I never meant to hurt you. I really hope everything goes well for Tilly today. Take care, Alex x

From what I had managed to find out, Charlie and Alex were still a little tense with each other but I truly hoped they'd sort that out in time, and that meant I'd probably end up having to see Alex again at some point. But that still didn't mean I was ready to forgive him quite yet.

I shoved the phone back in my pocket, shook the thought from my head and, refocusing, wandered over to where Charlie stood. He sensed me standing there and gave a 'two seconds' signal. The camera rolled off a few more frames and he turned to me, leaving the girls to their own devices for a few minutes.

'All right?' I asked.

'Girls!' a voice called up the stairs. 'The flowers are here! Come and see!'

Four bridesmaids and one bride rushed towards the door. Charlie hooked an arm out and scooped me out of the way before I got mown down in the melee. He put the camera down and perched on the edge of a bedroom chair.

'You seem to have all this in hand. I'm not sure you need me at all. Quite the charmer under all that, it would seem,' I teased.

His head snapped up. 'It's all bravado, believe me. Don't you dare leave!' I was slightly relieved to see that the Charlie we all knew and loved was still there. 'I'm just trying to get the shots.'

'Let me see?' I scooted over and sat on the floor next to him for a minute. He handed me the camera and I rested it on one of his legs, and leant on the other one, as I cycled through the shots he'd taken so far. 'Charlie!'

'What? What's wrong? Are they not what she wants?'

'No! I mean, yes. They're perfect. They're absolutely perfect! She'll love them! Promise me you'll take my wedding photos!' I laughed.

He looked down at me. 'I thought you said you didn't see yourself getting married.'

I tilted my head, still looking at the shots on the screen on the back of the camera. 'True. But these are so beautiful. You might change my mind.'

'Might I?'

I looked up and met his eyes, their blue enhanced by the deeper tan he'd acquired from travelling, alongside the great weather here at home. The white shirt he wore, sleeves rolled up to mid forearm, set both off perfectly. It was pretty damn easy to see why the bridesmaids were falling over themselves to call his attention. I was half tempted to find a spare corset and try it on myself.

'What?'

'Huh?'

'You said something about corsets.'

Oops.

'Oh, something for the blog,' I blustered. 'Thinking out loud. Sorry. Concentrating now. Promise.'

I pushed myself up from the floor, using Charlie's knee as a crutch. 'Right, Bailey, are you ready for round two?'

'Will you throw in the towel for me if it looks like I'm losing?'

'Nope. Not an option. Go get 'em, Tiger!'

He stopped and looked at me. 'Go get 'em, Tiger?'

I shrugged. 'I don't know. It just came out.'

He gave me a full-wattage grin, snagged my hand with his free one and pulled me along to go get 'em together.

* * *

It was half past ten and Charlie and I were sitting, or rather slumped, on his sofa, each holding a very large glass of wine, and both trying to find the energy to actually make the move to bring them to our lips. The large windows were open and the muffled sounds of a summer evening in the city blew in on the faint breeze. A single lamp lit the room as the sky outside lost the last deep blue of twilight.

'I'm shattered,' Charlie said, eventually.

I made a 'mmh hmmn' sound of agreement and took a swig of wine.

'Lie in tomorrow?'

Charlie rolled his head on the back of the couch to look at me. 'I think we both deserve it, don't you?'

'I do. But I'm having the boys tomorrow. So, think of me when you're lying sprawled in your bed with nothing to do all day.'

He raised one tired brow. 'You probably shouldn't tell blokes to think of you when they're lying in bed.'

I whacked him with a cushion.

'I get the hint. But my point still stands.'

I whacked him again because I was too tired to think up a clever reply right now. I'd probably have a zinger of one ready for tomorrow. He took the cushion off me and tucked it down the side of his hip.

'What have you got planned with the boys?'

'I honestly don't know yet. I haven't thought that far.'

'Have they been to Legoland?' he asked after a pause.

'Ugh. No. They haven't, much to their disgust. Matt's said he'll take them but it's been a case of finding the right time.'

'What about tomorrow?'

I looked at Charlie. 'I love those boys to bits, but I am not driving up to Windsor tomorrow to spend most of my day standing in lines, waiting to go on a two-minute ride.'

'I could drive you. And there are special passes that mean you don't have to queue.

I raised an eyebrow. 'You seem to know an awful lot about this.'

He brought his wine glass up and took a sip. 'I don't know what you mean.'

'I've a feeling there's another little boy who wants to go to Legoland...'

'Be careful where you're throwing that description around, won't you?'

I laughed. 'Afraid Elaine might change her mind?' I said, referring to his Marilyn-esqe neighbour. 'Is she still after you, by the way?'

'I don't think "after me" is the right description. But she has invited me over a couple more times, yes.'

'Then "after you" is exactly the right description.'

'Can we get back to Legoland?'

'I can text Matt and ask him what he thinks. You just said you were shattered though. It might be better to have a rest tomorrow. We can always go another time if you're still up for it.'

He turned his attention to the stem of his wine glass, its contents barely touched. 'I'll be fine after a good sleep. And I know I'm free tomorrow.'

I let out a sigh and pulled my phone from my bag.

'I'll ask him. It's hardly a cheap day out so I'd better check first.'

Pushing himself up off the sofa, Charlie crossed the room and began rummaging through some paperwork that sat piled on the corner of the dresser.

✉ Hi. Are the boys still wanting to go to Legoland?

I messaged my brother.

His reply came back swiftly. An emoticon with a wiggly line for a mouth. I got the idea. Another message immediately followed.

✉ Yes. Gonna have to bite the bullet some time and actually take them. Have you seen the prices??!! Why are you asking?

Charlie padded back across the room and held some papers in front of my face. I reached up and took them. Four complimentary VIP passes to Legoland Windsor.

'Seriously?'

He sat back down next to me.

'A client gave them to me the other day. I'd rather they got used than went to waste.'

'And you want to go to Legoland.' I smiled.

'I'm just offering to drive.'

'Oh, so you're going to stay in the car?'

'Well, if I'm there, I may as well go in.'

I smiled. 'Of course.' I looked at the tickets again. 'Are you serious about this? I mean, the boys will be ecstatic, but you've had a long day today.'

'It's fine. I wouldn't have suggested it otherwise. I can lie in bed another day. I'd enjoy spending the day with you and the kids. Especially if it's something they want to do anyway. Seems a shame not to.'

'Wow. First the James Bond car and now Legoland. I hope you're ready for a bit of hero worship.'

'Always.'

I rolled my eyes at him but couldn't help grinning. I started typing another text out to my brother.

✉ Would it be OK to take them tomorrow? Charlie
has free VIP tickets and has offered to drive us.

The reply came back so fast I imagined Matt's fingers smoking.

✉ Yes! Absolutely! Yes! You are the best sister
ever! Maria says you totally need to marry Charlie. I agree. The sooner the better preferably!

I told Charlie that they were happy with the plan – a massive understatement. I didn't mention the second bit of the text.

'What time should I say we can pick them up?'

'What time do they get up?'

'Oh, dark thirty, usually. Don't worry about that.'

'OK. Well, if we say pick them up at eight, if traffic's OK, we should be there about half nine or so.'

'Sounds good.' I texted Matt the details, and asked him not to tell the boys what was happening.

'We can tell them when we pick them up.'

Charlie grinned and his eyes sparkled in the soft light from the lamp.

'I'm not sure who's going to be the most excited. Them or you.'

'Could be close.'

I flopped my head back on the sofa. Charlie moved and the sofa dipped. I opened my eyes to find him shifting position, and now facing me.

'You sure you're going to be OK? I'm sorry. I didn't think to ask. I got sort of carried away.'

'I'll be fine. Although I do need to get home and get to bed.' I glanced at the wine in his hand. 'I'll call a taxi.'

'I've only had two sips, literally.'

'No, it's fine. You enjoy your wine.'

'Look. Why don't I whizz you home, collect your stuff for tomorrow then come back here and we can both enjoy our wine? I've only got to come and get you in the morning anyway.'

'I could always drive here first. Or meet you at Matt's.'

Charlie looked at me for a moment. 'Yes. Both good options. But I'll run you home now anyway.' He placed his glass down, grabbed his keys from the side table he'd put them on earlier, and pushed himself up.

I was reluctant to move, having now found an exceptionally comfortable position.

He glanced at me and then turned to study me more intently.

'You look comfy.'

'I am,' I said, sounding none too happy about it.

'You know you're going to have to move whatever decision you make.'

'I know.' I let out a sigh, but still made no effort to move.

'You can come back and sit in that exact position.'

'It won't be the same.'

'Come on, Goldilocks.' Charlie leant down and scooted his hands underneath my arms, then lifted me out of the sofa and stood me up.

'That's cheating.'

'I want my wine.'

'I said I'd get a cab.'

'And I said I'd drive you. So, come on.' He took my hand and led me down the stairs to where we'd both kicked off our shoes earlier.

'So, what's the plan?' Charlie asked as he pulled up outside the flats. 'Am I waiting now or what?'

I'd opened the door and had one leg out.

'I—'

'Well, don't you just keep getting better and better?' Rula's husky voice drifted in as she stopped by my open door and bent to look in at Charlie, running her hand sensually over the paintwork of his Aston as she did so. I squashed myself back in my seat to avoid losing an eye. The low-cut sundress was apparently the only piece of clothing being pressed into service right now. A wrap dangled from her hand but she made no move to put it on. Bearing in mind the cooler night air, it might have been a good option. Or not. Depending on who you spoke to. Either way, it was pretty clear that Charlie was being treated to the full spectacle.

'Evening,' he said.

'Isn't this beautiful?' she said, drawing her hand over the car again.

'Thank you. I like it.'

Rula threw me a look. Friendly. Assessing. Trying to work out whether I was sleeping with Charlie. I was pretty sure she came up with a negative answer because she carried on flirting for another few minutes, with me feeling very much the third wheel and unable to do anything about it as she leaned across me and batted her false eyelashes at Charlie. Every time she laughed, she threw her head back and I got a mouthful of hair whilst Charlie got a full eyeful of her cleavage standing to attention.

'We'd better get going,' Charlie said, at the first opportunity that didn't feel like an immediate brush-off.

Rula gave one last rake of her eyes over his body. 'Shame. But you know where I am.'

'Um hmm.' Charlie smiled brightly, and I stifled a laugh.

Rula stood and smoothed down her dress as I exited the car. Charlie stepped out the other side and the doors locked.

'Have a good evening,' I called as she turned to go.

She flicked her gaze between us. 'And you. Oh, by the way, there's no hot water in our block. They're supposed to be sending someone out tomorrow. Apparently.' She gave a wave of her hand as if to say she would believe that when she saw it, which was sometimes the case in these circumstances.

'Great,' I said.

'There's your decision, then. Grab your stuff and you can come back to my place and I don't have to detour in the morning.'

I chewed my lip and looked at him.

'There's lots of lovely hot water at my place...' he said, and began to mime taking a shower, with the sort of enjoyment noises you heard on shampoo commercials.

I nudged him. 'You twit. And if Rula hears you making those noises, she'll have you up against that wall before you know what's happening. And don't expect me to come to your rescue.'

Charlie glanced at the wall.

'You wouldn't leave me to her mercy.'

'I don't think she shows her men any mercy.'

Charlie took a deep breath.

'Oh, stop it. You love it.' I laughed.

His eyebrows shot up. 'What?'

'I saw you. You're getting quite the dab hand at flirting.'

'I wasn't flirting! I was talking. She's attractive, yes. But I'd like to live to see another day.'

'OK. I'll be sure to tell her you've no stamina the next time I see her. That should put her off. For a while at least.'

'I've plenty of stamina, thank you very much.'

I reached up and patted his cheek. 'There, there. No need to be touchy. Of course, you do.'

Charlie caught my hand. 'I'm thinking of withdrawing the hot-water offer.'

'Yes, but you won't, because you're lovely.' I winked at him.

He dropped my hand. 'Get your stuff quickly before I stop being lovely and consign you to a freezing shower.'

'I'm going!'

I scooted up the stairs and along to my flat, Charlie following behind, keeping up at a leisurely pace compared to my hurried one. Whizzing round, I grabbed a change of clothes, my PJs and travel washbag, along with my make-up and a hairbrush. I threw it all into a large tote and topped it off with a bottle of sun cream, and a wide-brimmed fabric hat that I could squash in on the top.

'Ready!'

'Blimey, that was quick.'

'There's wine waiting for me. And hot water.'

'There is indeed.'

Charlie stepped out and I turned and locked the door. He bent and took the bag off me then stood aside, allowing me to go first down the steps. We got to the car and he opened the passenger door. I slid in and waited whilst he popped the boot and laid my bag inside. A minute later he was in and belted and we were heading back to the land where wine waited and hot water flowed.

33

'You need a hat. I've just looked at the expected temperatures today.'

'Yes, Mum,' Charlie said, snagging a peaked cap off a coat hook.

I gave him a look.

'Do we need to stop and get anything? Water, snacks?'

'Nope. Maria is a machine when it comes to things like this. It's great. I just pick them up and go. There'll even be first-aid supplies in there.'

'Reassuring bearing in mind you're coming.'

'Oi. You shut that damn window in the first place! So technically, that was your fault.'

'I thought it might be.'

'I'm glad you agree.'

'I didn't say I agreed.'

'Look, if you don't behave I won't take you to Legoland.'

Charlie stared at me and then his face crumpled. He put his hands up to cover it.

I stared, open-mouthed, for a second until I saw his shoulders shaking. He looked up, his blue eyes shining with tears – of laughter!

'You should have seen your face!'

'You're such an arse,' I stated. 'I used to think you were this serious, intelligent man but in reality, you're just an arse.'

'Thank you.'

'You're welcome,' I said, getting in the car and pulling the door closed behind me.

Charlie slid in the other side. He glanced across at me, a smirk on his face. I stuck my tongue out at him, but I couldn't stop the grin that arrived at the same time. He laughed and squeezed my knee, then blipped the throttle on and set off.

'Charlie!' the boys chorused as they rushed out, pushing past Matt and Maria, both of whom were still in their dressing gowns, for which I had a moment of jealousy. Charlie scooped up the boys as they ran towards him, one in each arm. They giggled and Niall wrapped his hands around Charlie's neck whilst Liam rested an arm across his shoulder, enjoying the much higher viewpoint than he normally experienced.

'Auntie Libby!' they called, as Charlie brought them back towards the house.

'Oh. You noticed me, did you?' I said, teasing as they both leaned out to give me a kiss.

'Is Charlie spending the day with us?'

'Please?'

'It's amazing what a snazzy car can do. Busty women, small boys. They all love it,' I said to Maria as Matt and Charlie began chatting.

'Busty women?' Maria repeated, raising an eyebrow.

'Oh, you wouldn't believe the half of it!'

She cast a glance over Charlie, who was now happily laughing with my brother. 'Oh, I don't know. I might.' She laughed.

'I'm not sure having him for a mate is all that good for my ego, you know.'

'Maybe you should change that, then.'

I looked at her. 'I don't think I could. Not out of choice. I can hardly remember what it was like to not have Charlie as part of my life. And I don't really want to.'

'That wasn't exactly what I meant.' She gave me a minute.

'Ohhhhh! Oh, no. No, definitely not.'

'Why not? What's wrong with him?'

'Nothing! Nothing at all.'

'OK. Then what's wrong with you?'

I rolled my eyes at her for lack of something better to say.

'That's not an answer, Libs. He's funny, kind, stable, straight and stomach-meltingly gorgeous. So, I ask again. What's wrong with you?'

'It's just not like that between us. We're friends. We're kind of... beyond all that. It'd be weird.'

Maria fixed me with a look. 'Weird is not what I think it would be. And I don't think you do either.'

'Time to go!' I said, deciding this conversation was probably best ended.

'Where are we going?' The boys were now on the ground but jumping around, repeating the question.

Matt turned and looked at me. 'I didn't say anything.'

Charlie crooked a finger at me and beckoned me over.

'Hold out your hand,' he said, sandwiching mine within his own. I felt him pass me something and I curled my hand around it instinctively. I looked up and he gave a quick eyebrow raise and smiled.

'Where are we going?' the boys asked again.

Charlie nodded at me and I uncurled my hand in front of them. Sitting in my palm was a little Lego man.

The boys stared at it for a moment.

'Legoland?' they whispered together, not quite believing it.

I nodded.

Two minutes later we had bundled them in the car, having had a mad moment of corralling as their excitement threatened to wake the entire street. I took a rucksack from Maria with all the requisite supplies enclosed. Charlie took it straight off me and slung it in the boot.

'Where did the Lego man come from at such short notice?'

'That Happy Meal you mentioned me inhaling a while back.' He smiled and shut the boot.

'You sure about this?' Matt asked, as the boys continued to bounce about inside, restrained by their seat belts.

'What? Taking three children to Legoland?' I said, catching Charlie in my glance.

He grinned.

'It'll be fine,' he reassured Matt.

'Thanks for doing this, and the tickets,' my brother said.

'My pleasure.'

'Seriously. We're actually doing him a massive favour,' I said.

'Are you coming?'

'Do I have a choice?'

Charlie gave me a patient look.

'See you later!' I said, giving Matt and Maria a quick hug each. 'I'll keep you posted by text.'

'Have a great time!' They waved and we all replied in kind.

* * *

Nine hours later and the atmosphere in the car was very different from what it had been first thing this morning. Mellow was one word. Knackered was another. The boys had been asleep in the back seat before we'd even left the car park and I felt as though I could easily join them.

'Thanks for a great day,' I said, covering Charlie's hand for a moment as it rested on the centre console.

He flicked his glance briefly to me before returning it to the road. 'You're very welcome.' He turned his hand and squeezed mine. 'Thanks for letting me come along.'

'They were your tickets!' I laughed. Our voices were soft in deference to the children sleeping but, if I was honest, they'd had such a busy, exciting day, if we'd been talking with bull horns I still don't think they'd have stirred.

'Yes. But it wouldn't have been much fun on my own. I always have fun with you. And the boys seemed to really enjoy it.'

'I'll never hear the end of it now. It'll be Charlie this, and Charlie that. Your presence will be requested on every trip now. You do realise that.'

He gave my hand another squeeze but didn't answer. In the back seat, Niall stirred. I turned in my seat, letting go of Charlie's hand and reached down, picking up the cuddly toy Lego man we'd bought him earlier, who had now taken a dive to the floor. I wiggled again and leant back, tucking him close to Niall. Without waking, a little arm moved and snagged the toy, squashing him close. I watched for a moment, then turned back in my seat.

'They all right?' Charlie asked.

I nodded.

* * *

We handed the children over, still sleeping, to their parents and Charlie drove me home.

'Do you want to check and see if the hot water's back on? You're more than welcome to stay with me until it is.'

'I'm sure it will be.'

Charlie didn't seem all that thrilled with this gung-ho attitude, which for someone like him was probably a little too reckless in its approach.

'Why don't you check?'

'Charlie. You have to go to work tomorrow. And I'm not getting up at silly o'clock with you to get your train so that you can lock up.'

'I'd give you a key, you daft woman. I'd hardly turn you out of my bed – house! House! I meant house!' We were at the outer rim of a puddle of street light but even in the low light, I could see Charlie blush.

'You're definitely tired.'

'I am. I'm shattered. But I did have a great time. Yesterday and today.'

'Me too. It was fun.'

'You going to check that water situation?'

'Nope. I'm going to risk it.'

'That's not what I'd advise, you know. And this is my field of expertise.'

'Hot-water situations.'

He laughed. 'You'd be surprised.'

I reached up and gave him a big hug. 'It'll be fine, but I appreciate the advice and offer.'

Charlie hugged me back. I loved Charlie's hugs. He had a way of wrapping you up that made you feel as if you could stay there forever. Some people had a knack for great hugs. He was definitely one of those people.

'I love your hugs,' I said, and then looked up, surprised. 'Sorry. That wasn't meant to come out aloud.'

'That's all right. Good to know I'm doing something right.'

'Definitely.'

He laughed and swooped in for another. 'Now, come on. If you're insisting on staying here.'

'You don't have to walk me up every time, you know. It's quite safe.'

'I'm sure it is, but it makes me feel better if I do.'

'You're going to make someone a lovely boyfriend one day.' Maybe he could give Alex a few lessons in that area…

'Err, thank you. You do realise I heard that, don't you?'

'Yes, that one was meant for you to hear. But I'm going to stop thinking now, just in case anything unexpected comes out.'

'Possibly a good move.'

I did a thumbs up in place of speaking because there was a thought catapulting around my brain that had started off as a slow burn this morning. And if I was truly honest, it had been there for a while. I didn't know exactly when it had started, or where it had come from. Or what to do with it, now that it was there.

34

It was slightly strange seeing Charlie in his natural habitat of work. And, although I had no idea how this part of his world worked exactly, it was obvious to anyone that whatever it was he did, he was damn good at it. And he knew it. There was no arrogance. Just a quiet, assured, rather sexy confidence. Charlie finished his presentation and took a seat. I'd got the general gist of things but there were times he could have been speaking Venusian, for all I knew.

I'd taken those times to surreptitiously study the others in the room – most notably two women who were part of the team he'd apparently been having meetings with in New York. And, whatever their legitimate reason for being here, one of them most definitely had an extra line on her agenda, which was to lust over Charlie Richmond. I hadn't worked out whether he'd sussed this yet. Probably not, knowing Charlie. But certainly everyone else in the room had. I'd seen the look the two women exchanged when Charlie's eyes lowered to take a sip of water, and it didn't exactly say, 'Gosh, that was a thrilling presentation.' It was more, 'Him. Me. Stationery cupboard. Now.'

I pretended not to see and carried on watching the view from the window. Pleasure boats travelling up and down the Thames full of tourists, a police patrol boat and, closer to the building, HMS Belfast anchored, stalwart and steady. I didn't want to watch the woman smiling at him, laughing at a joke he made over something in his presentation – a joke that had gone completely over my head. I'd seen the women glance my way as they laughed. I'd smiled but they knew I hadn't understood. Flicking my glance to Charlie, I received the same reaction. His didn't have the same patronising look accompanying it but I felt awkward all the same. I gave a quick, tight smile before returning my gaze to the view as I tried to quell the uncomfortable feeling in my stomach.

I knew what the ache inside me was. Denial can only take you so far. Eventually everything will bust out, forcing you to see things as they really are. It had been happening for a while now but every time those feelings tried to bob to the top, I'd squelched them back down. But I knew things were changing. Those feelings were becoming harder and harder to contain. Driving home from Windsor, the two boys sleeping peacefully in the back as the car hummed along quietly, all of us cocooned in the warm, intimate space, I'd known. If I allowed myself to admit it, I'd known for a while. I was in love with Charlie Richmond.

I hadn't meant to fall for him. In fact, the more I knew of him, the more I'd known this would be a Bad Thing. I loved Charlie – as a friend. There was no way I wanted to lose that. As I'd told Marie, the thought of not having him in my life was just... I didn't even want to imagine it.

And, of course, the biggest obstacle was that I was pretty sure Charlie Richmond had absolutely no romantic interest in me whatsoever. In his own words, he'd said that having a partner in a similar field was ideal for him, providing a common ground for conversation at the least. Admittedly, we were never short of conversation as friends but still. He clearly had ideas as to the requirements of his perfect woman. And I didn't fit them.

I brought my gaze back to the room and found myself caught in Charlie's. He raised an eyebrow at me, a silent enquiry. If only he knew, I thought to myself. Instead I gave him a small smile, reassuring him I was just fine. He seemed to buy it. No surprise. I'd been practising that smile for years. The sympathetic smiles from my parents' friends, teachers who normally told me off for daydreaming had also used the same smile as they'd pulled my attention gently back to the room. And I knew that, even now, I did it on the blog. To the web, I was perfectly fine, and absolutely happy. They didn't know about the shock of losing my job and my boyfriend on the same day. They didn't know I still went and sat at Mum's grave, sometimes with a book, sometimes just to sit and tell her all the stuff that I wished I could tell her in person. They didn't know I had set up an email address for her that I wrote to in an effort to feel closer to her. They didn't know I'd been stood up in a romantic restaurant by a good-looking policeman who had already moved on without telling me.

I was happy, bubbly Libby. And sometimes keeping up that act was just exhausting. But I didn't see a way out of it. I'd made it part of my USP, not only for the blog, but also in my life, for better or worse. Mentally I gave myself a shake, smoothed my dress and returned my attention to the cool, air-conditioned office.

Tilly and I had absolutely loved the beauty products that Charlie had brought back from the States for us. Consequently, the company had sent the whole collection and done some more research into the market. Charlie's risk assessment of them branching out into Europe had obviously given them hope because it all seemed to be progressing well that way. And they wanted me along for the ride, helping to promote this new part of their venture. I was thrilled to do so. The products were great and I really liked the people I'd been dealing with over email. They'd advised that they were coming to London to have some more meetings regarding the expansion, including one with Charlie at his offices and had suggested I come along and sit in for part of it. Which was why I was there now. To be honest, I could have left after the first twenty minutes once my participation had been discussed and plans relating to that. From then on, the conversation and language had turned into one I didn't fluently speak, which had allowed my brain to go poking about for something else to think about. Which had turned out to be Charlie Richmond.

Finally, the meeting was over and everyone began filing out. The representatives from the beauty company came over to me, said lots of nice things and told me that they'd be in touch again shortly. We did the whole two-cheek-air-kiss thing, which they then repeated with Charlie before heading out. Charlie snagged me by the elbow as I made to leave, pulling me back.

'You OK?'

'Yes. Why?'

'You looked like you were glazing over a couple of times there. I was worried that I was boring you.'

'Pah! You didn't even know I was in the room.'

He dropped his glance for a moment. 'It's hard not to notice you in a room full of boring suits.'

I took his point. The heatwave was still engulfing the country, melting tarmac and cooking sunbathers to a fetching shade of lobster red. I'd decided to forego the black suit this time and had instead chosen a yellow and white Liberty print sundress with a light Chanel style jacket over it. The jacket had lasted about five minutes. I'd figured that the company had been studying my blog long enough now that they knew my style. And it wasn't as if I'd turned up in ripped jeans.

I chewed the inside of my mouth for a moment, before remembering my brother had commented that I bore a strong resemblance to Sonic the Hedgehog when I did so.

'Should I have gone with the suit?'

Charlie raised his eyebrows and shook his head. 'No! Not at all. It wasn't a criticism. It's kind of nice to look out and see a little ray of sunshine in the room. Not to mention a friendly face.'

'Thanks. Being a ray of sunshine is always nice. But I don't think you're short of people wanting to be friendly here.' I gave him a wink and made to walk out.

'What's that supposed to mean?' he asked, his face a mixture of confusion and amusement.

'Just saying.'

'Just saying what, exactly?'

'Oh, come on. Don't tell me you haven't notic—'

'Ready for lunch, Charlie?' The brunette interrupting us leant on the glass door in a way that looked both natural and incredibly sexy. I cast my mind back to my last experience with Charlie and a glass door. Definitely not sexy.

'Two minutes.' He turned to me. 'You ready?'

'For what?'

'Lunch.'

'Oh! I was just going to grab some sandwiches and have them on the train home.'

'You were?'

'Yes. I didn't know the day involved lunch.'

'Of course it does.'

I glanced out of the floor-to-ceiling windows that made up the wall of the office. Below us, the retired battleship sat steadfast, as all around it the water glittered as if a million stars had been tipped into the Thames. A tall ship was making its way down the centre of the river, and, to our right, traffic was backing up on Tower Bridge as the Victorian engineering began to go to work raising the middle, ready to allow the ship to pass through.

'I'm not really all that hungry, to be honest.' Actually, I was starving.

Charlie moved and stood to my side, watching the bridge. 'So, that wasn't your stomach I heard rumbling during my presentation then?'

Bugger. I thought I'd covered that.

'The cough was a good attempt at disguise though.'

'I was too nervous for breakfast. Don't be mean.'

He squeezed my shoulders. 'No need to be nervous now. They loved you in person just as much as they thought they would from your blog and correspondence.'

'You think so?'

'I know so. I might be a bit crap at reading people socially but this?' He held his index finger in the air and made a small circle with it. 'This, I'm good at.'

'I can tell. And thank you.'

'No need to thank me. Just come to lunch. It'll be a lot more fun with you there.'

I watched the ship pass through the bridge and the cantilevers start moving immediately to bring it back down. London traffic snarled at the best of times, so there was no hanging around in getting it flowing again as soon as possible.

Ms Brunette was back at the door. 'Hey, Charlie, can I speak to you quickly, before we go?'

Charlie smiled. 'Sure.' He looked back to me. 'We'll meet you by the lift in a minute, OK?'

I guessed I was going to lunch with them, then.

'OK. I'm just going to nip to the...' I sort of pointed out of the door, and he got the idea.

I was just making sure everything was where it should be when I heard the door to the Ladies open and two pairs of stiletto-heeled shoes walk in. These were accompanied by American accents.

'Oh, my God. He is so hot! I have no idea what he said in that presentation, so I hope you took notes.' I imagined this was Ms Brunette. Brandy, Sandy, Mandy? I'd been introduced to seven people at the same time and could remember only the first two names. She hadn't been in the first two.

'Lucky for you, I did. Why don't you just ask him out?'

'I'm planning my moment.' I heard a bag zip pull, and some movement. I guessed they were fixing their hair.

'Ooh owe, I id ink ee ite ee eeing at ibby.' And doing their lipstick apparently. 'But I don't think so,' she finished, lipstick back to perfect now, I assumed.

My hand was on the door catch, but at this I stopped. I knew I should just go out there. Mum had always told us it was rude to listen at keyholes and that you risked hearing something you'd rather not. But it wasn't as if I were hearing anything new to me.

'But he doesn't look at her like that.'

'No. You're right. She's hardly his type anyway, is she? I mean, she's nice. Kind of cute. But she's way too dreamy for him. Charlie's sharp, smart, high-flying. He needs someone on that same level. Someone he can have an intellectual conversation with.'

My fingers closed around the catch as I felt colour rush to my face.

'She kind of looked a bit blank in there. She's pretty decoration but Charlie needs someone who totally understands what he does for a living and appreciates it.'

'And I suppose you would know just how to show that appreciation?'

'You know it. And, my God, did you see his hands? They're huge!'

This seemed a source of great amusement.

'Candy, you are the worst! Charlie Richmond is a fine, upstanding Brit. He is not going to be into spanking!'

My mother had been 100 per cent right. I was hearing plenty I didn't want to!

'You'd be surprised.'

'You asked him?' I imagined the other woman's jaw had dropped, just as mine had. I didn't entirely know if I wanted to hear the answer.

'Of course not. I'm just saying, you'd be surprised. They always say it's the quiet ones.'

'Come on, let's get to lunch. And try not to drool into your salad too much.'

I waited until the door closed and I was sure that they had gone before I came out of the stall. I quickly washed my hands, brushed my hair and slapped a top-up of lippy on. Straightening up, I tried to force the overheard words out of my head. Walking purposefully to the main door, I took a deep breath and headed out.

Charlie was waiting at the lifts, along with the two women and another man from the London office who'd been in the meeting. He'd been third in line to be introduced. I was fairly sure that his name was Stuart, but I wasn't putting money on it. Charlie smiled when I came into view and I did a little hurry-up walk as it was clear they'd been waiting for me. We rode down in the lift and walked across the minimalistic foyer, the women's shoes clacking loudly on the limestone tiled floor. My own platform sandals had a rubberised sole, and I squeaked along behind them. Charlie stood back and let me into the revolving door first. I pushed it round, popping out into the scorching summer air. I caught my breath as the heat hit me. Warmth radiated up from the paving stones and I could almost feel my skin turning pink as I waited. The other women exited and turned their faces to the sun, catching the rays and adding to their already perfect tans.

Stuart led the way as we turned and headed towards the river.

Charlie caught my arm as I moved closer to the buildings in order to grab some shade.

'You all right?'

I squinted up at him. 'Yes. Fine. Why?'

He looked at me a moment. 'You were kind of a long time. I was worried that you might be... unwell.' His voice was low, almost a whisper.

I stopped. 'No!'

Oh, great. Ms Brunette was definitely right. Charlie most certainly didn't think of me in a desirable way. At all. Apparently he thought of me with an upset stomach.

'The door in the stall got jammed. I was... stuck.'

Well, the last part was sort of true.

'Why didn't you call out?'

'Does it matter? I got out. I'm here now.'

'No. I'm just... what's up? You don't seem quite yourself.'

My normal, dreamy self. The woman's words made me feel as if I were back at school with the cool girls taking the piss out of me for my pale skin and red hair.

'I'm all right, Charlie. Really. Just a bit hot. It's a little above my melting temperature out here.'

He nodded, not looking entirely convinced. 'We're nearly there.'

A few minutes later and we were all sitting around a circular table in the window of an upscale restaurant. The Golden Table. Of course. The seating plan hardly surprised me as Charlie was undeniably gorgeous, and looked even more edible in his handmade suit than the food on the menu. The two women were incredibly well groomed, good-looking, with Miss Brunette well into the realm of beautiful. Stuart and I did OK, but I knew it was these three that had inspired the maître d' to have us directed to the most prominently viewed table from outside, the message being that, 'Beautiful people dine here. Come in and join the beautiful people.' It was an odd concept, I always thought, as I tended to look at the menu, not the other diners, when I chose a restaurant but it was widely practised, so I guessed the industry felt that there was some benefit.

Charlie ordered wine for the table along with some iced water. As soon as the latter arrived he poured some out, handing mine to me with a brief glance as Ms Brunette caught his attention with some clever piece of conversation. The restaurant had gone with a trendy retro theme and the two women chose fruit juices as starters, with salads to follow. Big surprise, I thought, having noted their teeny bums and superbly toned arms when they'd slipped off their jackets outside to reveal sleeveless blouses. My arms were OK but I wasn't exactly a slave to the gym. Perhaps I should have a fruit juice and salad.

'Prawn cocktail and the sea bass, please.' Oh well.

When the starters came, it was clear that although the theme was retro there was definitely a modern twist on it all. The cocktail had the biggest prawn I'd ever seen in my life hooked over the glass edge. I stared at mine as it looked back at me, accusation in its beady little black eyes.

Charlie was busy dismantling his own prawn when I saw him glance over at my plate, and then at my face. I hadn't moved.

'Libs?'

'Hmm?'

'Everything all right?'

I chewed my lip. 'It's looking at me,' I whispered.

The others were talking amongst themselves but I hadn't missed Ms Brunette's smirk when my order was placed in front of me. I never was very good at hiding my emotions. Mum said it was the Irish blood and that it was healthy. Right now, I wasn't sure I agreed that it was such a helpful trait.

I saw him try to cover a smile. 'I'm pretty sure it's not.'

I flicked a glance to him.

'I thought you liked seafood.'

'I do. I just don't like my food looking back at me.'

He did the smile again and reached across, made some crunching noises and plopped the now naked prawn on top of my cocktail. He took the shell away and put it on the far side of his own plate.

''Scuse fingers,' he said, and then set back to eating his own starter.

I was aware that the others at the table hadn't missed any of the procedure. The women had exchanged a look that even I, with my innate want to see the best in people, had interpreted as pity. I pushed the thought away and stabbed the offending prawn with my fork, delivering it to my mouth with a controlled calmness I didn't feel.

'So, Libby. What do you think of Charlie moving to New York? Isn't it exciting?'

35

I snapped my head up at the question and the huge prawn slid down my throat before I got a chance to give it even one chew. My eyes bulged and I felt my throat close as I tried to draw breath – something my body had apparently decided it didn't really feel like doing right now. Grabbing for the water glass to wash it down, I took a swig but it didn't budge. I was starting to panic now and the others on the table were looking around awkwardly as I felt myself growing redder and redder from alarm and shock. There was probably embarrassment mixed in there somewhere too, but right now I was focused more on trying not to die of choking. I could always worry about dying of embarrassment later, if I got that far.

'Excuse us.' Charlie's arms wrapped around me and moments later we were out of the door and around the corner, away from the prying eyes of our fellow diners. A group of teenagers were hanging around, laughing too loudly and shoving each other, as tourists scuttled past, too busy capturing the scenery with their phones to actually look at it with their eyes. I was still making ghastly noises as I tried to breathe and my eyes were streaming. I wasn't sure if I was crying or if it was just from trying not to die. Either way, I was pretty sure my make-up was taking a hammering. Bizarrely, I suddenly had the thought that I hoped Charlie had the sense to wipe off the mascara stains before they zipped me up into a bag. But he was a bloke. A blokey bloke. Of course it wouldn't occur to him! I flapped my arms some more. Oh God, I was going to die *and* look a mess!

Charlie gave me a heft on the back that did nothing but send me flying forwards. Luckily, he had his other arm around my waist so I didn't face-plant straight onto the pavement. He moved behind me, wrapped both arms around my middle and pulled in and up. The prawn released itself, exited through my open mouth and sailed gracefully through the air, before landing safely in the hoody of one of the teenagers.

Charlie and I both stared for a moment. I knew that really I should go over and tell him, and apologise. But right now I was busy gulping air into my lungs and trying to return to a colour vaguely reminiscent of the one I normally was. Plus, the kid in question was wearing his trousers so low that he had to walk like an arthritic pirate just to keep them up. I had no desire to see random men's underwear and didn't appreciate it being shown without my asking. So I kept quiet about the prawn. Call it karma.

'Jesus, Libby. You had me worried there.'

I nodded. That made two of us. But my mind was already floating back to what had caused me to swallow the damn thing whole in the first place.

What do you think of Charlie moving to New York?

'You should go back to your colleagues.'

'It's all right. I can wait with you for a bit.'

The truth was, I didn't want to go back in there. I'd happily leave right this minute, but my bag was back in the restaurant and it had my train ticket, money, phone – everything – in it.

I ran my hands over my face and pushed my hair back, lifting it up at the nape where it was sticking.

For once, I wished I could keep my feelings to myself, and not have them spill out. This was another trait I'd inherited from my mother's side, and another she'd told us was healthy. But right now I was desperately trying to channel the English, traditionally repressed side of the bloodline. I failed.

'Why didn't you tell me you were moving to New York?'

I saw Charlie stiffen and scratch the back of his head. He didn't reply.

I moved and found some shade. He came and stood near me, but he still didn't speak.

'Charlie?' I prompted, 'Why didn't—?'

'I didn't know how,' he broke in, running both hands through his hair, having apparently gone way past the head-scratching stage.

'How long have you known?'

He looked away and I knew the answer wasn't going to be good.

'It was confirmed about six weeks ago.'

'Six weeks!'

'I know! Look, I've been trying to find a way to tell you.'

'Not very hard, apparently!'

'Libby, you don't understand.'

'You're bloody right, I don't understand! How could you not tell me this? We're supposed to be friends! Good friends.'

'We are! That's what's made it so bloody difficult! How could I tell you I wouldn't be able to come and chat to you whenever I wanted, drop round after a crappy day and have you cheer me up just by opening the door and smiling at me?'

'Don't! Don't do that.'

'Do what?'

'Make it worse!'

'I'm just trying to explain!' He threw his hands in the air. 'Libby, I didn't even know you at the beginning of the year and now I can't remember what life was like without you in it. And I don't want to. You're an amazing friend and I knew you'd be upset when I told you I was leaving. I didn't want to hurt you. I was trying to find a way to tell you.'

'There have been plenty of times in the last six weeks that you could have told me, Charlie. Times when it was just you and me. But no, you couldn't do that. You took the coward's way out and let someone else do it for you!'

'I never meant for it to come out like this! That's not fair. You know I wouldn't do that to you.'

'You just did, Charlie!' I yelled at him. 'You just did!'

We both stood there for a moment, just looking at each other. I realised I had tears streaming and this time I knew the exact reason for them. I was in love with Charlie Richmond, and he'd just broken my heart.

'You should have told me yourself, Charlie,' I said, and began walking back to the restaurant. I needed to get my bag. I swiped under my eyes with my fingers and hoped that the worst of the make-up trails had gone. He caught me up in two strides, and we entered the restaurant together.

'Are you OK?' Ms Blonde asked.

'Yes, thanks. I'm sorry to disturb your lunch. It was nice to meet you.'

'You're leaving?' Ms Brunette asked.

'Yes. Enjoy your stay in London.' I nodded and left.

Charlie followed me out. I turned and he bumped into me, his arms moving quickly to my waist to steady me.

'You should go back inside,' I said, pushing away. 'I've already caused enough disruption and embarrassment.'

'There's nothing to be embarrassed about, and frankly I'm glad of the disruption. We obviously have something to talk about.'

I threw my hands up in the air. 'So now you want to talk?'

'Yes.'

'Fine. What do you want to talk about? How we're supposed to be friends but I'm the last one to know that you're moving thousands of miles away? You say you didn't want to upset me – how the hell do you think it makes me feel to be the last one to be told? And in front of a bunch of strangers who already think I'm an idiot!'

'I didn't mean for you to find out like that. I didn't know Candy was going to say anything at lunch. And nobody thinks you're an idiot. You're overreacting.'

I glared at him. 'Seriously? That's your excuse? You didn't realise it was going to come up?'

Charlie started to open his mouth but I wasn't done. I wasn't anywhere near done.

'And whilst we're on the subject, how the hell does she know anyway? Are you seeing her?'

'No, I'm not.'

'Well, hold that thought, Buster, because she's got plans on that front. And, just so you know, she's into spanking, and apparently hoping that you're going to provide that service, so there's something for you to look forward to!'

Charlie's eyebrows were currently up in his hairline.

'Either way, the least you could have done is afforded me the same courtesy as her!'

He looked at me, and gave a little shake of his head, combined with a head scratch. 'Wait. I'm confused. Are you still talking about the spanking thing? Now you're pissed off that I never offered to spank you?'

The question hung there for a moment between us and, even though I was long lapsed, I still fought the urge to drop to my knees and fire off a handful of Hail Marys for the thought that momentarily shot through my brain.

'What? No, of course not!' Which led me to another question that, me being me, I couldn't keep locked inside where it should have stayed.

'Did you make an offer to spank her, then?'

'No!' Charlie's eyes were wide and confused. 'Look, can we back up a bit?'

That seemed like a really good idea. The best idea would have been for the ground to open up but I didn't see that happening, so I had to go with his. I nodded.

'What courtesy are you talking about?'

'Telling me about New York. Obviously.'

He rolled his eyes. 'Obviously.'

'You told strangers before me.'

'They only know because they're going to be working in the office over there with me.'

I felt sick.

Charlie pulled me to the side of the pavement. 'Look, Libs. I'm really sorry. I wanted to tell you. I really did, but every time I got the chance, it was always when we were having a great time, and I guess, a little selfishly, I didn't want to spoil the day.'

'OK. Can I ask you something else?' My mother was so right about not listening at keyholes.

'Of course.'

'Do you think I'm a bit... dreamy?'

'Dreamy?'

'Yes.'

'Yes. I do.'

Oh.

'And do you feel that you have to dumb down your conversation with me because of that?'

'What?' He jolted his head back, his brows knitting together. 'No, of course not! Where the hell is all this coming from?'

'It doesn't matter. I just wanted to know. I have to go. I'll miss my train.'

Charlie caught my wrist. 'There'll be another train. And it does matter. What's going on? This isn't like you, Libs. You are who you are and you're happy with that. Which is good, because you should be. I love that you're a bit dreamy. It's all part of who you are, and I really like who you are. I'm going to miss you like you crazy when I go to New York, which is why telling you was such a bloody problem.'

'Well, I guess I know now.'

Charlie let his shoulders go slack. 'I guess you do.'

'When do you leave?'

I saw his glance flick to the paving slabs. 'In a month's time.'

My temper flared up. Again. I couldn't help it. Blame my genes. 'Seriously? So, when exactly were you going to tell me? What were you planning to do? Drop a note from the plane? "By the way, Libs, I'm moving to the Big Apple with Miss Spanky Pants. Have a nice life!"'

'You're being dramatic.'

'I don't care! I'm entitled to be dramatic. It's part of my "dreamy" personality.'

Charlie scratched the back of his head.

'Libby—'

'I'm assuming Alex and everyone knows.'

He blew out a sigh. 'Yes.'

'And Marcus, and Amy?'

Charlie nodded.

'I can't believe Amy didn't tell me!'

'I asked her not to. But she said if I didn't tell you this week, she was going to.'

'I see.'

'Don't be angry at her.'

'Oh, don't worry, I'm not. I'm angry at you.'

'Great.' He did the head scratch again and then ran his hands through his hair, mussing it up completely. 'I don't know what you want me to say, Libs. I'm sorry I didn't tell you earlier. And I'm sorry you had to find out like this, but what's done is done. I can't change it.'

I felt the fight go out of me. 'No. I know.'

Charlie sensed a break in the battle and took a tentative step towards me.

'Please don't cry. I can't bear seeing you upset.'

I swiped at my nose with a tissue from my bag. I was pretty much resigned to the fact that my make-up was now way beyond help. All I needed now was to run into the cosmetics company executives in my current state and my day would be perfect.

'Is it forever – this move?'

'No. Maybe a year, depending on how things go.'

I rested my head on his chest for a moment. His heart began to slow as we stood there, his hand moving rhythmically over my hair, down my back.

'May I ask a question?'

'Mmh hmm.' I tilted my head back to meet his eyes.

'How on Earth do you know about Candy's... persuasions?'

'I overheard her saying it when I was in the loo.'

He brushed my hair back off my shoulder. 'Something tells me that wasn't the only thing you overheard in there.'

I didn't reply.

'I don't understand. You don't let stuff like that bother you normally. You've said yourself you have to find a way to not let people's opinions get to you if they say something mean. You know all that from doing the blog.'

'I know. I guess it's different when it's said in your hearing.'

'Well, it shouldn't be. You're just different from them. And, in my opinion, that's a good thing. Don't ever think that it isn't.'

I gave him a squeeze in silent thanks, and he returned it.

'Did you know already?'

'About what?'

'Miss Spanky Pants.'

I saw his mouth twitch at the moniker I'd dubbed her with. 'Yes.'

My heart did a lurch thing and my stomach contracted, as I wondered how he knew.

'Office gossip can be a very informative thing.'

'You're not one for gossip.'

'Nope. But my assistant always passes on information that she thinks might be pertinent.'

'What would she have done if your eyes had lit up when she passed on that particular bit of vital information?'

'She's harder to shock than you might think. Besides, she's already informed me that she doesn't think Candy and I would be a good match.'

'Really?'

'Apparently.'

'What do you think?'

'I think she's never given me bad advice. Besides, I'm not interested in her anyway. Dating someone you work with can get messy.'

'Would you date her if you weren't going to be working with her?'

'I hadn't really thought about it. I will be working with her, so it's kind of a moot point. My brain doesn't go to the same places yours does, with all those "what ifs".'

Logical, as always.

'You should really go back to them. I'm sorry I messed up lunch.'

'You didn't. Don't worry. Why don't you come? You haven't eaten anything yet.'

'I sort of lost my appetite.' I gave a little shrug. 'Only to be expected when you find out the man you've fallen in love with is about to put a whole ocean between you.'

Charlie's hand stilled on my hair and I felt his body stiffen.

I looked up. He was looking out across the river.

'What's the matter?'

He didn't move his gaze. 'What you just said. Did you actually mean exactly what you just said, or did it come out a bit... wrong?'

I rewound the conversation in my head.

Oh. Crap. Not quite how I had planned for that particular revelation to happen. In fact, I hadn't planned for it to be a revelation at all. In my messed-up state, I'd just gone blathering on. But I guessed it was out there now.

I drew in a sigh. 'No. I mean, yes.'

Charlie turned his head, stepping back from me as he held up his hands in question.

'So, which is it, Libby? No or yes.'

His voice was tight, his face serious.

I swallowed. 'It's both. No, it didn't come out wrong. And yes, I meant it.'

Charlie looked away, squinting as the sunlight bounced off the Thames. After a moment he shook his head, his eyes still averted.

'I have to get back to work.'

'Charlie.' I stepped towards him. 'I didn't mean to tell you like this.'

'Don't, Libby, please. You've just berated me for not telling you I was leaving and all this time, you've been holding onto something like that!'

'There's no "all this time"! I didn't even know until recently, and I wasn't about to blurt it out if I wasn't sure and risk ruining our friendship!'

'I have to go,' he said again, not looking at me.

'So go, then!'

He flicked his glance down to me, held mine a moment, then turned on his expensive heel and began walking back towards the restaurant. I watched him stride off, my chest burning as it struggled to keep all the hurt inside. Turning away, I put my head down and began heading for London Bridge station.

Hearing footsteps approaching fast behind me, I made to move out of the way, only to find Charlie back beside me. He caught my arm and pulled me to the side.

'You can't just go around doing that, you know!'

'I don't... doing what?'

'Telling people you're in love with them with no warning. It's just not... you just can't do it!'

I threw off his hand in anger. 'It's not something I make a habit of, Charlie! And I realise that I didn't do it in the best way possible, but it wasn't supposed to happen like that.'

'But you did plan on telling me?'

'Yes. Maybe...'

'Why?'

I looked up and met his eyes. There was none of the warmth

there that I was used to seeing when he looked at me. Today they were the blue of glacier ice.

I hesitated, feeling the chill through my bones. 'Because when something's important, you should say it.'

'Even if it means ruining a friendship.'

I swallowed hard.

'Does it mean that, then?'

He scratched the back of his head. Dropped his hand. Then repeated the action with his other one.

'Look. I know you believe in all this being open stuff. But sometimes it's best to keep things to yourself.'

'So, is that a yes to the friendship ruination question, then?'

'I don't know. Five minutes ago you were in love with my best mate, and now this? What am I supposed to think?'

The tears that had been pooling spilled out.

'That's unfair, and you know it! I never said I was in love with Alex. I liked him, but it didn't work out.'

'So what? You thought you'd try the next one in line?'

His words were like a punch to my heart. My mouth dropped open and it took me a moment to find my voice as I desperately tried to keep the pieces of my heart together.

'You're right, Charlie. I never should have said anything. I realise that now. But maybe it was a good thing because at least now I know what you really think of me. Enjoy your lunch. Try not to choke on it!'

I stepped around him and stalked off down the alleyway, all the while trying to stop his words ringing in my head. Suddenly I wished Charlie Richmond were already in New York and out of my life. Although I made a guess that the second part of that had now begun. Fishing in my bag, I pulled out my bug-eye, Audrey-Hepburn-style sunglasses and shoved them onto my face, hoping to conceal as much as possible from the world at large.

Standing looking up at the destination board, I watched the display change. The platform number for the next train to Brighton showed and a bunch of people began heading off towards it. I remained staring at the board. And then I turned and headed downstairs towards the Tube.

36

'Darling!' Gina threw out her arms in her usual ebullient manner of greeting, and then stopped. Reaching out with perfectly manicured, shocking-pink nails, she slid my sunglasses gently off my face. Without another word, she pulled me close in to her sizeable bosom and wrapped her arms around me. I stood there for a moment and then my shoulders started to shake. Gina made soothing sounds and ushered us both inside.

I was lying on the couch, idly tracing the flowers of its expensive chintz fabric with my finger, when Dad came in an hour later. Gina had obviously filled him in and he came straight over to me, scooched me up and gave me a big cuddle. Which set me off again.

'He'll come round,' Dad said eventually as my sobs subsided once more.

'No, he won't. Besides, I don't want him to come round. He said something he can't take back.'

'We all say things we don't mean in the heat of the moment. It's human nature, I'm afraid. Not a great trait, but not one that's easy to erase.'

'I shouldn't have told him.'

'Do you love him?'

I didn't even need to think about it. 'Yes.'

'Then it was right to tell him.'

'Even if I've ruined everything?'

'Even if that is the case.' Dad sat me back so that he could look at me. 'Libby. We both know you're far too much like your mother to have ever kept this inside. You're always bursting with things to say and feel. And Charlie knows that's just your way, too. He knows you couldn't have not told him. It's just taken him by surprise.'

'He doesn't want me to be in love with him.'

'Well, if that is the case, then he's not as smart as he thinks he is.'

I gave a small, sniffly laugh. 'Obviously.'

'I nearly missed out on having my time with your mum because I was too much like Charlie and not enough like you.'

'Really?'

Dad smiled, a mix of joy and sorrow. 'Yes. And although there were times after she passed away that I thought I might never get through her loss, I wouldn't have missed that time with her for anything. And I wouldn't have two wonderful children, and two beautiful grandchildren and all the irreplaceable joy that all of those things have brought me. I nearly kept everything to myself. Terribly British and all that. And suddenly I realised that if I didn't make my move, then someone else would. They'd see just how amazing she was and I'd have missed my chance. So, I put myself and my heart out there on display for her to see. It was one of the hardest things I've ever done. And the best thing I've ever done.'

'But she loved you back.'

'That's true. I was lucky.'

'Charlie doesn't love me back. It's not the same.'

'But could you have gone through life wondering what if? At least this way you know.'

We were back to the what ifs. Yet another difference between me and Charlie. What had I even been thinking, falling for him? I hadn't been thinking. That was just it. It had just happened. Either way, we were far too different. It was never going to work.

'Can I stay here for a few days?'

'Of course you can. You know you never need to ask. Stay as long as you like.'

'I need to go out and get some bits.'

'Why don't you go with Gina? She'd love to go shopping with you.'

I smiled at him. 'I think that would be lovely.'

His own smile broadened.

* * *

'So, I'll meet you at Selfridges at eight and let you know where I've booked. Sure you don't have any preferences?' Dad asked me.

I shook my head. To be honest, I still didn't have much of an appetite but I wasn't about to waste away over Charlie Richmond, so I would find something delicious on the menu and bloody well enjoy it.

I called Amy and told her the whole story, including where I was staying, but asked her not to tell anyone else, especially Marcus. She was just to say that I'd gone away for a few days. I checked on my blog and responded to questions and comments. There were a bunch of posts scheduled to go up over the next few weeks that Tilly and I had done before she went on honeymoon and I was enormously grateful now that we'd put in that time. It gave me a chance to relax and just think. Everything had been such a blur for the past year, and now this whole thing with Charlie. I was exhausted.

I spent the time at Dad's dozing and reading. We took trips to the park with picnics, and visited exhibitions and museums. What we didn't do was have anyone 'just drop in for dinner' for which I was unbelievably grateful. Although it had been a messy way to get the message across, Dad seemed to have finally realised that I had to make my own mistakes and find my own way when it came to love. As I was apparently on a roll with admissions, I finally told him that I'd always felt he was a little disappointed with me because I'd gone a different path from Matt.

The look of hurt on my dad's face in that moment told me I couldn't have been more wrong as he admitted that he wasn't quite sure how things like blogs worked. His lack of questioning about my work was down to him feeling embarrassed that he didn't understand more about his daughter's career, not because of any lack of pride in me. I'd seen the tears shining in his eyes as he enveloped me in a huge, reassuring hug.

* * *

After nearly a fortnight at Dad's, although my heart was in just as many pieces as it had shattered into when Charlie had turned his back on me and stalked off, I was beginning to feel a little more like myself again. Perhaps I had just needed a break after spending so much time working on the blog and trying to grow the business? Perhaps none of this was really to do with Charlie Richmond at all? My mind did its best to try and find a way out of the situation, but the moment Charlie popped into my brain, I felt the pieces of my heart squeeze and crack. I might well have been in need of a rest but the heartbreak was still real.

I sighed, took a deep breath and tried to push everything to the back of my mind. It had been a few days since I'd signed into the blog and I knew I ought to check for any messages or comments that I needed to vet or reply to. I had no desire to do much else online at the moment. Being unplugged for most of the time felt refreshing and I had made a mental note to take time to do this occasionally in the future. Hopefully with far less drama attached.

Switching on my phone, I tucked myself into the corner of the velvet Chesterfield that gave a view out of huge sash windows to the avenue and park below. The phone got signal and a barrage of pings and bleeps sounded as various apps downloaded the messages and emails sent via them. Scanning them quickly, I noticed there were several from Charlie. My voicemail counter was blinking nine and I hesitated before dialling to pick them up. I didn't need to hear Charlie berate me any more right now. It wasn't as if I'd planned to fall for him, and certainly not as hard as I had! Sometimes we had very little control over these things. Our emotions did what they wanted, overruling any sensible, logical instructions the brain valiantly tried to give. The voicemail started and at the first word Charlie spoke, I hit delete and moved to the next. I did the same with the next eight. As I got to the last, the band around my chest was almost suffocating and the screen had become blurry with my unshed tears. Every one was deleted without playing it.

Squishing the heel of my hand against my eyes to clear them, I scanned the message apps. Most were ones that could wait. Amy and Matt both knew where I was and had rung on Dad's landline. Again, there were more here from Charlie but I knew I couldn't deal with those feelings right now. Perhaps once there were thousands of miles and an ocean between us, I'd be able to look at them and deal with his no doubt logical, angry arguments as to why I'd had to upset the balance of our friendship. But until then, they would have to wait.

There was one message I did open. It was from Tilly, who still had another week of honeymoon left and should be doing a whole bunch of things far more interesting than emailing me. The message had come in late yesterday and didn't have a proper title, just a string of exclamation marks. Frowning, I opened the mail.

Oh, Libby! My cousin just sent me a photo of this clipping. Apparently, it was in a couple of national newspapers, both in the paper and online. I assume they didn't contact you as what they're saying is so totally wrong! Sam has told me not to get upset and that the media always blow things out of proportion and it will soon be yesterday's news. I know he's right but it's still upsetting and I hate what they've said, especially as you really are one of the very nicest people I know. I hope you are OK and am sending love. I'm sure Charlie will have a brilliant, logical view of it and hopefully will help you feel better.
Lots of love, Tilly xxxxx

I read the email again and then clicked on the link Tilly had included alongside the screenshot she'd been sent. My stomach churned and knotted as the page loaded and I saw the title.

How To Be Perfect And Live A Perfect Life – The Fraudster Bloggers That Damage Our Self-Esteem.

I forced myself to read the article. The byline read 'Miss Anthrope', which I guessed should have warned me as to the content. With a harshly sceptical tone, the writer blasted what she called aspirational blogs as damaging, false and another scourge from the Instagram Generation. Miss Anthrope had singled a few blogs out, including a couple extremely well known for generating their idea of a perfect life. The suggestion being that if followers just bought this dress, or that make-up, then they too could be like the blogger whose perfect life/house/body/teeth/hair was an achievable goal. She berated blogs for peddling this belief and then turned her attention to what she called up-and-coming blogs of the same ilk, including Brighton Belle. Absent-mindedly I pulled a cushion from the sofa and hugged it against me as though the soft stuffing would absorb the vitriol dripping from the pen – or keyboard – of this anonymous attack.

> The 'Brighton Belle' blog is just one of the many new blogs taking over the baton of pushing unachievable perfectionism from some of the more established names. According to Libby Cartright, the perky redhead behind this blog, mere mortals like you and I can make up for our drab and dreary lives by buying Fairtrade clothes, and ecologically sound make-up. Follow her advice and soon you too could be sitting on the balcony of your swanky marina apartment, sipping cocktails as the breeze gently tousles your tumbling, abundant tresses and a deliciously gorgeous man dotes on your every word and move.
>
> Bloggers like Cartright are a danger, especially to teenagers or anyone who may already be suffering low self-esteem. Self-harm statistics in this group are on the rise, with experts pointing to social media as one of the main culprits. Cartright and her fellow bloggers flaunt their perfect lives, making readers feel that they are less worthy when they don't achieve the same status.

I began reading some of the comments under the article but soon stopped, knowing it would only make it all so much worse. Staring out of the window, I watched two toddlers in the park below playing in the sunshine, their nannies conversing and laughing with their charges. I wanted to breathe in that happiness, that simplicity, and have it smother the roiling nausea that now filled me. Reaching for my phone, I pulled up Tilly's email and pressed reply.

Dear Tilly, please don't worry about all this. I'm fine and am not letting it bother me. As Sam says, it will soon be yesterday's news.

I added a smiley face here.

Just unplug, relax and enjoy the rest of your honeymoon! Everything is under control. Lots of love, Libby xxx

I felt bad lying to Tilly, but it was done with love. She didn't need to know that I felt as if my life was spinning out of control. My business had been attacked and criticised in a national paper, as well as online – I didn't yet know what that would mean for the blog or its sponsors. It could follow the 'any publicity is good publicity' route or it could go the opposite way entirely. The theme of making a good and happy life, rather than a perfect one, was a soundbite that was gaining traction. It was also one I totally agreed with. I'd never set out to give off some pretence of perfection. Was that really how people saw my blog? Had anyone ever read my blog, or watched a video, and come away from it feeling less worthy? The thought of that physically sickened me.

I wrapped my arms around my stomach and tried to calm my spinning mind. Tilly was right. Charlie probably would have something logical and comforting to say about it all. But I'd forfeited my chance to ever again ask him for such wisdom. A sad, strangulated laugh escaped from me – a perfect life? Hardly! That anonymous writer knew nothing about me. They had made suppositions, applied their own beliefs to my posts and made assumptions far from the truth. But there it was in black and white. My shallow, narcissistic values on display to the world. It didn't matter whether the words were true or not. The damage was done.

* * *

'You must ignore them!' Gina's hands flew as she talked, rings glinting as they caught the low sun as we sat together for our evening meal. 'These people, they know nothing about you. They are ignorant and small-minded.'

'I know. I keep telling myself that.'

Dad broke off a piece of the warm, crusty bread Gina had brought home to go with a lavish salad spread over the rich oak dining table. 'It doesn't sound like you are doing a very good job at convincing yourself.'

I speared a cherry tomato and popped it in my mouth. To be

honest, I hadn't been hungry but, being Italian, Gina had insisted, telling me that her family always discussed the most important things over food. I shrugged my shoulders at Dad's comment.

'One minute I think I am but there's something in the back of my mind that keeps niggling at me.'

'Which is?' Dad topped off my wine glass before moving to Gina's and his own.

'What if this person was right? What if I am, without meaning to, giving readers an idea of how they are supposed to dress, or act, or live?'

'People are usually intelligent enough to make up their own minds, Libby.'

'I know. But what if some insecure teenager watched a video or read a post and thought it meant more than it should have. I've never shared the bad stuff on my blog. I didn't think it was anything people would want to see. There's enough bad stuff going on in the world without me doing a video about having a crappy day. I suppose it also felt a bit too... I don't know, a bit too personal. I wanted people to read my blog or watch a post and feel cheered up by it.'

'Which they do. Your comments speak for themselves. Also, didn't you say the solicitor who helped you with the contract said that your blog had kept his wife company nursing her babies?'

I smiled at the reminder, but it was now a bitter-sweet memory because it had also involved Charlie. 'He did.'

'There you go, then.'

'But what if for every, say, five or ten people like that, there's one who thinks I'm living this perfect life and, unless they are doing the same, they're less of a person? What if I'm doing more harm than good?' My voice had risen in pitch as tears pushed their way from my eyes and trickled down my cheeks. A gnawing, panicky gripe twisted inside me. I pushed my plate away, the food I'd eaten suddenly sitting heavy in my stomach.

'You're not going to let a stranger's vitriolic tirade ruin something you've worked so hard on and that makes you happy, are you?' Dad asked, his brow creased with concern.

I wiped my tears away with the crisp linen napkin. 'I'm not exactly sure what I'm going to do.'

A couple of days later I'd made my decision. I quickly opened an email.

Here goes nothing. Wish me luck, Mum. Love you. Wish you were here xxx

Balancing my phone on the dressing table in the guest room Gina and Dad had prepared for me over a fortnight ago now, I squared my shoulders, took a couple of deep breaths and pressed record.

'Hi, everyone. Apologies for the different setting and quality of this video but I'm away from home and so making the best of what I have available.

'This isn't a post I had ever planned to make and, as you can see, it's not just the setting that's changed. I expect many of you know about the article that was in the news a few days ago, berating certain bloggers for pushing a vision of unattainable perfection, which for some followers could have serious consequences. Brighton Belle was named as one of the blogs accused of this. I've spent the last few days turning this over and over in my mind. I never meant for the blog to be taken like that and I can only hope that it isn't. I don't have a perfect life, and I never meant to give the impression that I have. I just wanted to create something that lifted my spirit and if it lifted someone else's too, that would be an amazing bonus.

'I first created my blog as an online journal – just for me, and, although it probably sounds a bit strange, it was a way for me to share my love of fashion, and beauty and design with my mum. Even though she would never read it. Like I said, that might sound a bit weird but the first post I did, it helped me feel close to her.

'My mum was amazing. Beautiful, clever, funny and joyful. She loved all the things this blog is about but I never got much of a chance to share them with her. When I was thirteen, she suffered a brain aneurysm. One moment she was there, laughing with us, and then she had gone. My bright, vibrant, full of life, wonderful mum...'

I scrunched the tissue in my hand and wiped my cheek with the back of my hand before carrying on.

'I miss her every single day. I think of her every day, and there's not a day I don't wish that she were here with me, so we could do all the things mums and daughters are supposed to do together. I created this blog as a way to keep a link with her. It's sort of like my own memorial to her. With every post or video, I feel closer to her. But it was never supposed to project an image of perfection and if I ever did that, if anyone ever thought that, then I'm truly, truly sorry.

'Life isn't perfect, and mine certainly isn't. I'm lucky in a lot of ways – I have a wonderful family who support me in my artistic endeavours, even though it's completely different from their more academic bent. But I am not perfect. I'm never seen without my make-up on in my videos, or in real life. Until today, as I'm sure you've noticed. My make-up is my armour, and it has been for years. I didn't have the self-belief that I could be seen without it, or that people would accept me just as well without that polished finish. It's my insecurities that have led to me being that way, not any natural ability to casually capture that perfect Instagram moment. Those candid moments aren't real. Not on my feed or anyone else's. We are all just trying to put our best selves out there. And for many, including me, it's because we're a little afraid that we might not be accepted, or loved, or thought worthy of attention if we do anything less.

'But we should never think that. I know that now. The people that care about us don't care if our make-up isn't perfect, or if our hair isn't stylishly tousled, or if we're wearing the right clothes – whatever those are. The people that matter are the ones that take care of you when you come to them with a heart so broken, you wonder if it will ever mend. The ones that let you sob when you've fallen so hard in love with a man you never meant to, and who doesn't love you back. And in telling him that fact, realising you've lost a best friend who you know you will never, can never, replace.'

My throat sounded croaky and rough and I tried to smile through the fresh wave of tears that now trickled down my cheeks.

'It wouldn't surprise me if Miss Anthrope attacks this post as a carefully constructed PR stunt and if she wants to think that, I can't stop her. But it's not. She was right in that I always posted about happy, bubbly Libby, but it wasn't to push some unattainable vision. It was to make myself happy because life isn't perfect. And because I miss my mum every single day. Some days it's a real, physical pain and I'd do anything to have her back. It's to offer ideas and advice that I wish I'd been told when I was young, and shy and feeling out of things because I was trying to be something I wasn't.

'It's just a blog. It wasn't meant to change the world. It was just something to help change my own a little.

'So!'

I did my best to wipe away the tears and smile at the camera phone.

'Now you know. This is me. The currently heartbroken, unadulterated pure Libby. With her red eyes, red nose and not a splash of make-up in sight. The thought of doing this made me feel sick, if I'm honest. But I needed to do it. Whatever you, or anyone, thinks of it is something I can't change. All I can hope is that you know you are everything you need to be. It doesn't matter what you wear, who you know, what you know, what colour your skin is. You are unique. And, more importantly, you are more than good enough.'

I gave a final smile and a little wave then leaned in and stopped the recording. Before I could change my mind, I pulled up the admin for my blog and posted the video. What reaction, if any, it might generate was out of my control.

38

The sound of shingle shifting close behind me made me turn. I shaded my eyes with my hand against the early morning sun as I looked up and saw two uniformed police officers standing to my left.

'Oh no.' I let out a sigh.

'Funny how about 80 per cent of women greet you with that phrase, Alex.' The shorter officer grinned.

'Give us a minute, will you, funny guy?'

Alex's partner nodded and scuffed off up the beach a little, his fingers hooked in the front of his stab vest. Alex watched him go for a moment and then crouched down next to me.

'Hi.'

'Just passing?'

He picked up a pebble and tossed it to and fro between his hands. 'Got a call that there was a woman looking suspicious near the pier.'

I turned to him, gave a quick glance around then looked back at him. 'Me?'

Alex nodded.

'I'm not suspicious! I'm just sitting here.'

'Yep. And apparently you've been just sitting there for the past two hours. With a piece of rope.'

'What? Don't be ridiculous. I don't have any rope!'

Alex reached around me and picked up the wrap I'd been fiddling with. It was cream and currently rolled into a thin snake.

My eyebrows rose. 'Oh! Oh no. I didn't even think... I'm so sorry. I didn't mean to waste anyone's time.'

He gave a smile that crinkled the corners of his eyes. 'Don't worry about it. Believe me, this is a much nicer surprise. Every once in a while stats about the town apparently having a higher than average suicide rate pop up. It can make some people a bit jumpy.'

'I guess it's nice that people are looking out for others.'

'There's that.'

We sat in silence for a few minutes. It was still early on a Saturday and the city wasn't yet fully awake. The sea slooshed over the pebbles, rattling them each time it withdrew.

'People have been looking for you.'

I didn't meet his eyes, instead trailing my finger over the bumps of the stones beside me.

'What for?'

'Because they were worried about you. Because they saw a heartbroken post on your blog. Because you wouldn't answer their calls.'

'It's better that way.'

Alex rolled his lips together. 'Nope. Not sure it is. Besides, from what I know of you, you're not the kind of person to let something stew.'

'I wasn't letting anything stew. I was clearing my head.'

'Uh huh. And is it clear now?'

'Pretty much.'

'Is that why you've been gazing out to sea since five a.m. on a weekend?'

'Is there a law against that, then Officer?' I quirked an eyebrow.

He smirked. 'Smart arse. And no, there isn't a law against it. But I still think you need to speak to him.'

'Who?'

Alex gave me a look.

Worth a try.

I blew out a sigh. 'I think everything has been said.'

'So, why's he been driving himself crazy to try and talk to you, then?'

I shrugged.

The silence hung again.

'I didn't know. When I went out with you, I mean. I honestly didn't know that I felt that way about Charlie. It's all been a bit of a surprise, to be honest. To everyone, it would seem. And not exactly a welcome one.'

'I know things weren't like that then – don't worry about it.'

'He hates me.'

Alex threw his head back and laughed. 'Women.'

I narrowed my eyes at him. 'Oh! Because men are so bloody perfect!'

He laughed again.

'I can assure you Charlie does not hate you. Just talk to him.'

'No,' I said, standing. 'There's nothing to say. And he'll be off to New York soon anyway and it'll be done.'

Alex followed me to a standing position and stood looking down at me.

'And you think all those feelings are just going to disappear because you shove a few thousand miles between you?'

'What's the point?' I whispered, noticing his partner heading back towards us.

'The point is, if you don't, I'm going to arrest you.'

'What? You are not. What for?'

'Loitering.'

'Don't be ridiculous.'

Alex slid his hand to his back and lifted his cuffs, before reaching out to catch my hand. I jumped back.

'Stop it! What if someone sees? They don't know you're mucking about! You could trash my blog's reputation! Although that seems to be a popular pastime at the moment.'

Alex gave a derisive snort. 'These days it'd probably up your numbers. But, if you don't want to prove that point, then go and talk to Charlie. Please. I'm asking you as a friend.'

'To whom? Him or me?'

'Both of you.'

'Cop-out answer. Excuse the pun.'

'Excused. Are you going to do it?'

'Yes. Fine. I'll talk to him.'

'When?'

'Later.'

'Not good enough. I'll drop you off now. The car's up there. And that way, the concerned citizen who's been keeping an eye on you all morning will know you're being taken somewhere safe.'

I rolled my eyes. 'What a crock.'

Alex gave me a 'whatever works' kind of look.

'Fine. Just put those damn cuffs back, will you? You're making me nervous.' I said, as we began walking towards the road.

'Bet ole Miss Spanky Pants wouldn't be so nervous about them.'

I cut my eyes to him. 'Charlie really did tell you everything, didn't he?'

'Oh, yeah.'

'I assume you're taking the first flight you can to New York once he's settled in, and looking for an introduction?' I said, standing next to the police car.

Alex grinned. 'In you hop.'

'It's seven o'clock in the morning. He's probably not even up yet.'

'That's what a doorbell is for. Come on. In.'

I huffed and slid in the back seat. Alex and his partner got in the front and pulled out onto the main road. A few minutes later they'd turned off and parked the car in the crescent that Charlie's house stood in.

Alex got out from the driver's side and came round to open my door. I saw a curtain twitch at one of the windows. Charlie's house was still in darkness.

'Great. Nosy neighbours. And it doesn't look like he's up.'

'Like I said—'

'Doorbell. Yes, I know. But it hardly seems fair to wake him on a Saturday when I could just as well talk to him later.'

Our voices were low in deference to the early hour and the open windows in several of the neighbouring houses.

'He won't mind. Stop stalling.'

'It's just that—'

'Libby?' We both turned. Charlie stood on his front step. He wore pyjama bottoms and a slightly misshapen white T-shirt. His hair was uncombed and his feet were bare and tanned against the white stone of the porch. He took a step towards us.

'Is everything all right?' Concern creased his face as he looked first at Alex, and then back at me.

Alex moved first. 'Yep. All good. We bumped into Libby on the beach and gave her a lift as we were coming this way.'

Charlie took a step towards me.

'Is that true?'

I drew myself up. 'Not exactly. Apparently sitting on the beach in the morning is suspicious. Alex got a call to check it out and found me minding my own business, watching the waves. He then said if I didn't come here and talk to you, he'd arrest me for loitering.'

Charlie looked at Alex. 'That sounds like it might be more accurate.'

'She can be stubborn. And you two need to talk.' He watched us for a moment and then dangled the cuffs. 'Don't make me use these.'

I tilted my head at Charlie. 'He has other plans for those.'

A flicker of a smile crossed Charlie's face.

'I'd hate to deprive you, mate,' Charlie said. 'Libby. Please, would you come in?'

Alex gave me a kiss on the cheek and headed back to his car. I hesitated, wondering about scooting off the moment they were out of sight.

'Don't even think about it,' Alex said, without turning his head.

I turned quickly to Charlie, a question on my face.

'He's been doing this a long time.'

'What? Delivering women to your door in the early hours?'

Charlie smiled. 'Being a policeman.'

'Oh.'

He looked down at me. 'Are you coming in?'

'Is there any chance I'd get back to my flat without being picked up for something else?'

'I doubt it.'

I let out a sigh and walked past him into the chequerboard-floor foyer. Charlie followed and closed the door. The air was cool here and light filtered in through the stained-glass panels above the door, making pools of bright colours on the tiles.

We stood there.

'I'll go and get dressed.'

'Don't worry on my account. I'm not staying long and you look tired. You should go back to bed.'

'I wasn't in bed. I've been up since five.'

'Why?'

Charlie turned and headed off towards the kitchen. I hesitated, then followed. He poured water from a filter jug into the kettle. Flicking it on, he leant back with his hands on the worktop, legs straight, ankles crossed loosely.

'Thinking.'

'About what?' I wasn't sure I wanted to hear the answer, but I needed to.

'About what you said the very first time we met.'

A laugh bubbled out of me unexpectedly, partly from nerves. 'I probably said a lot, knowing me. You'll have to narrow it down a bit.'

Charlie smiled. 'You have a point. I was thinking about what you said about life not being black and white and that it was messy, and that sometimes things don't make sense but we have to muddle through them as best we can.'

'Oh. Yes. Well, that does sound like me.'

He smiled, then looked down at his feet. The kettle reached a boil and Charlie turned and knocked the switch. When he looked back at me, his face was serious.

'I'm sorry about what I said. I didn't mean it. If I could take it back, I would.'

'I think we'd both take things back if we could.'

Charlie flicked his glance to a bird as it landed on his patio table and began sunning itself.

'What would you take back?' he asked.

This was it. This was the opportunity to fix everything. To try and put things back together the way that they had been before. It wasn't going to be exactly the same. I knew that, but maybe in time... I couldn't do it. I couldn't say something I didn't mean.

'Nothing,' I replied.

I walked to the patio door. The bird cocked its head and peered at me for a moment before fluffing its feathers, continuing to soak up the early morning warmth. 'I know that's not the right answer.

And I've ruined one of the best, if not the best, friendships that I've ever had, or probably ever will have, but what's the point of carrying on if I have to lie?'

'You wouldn't last five minutes without bursting.'

'Exactly.' I tried to laugh but it was so hard with him standing there, looking all ruffled and big and gorgeous.

'You know you and I don't make sense in my world of logic and patterns—'

I held up my hands, palms toward him. I didn't need it explained to me. 'I know, I know. You don't need—' I stopped as Charlie caught my hands and held them.

'I'm not finished.'

My stomach went all soft and heat rippled through me. This wasn't good. I mean, it felt *great*, but it wasn't good.

'Oh.'

'We don't make sense. But we still work. We work great. It's like you said. Sometimes things don't make sense but you have to muddle through.' He looked down at his hands, mine disappearing into his own. 'I really want to muddle through all this with you, Libby. As a whole lot more than just friends. You and I might not make sense on paper but in the real world, we do. Becoming your friend is the best thing that's ever happened to me. You've helped me see that sometimes things don't make sense but that's no reason not to go ahead and do them because it can bring joy and happiness and that sometimes it's good to do things just because! For no other reason than that.'

I searched his face.

'What?'

'You've never done anything in your life without thinking about it. I love you, Charlie. I do. But I don't want you to go into this just "because". That's not enough for you. And I know I'm probably driving you crazy and acting like I'm contradicting myself but I'm not. I can get over you now – in time. But if I let you in, really let you in, then I know how much harder I'll fall for you. And when you decide that you've had enough of "just because" and want someone you can discuss the world's great questions and, oh, I don't know, accountancy trivia with, having to get over you then will be so much harder. I can't put myself through that.'

'Come here.' Charlie led me to the small couch that sat at one end of the kitchen. It had a view of the patio and I could still see the little chaffinch preening in the early sun. Charlie sat and pulled me down beside him.

'First off, I can talk about everything and anything with you. And don't ever believe anything different. On the other point, yes, you're right. I don't make any big decisions without thinking about it. That's probably not going to change. Which is why I've done nothing but think about this since you walked off three weeks ago.'

I watched his face. 'Truth is, I've been thinking about it, on and off, since the day I first met you.'

39

'I don't understand.'

Charlie tucked a knee up and concentrated on playing with my fingers, lifting one to study the tiny painting the nail artist had done on them when I'd gone out for a girls' day with Gina.

'I had a massive crush on you before we even got to lunch that first day.'

'You did not!'

He laughed and nodded. 'I did indeed. Which sort of took me by surprise a bit because I'm not exactly prone to things like that.'

'Because crushes aren't black and white.'

'Exactly. I think the final straw was when you reached up and rubbed in the sun cream on my face. It was all I could do not to scoop you up and kiss the living daylights out of you.'

'I... I didn't have a clue.'

Charlie laughed again. 'Yes, I got the impression that I hadn't entirely blown my cover when you told me to feel free to accept the waiter's advances, if I felt so inclined.'

I shrugged, smiling. 'I didn't want to stand in the way.'

'That's because you're kind, and lovely, and you.'

'But you never...'

Charlie went back to studying my hands. 'I convinced myself that it was just a crush. Because you put me at my ease faster than anyone I've ever met. Because I felt I could be myself so easily with you. That wasn't something I'd ever experienced with a woman before. You were just so different from anyone I've ever been out with. Anyone I've ever met, in fact. I thought it was the uniqueness of you that I was falling for – not actually you. If that makes sense. At least that's what I thought. And, to be honest, you never gave me any hint that any advance would be welcome and I didn't want to lose you as a friend. So, I took what I could get and convinced myself that it was a crush that I would get over. I did a pretty good job of it too. Until Alex asked you out.'

'You weren't happy about it? Why didn't you say something?'

'I saw the way you two were with each other. Both easy-going, open, and I could see that you liked him. I suppose I sort of knew it would happen anyway once he saw you and found out you were single.'

'He wouldn't have asked me out if he'd known... about you.'

'I told him we were just friends. Which we were. And he believed me because, like I said, I'd done a fairly good job of convincing myself.'

'You know I never... we never... you know...'

Charlie nodded. 'I do. I wondered about that.'

I pulled a face.

'Not like that. It's just not like Alex to wait very long.'

'We didn't really get a lot of time together with one thing and another.'

'Normally, Alex makes time. Believe me.'

'Well, maybe he wasn't as keen on me as he thought he was.'

'Nope. Not that.'

'How do you know?'

'I asked him.'

'What?'

'I asked him.'

'I see. And what did he say?'

'The same as you. That you didn't really get a lot of time, yada yada.'

'We didn't. And it may be old-fashioned but I have to be seeing someone for a little while before I go that far.'

Charlie made a dismissive noise. 'Alex could charm a nun to

throw her knickers in the air if he wanted to. If he'd wanted to, you'd have been toast.'

I moved and thumped him on the arm. 'I would not! I have principles. Thank you.'

He grinned and rubbed his arm. 'Ow, by the way. Anyway, it turned out there was more to it.'

'There was?'

Charlie dragged a hand across his unshaven jaw. 'Yeah. We kind of had a bit of a bust-up over it?'

'Oh no! Oh, Charlie. I'm so sorry. I never meant any of this to come between you and Alex!'

He caught hold of one of my flapping hands and gently caressed the back of it with his thumb.

'It's OK. We're good now. To be honest, it's been building up for a while, I just don't think either of us wanted to face it. You might have been the catalyst, but you weren't the cause.'

'What was the cause?' I asked, feeling my heart rate slow at Charlie's gentle, rhythmic touch on my skin.

'Male ego. Too much testosterone and everything that circumstance brings along with it.' He shook his head. 'Ridiculous really. I was jealous of him being so capable of talking to anyone, being able to charm anyone he wanted when it's something I've always struggled with. Alex, in turn, was feeling like he was second best because of the difference in our salaries, and what goes along with that. We'd both gone to the same school, had the same privileges but had just chosen different paths, which led to different things.'

'But he loves his job!'

'He does. But a while back there was a girl who showed interest in him when we were out together somewhere. He really liked her but part way through the evening, something came up, I don't even remember what it was now, and she obviously realised that, as much as she thought Alex was hot and charming, he wouldn't be able to provide her with the trinkets someone on a higher salary might. At that point, she switched allegiances.'

'And you let her?' I raised an eyebrow.

'Aww, don't look at me like that. You know me and women. I'm not exactly fluent in them. Besides, we'd all had a couple of drinks by then and, to start with, I didn't even realise what she was doing. When I did, I made a polite excuse and extracted myself.'

'And Alex was mad at you?'

'We talked it over briefly and he said it didn't matter. That he hadn't particularly liked her anyway. He was just passing the time.'

'And you believed him?'

'Honestly, I'm not sure. But it was easier if I did.'

'But? I assume there is a but?'

'Yes. Things seemed OK and most of the time they were. But it felt like there was always this slight undercurrent of wariness. I hated it, if I'm honest. But I didn't know how to fix things. Alex says now that he felt the same.'

'So, what happened?'

'You happened.'

I shifted position on the sofa, my internal feeling of being suddenly uncomfortable translating itself to my body. Charlie patiently waited for me to stop fidgeting before he continued.

'I'd told Alex that I was helping you with your accounts and he asked about you. I kind of kept it all rather non-committal and tried to be blasé. I wasn't even allowing myself to admit I liked you, so telling someone else? That just wasn't going to happen.'

'Full state of denial, then.'

'Oh, absolutely. But the moment Alex saw you at Mum and Dad's party, he knew. He can probably read me better than anyone. And, like he said, I'd left out the part about you being gorgeous, so really that was all the confirmation he needed.'

'So, he asked me out to get back at you for feeling somehow less than you?'

'Yes and no.'

I frowned at him.

'Despite what I'd said, once he saw you and saw me with you, he knew what I felt for you was way past just liking you as a friend. But Alex really did like you too. I don't want you thinking he was just using you to get back at me for something.'

'But he kind of was...'

Charlie let out a deep sigh. 'Yes. I suppose so, in a way. But if I hadn't been on the scene he would have still asked you out. But, once it came to it, as much as he liked you, he couldn't go through with it. He knew, probably even better than I did, what you meant, and do mean, to me. When extra shifts came up, he'd take them, just so that he'd have a valid excuse for not seeing you. Like I said earlier, normally Alex is pretty charming as regards to sex but he couldn't go through with it with you. He cared about you too much... and he knew that once he went there, our friendship would never be the same.'

Shaking my head, I blew my fringe up out of my eyes. 'Why don't men just talk about things?'

Charlie let out a breath that contained a laugh. 'God knows. It would probably make things a lot less complicated.'

'It really would.'

'When I found out he'd stood you up that night, I was so angry with him! I hated to think of you just sat there alone. I stormed round to see him the next morning and everything kind of blew up! We were both yelling at each other and every insecurity we each had came shooting out.'

'Oh, Charlie.'

'No! Don't look like that. Honestly, it was the best thing that could have happened. It totally cleared the air and by the time we had finished I think we both understood each other a lot better.'

He ran a hand down my hair. 'I hate that you ended up being a pawn in all this, though.'

'It's OK. He didn't hurt me. I felt a bit of an idiot in that restaurant but apart from that I was OK. Although I will say seeing the look of abject horror on his face when I opened the door to him whilst wearing a wedding gown didn't do all that much for my ego either!'

Charlie grinned. 'Yeah, I think he was suddenly panicking that things might have got a little out of hand.'

I rolled my eyes.

'You kind of did both our heads in with that.'

'You too? But you knew it was all pretend. All just for the blog.'

'I did. But, God, Libby, you looked so... incredibly beautiful. You took my breath away. I had to keep myself busy so that I couldn't focus on the thought that one day some unbelievably lucky guy was going to see you like that for real. I didn't want it to be anyone else. I wanted it to be me and the thought of it being someone else just drove me nuts.'

'Charlie,' I whispered, as he rested his forehead against mine.

'I know you've said you might not want to get married, and if that's what you want, I can live with that. As long as you're only not getting married with me.'

'I've had some long talks with my dad over the past few weeks and I might have changed my mind on that...'

His smile said more than words ever could.

'But you and Alex?'

'We're good. I promise. He's been brilliant these last few weeks. I was going crazy and he kept me mostly sane.'

'I'm sorry I caused you pain, Charlie. I really am.'

'Don't even think about it now. If I'd been more brave and just admitted I was head over heels with you in the first place, it probably would have saved everyone a lot of heartache.'

Charlie twiddled the ring I always wore on my right hand. My mum's emerald engagement ring.

'I thought if I just packed it all away and concentrated on being a friend to you, the rest of the feelings would go away. And I convinced myself that they had.'

He sat back a little, his intense blue gaze focusing on me.

'Until you were nearly taken out by a king prawn and blurted something about being in love in the middle of a London street. Then everything came tumbling back.'

'So why not tell me then? Why make me feel like it was the worst thing I could have possibly done? Why say what you did?'

'Because I'm about to leave the country and because I thought I'd already dealt with my feelings towards you. I thought they were all nicely packaged away and labelled as "Past Crush". The fact that I'd never picked up any inkling of encouragement made it easier to deal with in a way. And then there you were saying that and ripping off the Band-Aid. I've never felt like this, Libs. I've never been surprised or swept up by someone before and you keep surprising the hell out of me, usually in a good way. I didn't know what to do. How to handle it. And I didn't react well, for which I apologise.'

Charlie turned towards me and scratched the back of his head. 'I was going crazy trying to get hold of you.'

'I didn't really want to talk to anyone.'

'I know. And I understand. But, please, please, never do that again. Please, just talk to me. Even if it means you're going to scream and shout at me. I'd rather that than not know where you are, not know if you were safe.'

'That's why I told Amy that I was OK.'

'Yes, but you could have been anywhere. On your own. You know the sort of statistics that would have been going through my head. Especially after I saw that video on your blog.'

'You and your statistics.'

'I know. Which is why I need you and your irrationality to balance me out.'

'I am not irrational.'

'You are sometimes.'

I opened my mouth to protest again but Charlie cut me off.

'It's one of the many things I love about you.'

I closed my mouth. Charlie's gaze dropped to my lips momentarily before it lifted back to lock with mine. Heat seared through me at the look of unrestrained longing in his eyes. His hands moved, releasing my fingers and sliding up my arms, brushing the straps on my shoulders, softly tracing along my neck until he held my face in his hands. Desire engulfed me as Charlie bent his head towards mine.

After the softest of kisses, Charlie pulled me towards him, holding me close, and I laid my head on his strong, solid chest and knew I was exactly where I was supposed to be.

40

'So, does this mean we're officially going out?' Charlie said, one leg draped lazily across me, the expensive white cotton sheet contrasting with his tanned skin.

Whatever I had expected to happen when Alex dropped me off at Charlie's house this morning, not once had I thought that it would be me ending up in Charlie Richmond's bed, by way of his kitchen sofa, not to mention the second-floor landing. He might not be comfortable with chatting up women, but it would seem once he got over that hurdle then the whole shy, retiring thing most definitely wasn't a problem any more. Charlie Richmond had skills. Boy, did he have skills! And then some.

'What are you smiling at?'

I scooted back in the bed so that I could tip my head back a little on his chest and meet his eyes.

'How did you know I was smiling?'

'I could feel it on my chest.'

I grinned again.

He caught a hand under my chin and moved to kiss me.

'You didn't answer.'

'About going out together?'

'Mm hmm.'

I looked back up at him. 'I don't know. You haven't actually asked me yet. You know. Formally.'

He made a face, considering it.

'That's true. We got a little carried away before I could get to that bit.' He flashed his eyes at me and my body responded.

'It's probably a good thing you didn't say anything that first time you came over, you know.'

Charlie traced a finger along my shoulder. 'What makes you say that?'

'Because I'm not sure we would have got much done.'

He followed his finger with his lips, dropping tiny butterfly kisses along my skin, following it up my neck before moving lower. 'I don't know,' he said. 'I think we might have got plenty done.' He gave me a look under his lashes and I caught my fingers in his hair.

'I once said that you only had the body of a bad boy. I'm beginning to reassess that. In fact, I think you may actually be a very bad influence indeed.'

He gave me a look that confirmed I might well be right.

'Would it make you feel better if I asked you out? Formally?'

I smiled. 'Maybe.'

'All right.' He pushed himself up onto his elbows and rolled so that he was on his side, propped up on one elbow. Reaching over, he took my hand. 'Libby Cartright, would you go out with me?'

I pulled a face as if I were thinking about it.

'Although, it's funny. I heard that you had this thing about never sleeping with a man on the first date...'

He ran his eyes over me, teasing.

I narrowed my eyes at him, and he waggled his eyebrows.

'Not quite so principled after all, then?'

'You know you're going to pay for that, don't you?'

He reached over and ran an arm underneath my body, flipping me so that I was on my back, looking up at him now supported on muscular arms above me.

'Oh, I hope so.'

ACKNOWLEDGMENTS

As ever, thank you to James. This is my ninth book, and my eighth novel. Without your belief and support, it's unlikely there would ever have even been one.

A huge thank you to the amazing team at Boldwood Books for choosing me to be a part of their inaugural launch list, and for the belief that they have shown in me and my writing. Special thanks go to Sarah Ritherdon, my editor, for loving Libby and Charlie's story so much and for helping me make it the best it can be. Extra thanks also go to Nia Beynon for answering all my random, pondery questions, and for her incredible energy and enthusiasm.

Thanks to copy editor, Sue Smith, and proof reader, Susan Lamprell, who worked their magic in cleaning up the gaffes.

Of course, a shout out goes to my writer-y pals – I'm wary to accidentally leave anyone out in a list but you know who you are. Thank you, lovelies!

A big thank you to Jo P for listening, laughing and for the Afternoon Teas.

I'd also like to thank the bloggers who help spread the word about my books. Your help, reviews and support are always appreciated and I'm extremely grateful to every single one of you.

And last, but not least, thank you to everyone who has ever read and loved one of my books. Without these fabulous readers, we are just dropping words into a void, so hearing that my book has made someone smile, laugh, cry and hopefully want to read another one fills my heart to the brim. Thank you.

MORE FROM MAXINE MORREY

We hope you enjoyed reading *#No Filter*. If you did, please leave a review.

If you'd like to gift a copy, this book is also available as an ebook, digital audio download and audiobook CD.

Sign up to Maxine Morrey's mailing list for news, competitions and updates on future books.

http://bit.ly/MaxineMorreyNewsletter

ABOUT THE AUTHOR

Maxine Morrey is a bestselling romantic comedy author with eight books to her name including *Winter's Fairytale* and the top ten hit *The Christmas Project*. She lives in West Sussex.

Visit Maxine's website: www.scribblermaxi.co.uk

Follow Maxine on social media:

facebook.com/MaxineMorreyAuthor

twitter.com/Scribbler_Maxi

instagram.com/Scribbler_Maxi

bookbub.com/authors/maxine-morrey

ABOUT BOLDWOOD BOOKS

Boldwood Books is a fiction publishing company seeking out the best stories from around the world.

Find out more at www.boldwoodbooks.com

Sign up to the Book and Tonic newsletter for news, offers and competitions from Boldwood Books!

http://www.bit.ly/bookandtonic

We'd love to hear from you, follow us on social media:

facebook.com/BookandTonic

twitter.com/BoldwoodBooks

instagram.com/BookandTonic